REVELATIONS

ANCIENT ORIGINS BOOK ONE

ROBERT STOREY

Adversity is a fact of life. It can't be controlled.
What we can control is how we react to it.

– Unknown

FACT:

On the 8th January 2011 an asteroid with the potential to impact Earth in 2040 was discovered by the Mount Lemmon Survey. This near-Earth object was given the designation 2011 AG5.

The majority of locations and organisations referenced in this book are real.

Many of the world's most powerful governments build and operate large clandestine subterranean facilities

PROLOGUE

NOVEMBER 13TH, 2017

Professor Steiner buzzed with suppressed excitement. This didn't happen often as his job was mundane, to him anyway. As head of a highly classified government subterranean research project, his job was an important one. He managed thousands of staff, allocated budgets and ensured the facility ran smoothly year in and year out, regardless of the many difficulties that arose. People's lives depended upon the decisions he made. Most other people would find the job extremely challenging, even stressful; he did not, however. Graduating top of his class from Harvard in engineering, physics and computer science, with PHDs in all three subjects, he had lectured all around the world including CIT, Stanford, Oxford, Cambridge and Tokyo. At the forefront of various research projects, he'd also authored numerous acclaimed scientific papers.

So why had this emotional transformation occurred? He'd been called to the White House on a matter of national security. The national security part was old hat to Steiner, of course; it was part of his daily work. The White House, on the other hand, certainly was not. Like many people he'd only seen inside it on TV and most of the time that was probably a mock up on a movie set or in a TV studio; this, however, was the real deal.

'Professor Steiner.'

Snapping out of his reverie he looked up from his seat as a woman dressed in a smart suit approached him.

'Would you like to come this way, please?'

Standing up he smoothed down his trousers, making himself presentable, and followed her through a door and into a large hallway. As they walked he took in the sumptuous surroundings of the residency of the most powerful man in the modern world.

Apparently the Oval Office was under renovation, otherwise he'd have asked for a quick peek inside. This hadn't dampened his mood, though, and neither did the fact that he wasn't meeting the President, who was off on important business at the 2017 G13 summit meeting in Shanghai. Just being in the White House was enough for him.

The woman opened a door and waved him through. 'Take a seat, Professor; they will be with you shortly.'

Thanking her, he settled down again to wait.

As Steiner sat there, his gaze was drawn to a magnificent oil painting that hung on the wall opposite. Captivating in its depth and energy, the picture depicted the Greek god Hephaestus wielding stonemasons' and blacksmiths' tools against the Earth. Great fire and gasses spewed forth at the sites of impact while gaping rents in the planet's crust branched out across its spherical mass, revealing the molten core beneath; the detail astounded him. He wondered how long it would take someone to paint such a masterpiece. Hundreds of hours, he presumed, preceded by a lifetime of mastering the discipline's finer points. Steiner's eyes soaked up the exquisite brush strokes, his thoughts becoming entranced by the scene's dynamic power. Sometime later, as he continued to study the great work framed within its ornate border of plaster and gold leaf, a young man appeared in a doorway off to his right.

'Professor, good to see you again. Sorry to keep you waiting. Come in, come in.'

Steiner couldn't remember the man's name. Not one of his strongest points, names and faces. Give him a mathematical proof to remember any day of the week. Entering the room, he saw that four people sat waiting informally on sofas and chairs, papers, files and laptops arranged haphazardly around them.

'Madam Vice President,' Steiner heard himself say.

The VP stood and shook his hand, the greeting as genuine as the warmth in her eyes.

Her entourage included one of the Joint Chiefs, a couple of suits and the man who'd let him in.

'Professor,' the Vice President said, 'thank you for coming on such short notice. I hope we haven't inconvenienced you too much by interrupting your important work. This is General Redshaw; I think you may have met previously?'

Steiner nodded giving the general a small smile as he was reintroduced. The fact was he didn't remember the man at all, but not wanting to appear incompetent he refrained from disclosing this fact.

'My Chief of Staff, David Broad,' the VP continued.

A sallow faced man moved forwards and shook Steiner's hand firmly. 'Professor, it's nice to meet you at last.'

Steiner gave another nod of his head as he returned the handshake.

'Malcolm Joiner, Principal Deputy Director of National Intelligence,' said the VP, indicating a tall, wiry man with jet black hair, who remained sitting, merely lifting a couple of fingers from his knee in recognition. The VP then put one hand on the young man's shoulder. 'And of course, my personal aide, Nathan Bryant, who you already know.'

Ah, that's his name, Steiner recalled belatedly.

'We have a lot to discuss, Professor,' she told him, gesturing with a measured hand for him to take a seat, 'so let's get straight down to business.'

Steiner sat down at the end of one of the sofas and Nathan handed him a cup of tea. For many days Steiner had been wondering why he had been called to this meeting, the prestigious surroundings and company meant it must be important; just how important he was about to find out.

Malcolm Joiner cleared his throat. 'Professor, in January, 2011 an observatory in Tucson, Arizona sighted an asteroid that had the potential to impact earth in 2040.' He handed him a grainy printout of the object in question.

'As you are probably aware, there are many potential objects in space that are likely to collide with the Earth at some point in the future. Unfortunately we have since verified that this rock, some four miles in length and half that in diameter, will almost certainly collide with us in 2040.

'To give you an idea of the scale of this threat scientists originally estimated the infamous meteor that wiped out the dinosaurs was about nine miles across; however, new estimates have the dino killer at a mere three to four miles in length. If this new data is true – and we believe it is – then we can expect—'

'An initial impact devastation zone,' Steiner said, cutting in, 'earthquakes and possibly volcanic activity. Tsunamis and destruction of the ozone layer, if the impact is in an ocean or sea, followed by acid rain and intense localised fires. The resulting dust cloud kicked up on impact will encase the planet for a number of years, killing off crops and plant life globally, not to mention the impact on human and animal life.' As Steiner finished his sentence it dawned on him the immense implications of what he'd just described.

'Indeed,' Joiner said, his tone solemn. 'Not a pretty picture. Yet, unlike in Hollywood movies, our top scientists tell us we do not currently have the capability to divert or destroy any asteroids that are heading our way. This won't stop us from trying, of course, but since the whole of our species is threatened with extinction we prefer to have plans with as close to a one hundred per cent chance of survival as possible. Not just survival, but a means by which to continue our way of life.'

'What about putting bases on the Moon or Mars?' Steiner said without thinking.

Joiner's mouth twitched, which may have been the man's attempt at a smile. 'Again, contrary to popular culture, we are even further away from attempting to populate other celestial bodies. So what do we do to counter these horrific after-effects? There are a few options open to us.'

Turning, Joiner pressed a remote button to bring up large slides on the huge flat screens behind him. He pointed to the first. 'Option one, underground shelters. Perhaps the most effective solution available to us at present. Any such subterranean facilities will be able to preserve our way of life, our species and the many other forms of life on the planet which may – although unlikely in this instance – be utterly wiped out by any impact blast and fallout. Option two.' He pointed to the next screen along.

'Space stations. Much more expensive in every respect; however, they have the significant advantage of manoeuvrability, enabling them to avoid direct impacts in Earth's orbit. And option three,' he said, motioning at the final screen, 'adaptive measures. Genetically modified crops, plants and trees which can withstand little to no sunlight for long periods. Food stockpiling and water storage. Infrastructure strengthening and adaptation. Conservation investment. Population education, leading up to impact – eternal darkness for many years will lead to mass panic and potentially wars and the breakdown of civilisation, unless pre-empted and diffused. Population evacuation of impact zone and any mega tsunami pathways.

'Since we have a finite time-frame of twenty-three years to prepare for impact, it was decided that the most viable options were one and three. Option two will be considered on a very small scale, utilising current projects.'

'Are you with us, Professor?' the Vice President said.

Tearing his eyes away from the screen Steiner focused on the VP, his mind racing and his excitement a distant memory. His expression became serious. 'I am, Madam Vice President,' he said confidently.

'Good. I knew you were going to be up to the task.' She turned back to look at the Deputy Intelligence Director. 'Proceed, Malcolm.'

'For the past few years all the major nations of the world have been in intense discussions on how to combat this distant threat,'

Malcolm Joiner continued. 'Not acting now may prove catastrophic in the future. Your work, Professor, since this discovery, has become more important than ever, which is why you will have seen a large increase in your budget year on year.

'Not only do subterranean facilities help to protect against meteor strikes, they will also be our first defence against super volcanoes and infrastructure-damaging solar flares and coronal mass ejections. These facilities, as you are well aware, will also lend themselves to protecting us from other pressing threats, such as pandemics, biological and nuclear warfare, and so on. Due to the urgency and severity of the threat to the planet we have been able to cut through a lot of red tape to speed up the planning of our defences; redirecting resources to and from the varying nations and multinational companies around the world.

'This process has inevitably been hindered by the need to ensure that the reason for such large scale unilateral cooperation between nations and private enterprises, initially, is known to only a select few. Fortunately the need for such secrecy has been aided by organisations that have been operating with complete – how should I put it? – *un-transparency* for generations, operating around the world unseen by the majority of the populace. They have proved very useful in averting suspicions and minimising the potential for mass panic and the breakdown of civilisation.

'We need the world's economy and people to go about their daily lives in as normal a way as possible, which will give humanity its best chance of survival in the future. Apart from the people in this room there are only a handful of people in the U.S. who know about this situation. Needless to say, everything you have been told falls under the official secrets act, to which you are already bound via your current position.' The intelligence agent looked over to the VP. 'Madam Vice President?'

'Thank you, Malcolm. So, Professor, what do think?'

'I'm thinking you want me to help you build a facility,' Steiner said.

'Well, yes and no. We need you to head up a programme,' she told him, 'globally.'

Steiner's eyes widened in shock.

'We are setting up an organisation called the Global Meteor Response Council, or GMRC for short,' the VP continued. 'The GMRC will be operating under the banner of the United Nations, but in fact it will have significantly more powers and will operate and virtually control every nation's response to the asteroid and its eventual impact and fallout. You will not be required to operate in the public domain as it would merely serve to nullify your skill set. No, you will help lead the council from behind the scenes and concentrate on the worldwide subterranean response.

'You were our chosen candidate from the United States, and while your Chinese and British counterparts also had excellent credentials, you won out on the fourth round of voting.' She smiled at him, her eyes sparkling with the glimmer of mischief. 'So, I believe congratulations are in order.'

Globally, Steiner thought, *in command of preserving civilisation, humanity and virtually all life on Earth? No pressure then!* 'Thank you, Madam Vice President,' he said dryly. 'You didn't think I should be informed about my involuntary candidacy prior to the voting?'

'Would it have made any difference?'

'I suppose not,' he conceded.

'Excellent.' She turned to her right. 'General?'

'Yes, Madam Vice President. Thank you.' General Redshaw considered Steiner for a moment. 'Professor, your job is going to be incredibly difficult; however, you will have a good team to support you.'

'Do I not get to pick my own support staff?' Steiner said.

'Unfortunately no, due to the sensitivity of the programme, team members will be allocated as we see fit. If you have any problems, come to us; the five people in this room are from this point on your core support. We are your team.'

'Hang on; you're saying I'm in charge of you, a member of the Joint Chiefs?'

'In a manner of speaking, yes. You will encounter many problems in the next twenty-three years and I am here to ensure you have the full backing of the United States military when and where needed. Hard decisions will need to be made.'

'Does the President know the full picture?'

The Chief of Staff stepped in to answer. 'No. He knows what he needs to know to do his job. He won't be in office long enough to warrant full disclosure.'

'Doesn't that also apply to you, Madam Vice President?' Steiner said.

'No, once my tenure is at an end we will remain as a team to ensure stability is maintained. Personnel change is neither efficient nor cost effective, and increases the risk of intelligence exposure – or so I'm told,' she said looking over at Malcolm Joiner, who nodded in agreement. She turned back to Steiner, a small smile creeping onto her face once more.

'Hang on, doesn't that mean I'm also in charge of you, Madam Vice President? Or will be?'

'It does indeed, Professor.' Her smile widened.

'Right – err – okay then, just making sure.' Dear lord what am I getting into? he thought to himself. In charge of the Vice President of the United States and one of the Joint Chiefs, not to mention the Deputy Intelligence Director.

'Your job at the China Lake facility will terminate immediately,' the General continued, 'your home and work will now be moved to a location on the border of New Mexico and Colorado, near a town called Dulce.'

Stunned, Steiner looked at them in amazement. 'I thought the Dulce underground base was just some bunkum made up by conspiracy theorists and alien nuts. You're telling me it actually exists?'

'The Dulce project has been underway for two decades,' General Redshaw told him. 'With this new *situation* we have simply adapted it to suit.'

'How large is its subterranean footprint and how on God's green earth have you kept it a secret? I'm in the same field with high clearance; I haven't even suspected that there was something going on there.'

'The footprint is approximately twenty square miles. As to how we keep it so well concealed, our friends in the intelligence community can be thanked for that.'

'We aim to please,' Joiner said, with an air of nonchalance.

'Twenty square miles, but that's ten times bigger than China Lake!'

'It will actually be a lot bigger than that, Professor,' General Redshaw said, 'as it will utilise the cascading chamber design that you invented. We've simply scaled it up. Final preliminary testing is progressing and the forecasts look very good for a fully functional multi-level facility to be viable in less than ten years. The top of the complex is three thousand feet beneath the surface while the bottom, when it is finished, will be over ten thousand feet down. It is truly an astounding feat of engineering on a scale humankind has never seen before.'

'So you must have been using nano tubes to strengthen the chambers,' Steiner said, gazing down at the floor in thought, 'otherwise the depth would have been too great to support the vast pressures above.' He looked back up. 'How have you managed to go so deep? Unless you've devised a new extraction method, of course, but then—'

'Professor,' the VP said, interrupting him.

'What? – yes, of course – sorry.'

'Don't apologise, Professor. This is what you have been hired to do, but you will have time enough to think and plan to your heart's content.' The VP stood up, with everyone following suit.

Steiner, caught on the hop, rose last.

'Nathan will take you to your new home and help you settle in. All your research and equipment will be shipped to the Dulce facility in due course,' the VP said. 'I'm sorry to have to drop all this on you so suddenly, Professor, you are coping remarkably well, which confirms our choice was a sound one. We will be meeting again very soon, but until then Nathan will be able to answer any further questions you may have.'

Steiner shook hands with them all, feeling a little bewildered by this sudden life-altering turn of events. At the door he turned. 'I won't let you down, Madam Vice President.'

'I have every confidence in you, Professor. We all do.'

Steiner gave her a nod of his head in acknowledgement and let himself be led out the door and into his new life.

After everyone else had left, Deputy Intelligence Director Malcolm Joiner turned to the Vice President. 'Let's hope he delivers,' he said.

The Vice President poured some scotch into two tumblers and handed one to him. 'Oh, he will deliver. We're here to help, after all; he's by no means alone in this.'

'The other nations will not want to follow him.'

'He'll win them round, you'll see.'

'Perhaps we should have told him everything? I believe he could handle it.'

'Hmm, perhaps.' She sipped her drink, the ice cubes rattling softly inside the glass. 'We will feed him more information pertinent to his job when necessary. He knows what he needs to know ... for now.'

CHAPTER ONE

TWENTY-TWO YEARS LATER. LONDON, ENGLAND. 2040.

TRISH LOOKED AT HER WATCH – again. Twenty minutes past the hour and Sarah had yet to arrive. Trish wasn't surprised at the tardiness; she'd known Sarah too long to expect anything else. Waiting around did grate after a while but something else bothered her much more. She'd been concerned about her friend's recent behaviour. Sarah hadn't seemed happy or even remotely motivated for some time. Less focused, more introverted and less sociable, very un-Sarah like. Trish hadn't seen her like that since Sarah's mother had died tragically in a fire five years ago. *How time flies*, she thought; it seemed like it had been only a couple of years since that fateful day. She took an idle sip of her tea and heaved a small sigh.

Trish had decided to meet Sarah for a drink at the new café located near the top of the Sky Pillar, the latest and by far the tallest London skyscraper, recently opened to great fanfare. An awe inspiring spectacle, the tower rose up over two thousand feet into the crisp blue sky, shining like a beacon of light across the city as the sun glinted from its smooth, glass-clad surface.

Looking down from her vantage point Trish could see the tops of some of the smaller towers far below, One Canada Square, The Shard, and its sister tower, The Spire. The building was so high it granted the observer a clear view of aeroplanes and helicopters as they bustled their way around the city. As she took another sip of her drink, she caught sight of Sarah stepping off the escalator and gave her a wave to catch her attention. Seeing the movement, Sarah waved back and began wending her way through the tables and chairs towards her friend.

Sarah was quite tall, taller than Trish, anyway, and at five eight she wasn't particularly short. Sarah also managed to catch the attention of many a passing man as she was a true blonde with a beauty, figure and complexion many models would envy. Sarah complained her looks were the bane of her life as many people only saw her features rather than the actual person behind them. Trish could see her point – she could, although she wouldn't have minded the attention that Sarah enjoyed. Her friend's physical attributes also helped her in the befuddlement and – usually inadvertent – manoeuvring of the opposite sex. This sparked jealousy in some women, but Trish knew it was a woman's prerogative, whether intentional or otherwise; men had testosterone and women had their wiles, it was just the way things were. "Gotta make use of what God gave you," her ma always said.

Unfortunately Sarah's looks had also helped to curtail her career prospects as an archaeologist. Strangely, many people didn't take her friend seriously, even though she was quite brilliant in her chosen field of anthropology. Trish knew Sarah had noticed people's attitude towards her, too; not everyone, but a reasonable proportion, enough to make it a recognisable problem. Some of her colleagues had even purposefully ignored her, and in some instances during her PhD studies their behaviour could have been classed as psychological bullying. Dealing with these attitudes shown Sarah by her peers had made her a little intense and insular at times. They had also undoubtedly been a factor in her decision to investigate the more dubious and obscure subject matters on offer; but then if you weren't respected or aided by your peers you would have to forge your own routes or face mediocrity, and Sarah wasn't one to settle for that.

Sarah dumped her bags down next to the table and gave Trish a hug in greeting.

'So, how are you keeping?' Trish said, as Sarah sat down and picked up a menu to browse.

'Fine, thanks.' Sarah glanced in her direction but didn't make eye contact. 'Busy, as normal. You?'

Trish wasn't convinced her friend was fine at all. In fact she looked like she'd been crying.

'How's Mark?'

'Yes, he's fine too,' Sarah said, still looking firmly at the menu.

'Sarah.'

'Hmm?'

'Sarah.' Trish leaned forward and eased the menu out of her hands. 'Look at me, will you? I know there's something wrong. For a while now you haven't been yourself. You can tell me. Whatever it is, I won't judge, you know that.'

Sarah looked at her friend, anguish suddenly coming to the surface; she quickly looked away again, out over the city. A waiter came over and Sarah ordered a half-caf and a piece of chocolate cake with whipped cream. Trish raised an eyebrow. Sarah normally took great care with her figure, so whatever troubled her must be serious.

Sarah caught the look. 'It's nothing, really,' she said, unconsciously wringing her hands together, which belied her words. 'Mark and I are just going through a bad patch; everyone does, right?'

'Of course, but it seems a bit more than that. You haven't been out much and when I've tried to talk to you about it you've fobbed me off with lame excuses. I'm worried about you, Saz.'

Sarah turned away again, her arms folding protectively against her chest. Trish noticed the tension in the movements. *She's not going to tell me*, she thought, but then Sarah's shoulders dropped and she sighed.

'Mark hit me,' Sarah said, her voice breaking.

'What! When?' Trish said, shocked that he could do such a thing. He wasn't perfect, but hey, who was? However, she was even more shocked that Sarah was still with him and had taken it. The fire that had taken her mother had mentally scarred Sarah, making her more vulnerable; could this be the reason she now found herself in such a position?

'A few weeks ago,' Sarah said, 'and yes, before you say anything, I should have left him but he was so sorry about it. He got really upset. He didn't mean to, he just lashed out, he'd been drinking.'

'Oh, my God, Sarah, are you listening to yourself? He friggin' hit you, the piece of shit. I don't care how sorry he was or what it was about, it's unforgivable.'

'I know – I know. He won't do it again, he promised me and I believe him. I love him, Trish, I do.'

Trish groaned inwardly; she knew her friend was wont to fall in love quite easily. Sadly this had left Sarah in some emotionally retarded relationships. She'd hoped Mark would be different, but it seemed those expectations had been well and truly dashed now. She had suspected Mark of trying to control Sarah; over time she'd seen warning signs, but when she'd raised the subject Sarah had dismissed her concerns out of hand. What else could she have done? It was her life after all.

'Hang on,' Trish said, 'is that why you didn't go to Marta and Keith's wedding reception the other day, when you said you were too tired? I thought that wasn't like you.'

Sarah's hand went to her left cheek.

Trish took her other hand to comfort her, but Sarah pulled it away.

'How hard did he hit you?' she said, softening her voice but finding it difficult to hide her anger.

'It left a bruise; it was a slap, really, not a punch or anything.'

'Bollocks!' Trish said vehemently.

A couple sitting at a nearby table looked round but Trish ignored them. 'That's fucking bollocks and you know it,' she said, a little more quietly. 'Punch or slap, it's the same thing. If it's hard enough to leave a bruise or otherwise, he hit you.'

'I know. Look, I'll wait a while and see how things go. It won't happen again. He'd had a bad day at work, you know how it goes.'

'Err, hello? I don't think so. A bad day at work doesn't give you carte blanche to beat up on the ones you supposedly love. Nothing does.'

'Trish, I know you mean well, but I can handle this. I'm fine, honestly. Can we talk about something else, please?'

Trish didn't want to push it. At least she's opened up about it, she thought, that's a major breakthrough. I'll raise the subject later, perhaps speak to—

'And no, I know what you're thinking. You will not call my brother, and besides he's off God knows where with God knows who.'

Trish gave a sheepish half-smile. 'You know me too well. Seriously though, Saz, if he does it again—'

'I know – I will – promise.'

'Good. And you best keep him away from me for a while, too, as I won't be responsible for my actions.'

Sarah didn't reply as a waitress arrived with her order. She dug into the cake with gusto while Trish considered her in silence.

'Sarah?' she said at last.

Sarah glanced up at her between mouthfuls.

'I wanted to meet not just out of concern,' Trish said. 'Well, that was the main reason, but there's something else. You know that dig a year or so ago where we found those artefacts that you got so excited about?'

Sarah's head came up quickly, any distress vanishing from her expression as her eyes came alive. 'Of course, I've been waiting over a year for the crossmatch carbon dating on those bits of bone. Have you got the results? Why didn't you tell me over the phone?'

'I didn't say over the phone as I was more concerned about you. I wanted to see you and I'm glad I did.'

A pained look crept back onto Sarah's face, only to be replaced with a sterner resolve. 'Get on with it, then,' she said, sounding impatient.

Trish concealed a grin; that was the Sarah she knew and loved.

Sarah's expression grew annoyed as she caught her friend's amusement. 'What?'

'Eh? Nothing,' Trish said hastily, losing the upturned corners of her mouth under her friend's penetrating gaze. 'Anyway,' Trish continued, 'the lab tech, some newbie, got the items to be dated mixed up and the bone fragments weren't done.'

Sarah swore loudly and the couple near them looked over again in disapproval.

'That's not all; after I gave them an earful I took a cab and went down there to find out what was going on. It was as they'd told me; they'd dated the wrong item, which is obviously bad.' Sarah was about to say something, but Trish held her hand up, cutting her off. 'Turns out this guy had actually dated some of that stringy rope we found wrapped round what looked like a phalange bone, except it turns out it wasn't rope at all – it was hair!'

'Hair? No way!'

'Yes, way, and what's more, and this is the really good bit,' Trish said, pausing for dramatic effect.

'Arrgh – get on with it already!'

'Well, they dated it and it was five hundred THOUSAND years old. I thought, what – that's rubbish, as your trinket, that pendant thing the hair had been bound around, was properly cast. So I told them to test it again, but they said they already had, three times, and the results came back the same.'

'I knew it!' Sarah reached across and gave Trish a big smacker full on the lips.

'Yuck.' Trish wiped her mouth with the back of her sleeve; she couldn't help but grin, though, as Sarah sat back down.

'Oh, Trish, this could be the break I've been looking for these past years, finally some more hard evidence!'

'Okay, I thought you might act like this. It's not really sufficient proof for your theory, though, is it? A few odds and ends?'

Sarah's eyes blazed with defiance. 'It will be when I get those bones dated too.'

'Hey, I'm on your side here, but you've got to think how they will look at it. You need supporting evidence, you know that, otherwise it will hold no water. Even if you did have supporting evidence, many would still dismiss the claims and say the conclusions are wrong. They will pick it apart piece by piece and you will be ridiculed. We've seen it before and we'll see it again. It's the game; it's just how it works.'

'You think I don't know that? Friggin' Ada, of course I know that, but it won't stop me from trying. If I still had those parchments—'

Trish didn't comment; she didn't want Sarah to dwell on that period of her life, especially considering her already fragile state of mind. The parchments in question, destroyed in the same fire that claimed her mother's life, were discovered by Sarah many years ago on a remote dig in the Zagros Mountains in Iran. Sarah had claimed they were from an advanced, extremely ancient human ancestor, since they had shown detailed maps of the continents equivalent to those that we have today; including Antarctica, which has only been mapped with any degree of accuracy in recent times. This theory was much more out there than another, which claimed a pre historical human civilisation existed around ten thousand years ago, one that was wiped out in a great flood when the ice caps melted. While this idea would also account for the maps, Sarah had other *evidence* to the contrary.

Sarah theorised a race of larger humans existed hundreds of thousands of years in the past alongside Homo erectus, cited by the scientific community as the direct ancestor for Homo sapiens and Homo neanderthalensis. She'd become obsessed with this theory after finding an oversized femur bone and subsequently meeting other like-minded archaeologists, mostly amateurs, following the completion of her PhD in her mid-twenties. Sarah, and her *group*, had gone from country to country following up on leads found on the net and in medieval documents contained within libraries of obscure religious orders with tenuous links to the Catholic Church.

Trish had always been open to her friend's ideas on the subject, but had never really believed in the theory like Sarah did. It was interesting, exciting and more than a little mysterious, but to prove it as fact was nigh on impossible. If *she* needed convincing, and she had an open mind, then sceptics making up the majority of the scientific community would need more than a few scraps to even begin to change their views.

'Five hundred thousand years old,' Sarah murmured to herself. 'Do you know what that means?'

'I'm not sure,' Trish said, trying to keep her tone conservative. The dating was intriguing, but no more than that.

'It means modern humans didn't cast the pendant we found with the bones,' Sarah told her, 'as according to accepted theories, Homo sapiens didn't even evolve until what? – an absolute maximum of four hundred thousand years ago. The earliest evidence of sophisticated casting equivalent to what we found was made by humans perhaps only four thousand years ago. So who made it, Homo erectus? Possibly, but extremely unlikely since there is no evidence they had the capability to cast anything. Couple this with the massive finger bones we found that indicate the individual's height was about ten feet and—'

'Come on, Sarah,' Trish said chidingly, 'that's pure conjecture verging on fantasy.'

'All right,' – Sarah raised her hands to placate her friend – 'perhaps eight feet. But considering Homo erectus, neanderthalis and sapiens all average roughly five to six feet, then eight is enormous. I have to get to the lab and get them to date the bones.'

Excited, Sarah jumped up and grabbed her bags, hugged her friend and zoomed off, leaving Trish sitting alone, bemused and left staring at the remains of a piece of chocolate cake discarded and forgotten on a plate.

Trish picked up Sarah's unwanted morsel and popped it in her mouth, savouring the rich taste as she chewed. *Waste not want not*, she thought, unsure if she'd helped her friend or just put her onto another destructive path; she was the one, after all, who'd introduced her to Mark in the first place. Heaving a sigh, she gazed out across the extensive metropolis of London, laid out like a beautifully crafted urban tapestry below, and thought, *I love this city*.

CHAPTER TWO

IT WAS seven o'clock post meridiem by the time Sarah reached the Oxford Radiocarbon Accelerator Unit. Fortunately, the recently upgraded Research Laboratory for Archaeology was still open as the lights blazed forth from the Dyson Perrins Building where it was housed. Dean, an old flame, would hopefully be working late. He had a soft spot for her and he might push through the bone fragments for analysis. She was lucky; about ten years ago this process had taken a few days or even a couple of weeks, but a new technique pioneered at this very lab had changed all that. Radiocarbon dating could now be carried out in a matter of hours, regardless of the age of the sample or its composition. And if this advance wasn't enough, another even bigger breakthrough made by the Chinese a few years later, enabled carbon dating's seventy-five thousand year limit to be extended tenfold. This new process, known as crossmatch radiocarbon dating, utilised big data arrays, stratigraphy, quantum modelling and molecular retracing, which had shepherded in a new era of accurate dating techniques; and Sarah knew if she was ever to make use of them, the time was now.

As she entered the building she checked her watch before taking the stairs up to the top floor. Turning left, she headed down the main corridor, passing a few students on the way. A moment later she'd reached Dean's door; the sign read Mass Spectrometry Manager. Giving a swift couple of knocks, she entered without waiting for a response. Dean's desk was empty but a furtive-looking woman shuffled through papers over on the right hand side of the room.

'Can I help you?' she asked Sarah, evidently annoyed at the intrusion.

'Err no – I mean yes – is Dean about?'

'No, he hasn't been in today. He'll be back next week.'

Sarah was crestfallen. She'd come all this way for no reason and the chances of getting any carbon dating done that evening had gone out of the window. *I knew I should have called him first*, she thought; *idiot*. 'All right,' – she gave the woman an apologetic smile – 'no problem. Thanks anyway.'

She wandered back into the hall and considered her options. Get the train back to London tonight or get a room at a local hotel and head back tomorrow. She rubbed the back of her neck, unconsciously easing some tension. Frustratingly, her efforts to get here quickly had proved fruitless. Plus, telling Trish about her problems with Mark had brought up memories she wanted to bury. Sadly, though, her friend wasn't really the problem as no matter how hard she tried to forget the incident with Mark, she couldn't seem to shake it.

I need a drink, she decided. The Turf Tavern was close by. Dean had taken her to it a few times back in the day. It was mostly students and tourists, so not her usual cup of tea these days, but it was familiar and friendly.

Having made her way back out of the building, a few minutes later she was nearing the pub when her phone rang. She looked at the screen; it displayed Mark's face and he looked agitated. *Great*, she thought, *that's all I need*. Pressing a button on the screen expanded the image; it also enabled Mark to see her.

'Where are you? I was worried. Do you know what time it is? It's getting dark ... and who are those people?'

Sarah looked round as some raucous college girls passed by her as she slowed.

'Just some students from the campus,' she said. 'Look, Mark, you're right, it's getting late and I'm in Oxford. I'm checking into a hotel. I'll see you tomorrow evening.'

'Oxford? What are you doing all the way out there? I thought you were meeting Trish at The Pillar.'

'I was – I did. She told me some information about those bones we found a while back. You know the ones we were waiting to get carbon dated?'

'It's taken that long? I thought you said they'd sped the process up or something?'

'They have, but you still get dumped on a waiting list and with my rep everyone else gets priority. Finally someone got round to doing it, but they analysed the wrong thing so I came over to sort it out.'

'Sarah, haven't we discussed this? It will go nowhere. It's always gone nowhere and it always will go nowhere. Forget about it.'

'I'm not so sure. Trish—'

'So are you coming home, then?' he said, cutting her off.

She was getting irritated with him now. 'What? No. I told you I'm staying overnight; I've got to go, it's starting to rain.'

'Fine!' he said. The screen went blank; he'd hung up.

Bye then, she thought. Wrapping her coat around herself as the drizzle turned into a deluge, she hurried on.

Reaching The Tavern, Sarah pushed open the main door. A rush of warm air and noise greeted her, the smell of beer and damp clothing filling her nostrils. The pub heaved with people, the downpour having driven many inside. Not that students needed any excuse to drink and socialise. Ordering a glass of dry white wine, she settled in at the bar on a stool. A group of tourists huddled next to her examined a map and argued in a language she'd guess was Indonesian, although she couldn't be sure.

A young man came and hunkered down on the bar stool next to her, a tad too close for her liking. He gave her a grin as he called the barman over. Despite herself she smiled back; it was hard not to, he was pretty cute if you liked the young cheeky chappie type, which she had in her younger days.

'So are you here for business or pleasure?' he asked her, raising his voice to be heard above the cacophony of noise filling the low-ceilinged room.

'Neither,' she said, hoping to confuse him.

'What else is there?'

'Education, or something non-pleasurable like a funeral?' she said pointedly. 'There are quite a lot of things really.'

'Shit sorry I—' he said, mortified – *which is appropriate*, she thought, chuckling inwardly.

'Don't be.' She laughed. 'I'm kidding.'

He indicated her clothes. 'You're wearing black, though.'

'You're quick,' she said, while smiling.

'Err, so—'

A large hand clamped down on his shoulder, halting him mid-sentence.

'I'm sorry, miss, is this fellow bothering you?'

She recognised that voice. 'No, it's fine, we're just chatting.'

The young man gave a nervous grin and made a swift exit.

Dean pulled up another stool and sat down next to her, a pint in one hand. 'Haven't seen you around for a while, what brings you to these parts of deepest darkest Oxfordshire?'

Sarah appraised him. It'd been a while since she'd seen him. He'd aged a little, now in his early forties, with some grey hair and a few more lines. Still easy on the eye, but he didn't seem that enamoured to see her. 'You don't seem pleased to see me,' she said.

'Why should I when the last time we met you left me hanging without another word? No sooner than you hear the word "excavation" or "expedition" you vanish quicker than a fart in a fan factory.'

Sarah gave a wry smile. 'Lovely analogy.'

Dean glowered at her from under his heavy brows.

'Oh calm down, Dean,' she said, and then assumed a pout while fluttering her eyelashes and looking pathetic. 'You can't hold a grudge with lil' ol' me, now, can you?'

He growled and took a swig of his drink, trying unsuccessfully to hide his smirk.

She pointed at him and laughed. 'Ha, caught ya!'

'Very good, I never could stay angry at you for long,' he said, relaxing a little and placing an arm on the bar. 'So, why are you are here? Not to see me, I take it?'

'Actually, yes, but not for what you're hoping for.'

'Get you with the big head; I'm actually seeing someone at the moment so I'm off limits.'

'Me too,' Sarah said, 'so we've agreed we're not interested in each other.'

'At the moment,' he said, with a twinkle in his eye.

She didn't reply, merely rolling her eyes in response. 'I'm down here to find out about a job one of your techs did for me recently. Unfortunately he's dated the wrong piece in the batch.'

Dean groaned. 'It's probably our new guy, Roland. He's gifted but a bit harebrained. I have to say, though, you don't seem that angry about it.'

'Well, I would have been, but the piece he dated actually produced something extremely useful. I just need him, or anyone, to date the correct pieces and I'll be a happy little camper.'

'Depending on the results,' Dean said.

'Of course, but I'm feeling confident.'

'So it would seem. Do you want another?' He beckoned the bartender.

She looked down to see her glass was empty. 'Sure. So who's this new assistant you've got working for you, have you had your wicked way with her yet? Sorry, I forgot, you're taken, aren't you.'

Dean looked at her, puzzled. 'What assistant?' he said, passing a fresh glass of wine to her.

'The brunette, slim about my height, suit. Seemed a bit smart for your office, but hey, it's your show.'

'I don't have a clue what you're going on about, Sarah; I haven't had an assistant for a while now. We've had a lot of cuts recently, every department has. For that matter nearly every government-run sector has, what with the impending doomsday and all these precautions they're taking. I think they've gone a bit too far recently, though, don't you think? Some people are saying the asteroid may even miss us altogether.'

'What? Oh, that. Yes not long till Impact Day now. It's a little exciting, don't you think? Takes the mundane out of everyday life.'

'I suppose, although since they've had to evacuate virtually the whole of southern Africa over the last few years, Africans may have a different viewpoint.'

'I guess,' she said with a chuckle. 'So who's this mysterious woman, then? She was in all your filing cabinets. There were quite a few documents spread about, I just assumed she worked for you. She also told me you wasn't at work today and would be back in next week.'

Dean looked worried now. 'Sarah, I really don't know who this person is and my cabinets are always locked; plus I've been in all day today. How long ago since you saw her?'

She looked at her watch. 'About an hour now.'

He got his phone out, hit a button, waited a few moments and then swore.

'What's wrong?' Sarah said.

'My camera's not working.'

'Camera?'

'Yeah, I've got a small security camera set-up in my office to prevent students nicking things, they're thieving little buggers.' He got up and drained the rest of his pint. 'Right, I'm going back to check this out. Coming with?'

Most of her wine was still in the glass, but she downed it, too. 'Sure, why not,' she said, and followed Dean out of the pub.

Total darkness had descended by the time they'd made their way back to the university. A few lights were still on and a lone student scuttled past them as they entered the building. Once in the office nothing appeared to be out of place. Dean went straight to the cabinets, which were locked with no apparent sign of tampering.

'Where's the camera?' Sarah said.

'Eh?' Turning around he went to the corner opposite the door and gazed up at the ceiling. 'There.' He pointed at a tiny dome-shaped object, its white surface making it all but invisible. 'It's got motion and heat sensors, time stamps, remote access, video conferencing, upload and download facilities, 32K definition playback and record, it's a fantastic bit of kit.'

'Apart from the fact that it doesn't work,' Sarah said, peering around the rest of the office.

'I know it was working yesterday, as I checked its feed.' He removed the device for inspection and then plugged it into his computer. 'Strange,' – he tapped a few keys – 'it seems to be okay now.' He went back to the cabinets and swiped across the locks with his phone to unlock them. Sarah sat down in his chair and fiddled with a stapler as he checked the files to see if anything was missing.

'So what gives, Dean?'

'Regarding?' he said, without taking his eyes off the cabinet he was now rifling through.

'Well, I've been waiting a year for my artefacts to be dated; couldn't you have pushed me up the list a bit?'

'I'm sorry, I should've done. I was angry with you after ... well, you know, and then I just forgot about it. I no longer prioritise the list these days.'

Accepting his explanation, Sarah watched as Dean continued to leaf through the documents while muttering to himself. A few minutes ticked by before he stopped and turned around. 'Shit!'

'What's up?' she said. 'Something missing?'

'No, nothing. Are you sure she had the cabinet open and this wasn't some ploy of yours to get me up here alone?'

'You wish. No, honestly, she was here and that was definitely open.'

'Well, I don't know what's going on then,' he said, looking at her in confusion.

'Don't look at me, I don't know either. Doesn't anyone else have the access code?'

'Roland does.'

'Isn't that the muppet who buggered up my tests?'

'The very same. Bloody hell, I bet he's let someone else come up here; if he has he's outta here. Come on.' He waved his hand for her to follow him as he locked up the cabinets and headed for the door. Sarah jumped up out of the chair and trailed after him.

The mass spectrometer was housed in the adjacent building and, according to Dean, Roland always worked late. *Probably because he has to correct all his mistakes*, she thought to herself. After a short walk they arrived to find Roland still there, as predicted, although he didn't appear to be working, as he lay sprawled out on a desk, asleep.

'Roland!' Dean's voice rang out.

Roland stirred and lifted a bespectacled head. 'Dean, is that you?'

Roland was a small rotund young man in his early twenties, although his clothes looked like they belonged to an elderly librarian.

'Yes, of course it's me,' Dean said with exasperation. 'Have you given your access code to some woman today? She was seen rifling through the secure cabinets in my office.'

Sitting upright, Roland straightened his glasses and blinked owlishly as he got his mind back into gear. 'Of course not, you specifically told me never to let anyone do that, so I haven't.'

'And you haven't told anyone the code or mislaid your phone?'

Roland checked his pockets. 'Nope,' – he patted his breast pocket – 'still here.'

Dean shook his head. 'I give up,' he told Sarah, 'nothing's been taken, so as far as I'm concerned there isn't a problem. I've got too many other things to worry about without this as well.'

Sarah shrugged and made a face to show Dean she wasn't that concerned either. She also had more important things to consider. 'Do you have the dating results for a job for Sarah Morgan?' she asked Roland.

Roland shifted his gaze to Sarah and broke into a broad smile. 'Oh, so you're The Giant Lady.'

Sarah sighed wearily; that was one of her nicknames in some archaeological circles. 'Yes, that's me, The Giant Lady.'

'I always thought you were quite small,' said Dean, looking at her with an impish grin.

'Funny,' Sarah said.

Roland rummaged around in some trays on one of the desks. After a while he stopped and held up a sheet of paper. 'Ah ha,' he said, waving it about in triumph, 'got them!'

He passed Sarah the paper and she read through the results. The hair was, indeed, approximately five hundred thousand years old. She felt exultant, relieved and amazed all at once, and having the proof in her hand was an unbelievable feeling. All she had to do now was get the bones tested and get a credible anthropologist to back up her assertions that they belonged to a very large member of the Homo genus.

'Dean, you couldn't do me a massive favour, could you?'

He eyed her with suspicion. 'That depends on what it is.'

'Is there any chance you could do an analysis of the bones I need tested, this evening?'

'Seriously, now – tonight? It's nearly nine.'

'I'd owe you big time,' she said, her eyes pleading with him.

'Yeah, ya would,' he said, mock vehemently.

'So you will, then?'

'Sure, just one item, though; I'm not going to stay here all night.'

'Oh, thank you.' She gave him a peck on the cheek. 'You're a real star, do you know that?'

Looking a little nonplussed, Dean sent Roland to get Sarah's artefacts from the security vault on the far side of the large room. Meanwhile he went about preparing the mass spectrometer for operation while Sarah re-read the results of the hair sample.

A couple of hours later, the analysis on the large near-complete finger bone finished, Dean printed out the data and took a look. Barely a moment passed before Sarah could contain herself no longer. She whisked the paper out of Dean's hands, much to his chagrin, and read the results.

'I can't believe it,' she said. 'It matches the hair sample. Five hundred and eleven thousand years old.'

'Give or take a few hundred years,' Dean said.

'This is fantastic!' she enthused, overjoyed at the news.

'That is impressive and certainly interesting,' Dean said. 'But it's late and I've done enough work for one day, so if it's all right with you two, I'm off home.'

With all in agreement, Dean locked up the building after they had shut down all the systems and turned off the lights. Outside, Roland gave them a parting wave of farewell before trundling off into the night in the opposite direction to the pub.

'Pleased?' Dean said as she found herself looking at the new results again, with a grin on her face.

'Yes, very. Thank you so much, you've been really great tonight.'

He smirked. 'I've heard you say that before.'

'Really, do you ever get your mind off sex?'

'You know me,' he said, grinning.

She laughed. 'That I do.' She looked down the street and then back at Dean. 'Anyway, I'm going to hit the sack.'

His expression turned serious. 'Do you have anywhere to stay?'

'I'll be fine, thanks. I'll check into that nice little hotel next to the Tavern, the one we—'

He was smiling again.

'Oh,' she said, blushing, 'never mind, yes, that one.'

Ever the gentleman, Dean escorted her to the hotel where she bade him goodnight.

'Are you sure you don't want to—?' he asked her, darting his eyes pointedly up at the hotel rooms above.

'You're terrible; I thought you were seeing someone, anyway?'

'I'm not really, I was hoping to make you jealous. Did it work?'

'No, 'fraid not,' she said, even though she was tempted to take up him up on his offer, what with her situation with Mark. She'd felt a lot happier today than she had for quite some time and a night with Dean would be very enjoyable, but she wanted to make it work with Mark.

'So?' he said.

'Sorry, Dean, I—'

He held a hand up. 'Don't worry, I'm fine. I'll see you tomorrow and we can finish off the rest of your tests if you want? Perhaps have lunch, strictly platonic. Sound good?'

'It does.' She smiled. 'I'll see you tomorrow, then.' With a wave goodbye, she turned and walked into the hotel. It had been a long day and she was looking forward to resting her head on a nice soft pillow.

Once in a room and tucked up, snug, ready for sleep, her mind wandered on the day's events, settling at last on the carbon dating breakthrough she'd been waiting for, seemingly for her whole life. As she drifted off to sleep she dreamt of receiving the International Archaeology Award for Archaeologist of the Year. *And this year's winner is ... Sarah Morgan.*

CHAPTER THREE

SARAH ARRIVED BACK bright and early the next day at the mass spectrometer building to find a police car parked outside. Wondering what was going on, she went inside to where Dean was talking to one of the officers, while a disconsolate Roland sat alone at one of the desks, around which papers were scattered and trays upended.

'Roland, what's happened? Is everything all right?'

'Hi, Sarah; no, not really. We've had a break-in; they trashed the office and broke into the vault.'

'What! Hell, no one was hurt, were they?'

'No, it must have happened some time late last night. The vault is like a bomb site, artefacts all over the place.'

Sarah looked at him suddenly feeling anxious. 'What about my bones and hair?'

Roland shrugged. 'I don't know. The police won't let us in there now. They want to take photos and see if they can get prints and that.'

Sarah had a dreadful sinking feeling in the pit of her stomach. Slumping down on a chair next to Roland, she ran one of her hands over her head, her brow furrowing. She'd suffered the loss of evidence a couple of times before, not only her mysterious maps, but also a bone she'd found early on in her career, a complete femur.

This fossilised limb had been massive in comparison to modern day humans. Dating revealed it to be two hundred thousand years old and she declared it as a previously undiscovered human ancestor or cousin, the ever elusive Homo gigantis.

The bone indicated the height of the individual must have been at least nine feet, fully erect. At the time she made comparisons with fossils of an animal known as *Gigantopithecus blacki*, a giant ape estimated to measure ten feet in a standing position. This massive creature lived between nine million and one hundred thousand years ago, in what was now India, China and Vietnam. That such an animal evolved, an animal that was a member of the Hominidae family – of which humans were also a member – added credence to Sarah's claims. The fact that massive giant apes had evolved in Earth's history opened up the door to the real possibility that humans, or more specifically, their ancestors, may also have grown much larger.

To some this sounded preposterous. Giant humans, people scoffed at the notion. This entrenched cultural scepticism, or modern day superiority complex, seemed to Sarah to be wholly out of touch with the palaeontological discoveries displayed in museums and taught in schools the world over. Huge great lumbering beasts had roamed the Earth for millions of years; none better known than the dinosaurs, pterosaurs and the fabled giant mammals of the ice age. Descendants of these colossi were even with us today in the form of elephants, giraffes, crocodiles, and the largest animal ever to have existed, the one hundred foot long blue whale.

These arguments began to gain purchase with a few academics – until, that was, the femur in question had been stolen from one of her cases soon after she had published a paper on Homo gigantis. Sarah's work had utilised a plethora of supporting data, written accounts, photos and videos she had compiled over the years, with the femur as the crowning evidence for the new species.

Of course she had been ridiculed by the general scientific community. She had expected resistance, as many of her friends outside of more credible circles had also received such treatment. Sarah, however, being an up and coming archaeologist at the time and predicted to do great things by some top academics, had believed she could give credence to the subject, especially with her new proof.

The intense scepticism shown by most had briefly waned when a couple of her colleagues had shown tentative interest after they had seen the bone in question. Sarah had been so excited when a senior scientist and her mentor, Dr. Middleton, had been willing to go out on a limb for her and take a look at the bone. This was when her world had been turned upside down by the theft. Without the bone, she had no hard evidence and without evidence, she had nothing. Her career had taken a nosedive since that fateful day and she had been treading water ever since.

The most disturbing thing was the fact that it wasn't just she who had been plagued by bad luck. Many of her friends and like-minded believers in the existence of Homo gigantis had also experienced many accidents and thefts of finds that may have proved their theories. Too many to be coincidence, many argued. Sarah had initially thought they were paranoid; however, she had come to feel the same way over the years. If this break-in had targeted her evidence then it was time to take a stand, but how? That was the question.

Sometime later, rousing her from these increasingly speculative musings, Dean finished talking to a policewoman and came over to Sarah and Roland. 'They're bringing in the investigators shortly to try and gather evidence but they seem to think it's a professional job, as the vault couldn't have been opened by amateurs. They knew what they were doing. I had a look around before I rang the police and it looks like a few things were taken, but most were just trashed mindlessly.' He looked at Sarah, his expression sad. 'Sarah, I'm so sorry, your pieces weren't there. I looked everywhere for them. There may be an outside chance they're amongst the debris, but the box they were in is one of the ones that are missing.'

So there it was, her proof gone – again. She put her head in her hands wondering why she deserved such bad luck.

'Roland, you didn't happen to see a woman hanging around here yesterday, did you?' Dean said.

Roland looked confused 'Can you be more specific?'

'Sarah, what did she look like, the woman in my office?'

'I don't know; my height, grey suit—'

'Dark curly hair and glasses?' Roland said, finishing her sentence.

Sarah's head shot up. 'Yeah – yes!'

'What was she doing here?' Dean asked him.

'She said she was meeting you here, but you never showed up. She waited a while and then went.'

'Me?' Dean said.

Roland nodded.

'Did she look at the vault?' Sarah asked him before Dean could say something else.

'Actually she did. She looked at everything, really, just wandered about. I didn't think anything of it then, but now—'

'Well, that's it then,' said Dean. 'We know who did it, this mysterious woman. You two had better tell the police and give them her description. I already told them about last night, Sarah, they were going to talk to you anyway.'

After Sarah and Roland had given their accounts to the police Roland went home and she and Dean went to a café around the corner for lunch.

'So what are you going to do now?' Dean asked her as a waiter cleared away their plates.

'I'm not giving up on this. There's something going on here, it's too much of a coincidence. Two times now this has happened to me.'

'They never did recover that femur, did they?'

She shook her head, not wanting to discuss it further. She was already too angry and upset to think about that right now.

'You think someone is deliberately preventing you from finding or going public with any evidence to support your theory?'

She heard the scepticism in Dean's tone even though he tried hard to hide it. She shrugged, not trusting herself to answer. *What can I do now?* she wondered. *I can't let this keep happening*. One thing was for certain, someone was doing their best to discredit her and prevent her theories from seeing the light of day and she would find out why or, at the very least, get the better of them. She stood up, suddenly knowing what she had to do.

'Are you going home?' Dean said.

'Yes and no.'

He looked puzzled by her answer.

Without elaborating, she thanked him for all his help, kissed him on the cheek goodbye and headed for home. No sooner was she out the door than she was on her phone, booking a flight to Turkey.

Sarah arrived back at her apartment early in the evening and went straight into the bedroom to pack her flight case. *First things first, though*, she thought to herself. Going to the closet she opened the double doors and parted the clothes hanging on the rail inside. Grabbing a stool, she climbed up, the top of her head now grazing the ceiling. At eye level a small air vent nestled off to one side behind some old musty smelling boxes on a shelf. Sarah pushed her hand over and popped off the plastic grate from the wall. Feeling around inside, her palm brushed against a flat metal object; curling her fingers around it, she pulled it out. For a moment she looked at it and then gave it a quick kiss before slipping it into her pocket; it represented her final piece of evidence and she felt a great sense of relief and comfort that she still had it in her possession.

As she walked back into the lounge to go into the bathroom to collect toiletries, something caught her eye. She slowed to a stop in front of the mantelpiece, on which sat a rustic oak picture frame. Sarah picked it up with care and stared into her mother's beautiful blue eyes. A thought suddenly struck her. Her discoveries – the femur, the finger bones, the hair – if they had all been taken from her due to some kind of conspiracy, then it stood to reason that the maps had been destroyed on purpose, too; especially considering the fire investigation report had been inconclusive, perhaps even hinting at foul play. *That means Mum didn't die in an accident at all,* Sarah thought in horror, *she was murdered!*

Memories of the fire all those years ago came flooding back to her, the smell of the smoke and the intense heat of the blaze. She remembered the noise of the flames as they consumed her mother's house. Perhaps the most vivid recollection of that terrible day was the sound of her own screams as firemen fought to hold her back as she tried in vain to get into the house to save her mum's life.

Sarah felt faint and put her hand against the wall to steady herself. Her head swam and the room grew dim. The thought was too much to take and she crumpled slowly to the floor, the picture frame falling with a clatter from her hand. Her mind awash with emotion, she dragged the photo back towards her and stared at her mother's face through distorted vision as tears welled. A dark, slow realisation wound its way around her heart, constricting and restricting it; *it was my discoveries that killed Mum. If I hadn't taken the maps to the house she'd still be alive today*. Agony lanced through her stomach and she scrambled to her feet and rushed to the kitchen sink, where she retched until her throat burned with pain. She stood there for some time in silence, her head hanging limp; finally she turned on the tap, washed out her mouth and cleaned her face.

A couple of hours later Mark rolled in. He'd been out drinking with his friends by the look of it and he wasn't pleased to see her.

'So you're home, are you? About time,' he said, and then he noticed her cases by the door. 'What's that?' He pointed at them. 'Are you leaving me?!' His voice had gone up an octave. He came over to her, pushing his face into hers. She pulled back as his breath stank of lager, but he grabbed her arm.

'I'm not leaving you,' she said, subdued and without emotion. 'I'm going on a dig in Turkey. I leave tonight.'

'What? What you talking about, you're going to Turkey, for how long?'

'A few weeks, six at the most. Look, Mark, I've—'

'Six weeks!' His eyes bulged at the thought. 'I don't think so! I've got a work do next week and the week after that it's my sister's wedding, and you're not going to let me down on that. I'll show my sister I'm better than her. She said I'd never get married, but I'll show her!' He pushed Sarah away and stumbled over to an oak cabinet against the wall to get another drink.

Sarah saw this wasn't going to go well so she began collecting up her gloves, keys and phone. As she pulled on her coat, Mark swung her round and red hot pain exploded on the side of her face and she was flung to the floor. As her eyesight came back she saw him standing over her, swaying from side to side.

'I told you,' he said, a hint of madness in his eyes, 'you're not going anywhere.' He emphasised the last word with his hands.

Sarah managed to get to her feet with Mark looking on, an exultant look on his face. Calm settled upon her. She had been working on a numb sort of autopilot as she'd prepared to leave, but the blow had brought her to her senses and her mind felt strong, somehow, and needle sharp.

'Mark,' Sarah said softly as she laid a hand on his shoulder. He shrugged it off, but she took his hand with a tender touch and pulled him closer. He was about to say something when she rammed her knee with full force into his groin. He hit the floor hard, writhing in agony. Sarah bent down to him; her anger raised, and grabbed his cheeks between the fingers of her right hand making him look at her despite his pain. 'I'll go where I damn well please,' she said to him through gritted teeth.

Pushing him back to the floor, she picked up her bags, and as she walked out the door she turned back to see him staring up at her with undisguised hatred.

'By the way, Mark,' she said, 'I am leaving you now.' Slamming the door behind her, she walked off down the hall, looking at her watch; she had a flight to catch.

CHAPTER FOUR

DUST clouds swirled and streamed across the distant plains as fierce winds battered the tents at the base camp of Mount Ararat on Turkey's eastern border. Fabric panels rippled as the air drove against them, end flaps snapping as they whipped endlessly back and forth. Like an invisible assailant the storm whistled and screamed around a man who stood just outside one of the temporary shelters. Pulling his coat tighter about him he ducked back inside to rejoin his two team mates.

'It's colder than a frigid rat's arse out there,' he said, taking off his gloves and blowing into his hands.

'Is a frigid rat's arse colder than a sexually active one, then?' a man on the far side said.

A woman laughed. 'Perhaps he knows by experience. Have you been putting little Jimmy in places he shouldn't go, again, Jas?'

'You should know, Trish,' Jason said, grabbing himself and thrusting at her.

Trish wrinkled up her nose in disgust. 'Ew – you're gross!'

'Ha ha, bollocks, you'd love a bit of ol' Jas.'

Just then another gust of air ripped into the tent as someone else came in, wrapped in a thick red puffer coat.

'Don't you agree, Sazza?'

Sarah closed the tent flap behind her. 'Agree with what?' she asked, as Jason looked at her, waiting for a response.

'He reckons women find him irresistible,' Trish said.

Sarah looked at her friend with a serious expression on her face. 'Irresistible? Course, I know plenty of women who find Jason the dog's doodahs.'

Jason clapped his hands together in jubilation. 'See? I told you so!' he said, while Trish looked at Sarah in disbelief.

'Although these women have been mummified for five thousand years,' Sarah continued, 'and would find a rotten turnip an attractive proposition.'

Trish doubled up and Jason's exuberant grin turned into a hurt scowl. As Sarah walked past she gave him a friendly whack on the back of his head with her gloved hand.

'Carl, do you know how long this weather is likely to last?' Sarah said.

The man across from Trish made a face and shook his head. 'Hopefully it should be only a few hours; it's a fairly regular occurrence at this time of year.'

Sarah nodded and then lay down on a sleeping bag, zoning out while Trish and Jason argued over whose turn it was to cook. She was glad to be out there, away from all her troubles. Surprisingly Mark had tried ringing her, but she had just blocked his calls. The only thing she regretted about that night was that she hadn't kneed him harder.

The stolen bone fragments still gnawed away at her, although the theft was a welcome distraction from the terrible guilt over her mother's death, something that dwelt immovable in the recesses of her mind.

Who's sabotaging my work? she asked herself for the umpteenth time. She'd been in touch with her *group*, people who, like her, believed that a large human ancestor lived and flourished in the distant past. They had suggested the Catholic Church as a culprit, as according to some it had been covering up the existence of *giants* for a very long time. Sarah was unsure if such claims had any credibility, but it was put to her that the Church covered it up because it proved that an advanced race populated the world prior to – according to the Bible – the creation of the universe. This was a fact the Church could not allow to become common knowledge as it directly challenged and fundamentally undermined their whole faith.

She had to admit looking at it that way made it seem much more plausible. It was well documented that the Vatican had banned and destroyed many books, along with any other evidence that contradicted their teachings, over the centuries, so why not this, too? The answer, Sarah reasoned, was that such a theory falls down when you think about the scale of the potential cover up. Could they really police the whole world so thoroughly?

Once again there was a counter-argument. What if the population of Homo gigantis hadn't been that large, or had been condensed into certain areas? Not to mention the fact that fossil records, while appearing comprehensive, are anything but; this misconception was mainly due to the sheer mass of media coverage, films and books warping our sense of perspective. Conventional predictions indicate that a mere two per cent of all species that have ever lived will have been preserved. In many instances, millions of years go unaccounted for in terms of any kind of significant animal finds and evolutionary continuity is ridiculously underpinned. There is little to no proof that anything actually evolved at all, apart from the more recent biological remains and the observation of evolution in modern times.

The fact that evolutionary theory was correct was not in question in this instance. What was in question was the fact that it was not currently proved by the fossil record or by any other means of using ancient records. Extremely old, preserved DNA may begin to make this argument redundant, but for now it is a very real fact; we know very little about Earth's evolutionary history and have only scratched the surface of what was in our past.

All these assertions, according to Sarah's circle of like-minded individuals, were why a single powerful organisation such as the

Catholic Church had the motivation, means and opportunity to be able to cover up the existence of a whole species.

A flaw still existed, however. Over the last hundred years many scientific discoveries had been made to challenge a whole raft of religious teachings, Catholic or otherwise. So why still cover it up? Something else must be going on, some other reason to hide this from the world. Wild claims suggested by her friends swirled dizzyingly around in her head as she drifted into a deeper sleep.

———

'Sarah!'

'What?' she murmured, rolling over, away from the sound.

'Sarah, wake up will you.'

She felt a foot nudging her side; groaning, she opened bleary eyes and saw Trish looming large above her.

'Sarah, I've been calling you for ages. The winds have died down, come on, we've got a few hours left till nightfall, let's get to the dig site.'

'Sorry, I must have been dozing.'

'Sound-O is more like it,' Trish said, amused. 'Come on, Saz, let's get going!'

Grunting a little, and accepting a helping hand from her friend, Sarah pushed herself up. 'You've got far too much energy for your own good,' she grumbled.

Trish laughed. 'Ha! Pot, kettle, black is all I have to say to that.'

She had a point, Sarah had been like a woman possessed these past few weeks. She'd pushed her small team to the limits to cover as much ground as possible around the area where she had discovered the previous year's finds, which included the hair, finger bones and the small cast metal pentagonal disc. The disc had a small hoop on one edge, like a pendant, enabling her to hang it in on a chain around her neck. Instinctively she pushed a hand onto her thick puffer jacket and felt the object press reassuringly against her chest. This was one thing she was determined never to let out of her sight again, doubly so in light of recent events. She'd been keeping it at her apartment while she waited for the other artefacts to be dated at the lab. Initial tests had revealed no residual presence of carbon-14 outside or within the disc, rendering it impervious to the dating technique. Luckily this had ensured it was not amongst the other objects when the vault was broken into back in Oxford.

With Trish by her side, Sarah made her way to the current site of excavation. A number of hours soon passed and after much digging and relocating, Sarah found herself off on her own on a particular bit of ground, slowly removing earth and rock with her pick and shovel. She'd found anomalies there with her favourite bit of kit, a hand-held ground-penetrating imager, which made finding fossils and buried objects much easier as the resolution meant you could virtually see through stone. It cut days or even weeks off normal dig times.

The imager had been around for some time, but it used to be extremely expensive and unwieldy; however, with innovative technical advances in its manufacture, it was now lightweight and a lot cheaper – still expensive, but well worth the money. Sarah had also upgraded the scanner's software and added some lines of code herself to further improve performance, something she felt quite proud of.

Prior to Sarah's reputation going down the plughole she had also managed to acquire some much sought-after satellite time. Using infra-red satellite technology enabled massive areas to be scanned from space, resulting in spectacular finds. The idea had been pioneered in the early twenty-first century when it had unveiled the lost cityscapes of Egypt, including the phenomenal finds of seventeen pyramids buried for millennia in the desert sands. Since then many lost tombs and treasures had been unearthed, eclipsing even those of the infamous Tutankhamun. It was truly a new golden age of archaeological discovery and Sarah had got in on the act and requisitioned mapping of some areas around Mount Ararat. At the time people bemoaned the waste of such resources on an innocuous piece of land, but Sarah knew that significant finds had been made there in the fifteenth and sixteenth centuries, when an Islamic expedition from within the Ottoman Empire had unearthed bones of giant humans.

The scriptures that indicated this had been found in an old Islamic library in the city of Samsun, Turkey. Supposedly Samsun also had many caves which had contained the bones of seven foot tall humans; none had been recovered, however. Sarah herself had been there many times without her searches coming to fruition. Obviously she hadn't said in the official mapping request form that she was searching for giants based on passages contained within old Islamic texts. Instead she put together a feasible yet flimsy argument for finding Noah's Ark on the plains around Ararat Lesser, the smaller of the two peaks of the Mount.

She hadn't expected to get approval, truth be known, and when it came she had nearly fallen off her seat. The resulting scans revealed various anomalies, although none were boat-like or large enough to warrant further study – officially. Sarah kept the scans, however, and in her own time she went out on numerous occasions to the large expanse to unearth the more promising areas. That was how she had found the maps, fragments, hair and her pendant. If she were to find further evidence, it would be here.

Getting down on her hands and knees she heaved over a large stone to reveal – she held her breath – the skeleton of a long dead sheep. Cursing her luck she stood up and took a swig of water. That was the only downside to the imager, you may be able to find various things that looked like finds of the century, but ninety-nine times out of a hundred you'd end up with bugger all.

Jason came over to see how she was faring. 'Anything?' he said.

She pointed at the very ordinary bones with her foot.

He put his hand on her shoulder consolingly. 'Shall we call it a night? The light's almost gone.'

She looked up at the sky; night approached, its blackness seeing off its antithesis, the colours of the day. 'Let's get the generators out; we can get in another five hours minimum.'

'Seriously? We haven't got that much fuel left,' he said, looking dubious. 'If we run out it's a long way back to the nearest town that can supply us with more.'

'If we have to go back, we have to go back. It doesn't make much difference if it's in a couple of days or a week. Let's push on now; we always get more done when we're in the groove.'

'You're the boss, boss.' He mock-saluted and went off to set up the lighting rigs, Sarah following to get the gennies started.

Sarah and Trish were scanning a new section of land some time later when a shout went up a hundred metres away. Sarah looked at Trish, who appeared as surprised as she must have done. They dropped their tools and half-ran half-leapt over the rough terrain to where Jason and Carl had excavated a deep trench. Lights blazed down as a generator chugged away in the background. A small digger sat motionless off to one side of the hole. They were lucky to have been able to hire one on such short notice, and Sarah hoped it was worth the money as she crouched down and peered into the pit, Trish alongside her. Jason danced a jig and whooped in joy while Carl, hunkered down against a wall of sediment, teased something from its vertical face, brushing round it with care. She caught a glimpse of what looked like bone.

'What is it? What have you found, you fool?!' Trish said to the exuberant Jason.

'It's only bloody amazing, it's bloody beautiful is what it is!' He came over and gave Trish a big hug and a kiss.

'Argg, get off you big oaf!'

Sarah wasn't listening to them; she was transfixed by what Carl was extracting from the crumbling layers. Finally, after what seemed an eternity, he moved it clear and held it up to the light for everyone to see. Trish gasped. Jason was ranting loudly and Sarah just stared in disbelief. Carl held aloft a skull. Not an animal skull, but a human one, and it was big ... very big.

Cradling the object like a mother with a newborn child, Carl brought the skull over and passed it to Sarah, who gingerly, almost reverently, placed it on the ground so Trish and Jason could look without fear of it dropping and, heaven forbid, breaking apart. On closer inspection it wasn't Homo sapiens, not just because of its size, but due to the massive ridges on the frontal bone, large nasal cavity, wide zygomatic bone and subtle elliptical orbits. This was not from an abnormally large human and nor was it a deformation, or not any that she knew of. Coupled with its location and her previous finds, there was only one conclusion, this was Homo gigantis. This was the holy grail of her quest. Proof beyond doubt!

A hand touched her shoulder, it was Trish. 'Sarah, are you okay?'

'I—' She glanced at her friend. 'Yes, more than okay.'

'Only you're crying,' Jason said.

'Am I?' She wiped her face with the back of a grubby hand; looking at it she noticed wet streaks cutting through the dirt. She went back to looking at the skull, turning it over with the gentleness of a lover. With the greatest care she prised off some hard earth to reveal very human-looking teeth; very large teeth, but very human nonetheless.

Carl went to retrieve a secure container from the utility vehicle and on his return Sarah placed the skull inside, making sure it was well protected by surrounding materials inside the box. They all looked at Sarah in expectation, wondering what she wanted them to do next.

'I think an all-nighter is in order,' she said, staying calm. However, the sparkle in her eyes betrayed her excitement.

'I suddenly don't feel tired any more,' said Jason.

Trish grinned. 'Me neither.'

They turned to Carl, who just gave a solemn nod in agreement.

'Let's get to it then, people,' Sarah said, clapping her hands together to gee them up.

By first light they had unearthed nearly a full skeleton, approximately eight and a half feet long, and that wasn't all; after a few hours working in the trench, Sarah had gone back to the scan site that she had been surveying prior to the skull being found. She'd noticed a very strange reading; the imager's OLED display appeared to indicate that there was solid metal below the ground.

Knowing the others still had their work cut out with the skeleton,

Sarah desperately wanted to make a personal find of her own. She felt the anticipation growing within her as the hours passed, digging down ever deeper. A loud metallic clank accompanied by a vibration through the pick handle told her she'd hit whatever lurked buried below. Cursing her stupidity, she switched to a trowel. She prayed she hadn't damaged whatever lay down there; she was getting tired, making mistakes. She was still annoyed at herself for letting the skull be taken out of the ground prior to in situ photos and other data being taken and catalogued. *Get a grip, Morgan*, she berated herself.

Taking a long draught of gasoline-strength coffee from her flask, she continued more warily.

More time came and went and sunlight blazed forth, announcing a new day, as she finally hauled out a strange oval metal casket. She caressed its smooth, unmarked surface. The pick had not made a scratch; it looked polished and shone as if it had been made only the day before. Brushing off the remaining dirt and dust, she pulled it a little further out of the deep hole she'd dug. It was heavy, perhaps thirty kilos. She hadn't realised she'd been holding her breath; she let it out with a whooshing noise. She wasn't sure what was more amazing, the skeleton or this. *The skeleton*, she decided, *still the skeleton. But this – what is it? Is it related to the skeleton or is it Islamic buried treasure? It doesn't look like any Islamic artefact I've ever seen.*

It wasn't, as Sarah had first thought, solid, as a fine gap encircled it. She ran her fingers along the line and around its whole circumference. Picking up the shovel, she noticed its flat straight blade and then looked at the casket. *Well, the pick had no effect and it hit it hard*, she reasoned, *so prising it apart with this should be fine*. She braced the casket by putting it back in the hole, but tilted it upwards to expose the join. Placing the edge of the shovel along the line she took a deep breath and brought her foot down with half-force – nothing. No movement at all. She tried again with full force – still nothing. Frustrated, she threw down the shovel and went to the pickup for a set of fine-edged bolster chisels, a club hammer and a pry bar. As she neared the main site, she noticed Jason at the side of the utility vehicle where the skull and other bones were being stored, looking furtive.

'You all right, Jas?' Sarah said, as she approached.

He spun round, looking a little worried that she was there. 'Yeah, I'm fine, just putting some bones in for storage.'

She noticed he slipped something into his pocket as he turned round and made his way back to the trench. She watched him walk away, wondering what he was up to. Too wired and in the zone to give it any more thought, she collected the tools she wanted and went back to the casket. After a while she had all the chisels inserted evenly around the gap. Going to each one in turn, she knocked them in a little further every time around until the top popped up by half an inch.

With her heart racing again, saliva built up in her mouth in anticipation; she swallowed and calmed herself. Most of the chisels had dropped onto the dirt, so she pulled the last couple out and lifted the lid upwards. Since the winds had died down overnight it was very still out on the edge of the Turkish plain, and an odd metallic smell lingered in the air as she moved the lid away and looked inside. Sunken into a circular hole, the size of a dinner plate, a large handle protruded. She gripped it with both hands and pulled hard; it came out in one smooth motion with a satisfying sucking pop. Sarah stumbled back before regaining her balance, then put the insert to one side and looked into the now unobstructed opening.

A number of objects nestled inside; all were quite strange and nothing like anything she had seen before, apart from something that looked like a larger version of her pendant. Reaching in, she drew it out. Measuring two and a half inches in diameter, it felt cold to the touch, as if it had been stored in a fridge. It was also slightly different to her artefact, not only in size, but in design. Whereas hers was quite simple, pentagonal with a single circle in the middle, this was ornate in comparison. Multiple symbols had been embossed onto its surface in what appeared to be some kind of text, although it didn't look like any script she'd ever seen. They weren't pictograms so it was either made before the earliest major civilisations or later. Considering where it was and what they had just found, she was betting it was pre-Babylonian by a long shot; perhaps even pre-human.

She noted that, unlike hers, this one had a metal clip at one end which she easily popped open using a couple of fingers. She looked inside to see it contained a roll of parchment. With her fingertips, she managed to coax it out. About to unfurl it, she paused. Was that an approaching vehicle she could hear? Slipping the paper-like material back into the large pendant, for it too had a hoop at one end, Sarah moved around from behind the craggy outcrop of rock where she'd been working to see that it wasn't one vehicle, but five. Two black military looking short wheel-based lorries and three large desert-coloured SUVs roared up around the dig site, one peeling off towards Sarah, who rushed back to the canister-like box she'd just dug up. Yanking out items she stuffed them into her pockets; chucked a few under some rocks, and then they were on her. Two armed men jumped out of the SUV and grabbed her from behind, dragging her backwards as she tried to escape. She kicked, struggled and shouted at them before being slammed up against the side of the vehicle for her troubles. With rough efficiency, they then stripped her down to her underwear and removed all the artefacts she'd concealed in her clothing.

She started to shiver as the two men swept the area. 'Is that everything?' one of them asked her after they had gathered together most of the items she'd hidden. Sarah glared at him with baleful eyes and didn't answer.

'It doesn't matter,' said the second man, 'we'll pick this site clean when the others get here.'

'What others?' Sarah said. 'Who the fuck are you?'

The men ignored her. One of them picked up her clothes and shoved them into her midriff. After she had dressed they marched her over to the others. Trish looked terrified and Jason bled from a gash to his head. There was no sign of Carl.

Amongst the desert camo-clad soldiers, who now seemed to be everywhere, a tall, imperious man strode around issuing orders. He wore a pinstripe suit and looked extremely out of place, almost comically so, and yet the men obeyed him without question as he directed them this way and that. Then, appearing from behind one of the trucks, Carl came into view.

'You fucking bastard piece of shit!' Jason shouted, rushing at him.

Carl sidestepped the attack and stuck out a leg, and Jason hit the ground hard. They grappled for a moment in the dust, but Jason was soon overcome. Now on top, with Jason face down, Carl knelt on Jason's back and twisted his arms behind him until he cried out in pain.

'Stop it!' Trish pleaded, in tears. 'You're hurting him!'

At that moment the suited man approached. He surveyed the scene with a critical eye, looking at Jason, Trish and then finally Sarah. 'Get rid of them,' he said to Carl in a strong and unmistakable Italian accent.

Carl hauled Jason up, dragged him over to a nearby vehicle and thrust him into the back seat. Trish and Sarah were forced forwards and Carl unceremoniously pushed them in to join their friend. As Carl walked off, one of his colleagues noticed Sarah's pendant.

'Sir, what about that?' he said pointing at the dangling pentagon.

Carl paused to glance at the metal disc hanging around Sarah's neck. He looked her in the eye. 'It's nothing,' he said, moving away, 'just some cheap trinket.'

Satisfied with his superior's judgement the man slammed the door shut on the three archaeologists with an ominous finality.

'Sarah, what's going on?' Trish said. 'Who are these people?'

'I don't know.' Sarah looked out of the window at the men as they went through their gear, throwing boxes of precious bones to the ground as if they were worthless pieces of junk. 'Although I'm beginning to get an idea.' She turned to look at her friends. 'Did they take everything you had?'

Trish nodded.

'I tried to stop Carl taking the skull,' Jason said, 'but got this for my troubles.' He pointed at his battered face.

The front doors of the SUV opened and they fell silent; Carl got into the driver's seat and another man climbed into the passenger side. The suit and his mercenaries stayed behind while Carl drove them back towards base camp. As they bumped along the uneven road, no one spoke, each immersed in their own thoughts. Reaching the site Carl jumped out and ducked into the main tent. After a minute he was back and they were driving again, this time on the road towards the nearest town. Miles before they got there he slammed on the brakes and the vehicle skidded to a stop. Turning round he chucked each of their passports at them and some cash at Sarah.

'Do yourselves a favour and don't speak of this to anyone,' he said, his eyes steely cold. 'Now get out.'

The three did as they were told and as the SUV turned round and headed back towards the camp, Trish yelled some obscenities after them.

Dejected, Jason looked around at the barren wilderness that surrounded them. 'Now what?'

'Now,' Sarah said, her face grim, 'we walk.'

CHAPTER FIVE

Richard Goodwin waited in his office. He looked out at the lush, green, Brazilian rainforest, which stretched to the distant horizon and beyond. It was a wondrous sight; it was also an illusion, albeit a real-time one. Cameras around the world were trained on various landscapes that you could select, much like the allocation of a backdrop on a user interface. Once a vista was chosen, you couldn't change it again for at least six months as, according to scientific research, for the brain to train the subconscious into believing it was real it had to remain constant for that minimum duration; altering the scene every day to different locations negated the effect. He still knew it was fake, but it was soothingly familiar nonetheless.

Goodwin watched as a group of howler monkeys he'd grown to know worked their way through nearby treetops, adults foraging for leaves and berries and juveniles playing and learning to survive. Exotic birds preened and sang as the sun rose high in the crystal clear sky above.

The three hundred and sixty degree views plus domed ceiling display all seamlessly knitted together, producing a 64K visual marvel; it was truly an immersive 3D experience and yet for all its wonder it brought an ache to his heart as he knew the darkness was coming. Soon the meteor would hit and the planet would become encased in a thick, pervasive dust cloud, choking the life out of the plants, trees, birds and animals indiscriminately. Only a tiny minority would survive and they would be entrusted to start their species anew; along with human help, of course. Zoo funding had gone through the roof and conservation, or *Genesisity* as it had become known, was very big business, much like the *Green* movement at the turn of the century, forty years earlier.

A bell chimed on his desk. 'He's here, Director,' said the familiar voice of his secretary.

Goodwin pressed a button. 'Thank you, Leah, send him in, please.'

A few seconds later a soft yet purposeful knock came on the door.

'Come in,' Goodwin said.

The door opened, shifting the image to one side and revealing the reception office beyond and a short man with silver hair and a bushy brown-grey beard.

'Professor Steiner,' Goodwin said, walking forward and shaking his hand. The door closed behind him and the illusion resumed once more.

The professor looked around the room at the beautiful setting.

'Did you have a good journey, Professor?'

'I did, Richard, thank you,' the professor said, his strong voice belaying his age and appearance. He wasn't the most powerful person on the planet, but he was right up there. Able to call upon massive resources from around the world, governments bent to his will. He was perhaps the most important man on the planet in terms of ensuring the continued functioning of civilisation as they knew it. He was also Goodwin's direct superior, in principle, anyway; he rarely got to see the man due to his never-ending workload.

Goodwin was the operational director of the Dulce underground facility, officially called the United States Subterranean Base Steadfast, or U.S.S.B. Steadfast for short. Located on the border of Colorado and New Mexico, it was the second largest of the U.S. bases which had been constructed deep underground to preserve not only human life, but all other life on the planet. Of course, the United States wasn't the only country with such bases. They also weren't just there to protect against acts of God, such as meteors, solar flares and the like, as they also protected against nuclear war, plague, biological war and other catastrophes devised and unleashed by nature or man.

Goodwin had worked on the base for ten years and had led it for four. More than a kilometre below the surface at its uppermost point to over three kilometres at its deepest, the complex housed nuclear reactors; weapons depots, five hundred thousand residents and staff, offices, laboratories, engineering and computer suites and a huge multifaceted living ecosystem. Alongside the Chinese Shanxi base, U.S.S.B. Steadfast contained the largest manmade partial self-sustaining biological organism (P.S.S.B.O.) in the world. The P.S.S.B.O. utilised fully integrated technology, including water recycling, air regeneration, horticultural and microbiological continuity manipulation and sunlight wave systems, representing human ingenuity at its finest.

'How goes Steadfast, Richard?' the professor asked him as he walked around the room taking in the view.

'I sent you a report last week, Professor,' Goodwin said with concern. 'Didn't you get it?'

'Yes, of course; however, you can never really gauge a situation until you have seen it first-hand.'

'It also means you don't get stuck in an office all the time, either,' Goodwin said in jest, and then regretted it instantly; *crap*, he thought, *have I angered him? That sounded like I think he's lazy or something.*

Luckily Professor Steiner just chuckled. 'There is that advantage, although,' – he looked about the room – 'this projection makes real life seem bland, office or no.'

Goodwin coughed in discomfort. He'd requisitioned the room's screen tech to combat the depression he suffered from being underground on such a long term basis. He occasionally took time out to walk through some of Steadfast's gardens and forests, but even that wasn't really enough for him.

'It is very soothing, it helps me work better,' Goodwin said, his reasoning sounding lame even to his ears.

'Then it's worth every dime, you have done some excellent work here, Richard. A few perks merit the investment, I think,' – Steiner flashed him a wink and smiled – 'we have the budget, after all.'

Goodwin grinned back at him, relaxing a little. The professor was right, though, their budget was enormous. Virtually anything they needed, they got. Goodwin wasn't sure how this near infinite supply of money had been cleared through congress, although it was a black project and as such mechanisms had been in place for nearly a century to ensure they passed through regardless. Some things were just too important to disclose to the public and even to politicians. It was concerning, though, even on this side of the curtain.

'How is morale,' the professor asked him, 'as a whole?'

'Very good,' Goodwin said with confidence. 'We're on schedule with every major programme and final preparations are being made for when Impact Day protocols are activated.'

'That's not what I asked, Richard. What I mean is, how are people coping generally with the fact that all overground leave has been cancelled for perhaps five years or more? Some loved ones and friends will not be seen in person for the same duration. The sun and our fine,' – he looked up – 'fine blue sky will also be disappearing, too. What is their mood, Richard? These are stressful times for all.'

'There is an air of excitement,' Goodwin said. 'This is what we have all trained for, some for many years or much longer in certain instances. There is also anxiety and agitation in some quarters, especially amongst the families of base personnel. Some of the military are also getting a little agitated; we had an incident the other day where a large fight broke out between air force and army officers, not an example they should be setting to their men.'

'That sounds a little serious, but we have been experiencing such instances in other bases around the world; although not usually with officers, mind you. Testosterone, fear and close quarters are not the best of bedfellows.'

'I agree. One of the Special Forces colonels took control of matters, although he was a little heavy handed for my liking.'

'Oh?' Steiner said, raising an eyebrow. 'How so?'

'He had some of the men locked down in solitary confinement,' Goodwin said, his tone disapproving. 'He also broke an air force major's jaw in the melee, which is when I had to step in to prevent further conflict. Colonel Samson was not too happy with my intervention, however.'

'It takes a tougher man to control tough men, Richard. The military and civilian directorship is always a flash point in any situation; however, it must be known that we are in charge. They are our tool to guide, not the other way round.'

Goodwin grimaced. 'That is a difficult message to get across sometimes.'

'And yet it is what we are paid to do,' Steiner said. 'The Chinese have another method, of course. Communism and strict governance allow little leeway for rule breakers. Their method has its advantages, although I believe those are outweighed by the negatives; but then, no one is perfect, are they?' He smiled again, lightening the mood a little.

'Apart from us, Professor,' Goodwin said, grinning.

Steiner laughed. 'Well, that goes without saying, of course,' he said, before continuing his stroll around the room as he immersed himself in the sights and sounds of the Amazon rainforest in all its glory.

Goodwin remained silent as he didn't like to interrupt the special moment people enjoyed when they were mentally transported to the idyllic location. It took people in various ways. Some liked to chat about every detail; others questioned less and soaked up the ambience. A few people didn't want to leave, so much so a business a few chambers over had installed a similar system, but much larger, for people to enjoy on lunch breaks and the like. He'd heard it had been a resounding success.

'Can you take me on a tour of the facility, Richard?' Steiner said at last.

'Of course, Professor.' Goodwin led the way to the door, and they emerged into a well-lit but mundane office. Out of the window the actual view was an odd one. Thousands of feet below the surface one would expect to see just rock; however, a major jump forward in excavation techniques enabled enormous chambers to be cut out of the Earth's crust. The principal and unusual process behind this success was called Thermal Density Reduction (T.D.R.), pioneered by renowned British scientists William and Thomas Wedgwood.

It was evening, so the chamber they were currently in – Alpha Chamber One, or AC1 for short – was under street lighting, much like any surface town or city. U.S.S.B. Steadfast was classified as a subterranean base, but since it housed five hundred thousand people it was really an underground city and as such would have qualified, if it wasn't clandestine, as the forty-fifth largest city out of two hundred and eighty-five in the United States.

A central road ran through the chamber and from the Command Centre, in which they were located, it could be seen disappearing off into the distance. Many roads branched out from this thoroughfare in a familiar grid system configuration, while emission-free cars, bikes and trucks criss-crossed smoothly throughout the transport network's intersections like data packets moving between computers. Of course the advantage of electric vehicles underground was obvious; a lack of pollutants prevented chambers from filling up with noxious gases. Induction track lines integrated on the main roads charged and powered vehicles while also preventing high speed crashes, which would likely have dire consequences in such an underground facility. Safety was paramount for all Steadfastians, as they liked to call themselves.

Once the two men had made their way outside, Goodwin hailed a cab and climbed inside after Steiner had boarded.

'Where to, Mr. Goodwin, sir?' the cabby said.

A certain loss of anonymity came with heading a project like Steadfast, and he was known throughout the base. He'd even appeared on the various media platforms run by the civilian sector, much to his dismay; he enjoyed his privacy and didn't like to be the centre of attention.

'Can you take us to the Bio Chamber System, please, BC5 would be good.'

'Will do, sir, should take about thirty-five minutes.'

Goodwin thanked him as the car effortlessly gained speed and linked onto the main trunk road. A loud clunk reverberated through the sub frame as the taxi locked onto one of the central track ways.

'How is Cathy?' the professor asked him as the scenery flashed by.

'We went our separate ways,' Goodwin said.

'I'm sorry to hear that, she was ...'

'Manic, is the word you're looking for.'

'I was going to say energetic,' Steiner said, with a small smile.

'That would be one way of putting it.'

'You've found no one else?'

'No, it's been a while now and I've gotten used to being on my own.'

'Richard, don't end up like me, wealthy, driven and successful and yet I am alone. It's not the sort of life you should be getting used to.'

'Did you never want to remarry?' Goodwin said, steering the conversation away from a topic he'd rather not discuss.

'Not for a long time.' Steiner sighed. 'I replaced companionship with my studies and work and when I did eventually consider it, I felt it too late in my life, I was stuck in my ways. Sad but true.'

Goodwin didn't reply. The professor was right, he didn't want to get used to being alone and yet he'd tired of the merry-go-round of the dating scene a while back. No, he was happy enough; he had good friends, excellent friends, and many interests. Besides, his work took up most of his time so he wouldn't be able to give a woman the attention she deserved anyway.

As they neared the bio chamber a while later, travelling along a seemingly endless low-lit tunnel, they passed a large digital road sign indicating entry into section BC5. The taxi swept around a tight bend and up a steep incline before bright, simulated natural light engulfed them as they exited into a truly cavernous area of the base. Trees pressed in all around the car and flocks of birds flew up as they glided by. After a few minutes the underground forest opened up on either side. Pushing a couple of buttons, the cabbie detached the vehicle from the main trunk road's induction track and drove into a gravel car park. Having arrived at their destination, Goodwin asked the driver to wait for their return before joining Steiner out in the fresh air. The two men then walked over to an oval shaped building which overlooked a large expanse of water. A plaque outside read:

M.E.C.A.
MANAGED ECOSYSTEM
CONTROL ARRAY

U.S.S.B. STEADFAST
BIO-CHAMBER FIVE
Protocols 6;12;56;57;58;81

Goodwin had his bio signatures confirmed and then unlocked the doors with a quick swipe of his phone. The two men entered the building and an elevator transported them up to the sixth, and top, floor. They exited at the centre of a large room that was encased in a single transparent dome, showing off the full glory of the forest and lake below, all the way to the distant edge of the chamber a couple of miles away.

A young looking woman greeted them. 'Richard,' she said in a rich South African accent, 'the system told me you were en route; it's good to see you, it's been a while.'

Goodwin kissed her on both cheeks and then introduced her to Professor Steiner.

'Professor, this is Dr. Kara Vandervoort, the head of our wonderful ecosystem.'

'It's a pleasure to finally meet you, my dear; you have quite the reputation amongst your international peers.'

'We call her Green Fingered Kara,' Goodwin said, smiling fondly at Kara, who blushed in response. 'How was your trip,' he asked her, 'did you get to see everything you wanted?'

Dr. Vandervoort shrugged. 'Yes, I suppose,' she said, a little downcast. 'I thought I had prepared myself for letting go, but I hadn't realised how hard it was going to be. Knowing the places you grew up, went to school, the national landmarks, everything, is soon going to disappear is ...' – she stared off into space – 'difficult.'

Goodwin laid a consoling hand on her shoulder. There wasn't much he could say, South Africa was to take the brunt of the impact and nothing would be left after AG5's arrival.

'These will be difficult times for us all,' Steiner said, turning serious. 'Your nation will be mourned, my dear, but it will not be forgotten.'

'And the country can be rebuilt when everything has settled down again in the future, isn't that right, Professor?' Goodwin said, catching a brief flicker of angst – or was it fear? – on the professor's face, before the warm smile came back as though it had never been away.

'Most definitely, all will be well.'

Goodwin felt a little uneasy after witnessing that micro expression. Did the professor think South Africa couldn't be rebuilt in the future? And if so, why? Unable to think of an answer, he shrugged it off while the doctor demonstrated for them the real-time monitoring systems and presented historical results and forecasts, all of which Goodwin had seen many times before. The professor, however, took it all in, asking numerous pertinent questions.

After leaving Kara to continue with her work, they spent a few hours taking in many of the other major systems and facilities throughout the base. Finally they took a cab back to the main Command Centre located in the middle of Steadfast. The building, a massive structure fifty floors high, cut through three chamber levels and housed the majority of Steadfast's high ranking civilian and operational personnel. Goodwin led the professor to the core observation deck located in the heavily reinforced interior. The large room comfortably held seventy systems operators, technicians and analysts. Each person had their own semi-wrapped crescent screen and operators flicked and gestured at their monitors, shifting information from location to location remotely. Complicated graphics, charts and telemetry cascaded down onto one large command screen which dominated the room.

'Would you like to take control, sir?' said a lead control centre analyst as an alarm sounded off to one side indicating some target or level had been reached on a particular system.

'I would, thank you, Rob.' Goodwin swiped his card over the analyst's handheld computer phone and then attaching a control circlet to his index finger. With a couple of quick movements, he brought up current trajectory data for the asteroid known as 2011 AG5.

'It looks as though it's increased in speed slightly,' Goodwin said, 'however, it hasn't affected predicted impact zones or forecast fallout data.'

'The increase in speed will be due to gravitational forces as AG5 passed close to Mars,' the professor told him. 'As you say, it's a negligible factor.'

Goodwin nodded; he might have known the professor would be up on such information. Goodwin brought up real-time footage of AG5's passage through space. A few workers looked up at it for a moment and then carried on with their duties. Goodwin marvelled at the object they had waited for so long to arrive. Colossal and sinister, and, according to a spectral composition analysis, it had almost the same mass as had been displaced from the entire base. Parts of its surface glistened with ice as light from the sun reflected off its great bulk as it drew ever nearer to Earth.

'She's quite a sight, isn't she?' Steiner said.

Goodwin looked at him. 'She?'

'The media, Richard, they named her Big Bertha years ago.'

'Did they? Oh yes, I vaguely remember, it's had so many names I lose track.'

'I like Big Bertha, it takes the sting out of it; it is, after all, only a bit of rock.'

Goodwin made a face. 'A very big bit of rock.'

'That she is,' Steiner said solemnly, 'that she is.'

Goodwin checked the countdown timer. 'Looks like we're going into the final stage.'

The professor nodded as they both watched the seconds tick away. A loud alarm sounded and a red flashing light indicated time until impact had passed the fourteen day threshold. Many more people took the opportunity to peer up from their desks this time, chattering to one another in mild animation. The flashing stopped, work resumed, and the timer continued its inevitable decline to zero.

The next day Goodwin had the unfortunate task of introducing Professor Steiner to the military liaison for a tour of the military installations of the base. Unfortunate, because the usual designated liaison had taken ill and the only on-site available ranking officer turned out to be the very one that Goodwin had recently clashed with, Colonel Samson.

Apparently Professor Steiner didn't seem to mind the man's curt and sometimes aggressive demeanour. Goodwin knew military people; a few were close friends, and none of them displayed that type of behaviour, not towards civilians, anyway. Goodwin did not care for such rudeness. He'd heard the man was ruthless in war and, if not to be respected, certainly to be feared. Goodwin didn't fear the man, although he definitely wouldn't fancy his chances against him in a physical contest. A veteran in the Special Forces, Samson had numerous honours and had received many accolades from senior ranks. 'He gets the job done,' Goodwin was told.

'That's not in dispute,' Goodwin had argued, 'it's how he gets it done that I don't care for.' Goodwin had seen first-hand how Samson ruled his command; fear and intimidation were paramount in the Samson guide to leadership, everything that Goodwin abhorred and the complete opposite to how he managed those below him.

Amazingly, Steiner didn't seem to be affronted by Samson, seemingly oblivious to his abrasiveness; *although that probably isn't surprising*, Goodwin thought, *considering the professor must deal with these sort of people, and perhaps worse, on a continuous basis*. His respect for the man, already considerable, increased even further.

'And where are the missiles stored, Colonel?' Steiner was asking.

'Right through there,' Samson said in his gruff manner, pointing to one side.

Steiner's placid demeanour remained unchanged as he waited for Samson to continue, his eyes asking the colonel a question.

Samson ground his teeth in frustration. 'Did you want to look?' he said, now clearly aggravated.

'Yes, thank you,' Steiner replied with flawless sincerity.

Samson swiped an access reader with a card and went through the bio scans. The outer doors whisked open while much thicker and larger inner doors parted slowly inwards. Lights flickered on inside the vast room where various types of military hardware had been crated up.

'There don't appear to be any missiles here, Colonel,' Steiner said.

Samson stifled an angry growl. 'That's because they're in the next room.'

Goodwin concealed a smile as the fuming colonel swept past him back into the hall and down the corridor leading to the missile room. Goodwin gave Steiner an apologetic look.

'I thought you'd have known the missiles were located down the hall, Richard?' Steiner said innocently, as the blast doors closed behind them.

Goodwin didn't reply, he had known, but he didn't know if the professor was jesting with him or reprimanding him. He believed it was the former, but he wasn't totally sure.

Later on, after the tour had ended, the professor bade them goodbye and left for a nearby hotel with a few of his aides who had been trailing after them during Samson's dire performance as military liaison. As Goodwin turned to leave after Steiner's departure, Samson said something to him; Goodwin, his mind elsewhere, didn't catch the remark.

'I'm sorry, Colonel, what did you say?'

Samson stepped in close, his face a mere inch from Goodwin's own.

Startled, Goodwin stepped back a pace.

'I said,' – Samson moved even closer than before, his breath on Goodwin's face and eyes bulging with rage – 'if you ever try to humiliate me like that again, I'll gut you like a pig.'

Goodwin froze in shock, unsure how to respond. The colonel meanwhile had already stormed away. Goodwin felt a little shaken, more than a little. Samson had intent in his eyes when he'd said it and Goodwin didn't doubt the man, given his reputation. What should he do? As leader of Steadfast he couldn't have a military officer threatening to kill him. But then, such an accusation, if submitted to the base's General, must have supporting evidence; a witness, which he didn't have. Clearly the man was unhinged. Perhaps he'd speak to the professor about it for some advice or assistance. He didn't want that kind of man on his base, more for the safety of those under his care than out of concern for himself. If anyone had the power to do something without needing a reason it was the professor, he was always the man in control.

CHAPTER SIX

PROFESSOR STEINER PACED AROUND his office, his concern mounting and frustration tangible. He'd been trying to obtain details about a large piece of Japanese equipment destined for Steadfast, a task he'd taken on prior to his arrival at the base; however his requisition orders kept getting delayed. This hadn't happened to him before – ever. Normally what he wanted, he got. It wasn't as if the machinery in question was still under manufacture, according to the usually one hundred per cent reliable GMRC global procurement database it waited in a warehouse just outside of Tokyo.

Sitting down he rhythmically tapped his fingers on the desk and then snapped up his phone and dialled the GMRC's U.S. Department in South Korea; they were the primary point of contact for all international freight forwarding in Asia.

'Yes, hello, can I speak to Nathan Bryant, please,' he said, and then waited as an operator put him through.

'Nathan Bryant,' said a familiar voice.

'Nathan, I need your assistance.'

'Professor! Nice to hear from you, it's been a while. I'm going doolally over here, I'm sure Joiner stuck me in this office out of spite,' he said, half joking, half voicing serious complaint.

'Indeed,' Steiner replied, recognising Nathan's plight, but currently not in a position to tackle it; he had more important matters at hand. 'Nathan, I need your help. I'm trying to get some important equipment through to Steadfast, but it keeps getting put back. Can you bang some heads together and sort it out for me as soon as possible, please? The order ref is Q R S nine nine one dash zero eight five six four dash A B.'

'Sure,' Nathan said, 'no problem, hold on and I'll check it right now for you.'

A tapping of keys echoed down the phone and then he came back on. 'Looks like that's been diverted to another base, Professor.'

'Which one?'

'U.S.S.B. Sanctuary.'

'What? How did that happen? Nathan, sort this out now. I want that equipment here yesterday.'

'Very good, Professor, I'll keep you updated.'

'Thank you, Nathan, it's appreciated.' Steiner hung up the phone, now in a furious mood. It wasn't often things went awry, but this was a large and very important piece of kit for the water purification system. He got up out of his chair and started pacing. He needed to keep his mind occupied while he waited, as he knew it might take Nathan a few hours to sort it all out. After a few minutes he had settled back down at his desk and was going through his itinerary when the phone rang.

'Yes?' he said.

'Professor, it's Nathan.' He sounded unusually nervous. 'It seems we have a problem, it seems—'

'Come on, out with it,' Steiner said, in no mood for indirectness.

'It seems your order was overridden.'

Steiner didn't say anything, his mind racing to digest the almost unbelievable information he'd just heard.

'Professor, are you still there?'

'What? Yes – yes of course. Who the hell overrode me?'

'It looks like the Secretary General of the UN—'

'He doesn't have the authority to overrule me,' Steiner said, cutting in.

'If you'd let me finish, Professor,' Nathan said, his tone placating. 'The Sec Gen's order was combined with one from the Joint Chiefs.'

'Which General or Admiral gave the order?'

'It was a full issue procedure, they all cleared it.'

Again, Steiner said nothing.

'It's odd though,' Nathan continued when there was no reply. 'It looks, as far as I can tell, like your request was intentionally buried in the system along with the override itself. This couldn't have happened by accident, it was deliberate. So not only did they override the order you gave, they tried to make sure it looked like a system or logistics error.'

Steiner frowned. 'You found it quickly enough.'

'Only because of my clearance level,' Nathan said, 'and due to the skills I picked up working alongside you on GMRC computer system architecture; anyone else would've missed it.'

Grim-faced, Steiner kept an iron hold on his emotions, which raged beneath the surface. 'Who has administrative access to that system?'

'There are a few people here, but I checked the logs in detail and it appears it was an outside source. I'd say high level military intervention; they're the only ones with the means and access codes.'

'So the Joint Chiefs are blocking me; for what reason?'

'I have no idea, Professor.'

Steiner thought for moment. 'Nathan, I want you back here immediately. I'm going to make some calls.'

'I'm on my way,' Nathan said and promptly hung up.

Steiner expected him to arrive within a few hours as he'd be utilising a Sabre propelled passenger plane for transport. In the meantime he had some markers to call in.

Some time later he was no longer angry or even frustrated, but very worried; every close contact he'd nurtured within the U.S. military had clammed up. They either told him they wouldn't be able to help or came up with some excuse not to. With his sources dried up, he had one last throw of the dice left. Picking up the phone, he re-routed the software protocol by altering the actual code, preventing any tracing or tapping of his call. He'd become that paranoid since, in all the years he'd been in command, not one time had he encountered anything like this type of resistance; something was seriously wrong. The phone rang for some time before being answered.

'Salt Lake Care Home.'

'Can I speak to Selena Adams, please?'

'I'm sorry, I don't recognise that name.'

'Ex Vice President Selena Adams?' Steiner said.

'Oh yes, of course, sorry I'm new here. She may be sleeping, I'll go and check.'

'It's quite important, so please wake her if she is.'

'I'm not sure—'

'Madam, this is extremely urgent and a matter of national security. Now, instead of me having to send a helicopter to pick Selena up and fly her halfway across the country I would appreciate your assistance.'

'Certainly, sir,' the woman said, sounding flustered, 'I will get her right away,'

A couple of minutes later a soft voice came on the phone. 'Hello. Who is it?'

'Selena, it's George.'

'George? I don't know any George.'

'Selena, it's Professor Steiner.'

'Oh, why didn't you say so? Hello, Professor.'

Steiner was concerned, he knew her memory had declined, but it must be more serious than he'd thought.

'Selena, are you alone?'

'I'm not sure what you mean, dear.'

'Madam Vice President, are you alone?' he said with authority.

'I am and you should watch your tone,' she said, her voice gaining strength and some semblance of its old power, 'do you know who I am?'

'I do, Madam Vice President, forgive me. I need your help. It's extremely important and I think you are the only one who can help me.'

'Go on,' she said, her voice a little weaker, but still much sharper than before.

'Selena, I'm being blocked by the Joint Chiefs on a very important piece of equipment for one of the bases, but much more than that I'm being stonewalled by the whole damn military fraternity. Do you know anyone that could help me? I need to know what's going on, and fast.'

'The military, you say. Well, there is General Hampton, he will be able to help you.'

Steiner cursed under his breath; General Hampton had died ten years previously.

'I'm sorry, dear, what did you say?'

He tried a different tack. 'I need a younger officer, one you can trust.'

'Oh that's easy, Colonel Ellwood. We were very close; he proposed, you know. I turned him down, I don't remember why. Do you know why?' she said, her frailty and confusion reasserting itself.

'I don't, Selena, I'm sorry. Will Colonel Ellwood be willing to help me?'

'No. Not you.'

'But he will help me as a favour to you?'

'He may, George,' she said, obviously remembering they were close friends by using his given name. 'We have a secret.'

'A secret?' His hopes rose. 'Can I use that to get him to help me?'

She didn't respond.

'Selena, how can I get Colonel Ellwood to know that you sent me? I need him to help me.'

'I'm sorry, dear; I have to go; they're serving lunch. It's my favourite, cheese and tomato sandwiches.'

'Madam Vice President,' he said, hoping to snap her back to the present once more. 'I need your help, please. What can I say to Colonel Ellwood?'

Silence followed and then, 'Amy Adams,' she whispered, her voice wavering in emotional distress, and then she was gone.

It took Professor Steiner a few hours to track down Colonel Ellwood, now another rung up the ladder and Brigadier General Ellwood. He'd been stationed at U.S.S.B. Sanctuary, which was convenient yet at the same time extremely unfortunate. Ellwood would know why Steiner suddenly found himself on the outside regarding the U.S. military, and seemingly U.S.S.B. Sanctuary in particular; however, he might be complicit in preventing his progress in the first place. Steiner had nothing to lose at this point so he picked up the phone, executed his previous protocol and code process to ensure a secure line, and waited for an answer.

'General Ellwood,' a gravelly voice said.

'General, this is Professor Steiner, GMRC Subterranean Director General Steiner. I need your assistance.'

The General's tone became guarded. 'How can I help you, Professor?'

'General, I'm having some issues with some equipment I procured which was bound for Steadfast; however, it appears to have found its way to Sanctuary instead. I need it to be shipped back here urgently, please.'

'I'm sorry, Professor, I can't help you with that. I don't deal with that side of things.'

'General, let's cut the crap, shall we? I've been getting the runaround all day and I need your help.'

'I'm sorry to hear that but, as I said, I can't help you.'

It sounded like he was going to put down the phone so Steiner crossed his fingers and prayed Ellwood owed Selena big time. 'Amy Adams,' he said.

There was a long pause. 'I'm sorry?' An edge of fear crept into Ellwood's voice. 'What did you just say?'

'I'm a very close friend of Selena Adams, Ex Vice President Selena Adams.'

'Yes, I am well aware who she is.'

'You owe her big time,' Steiner said confidently, although feeling anything but, 'and I'm here on her behalf to collect.'

Silence. Had he hung up? No, he could hear breathing and background noise.

'Look, General, I know everything there is to know about Amy and what went on between you and Selena. I'm not interested in that, what I am interested in is why I am being undermined by the military at such a crucial time and in connection with such an important piece of equipment.'

Still silence.

'Are you there, General?'

'Is this line secure?'

Steiner could have jumped with joy. 'It is,' he said, remaining calm.

'It better be. Have you checked your deep space imagery recently, Professor?'

'Of course. I am constantly updated on the progress of all deep space analysis.'

'Check it again. Clearance code H J K dash zero zero niner dash SANCTUARY dash I D star eight two five. All letters are uppercase.'

'And this is why the Joint Chiefs are blocking me?'

'The Joint Chiefs are involved, yes. But Joiner pulls all the strings.'

'Joiner, Director of Intelligence, Malcolm Joiner?'

'Yes,' Ellwood said, and hung up.

Steiner put down the phone. Well, it looked like the gamble had paid off, but now he felt even more worried than before. What could be going on that he wasn't aware of? He had top level clearance. He knew things that very few knew; for instance, no one else in Steadfast knew what he knew. So how did a lowly Brigadier General at U.S.S.B. Sanctuary know more than he? He took his personal computer phone from its induction dock and the screen went blank. It was probably wiser to find another station to work on rather than use his own again. Exiting his office, he walked down the hall, took an elevator down three floors and found a disaster recovery console. He hacked into the telemetry array and entered the security access code Ellwood had given him.

The data streams that came up on a monitor he had seen many times. He flicked the information onto a large screen display on the right wall of the room and brought up charts and graphs showing current and historical feeds. Entering a standard code, he was able to compare the two data sets against each other. He didn't know what he was looking for, so he studied the screen for some time until suddenly he spotted it. The data he normally had access to had been tampered with. This new feed was apparently the real stream. Now that he knew there was a problem, he quickly found the algorithm utilised in the deception. The discrepancies appeared tiny, but Steiner knew that when dealing with massive objects and trajectories, the resulting repercussions could be massive.

He extrapolated the numbers he needed and plugged them into a simulation programme. *That can't be right*, he thought, and he put them in again. The same result displayed. He did it again. Switched terminals and tried again. Went back to his office and tried again and again. There was no mistake; he'd been badly deceived and many people's lives were in mortal danger because of it. He needed to act, but how? He still had civilian support; he reached out and met little resistance as he probed people with searching yet subtle questions. The duplicity was seemingly a military affair, although what with the involvement of the UN Secretary General and Joiner he wasn't totally convinced of this assumption. He decided to mull over his options and discuss them with Nathan when he arrived. Sitting at his desk, Steiner absent-mindedly rotated the single gold band that adorned his ring finger, staring off into space, his mind racing and his mood dark.

———

Goodwin approached the professor's office, one of his many offices located in bases around the world. He knocked; Steiner called him inside.

'Professor, I need to talk to you about a problem that's arisen.' He stopped as he caught sight of Steiner; he looked exhausted. 'Are you all right, Professor? You look tired.'

'I'm fine, Richard,' he said wearily, 'please sit down.'

Goodwin took a seat and noticed for the first time that Steiner looked his age.

'What's troubling you?' the professor said.

Goodwin felt reluctant to pile any more pressure on the man, but Steiner noticed his reticence and waved him on with a hand.

'I had a very uncomfortable encounter with the colonel after our ... *tour*,' Goodwin said.

'Samson?'

Goodwin nodded. He was wondering how to put it to Steiner, but there was no easy way so he went down the direct route. 'He threatened to kill me.'

Steiner's eyes widened in shock.

'Well, he actually said he'd *"Gut me like a pig"* which amounts to the same thing, really.'

'Why on God's green Earth would he say such a thing?' Steiner said, incensed.

'Perhaps due to the altercation I broke up the other day. I undermined his authority in front of his men, so he might be holding a grudge. I think he also thought I was intentionally humiliating him during the tour of the facility, when he got the wrong room for the missiles. I suppose I could have said something, as I did know he'd gone to the wrong door, but then he'd probably have got equally as angry if I'd done that. I was just keeping my head down, really. Apparently he's a little sensitive when getting things wrong publicly.'

'That seems like an understatement in the circumstances,' Steiner said, wiping his brow with a handkerchief. 'To be frank, Richard, this couldn't have come at a worse time. I'm having some difficulties with the military myself at the moment.'

'I'm sorry, Professor, I didn't realise. I can take this to the colonel's superiors.'

'I doubt that would have the desired effect. In fact, it might make things worse. I think you may have guessed that already, hence you're here now.'

Goodwin nodded.

The professor appeared to be in thought for a moment. 'Leave it with me,' he said eventually, 'and I'll sort it out for you. I would steer clear of him for the time being, I will assign you two of my bodyguards. They will be discreet, so not to draw comment.'

'I don't think that will be necessary,' – Goodwin shifted in his seat, unnerved at the prospect – 'in truth, I'm actually more worried about others on the base. I'll be fine.'

'I'd rather not take that chance at the moment,' Steiner told him.

Goodwin wondered why that would be, but since Steiner didn't appear to be in the mood to elaborate, he didn't question it. 'Thank you, Professor, I can't tell you how much I appreciate this. If there's anything I can do for you just let me know.'

'No need, but thank you for the offer all the same. I have great admiration for you, Richard; I think of you as a friend rather than a colleague and friends help each other out and require nothing in return.'

Goodwin thanked him again and got up to leave, just as there was a knock on the door.

Nathan Bryant entered at the professor's behest.

'Richard, it's been a while,' Nathan said, briefly shaking his hand as they passed each other. Goodwin smiled and continued on his way; Nathan, seemingly too busy to chat, had already taken the chair recently vacated by Goodwin. That was fine by him as he felt exhausted himself now; he planned to have a long bath and a good night's sleep to ease his tired muscles. A short while later he reached his apartment to find two suited men standing guard outside his door, their chiselled physiques and holstered sidearms out of place in the residential neighbourhood. Steiner had been as good as his word.

Goodwin spoke to them briefly and then retired to recuperate for the following day.

Steiner sat at his desk across from Nathan as they discussed his options and the new information he had gained from his source. He didn't disclose Ellwood's name as he didn't want to put Nathan's position in jeopardy, even though the younger man pushed for it, saying he didn't mind taking the risk. Steiner also didn't want to betray Selena's trust in him; it was bad enough that he was using her secret for leverage, he wouldn't tell another and lower himself further. Of course his actions weren't completely altruistic as, while he hadn't wanted to blackmail Ellwood, he had and he knew he'd prefer not to publicise such a shameful act, even though in actuality he hadn't a clue what had occurred with Amy Adams and nor did he want to know.

'So there is only one route to take,' Steiner said, after they had weighed up all the options in their entirety.

'It's going to be hard to swing it,' Nathan said, 'especially if the Joint Chiefs are behind this for whatever reason.'

Steiner knew he was right, but it was beside the point. 'What can they do? If we mobilise and turn up on their doorstep they won't be able to turn us away as it may expose us all. They'd have no choice but to comply.'

'It's high risk; what if word got out?'

'It won't make any difference in the longer term,' Steiner said, his expression grim, 'it will merely make their life a lot harder overnight and we could just take our chances later on.'

'I would advise against it, Professor.'

'Duly noted,' Steiner said, indicating an end to the matter. Steiner had hoped for Nathan's full support, but it seemed he was to be disappointed. He'd have to go it alone on this one. *On my head be it*, he thought. It was the right thing to do, he knew it; he wasn't sure of Nathan's reasons to decide otherwise, but that was his prerogative.

Now he must begin preparations, plus he would sort out Samson for Goodwin. His anger swelled again at the thought of someone threatening his friend's life.

The next day Steiner made his way to Steadfast's military quarter. Once at the appropriate barracks, a guard informed him Samson conducted exercises for his men in a nearby training ground. Steiner had brought his last remaining bodyguard along with his aides as a matter of course. Hopefully this would deter Samson, who sounded like he could be borderline insane, from chopping Steiner down in front of witnesses. *I can't afford to die at the moment*, he thought to himself with more than a little sardonic humour.

'I'd like to speak with the colonel, please,' Steiner told one of Samson's troops, who lounged at the entrance to the compound.

'He's exercising with the men,' the soldier said, looking at his watch. 'He'll be finished in five, wait here and I'll let him know as soon as he's finished.'

'Thank you, Sergeant,' Steiner said, and moved away from his retinue to wait, which wasn't long as soon after Samson stalked out to meet him.

'You wanted to see me?' the colonel said, irritation written all over his face.

'I did.' Steiner moved further away from prying ears. 'I'm not going to beat about the proverbial bush, Colonel. You have threatened one of my personnel with physical violence; they also happen to be a friend of mine, so I shall put this very clearly. You will request a transfer to U.S.S.B. Haven immediately or I will have you forcibly removed and detained until I decide what to have done with you. Do you understand me, Colonel?'

Towering over him, Samson's face darkened and he leaned down menacingly. Steiner's bodyguard moved forwards, but Steiner held up his hand to stop him.

Samson looked round and laughed. 'Your bodyguard doesn't scare me and neither do your empty threats. I'm going nowhere.'

'That would be unwise,' Steiner said, holding his ground. 'You do not want to try me.'

The colonel smiled and walked off without another word, eyeballing Steiner's bodyguard as he went.

That went badly, Steiner thought. His threat of moving Samson by force was a weak one considering his current relations with the Joint Chiefs and the military fraternity. Apparently Samson knew that too, or else he just didn't give a crap. *At least Richard has my bodyguards for protection*, he reflected.

Looking at the bigger picture, Steiner decided he needed to call in some contractors as soon as possible. Now that the U.S. military essentially danced to their own tune, the GMRC itself had been compromised; his hand had been forced and he had to return the status quo. If the Joint Chiefs and Joiner wanted to play games, then he still had some final cards to play.

CHAPTER SEVEN

A PRIVATE PLANE touched down on a military airstrip five miles outside of the town of Dulce, New Mexico. A group of black SUVs made their way out from one of the hangars as the aircraft came to rest half a mile away. No sooner had the engines shut down than a ladder was manoeuvred into place as a door opened above. Men in dark suits exited, many donning shades to fend off the dazzling rays as the sun beat down overhead. As the SUVs came to a stop nearby, a final group of people emerged from the opening.

Malcolm Joiner, Director of National and GMRC Intelligence, stepped down onto the baking hot tarmac and moved to his waiting vehicle. He was glad to get inside the air-conditioned cabin as his men climbed in around him. The small convoy began to move and a short while later they were passing the checkpoint to the military compound guarding the primary surface entrance to U.S.S.B. Steadfast. The vehicles cleared a final security sweep and were then driven onto one of the enormous elevator mechanisms; an engineering marvel that had been utilised the world over in subterranean complexes as the principal surface-to-interior transportation system. Thick, super-hardened doors encapsulated the convoy on a wide, expansive oval platform, while teams of workers prepped the structure for departure. Ten, twenty and then thirty minutes ticked by as they waited for the other levels of the elevator to be loaded up, the system being too large an operation to warrant deployment for small parties and Joiner's arrival having been timed so that it coincided with that day's descent schedule.

Soon enough sirens sounded and beacons flashed as speakers announced magnetic coil locks had disengaged and surface departure was imminent. Grinding noises sent vibrations through the platform and a loud whining assaulted the senses, indicating the turbine engines had powered up. The super elevator gave a lurch and then descended steadily toward its destination, the huge engines ensuring the whole load didn't plummet in freefall towards the distant shaft floor thousands of feet below.

The small convoy arrived at the central chamber of the base two hours later. Joiner looked up as they passed underneath a large arch to see the Command Centre's building rise up to the ceiling and on into the chamber above. Huge letters ran vertically down the imposing structure spelling out the name *U.S.S.B. STEADFAST*.

Joiner was displeased at having to move his operational offices at such a late hour in the impact countdown calendar. Steiner was proving to be an annoyance; power had gone to the man's head. *Still*, he thought to himself with some satisfaction, *that will become less of a problem in the near future*. The winds of change above and below the surface grew in strength, a shift of power an inevitability. Steiner might think he had him under his command, but Joiner knew differently; many things were far from what they seemed. Even before Steiner had been brought onboard all those years ago at the White House, Joiner had been laying down plans which were only now reaching fruition some twenty-three years later.

Exiting the car and accompanied by his entourage of intelligence agents, Joiner entered the Command Centre. A few hours on, after he'd settled into his new surroundings, he summoned Nathan Bryant, the political aide who'd become an integral part of the U.S. and GMRC's management of the upcoming global event. Joiner had been surprised and momentarily vexed by Bryant's presence at Steadfast;

he had placed him in South Korea for a reason, but ever the adept at manipulating the unexpected to align with his own agenda, Joiner saw it as an advantageous opportunity.

His office door opened a while later and one of Joiner's agents ducked their head inside. 'Director?'

Joiner looked up from his desk.

'Nathan Bryant, sir,' the man informed him.

'Send him in,' Joiner said, turning off his screen with a flick of his infrared finger circlet.

Bryant entered the room looking relaxed and confident, as he usually did. 'Ah, Director, you wanted to see me?' he said, lacking his usual aggravating grin and sitting down before being invited to do so.

Joiner disliked Bryant immensely; cockiness and eternal happiness exuded from him like pus from a boil. No one should be happy all the time; it wasn't right. Joiner himself rarely felt happy and when he did it wasn't normally because he'd achieved something, it was because others had failed in their endeavours. He reasoned Bryant must always be gloating at others' failures, which infuriated Joiner more than he could say; he wondered what his secret was.

'Is everything proceeding as we arranged?' Joiner said.

Bryant looked uncomfortable and nodded, his sickly smile nowhere to be seen on his annoying face.

'He doesn't suspect you are not his man anymore?' Joiner said.

Bryant's expression stiffened. 'No.'

'It was unwise of you to tell him about the equipment and the military's involvement. I underestimated your stupidity; have you forgotten our little arrangement so quickly?'

Bryant shook his head. 'Of course not.'

'Then why are you here at Steadfast?'

'The professor asked me to come,' Bryant said, his voice a pathetic whine. 'I had no choice. It would have looked suspicious if I'd refused.'

'If you betray me again the consequences for you will be dire, but for others – fatal,' Joiner said, eagerly watching as Nathan squirmed in his seat, his fear plain to see. Every man had his price, Joiner knew, and Bryant was no different. 'So what is he up to, our beloved leader?'

'He's making final preparations for the impact; that's his job, after all.'

'Don't get cute with me,' Joiner said, eyes narrowing, 'or you'll find I can make your life quite unbearable.'

Bryant looked at him with hatred and Joiner smiled. That was something else that brought him pleasure; other people's discomfort and suffering, two things that his job enabled him to revel in on a regular basis.

'Steiner doesn't suspect my involvement behind the military's departure from his control,' Joiner said, 'or that the UN Secretary General is acting under my orders?'

'No, he seems to have his hands full with the military stonewalling him, a Colonel Samson threatening Richard Goodwin and the imminent meteor impact. Quite a lot to keep any man occupied, even one as gifted as the professor.'

'Excellent. Now, what aren't you telling me?' he said, catching Nathan on the hop. Joiner had unnerving powers of perception; he hadn't reached his position by chance. Secrecy, manipulation and anticipation were just a few of his skills.

'I don't know what you mean.' Nathan sounded unconvincing as Joiner's gimlet eyes bored into him.

Joiner didn't say anything, but piled the pressure on Bryant using silence as his weapon.

'He's bringing in contractors, private contractors,' Nathan said at last, breaking under Joiner's gaze.

'And?' he said, pressing him for more.

'He's pulled some strings,' – Nathan, still reluctant to give away his friend's secrets, paused before continuing – 'and redirected Darklight to Steadfast.'

Joiner didn't show his emotions, but inside he seethed with rage. Darklight, the world's leading private security firm, had huge resources and large numbers of personnel; an army for hire by the highest bidder, which in the current financial landscape meant only one organisation, the GMRC. In the past few years they had been used to spearhead the evacuation of South Africa and other southern African states, not to mention being employed by the Japanese and Chinese governments to protect key resources and projects pertinent to the global subterranean response to the looming disaster. Somehow Steiner had managed to requisition them under the radar; Joiner would have found out eventually, but by then it would have been too late; he knew he had to make counter preparations, and quickly.

Joiner, still distracted by the news, refocused on Bryant. 'What else?'

'That's it, unless you count the fact that he's very tired at the moment,' Nathan said, sounding concerned.

'How caring of you,' Joiner said with a sneer. 'Now get out of my sight, but don't go too far; I might have need of you again.'

After Bryant had scuttled off, Joiner picked up his phone to contact one of the Joint Chiefs. 'General, we have an imminent Dark-light infestation at Steadfast; you know what to do—' he said, and then promptly hung up. Pleased with the work he'd completed in such a short time, Joiner decided he'd have a swim in the plush Principal Hotel pool and then take afternoon tea, but he had one more quick call to make first. He pressed his intercom button. 'Operator, put me through to a Colonel Samson.'

Colonel Samson, dressed in civilian clothing, tapped his fingers in impatience as he waited at a private table in one of Steadfast's swanky hotels. Some spook had requested his presence. It seemed this person had substantial clout within the military as, soon after Samson had refused to meet the man, a call had come through from one of his superiors ordering him to go and give the man a fair hearing.

Wanting to be anywhere else but there, Samson continued to wait, and a little while later a thin, aging man in a suit came and sat down opposite him. A waiter approached and the newcomer ordered some fancy wine, which he then had poured for them both. Samson would have preferred a beer; he sloshed down the wine in a few gulps as the other man watched him, sipping his own drink in slow deliberation.

'I hear you are a man not to be trifled with,' the spy said to him, 'and that you don't care for civilian leadership.'

'You have good hearing,' Samson said, bored out of his mind, 'and who the fuck are you?'

'I'm someone not to be *fucked* with.' The man handed him a card.

MALCOLM JOINER
Principal Director of National
& GMRC Intelligence

'So you're some bigwig,' Samson said. 'What do you want with me?' He wasn't impressed by cards, hotels or titles.

'I'm just introducing myself. I heard about your situation with Professor Steiner and I thought I would offer you my support.'

'I don't need it,'

'You may have been told by your superiors that Steiner is no longer in full control of the military; however, recently a situation has arisen that may prove ... interesting. Have you heard of Darklight?'

'The security firm?' Samson said.

'The same. It seems our beloved professor is bringing them into Steadfast. This is going to cause some problems in the chain of command. I just want to make sure that you are aware that you may be vulnerable to reassignment if Steiner gets his way and that I can protect you.'

'I don't need protecting,' Samson said with a snarl.

'Of course not, what I meant was that I can prevent your transfer.'

'And why would you do that?' Samson looked at the intelligence director suspiciously.

'I may need your help at a certain point and if I scratch your back—'

'I'll do what I want, when I want,' Samson told him. 'If you need something that requires my skills we can speak again.'

'Very well,' Joiner said, unmoved by the colonel's animosity, 'that's good enough for me.'

'It'll have to be,' Samson said, and got up and left.

Richard Goodwin looked on as the impact countdown timer sank below ten days, signalling the initiation of the Final Protocols. In the Command Centre and around the whole of U.S.S.B. Steadfast EMERGCON (emergency readiness condition) and DEFCON (defence readiness condition) threat alert levels were displayed via screens and signs. The largest readiness display had been built onto the outside of the Command Centre building itself; at some forty feet in height, this provided a real-time visual indicator of current standings to passers-by and for workers in the vicinity.

2011 AG5, or Big Bertha as the professor liked to call it, had its trajectory mapped out in the centre of the display Goodwin now watched. Key Control Centre staff moved around the room as keyboards clicked, finger circlets flicked, voices chattered and phones rang. The implementation of final surface procedures had begun as U.S.S.B. Steadfast cycled towards complete isolated lockdown for the years ahead. This is what they had prepared for; everything was coming together, apart from one major piece of equipment that should have arrived. Goodwin had asked the professor about the back-up water purification machinery and its location, and he'd told Goodwin it would be there. Goodwin had pointed out its importance; however, the professor didn't seem to be worried, a small comfort as Goodwin knew the importance to the programme such a device represented.

He was also concerned that the professor had decided to set up his base of operations at Steadfast instead of U.S.S.B. Sanctuary where he had initially been scheduled to be during impact. It seemed a lot of new people had streamed into Steadfast at a time when he needed calm and familiar faces. He'd also been told by the professor to expect a large and heavily armed contingent from the Darklight security firm. Basic procedure, he had said, but Goodwin wasn't convinced. Something was going on, but he was far too busy to look into it further; *besides*, he reasoned, *the professor knows what he's doing ... doesn't he?*

U.S.S.B. Steadfast was being sealed indefinitely. Surface deployment could only be sanctioned under special conditions authorised by the Joint Chiefs, Professor Steiner or the President himself. While according to predictions AG5's impact wouldn't be apocalyptic, it did represent a severe threat, as it posed a multitude of scenarios that a subterranean base was designed to combat. These scenarios included unforeseen fallout due to unidentifiable parameters, atmospheric ignition triggered by the impact detonation and microbial contagions piggy backing in on the meteor's surface or within its structure.

Steadfast also helped to preserve plant life and protect U.S. command structure against possible nuclear or biological attack by a hostile nation during the potential chaos following the asteroid's arrival. The U.S.S.B. programme was a crucial and pivotal component in defending the United States; however, it also had offensive capabilities hence the civilian and military collaboration. Certain doomsayers within the subterranean base community said the meteor could be the prelude to a war with the Chinese. Goodwin doubted this; he knew people liked to imagine the worst to bring some excitement into their lives, as he'd done the same in his youth and even occasionally in later life. This train of thought, he theorised, was perhaps an unfortunate mental aberration in the human psyche in response to modern day life and all the rules and controls it brought with it. He had to admit to his older self, however, that he'd been getting excited as the asteroid drew closer. He shouldn't, he knew, because people's lives would be in danger even though mass evacuations had been made in Africa and beyond.

Goodwin had also noticed the change and buzz that circulated in and around the base as Impact Day grew ever closer, which was inevitable, really, since everyone had geared up for its arrival for so long. And despite the many years of preparations by virtually every nation on Earth, such a huge global event would spark worldwide panic, especially when the dust cloud brought with it an eternal night. It was said the younger generations would deal with the darkness better since they were biologically more resilient. They had also grown up knowing the impact would happen, what would ensue and how it would affect their lives. It had been ingrained into their education and very existence, whereas the majority of the adult population were set in their ways and used to a *normal* life, not the horror of a world without sunlight.

Goodwin told one of the analysts to bring up the nuclear reactors' live data feed.

'All reactors are operating within parameters, sir.'

'Air regeneration systems?' Goodwin said.

The analyst brought up more data. 'Five by five, sir.'

'Water?'

'Seventy five per cent efficiency.'

'Control systems?'

'One hundred per cent in the green.'

'Population anxiety levels?' Goodwin said. All underground citizens, civilian and military, had bio readers implanted under the skin, enabling numerous psychological and physical checks on whole or specific groups throughout the base. This was an extremely useful tool in the event of an emergency or to identify potential flash points. Population management in Steadfast, and for all U.S.S.B.s, played an integral role in the smooth running of a modern day subterranean facility.

'We have a few anxiety spikes, sir, mainly due to the EMERGCON and DEFCON display and sign activation, since it coincides with the time they went live around the base.'

'Very good,' Goodwin said, satisfied everything proceeded as planned.

Professor Steiner had managed to set up his global response centre using some of the disaster recovery rooms he had visited earlier. They had full GMRC database access, enormous screens and a plethora of workstations. Those of his personnel that had been destined for U.S.S.B. Sanctuary had been flown in from other locations, and communication networks had been rerouted to his new operational hub.

Sophie, Steiner's primary aide, stood by his side as images of various people appeared on a large grid live on screen.

'We have full connectivity, Professor,' Sophie told him. 'Shen Zhǔ Rèn is waiting to speak to you.'

Shen Zhǔ Rèn, or Director Shen, had been selected by the Chinese to run their meteor response programme and he had also been on the shortlist to co-ordinate the planetary response on behalf of the GMRC, the very position now held by Steiner himself. Typically relations between the United States and China were frosty at best, especially considering China's dominance in the fierce economic battle that had seen the U.S. increase its population twofold in the last twenty years in an attempt to keep pace. Such radical growth had been gained by opening the borders to the United States, plus the roll out of highly lucrative government incentives for couples who had five or more children. Both of these schemes proved extremely controversial and initially had caused the U.S. economy to stall; in the last five years, however, it had regained its power and closed the gap with its rival.

'Shen Zhǔ Rèn, *ni qi se bu cuo*,' the professor said in flawless Chinese.

'Professor Steiner, I am very well, thank you,' the Chinese Director replied. 'I notice you are at U.S.S.B. Steadfast rather than Sanctuary; is there any reason for this late change to your plans?'

Steiner glanced round to see the large Steadfast insignia on the wall behind him. 'You're very observant, Zhǔ Rèn,' Steiner said without a hint of sarcasm. 'No, there is nothing to be concerned about, we have just a few issues to smooth out here and it seemed better for all concerned if I stayed onsite rather than moving on to Sanctuary.'

'Can we assist you in any way?' Shen Zhǔ Rèn asked politely.

'No, thank you. How are your final preparations? I was told that you were experiencing rioting in a few of your larger cities.'

'That is being dealt with as we speak, Professor,' Shen said, radiating confidence. 'I think you should be more concerned with the EU's Austrian base, which seems to have experienced a breach to one of its chambers due to a gas explosion. Apparently it may have affected their water and air systems, although we haven't been able to confirm this directly. We did warn the Europeans against gas infrastructure, but we were ignored as usual.'

Steiner detected Shen seemed quite pleased that the Chinese advice had proved correct, although that might have been to do with the fact that it was the Germans' and the Italians' final votes that had ensured Steiner had received the position of GMRC Director General over Shen himself.

An image of a large, heavyset man appeared on the screen, the EU's Representative, Dr. Daniel Sidwell.

'Ah, Daniel, so nice to see you,' Steiner said, as Zhǔ Rèn's image grew smaller, indicating Steiner now conversed with another person, a situation mimicked on Shen's own screen in China.

'Professor, I hope you are well,' Dr. Sidwell said, giving him a warm smile. 'Director Shen's information is correct, but the issue has already been resolved so we won't be requiring assistance. Perhaps the Chinese should be ensuring their own ship is in order before criticising someone else's.'

Steiner knew Daniel well from a research project they had run together many years ago, but he wasn't about to start taking sides as it was his job to pull people together, not push them apart. 'I'm glad you've contained the problem, Daniel,' he said diplomatically. 'How are the satellite relays operating from your end? We read green across the board here.'

'There is some interference on a couple of frequencies, but nothing too serious. It's been caused by some small space debris from an old Russian rocket, robotic repairs are already underway.'

'These things are sent to try us,' Steiner said.

'We'd be out of a job if they didn't,' Daniel replied.

Steiner smiled. 'We'll talk again at the holo-conference tomorrow,' he said, before logging off the feed.

Sophie passed him an itinerary for the rest of the week just as Malcolm Joiner entered the room with Nathan at his side.

'Thank you, Sophie,' Steiner said, as the two men approached.

Sophie bobbed her head and moved off to speak to a couple of technicians who were busy installing a secure military network connection for Steiner's new command post.

'Gentlemen,' Steiner said in greeting.

Nathan nodded his head in acknowledgment.

'Professor,' Joiner said, before gazing around at Steiner's new hub of operations. 'So you've decided against Sanctuary?'

'I have, there was an equipment problem and I have a little issue with the military at the moment. You don't happen to know why, do you, Malcolm? You are head of intelligence, after all.'

'I've heard you may have fallen out of favour with the Joint Chiefs,' Joiner said, unfazed by the question. 'Did you want me to speak to them about it on your behalf?'

'If I thought it would do any good I'd have asked you already,' Steiner said as he studied Joiner's deadpan face, which – as usual – revealed nothing.

The intelligence director remained silent, but Steiner could see the cogs turning behind those cold, calculating eyes.

'I take it you know I have secured the services of a civilian contractor?' Steiner asked him.

'I heard it mentioned.'

'I thought you might have done,' Steiner said, wondering what else Joiner was hiding from him.

A sliding door opened behind them and they all looked in its direction. Three men had entered. They each wore a full suit of black state of the art body armour, and MX4 rifles hung from slings around their necks. The leader was tall and heavily built, with a face which looked like it was hewn from granite. A nasty scar ran down the middle of his face, a small bit of his nose was also missing as the scar carried on down to his chin.

'Ah, Commander, it's good of you to come up to see me.'

'Not a problem, Professor,' the man said, his voice deep and powerful.

'Gentlemen, this is Commander Hilt,' Steiner said, 'he and his division will now be taking charge of the weapons systems and security details here at Steadfast.'

Joiner's face looked like it was very slowly being inflated from the inside as his eyes bulged at the sight of the man before him.

'Nathan Bryant,' Nathan said, leaning forward and shaking the commander's hand. 'I didn't realise there was such a large Darklight contingent in these parts, Commander. A division: that's ten thousand men, isn't it?'

'We do operate covertly at times, Mr Bryant,' the Darklight officer said, sidestepping the question, 'and our base locations and troop movements are not always divulged.'

'Aren't the Joint Chiefs going to be a little put out by you taking over their main duties?' Nathan looked from Steiner to Hilt, and then to Joiner, who still hadn't said anything.

'They won't have a choice,' Steiner said. 'It's my show and what I say goes.' *Here, in any case*, he thought to himself.

'Our men are relieving them of duty as we speak, Professor,' Hilt told him.

'Very good, Commander, thank you.'

Hilt nodded and left; his two men, however, stayed flanking the door on either side of Steiner's new command post.

CHAPTER EIGHT

The door slammed hard as Joiner burst into his office. How the fuck did Steiner get Darklight into Steadfast so quickly? he thought, heart racing. And how did they avoid the blocks I ordered the military to impose on traffic and flight routes into Steadfast? Enraged by the deception, Joiner's blood seethed through his veins like acid. I need the base under my control if I'm to extract key personnel and equipment to Sanctuary.

The question he should have been asking himself was why had the professor really called in the mercs? It suddenly dawned on him: *he knows – Steiner knows!* Joiner didn't know how he'd done it, but he'd found out the asteroid's telemetry had been altered. He must react, and quickly, otherwise word might get out and his careful preparations would be compromised.

Joiner knew he wouldn't be able to acquire reinforcements to deal with the threat fast enough, and yet the base still had a U.S. military presence underground, which he could control. He checked his digital mailbox for the latest Steadfast intelligence reports. According to a base-wide personnel count, the influx of mercenaries was more substantial than he had initially feared, but fortunately Steadfast was heavily garrisoned and U.S. forces still outnumbered them by four to one. Steiner was craftier than he'd thought; he had underestimated him. Joiner calmed his racing thoughts, focusing his mind on the problem at hand. He picked up the phone and dialled a number.

'Yes?' a man answered.

'General, as you're no doubt aware Professor Steiner has managed to flood Steadfast with civilian contractors who now hold key positions throughout the base. What you don't know is that Steiner is now also privy to certain information that poses a direct threat to the United States and its allies. This information cannot be allowed to be disseminated as it will jeopardise the whole programme, and therefore he cannot be left in command.'

'That may prove difficult,' the general said, 'he is in charge on a global scale. People might notice if he's suddenly not on the scene.'

'Steiner's role is nearly at an end, he won't be missed for long and a stress-related illness will prove an adequate cover story.'

'What do you propose?'

'A swift strike on Darklight positions and the Command Centre, along with the extraction and detainment of Professor Steiner and other key personnel.'

'Engaging Darklight forces will result in casualties on both sides,' the general said, 'and civilian lives will also be put in jeopardy. Is this something you really want us to commit to?'

'We have no choice, the alternative is unthinkable.'

There was a long pause.

'General?' Joiner said.

'Very well, I'll keep you apprised.'

'Don't bother. I'll be sending in my own men to oversee critical targets.'

'That won't be necessary,' the general said, his tone stiffening.

'It is, General; do you have a problem with that or should I contact your colleagues? They might like to know how you've been spying on them and manipulating their careers to suit your own ends.'

'You snide little worm, it was you who helped me!'

'I don't suppose you have any proof of such heinous claims?' Joiner said, amused.

The general said nothing, but Joiner could sense his fury.

'I take it that's a "no" then. Oh, and General, let's be clear; I'm in charge here, not you or the Joint Chiefs. I'll be in touch.' Joiner hung up the phone.

Goodwin sat relaxing in his office chair, soaking up the forest scene around him. The familiar sounds washed over him as he closed his eyes; he gave a loud yawn and stretched out his arms and legs, easing away his stress. As he let his mind wander, his door burst inwards with a BANG, making his eyes flare open and stomach clench.

His secretary, Leah, stood in the doorway, wild-eyed. 'You better come out here!'

Confused and annoyed by the disturbance, he jumped up out of his chair and followed her into reception. At the window she pointed down below, where people ran in all directions.

'What on earth—' His voice petered out as from across a plaza to the right fifty men garbed in black appeared, moving backwards at speed with guns raised. The unmistakable shots of automatic gunfire rang out, coupled with bursts of muzzle flash expelled by the weapons. They both watched in horror as U.S. military troops erupted from either side of the retreating Darklight personnel. Men fell on both sides, some dropped like stones while others writhed in agony. What was a normal pedestrian scene had turned into a bloodbath as the two sides fought for a foothold.

Goodwin's adrenalin surged. He grabbed an arm of the mesmerised Leah and dragged her from the room and into the corridor. Panic was in the air. People's screams echoed up from the atrium below as they ran for cover. Darklight troops ran towards the gunfight, dodging in and out of people fleeing in the opposite direction. Goodwin headed up a staircase to the floor where he knew the professor's team was housed. Leah had other ideas and shrugged off his grip.

'Leah, where are you going?' he shouted after her, but she'd already dashed off into the melee, heading towards the back of the building. The shooting down below intensified and grew ever louder.

'Richard!'

Goodwin looked round and saw the professor striding towards him flanked by his one remaining bodyguard. He wasn't sure where his own had disappeared to.

'Where are your guards?'

'I have no idea,' Goodwin said, in shock. 'What's happening?'

'It seems our beloved Joiner is trying to wrest control away from me. I don't have time to explain, but you must gather as many people as you can and rendezvous with Commander Hilt in the forest outpost.'

'What are you going to do?'

'I must stay here and unlock the elevators so you can get out.'

'Get out, to where? The surface? What are you talking about?'

'Just do as I say, Richard, please.'

Before Goodwin could ask him anything else, gunshots exploded inside the building.

'Go!' Steiner said. 'I'll contact you on your phone to explain everything to you, now go!'

The professor turned and ran back down the corridor, closely shadowed by his protector.

Goodwin ducked as a bullet ricocheted off a pillar nearby, and he found himself running towards the back of the building to where all the other workers had fled. He rattled down another staircase and burst out of the doors, trying to get his bearings.

Before he'd decided on his next move, a massive transport vehicle screeched to halt fifty yards away and another two followed it.

The Darklight commander, Hilt, leaned out the door of the first vehicle with a megaphone. 'This is an evacuation emergency! Please make your way to Bio Chamber Five, BC5!'

Goodwin ran over as others from all around came streaming onto the passenger buses. As Goodwin reached one, his phone – and everyone else's – sounded a high pitched alarm. It was a Command Centre Alert message. The screen flashed and read:

PROTOCOL 9
BASE EVACUATION
PROCEED TO YOUR
DESIGNATED SECTOR
FOR SURFACE EVAC
THIS IS NOT A DRILL.

RELOCATE TO EVAC SECTOR: BC5

Goodwin knew the professor had activated the alert, but if what he said about Joiner was true then the military would be cutting off access routes as fast as they could.

'Where's the professor?!' Hilt said, raising his voice over the bedlam.

'He's back in there!' Goodwin pointed to the Command Centre. 'He's trying to unlock the elevator shafts and surface exits.'

Hilt swore and got on his radio. 'Major Davis, I need as many men as you can spare to the Command Centre a-sap.'

'Roger that,' came a swift reply.

Hilt gestured Goodwin onboard and the vehicles struck out for the Forest at full tilt.

Samson's anger simmered within, like a volcano ready to erupt. His superior had ordered him to let SOG, the CIA's Special Operations Group, lead the grunts in securing the Command Centre, which had since been reinforced by more Darklight troops. Ordinarily he'd have been pumped at an imminent combat situation; instead he felt deflated. He'd begun to suspect his commanding officers of being influenced by an outside source, perhaps even by that slippery bastard intelligence agent, Malcolm Joiner. *Still*, he told himself, *orders are orders*. His team, SFSD – Special Forces Subterranean

Detachment, also referred to as Terra Force – had instructions to rendezvous at the building, after having secured a nearby elevator shaft from Darklight control. This first objective had been easy; Darklight might pay well, but the U.S.S.B.s were afforded the pick of the best men and the elite Terra Force was no exception.

Their armoured transport roared into the huge central plaza which encircled the Command Centre on the lowest chamber. The men inside stood holding onto hand straps hanging from the roof; all were fully equipped in a similar fashion to the black-clad Darklight forces, but they'd had time to attach further protective armour for the assault. Their dark grey and green kit had a matte finish and many bore the scars of previous engagements with hostile forces, indicating to any observer their battle-hardened credentials.

The vehicles' sides shot upwards, allowing the soldiers to all disembark at once, and the noise of many heavy boots hitting the floor momentarily filled the air. Bodies littered the ground around them; most had been armed, but a few civilians lay amongst the dead. This didn't disturb Samson as he'd seen it all many times before, and worse, much worse.

The SOG's commander was organising U.S. military forces as Samson and his team approached.

'Ah, Colonel, good of you to join us. I'll need your team to be the tip of the spear on entry; your men look equipped for the job, good.'

'And you are?' Samson said.

'Agent in charge Myers. You can call me sir.'

Samson ignored him, although a vision of his fist smashing the man's teeth through the back of his head flashed up in his mind.

Agent Myers held up his hand to Samson indicating he wanted quiet as he put his other hand to his earpiece. 'Yes, sir,' Myers said and then waited as further instructions were relayed to him. 'Where is it located?' A pause. 'Okay, and the principal target?' Another pause. 'Right. Yes, sir, I'll contact you when it's done.'

Gunshots rang out once more inside the building they now had surrounded on all chamber levels. Agent Myers turned back to Samson, whose patience was ready to snap.

'Well?' Samson said.

'We need to cut the outgoing hard lines and wireless antennae array. You'll find them on level thirty-eight, rooms eighteen through to twenty-two. My man Henson,' – he indicated an agent over to his right – 'will guide you through the process. "Cut" doesn't mean physically chopping them in two; there are large lever handles to pull down, which will do the job.'

'Really?' Samson said, his voice loaded with scorn. 'I would never have guessed.'

Before Myers could respond Samson turned his back on him and addressed his men.

'You heard the S.O.G.,' Samson said, with a derogatory inflection which made a few of his men smirk. 'We're point, load up. Look and shoot sharp. We move.'

Terra Force dropped their visors as one, shouldered weapons and advanced on the building as the regular base troops parted to let them through.

Darklight personnel waited in nervous anticipation for the inevitable assault on the building's upper levels. They had been bolstered by their initial success in repelling attempts to breach their lines, but spotters had witnessed the arrival of a heavily shielded Terra Force detachment and morale had fallen in response.

Major Davis walked amongst his men offering encouragement and issuing orders. He knew they hadn't the numbers to hold for much longer, but his commander's final order was clear: hold at all costs. Major Davis moved down a corridor and entered a control room. He approached the GMRC head honcho, Professor Steiner, who furiously tapped on a keyboard while computer code flashed by on a screen in front of him.

'Do we really need to fight on, Professor?' Davis said. 'It's only a matter of time before they overwhelm us and Special Forces are moving in.'

'Major,' the professor said without turning round, 'I would not ask anyone to lay down their life if it wasn't absolutely necessary. Many more lives are in danger and I need to get these elevators and surface exits unlocked and overridden. The base must be evacuated before it's too late.'

'Too late for what?' Davis said.

The professor looked directly at him, his gaze determined and unwavering. 'That I cannot tell you, but believe me, you will be saving many lives by what you do now.'

Davis sighed. 'Very well, Professor, you obviously know what you're doing. We'll try and give you as much time as we can.'

'Thank you, Major,' the professor said, with heartfelt gratitude, and he resumed his task.

A shout came from down below as Major Davis moved back into the corridor. An eruption of blasts and gunfire signalled the final assault had begun. Davis took a small photo out of a pocket and kissed it before tucking it away, cocking his weapon and lowering his visor.

'Men, on me!' He commanded two soldiers who'd been guarding the room. Davis led them through a side exit into a stairwell and down. At the bottom one of his team lay unmoving as blood seeped onto the pristine white marble floor around him. The fighting was frenetic. Bullets flew through the double doors and zinged past his head. Another of his men went down before they were able to engage the enemy.

Davis took aim at one of many Terra Force targets on offer. He only had one clip of armour-piercing rounds so he had to make them count. Firing off shots, he cycled from target to target, taking down one and injuring three more. The rifle's bolt locked back and he dropped the clip and slammed in another. A bullet hit him in the shoulder, shifting his weight back.

He glanced around to see he was the last man standing. With no more time to think, he grabbed two grenades from his belt, dialled the time to five seconds, flicked off the pins and threw them into the main foyer. As they detonated, he made to head back the way he'd come, but he heard the telltale noise of a small metallic object bouncing off the hard floor nearby. *Too late!* he thought, before a lethal blast ripped him from his feet.

Samson moved the body of a Darklight officer out of his way with his foot, barely noticing the image of a mother and child as a photo dropped to the floor from the dead man's hand. He moved on up the stairs. U.S. forces had taken control and many Darklight soldiers had fallen, but some had been disarmed and rounded up for detention so the powers that be could decide what to do with them.

Samson didn't like or dislike killing, but he was good at it, very good. He knew his men called him *The Reaper* behind his back, but they knew better than to say it to his face.

They'd managed to shut down the communication lines and array in the Command Centre, although Myers wasn't happy as Steiner had managed to open up access to some of the elevator shafts and upper access doors and had then frozen the system so they couldn't be resealed.

'Where is the professor?' the CIA man asked him as he approached.

'Over there.' Samson pointed at a small room.

Myers went over to it and relieved the agent within, who went and stood guard outside. Samson followed him in. Myers noticed his presence, but said nothing. In front of them, Steiner sat on a chair behind a small table, a smashed console before him.

'My agent tells me you were trying to communicate with someone on that console, Professor,' Myers said. 'Who were you calling? Commander Hilt, perhaps, or some of your government friends?'

'I don't know what Joiner thinks he's playing at,' Steiner said, full of defiance, 'but when word of this gets out, and it will, heads will roll and yours will be one of them.'

Myers laughed with genuine humour. 'I don't think so, but I like your style, Professor. You have balls, I'll give you that.'

Steiner looked at Samson and then back to Myers again. 'Well? What are you going to do with me, then?'

'I'll leave that up to the Director, Professor,' Myers said, 'but trust me when I say it's in your best interests to co-operate.' With the brief exchange over, the two men departed the room, leaving the agent outside to lock the door and resume his guard duty.

A muffled ringing came from a compartment on Samson's chest armour. Taking off an armoured glove, he retrieved his personal computer phone, put it to his ear and moved away for some privacy. 'Yes?'

'Colonel, it's Malcolm Joiner.'

This just gets better and better, he thought. 'What do you want?' he said, offhandedly.

'I hear that Professor Steiner is under arrest.'

'Your man Myers has him under guard.'

'Are you able to get in to see him?'

'Yes.'

'That is convenient, Colonel. I need you to do me a favour.'

Samson said nothing and waited.

'This is an opportune time for everyone concerned, Colonel,' Joiner continued, undeterred by Samson's lack of commitment to the conversation.

Samson remained silent, so Joiner went on. 'I – *we* – could both be well served if our dear professor had not made it through the firefight.'

'What do you want?'

'I think that's obvious, Colonel.'

Samson's lip curled back in contempt and the phone in his hand creaked under pressure. 'I'm not an assassin,' he said vehemently, 'and I'm not your lackey. If you want a man killed, do it yourself or use Myers; he'd probably fuck him if you ordered him to.'

'I'm sorry to hear that, Colonel,' Joiner said, his tone hardening. 'I thought you a man of conviction, I was clearly mistaken.'

The line went dead; Joiner had hung up. Samson snorted in derision and put his phone away. He needed to get out of there, he felt confined, constricted. He called his team to him and without a backwards glance moved out of the building, his job done.

Approximately five per cent of Steadfast's population had managed to make it to the extraction zone in the forest, around twenty-five thousand people, plus Darklight forces. Commander Hilt had already loaded up the first elevator, which was surface bound. He'd also contacted Darklight units topside. They stood on full alert in case of outside U.S. military intervention.

Goodwin paced around inside the M.E.C.A. building where Dr. Kara Vandervoort helped bandage up some of the wounded civilians, the high tech office having been turned into a triage hospital. *We're evacuating these people*, Goodwin thought, *but why?* He knew the professor must have a good reason, but he couldn't guess what it could be. *Why isn't Steadfast safe any longer? And why is Malcolm Joiner, Director of Intelligence, trying to take over from the professor in some kind of military coup?* His confusion pressed down upon him like a large, cold stone on his shoulders, making him feel disorientated and drained. He slumped into a chair, his head in his hands.

A soft touch on his shoulder made him look up.

Kara looked at him with concern. 'Are you all right, Richard?'

He looked at his hands, they were covered in blood.

'I'm fine, it's not my blood,' he said, wondering how it had got there and who it belonged to.

'What is going on?' she said, sounding scared. 'People are saying the military opened fire on them and that the Darklight forces fought back to protect them.'

'No,' – he gave a weary shake of the head – 'the military took on Darklight and civilians got in the way.'

'Why?'

'I don't know.'

'Are you sure you're okay?'

He managed a small smile. 'Quite sure, thank you. I just feel exhausted for some reason.'

'That'll be the come down off of the adrenalin your body kicked out during the chaos,' said a deep voice.

Goodwin looked round as Darklight's leader approached. 'Commander, any news from the professor?'

'None, I'm afraid, sir,' Hilt said. 'I've lost contact with my men at the Command Centre, too; I fear it's been taken. We've set up a perimeter. This chamber is pretty easy to defend, so we won't have to worry about getting overrun. It also appears that the military aren't pursuing us, they've pulled back. They must have realised that this sector isn't worth losing more men over.'

'I hope you're right.'

'Time will tell,' Hilt said, before one of his men handed him a digital map. 'Where shall we go when we hit the surface, sir?'

'I have no idea, Commander.'

Hilt studied a hologram of the terrain. 'Darklight has a large compound about twenty clicks from Steadfast's surface location. It's well concealed and we could fit most of these people in there for the short term. We also have vehicles topside to get them there, although it will take multiple trips.'

'That sounds like a good plan to me,' Goodwin said, happy to let someone else take the lead.

'Sir,' Hilt continued, 'the civilians are getting a little out of control in some places. They want to know what's happening and where they're going.'

Goodwin sighed and pushed himself to his feet. 'Has this station got a public address system?' he asked Kara.

She shook her head.

'Don't worry, sir,' Hilt told him, 'we have a command unit with that capability. I'll take you to it.'

'Thank you, Commander, lead the way.' He gestured the military man forwards with a bloody hand.

'Perhaps you should clean that off,' Hilt said, noticing the stains, 'it won't help calm people's nerves.'

'Good idea. Kara, have you—' Goodwin's voice trailed off as Kara was already handing him a damp paper towel. 'Thanks,' he said, giving her a small smile.

She squeezed his arm in support.

Handing Kara the now bloody rag, he followed Hilt out of the building.

'It's right over there.' Hilt pointed at a large armoured van that had a plethora of domes and antennae on its roof.

The two men pushed their way through the milling crowd. Some people were crying, while many remained silent, in a state of shock. Others shouted out, calling people's names, trying to find friends, colleagues and loved ones they'd become separated from in the dash to the evacuation zone.

As Goodwin passed one group of what, from their clothing, looked like engineers, someone grabbed him and yanked him round.

'What the fuck is going on?!' a man screamed into his face as his friends struggled to pull him back. 'You're in charge. My wife is dead because of you, do you understand? DEAD!!'

Goodwin didn't know what to say, and he just stood there in horror as the man's grasp tightened, his eyes wide and staring in what looked like madness, the madness of grief.

'BACK UP!' Hilt detached the man's hands from Goodwin's shirt and pushed him back toward his friends, who encircled him as they attempted to calm him down.

Goodwin and Hilt moved off and increased their pace. 'Thanks,' said Goodwin, 'it's getting a bit ugly out here.'

'And it'll get ten times worse if nothing is done,' Hilt said, as they finally reached the armoured truck. 'Here, you better get up on top of the roof otherwise people won't be able to see you.'

Goodwin grasped the ladder which was built onto the side of the vehicle and pulled himself up onto the roof, wobbled, then stood up precariously. Hilt disappeared inside the van for a second or two and then reappeared with a microphone in his hand, which he passed up to Goodwin.

'Are we on?' he asked Hilt, but his voice echoing out of the domed speaker system answered his own question.

Goodwin looked out as a sea of faces all turned in his direction.

'Hello,' he said, his voice faltering.

Unsure as to how to proceed, Goodwin surveyed those gathered, the fear of public speaking upon him. The silence stretched on and he could see the microphone in his hand trembling from nervous tension. He caught sight of a scared looking little girl who perched on her father's shoulders some thirty feet away. She needed reassurance, they all did, and it was his job to give it to them.

Gaining confidence, he began again. 'Hello,' he said, his voice louder and steadier than before. 'The events of the last hour have been traumatic for us all and devastating for some.' He looked over to the group where the man had accosted him. 'There are some among you who have lost loved ones and friends.' He paused, his emotions almost getting the better of him as his compassion went out to the grief-stricken husband, who even now held his gaze. 'Some will blame me for their deaths,' he continued, looking around at the many faces staring up at him. 'Perhaps they're right. It is my job to look after you all and to ensure no lives are lost. But lives have been lost and for that I am so very sorry and my thoughts and prayers go out to you in this horrific time. I wish I could tell you why this has happened, but I am as much in the dark as you are.'

He paused again to gather his thoughts. 'For some reason the military who are supposed to protect us have, in fact, caused us harm, whether unintentionally or otherwise. We have all received the evacuation command to assemble at this location and this emergency protocol was issued by Professor Steiner himself. As yet I do not know the reasons for the alert, but we must take it seriously and head to the surface as fast as possible. Darklight sources tell us that the military are not pursuing us and that is a small comfort.

'Many of you will be wondering where we will be going. To ensure our safety and to find out what has transpired here, we will be relocating to a Darklight base on the surface, some twenty kilometres away. What I do know is that Professor Steiner believes that this base is not safe.' He held up his hand for silence as a swell of noise swept through the assembled crowd. 'I understand your concerns and confusion as I feel exactly the same way, but I trust the professor with my life and if he says that it's not safe, I believe him.

'If anyone wants to stay behind, that is their choice. And while I believe the military will not harm them, as the Command Centre and other exit points appear to have been their main targets – seemingly to secure us and prevent our escape from Steadfast – I cannot guarantee this fact.

'Rest assured that when I know more, you will know more. Please remain calm and organised, as we have small children and the injured to look after. Thank you for your time and I will speak to you all again when we have reached the Darklight outpost I mentioned previously. Thank you.'

Goodwin got down off the roof and handed the microphone to a woman waiting on the ground who wore a bright orange vest bearing the words *Evacuation Officer*.

'Some of us managed to action the procedure for an emergency,' she told him, stepping onto the bottom rung of the ladder.

Goodwin knew he ought to know her name, but it escaped him.

'It's Julia, sir,' she said, catching his look of semi-recognition. 'I work on the third floor, personnel.'

'Yes, of course, I remember, the charity tri-athlete, right?'

'Yes, that's me, sir. I'll try and get some organisation going for you.'

'Thank you,' he said, as she made her way up the ladder to address the people who now spoke amongst themselves, digesting the information Goodwin had just given them.

'Excellent speech,' Hilt said solemnly.

'Thanks, I hope it helps.'

'It already has,' the commander replied.

A siren wailed in the distance, momentarily drowning out Julia on the speaker system.

'Sir, the second elevator has been loaded and is about to depart,' a Darklight operative told Hilt.

'Very good, Lieutenant, thank you.'

'Richard!'

Goodwin looked round to see Kara fighting her way through the press of bodies.

'Come quickly,' she said as she reached them, 'it's the professor; he's making a video call, he wants to speak to you, it's urgent.'

Goodwin excused himself from the Darklight commander and followed Kara back to her building.

'He asked to be transferred to a private terminal,' she said, showing him into a small room.

Thanking her Goodwin shut the door behind him.

On the wall in front of him a screen displayed Professor Steiner's face; he was using his computer phone to make the call.

'Professor, why didn't you just go through to my personal device?' Goodwin said. 'More importantly, are you all right?'

'Yes, I'm fine; I'm going through a secure military network as they've shut down all other communications in the base. I haven't got much time; they've locked me in a room. Luckily they didn't confiscate this phone, it's my back-up and I keep it in an ankle holster.'

'What are they going to do with you?'

'I'm not sure, but I think Joiner wants me confined indefinitely so I can't disrupt his plans.'

'What plans?'

'Something is going on, Richard, that even I didn't know about. I can't tell you everything I want to right now, but I can tell you to get out of Steadfast. Get to U.S.S.B. Sanctuary as soon as you can, along with everyone you have with you. How many are at your location?'

'We estimate about twenty-five thousand, plus Darklight forces.'

The professor made a face. 'I was hoping for more than that.'

'I'm sorry, Professor.'

'It's not your fault. God, it's mine. I should have anticipated something like this happening.'

'Something like what? Damn it, Professor, what is going on? For pity's sake, tell me!'

'I would if I could, Richard, but my hands are tied. All you need to know is that you have to get to Sanctuary as quickly as you can.'

'But I thought Sanctuary was a military run operation?'

'It is, but I can get you access – well – I have the information to get you in, anyway.'

'Okay, but why would we want to be at Sanctuary surrounded by the military when they were trying to prevent us getting out of Steadfast? None of this is making any sense to me at all.'

'All I can tell you is that Steadfast is not safe.'

'I realise that,' Goodwin said irritably.

'Right, and that's all you need to know for now. Joiner won't permit you to stay above ground as you'll be deemed a security risk and they may detain or eliminate you.'

'Security risk?' Goodwin said, but Steiner had already continued.

'Once you're in Sanctuary they're unlikely to kick you out again and you can believe me when I say they have the room. When you get there, find my office and access my system with this code: J P one zero one CLARITY, all one word and capitals. Go into my video archive folder and access the file entitled *Fishing for trout*.'

Goodwin typed all the instructions into his phone.

The professor looked up for a moment, alert for sounds or signs of movement outside his room. Satisfied, he continued. 'Once you've watched the message, which explains everything, you will hopefully understand my reasons for not telling you previously.'

'So how do we get into the base? And where is it, for that matter?' Goodwin said.

'It has a few entrances, but the one you will need is an auxiliary gateway that is rarely used. I'm sending you an access program through this system now.' He went out of shot for a moment as he sent the file to Goodwin's location.

Goodwin placed his phone on the magnetic data transfer pad and the procedure was complete.

The professor came back on screen. 'Now, this will only get you so far, but I know someone on the inside who will help. His name is General Ellwood and his private phone number is now in your contacts list. All you need to tell him is that Professor Steiner needs one last favour. Do not tell him that you have thousands of people you want to get inside the base, just say it's you and a few others. Deceitful, I know, but needs must.'

'And Sanctuary's location?'

'Mexico; approximately two hundred miles north of Mexico City, to be more precise. The co-ordinates for the entrance are also now in your phone.'

'Mexico City? Why on earth would the Mexican government allow a major U.S. military base near its capital city? And how have they kept it a secret, for that matter?'

'Good questions. We have paid the Mexican federation massive sums of money and supplied them with military hardware and blueprints to some of our more sophisticated projects. The Mexicans also have a military contingent in and around the base to minimise outside interest and to police U.S. movements within their borders.'

'So they actually have personnel inside U.S.S.B. Sanctuary?' Goodwin said. 'I bet the Joint Chiefs love that.'

'It was unavoidable. They only have access to less sensitive areas, however.'

'It's going to take us some time to get down there, Professor. Won't the military try to prevent us?'

'Perhaps, but the Mexicans will be more of a problem, as you will be travelling in their territory. I think I'm about to get interrupted and I'm not sure when I will be able to speak to you again, so good luck and Godspeed. Take care, Richard, I hope—'

The phone went dead and the words *Channel Blocked* flashed on the display.

'Take care, Professor,' Goodwin said, full of sadness, and switched off the screen.

CHAPTER NINE

ALBUQUERQUE, UNITED STATES.

THE FOOD STORE bustled with activity. Chattering voices and the beeping of barcode readers resounded throughout. School holidays meant an influx of people to the local high street, which made Rebecca's job harder. She worked as a carer for adults with mental health problems and less people made her life much easier.

At the moment she was taking one of her primary wards out with her to get some weekly food supplies. Joseph required constant attention which made most activities difficult; he enjoyed the trips, however, so she did her best to make sure she took him as often as she could.

Picking up some bananas she placed them in the basket that Joseph held for her.

'Nanas!' Joseph said with a big grin on his face.

Rebecca smiled at him and touched his arm fondly. 'That's right, your favourite. Now I need some breakfast cereal,' she said to him, although it was more to herself as Joseph only had a very limited vocabulary and understanding of language. She'd spied what she wanted, but the next aisle was too crowded to take Joseph there without disturbing others and potentially scaring him. Bound to a tight schedule, she glanced at her watch.

'Joseph, stand here and I will be right back.' She put the basket on the floor by his feet and held both his arms by his side and pointed at the floor. 'Stay here, Joseph, okay?'

Joseph looked at her and beamed.

She couldn't help but smile back. 'Stay HERE. Okay? I won't be long.'

Joseph nodded his head and pointed at the floor. 'Here!' he repeated, still smiling.

'Yes, here.' She pointed at the floor again and then went off down the next aisle. As she neared the end, she looked round; the back of Joseph's head could just be seen peeking out past a shelf. Satisfied he was doing as he was told, she bent down and picked up the box she wanted. As she lifted it the bottom opened and the bag fell out and split, the contents going everywhere. People looked round at the noise and moved out of the way as she scrabbled to clear up the mess. A shop assistant who'd heard the commotion came round the corner and began helping her.

'I'm so sorry,' Rebecca said to her. 'The bottom was undone and the bag split and it just went whoosh!'

The woman laughed. 'Don't worry, dear, these things happen. No harm done.'

'Thank you, I—' She stood up, remembering Joseph was waiting for her. 'I'm sorry, I have to go.'

The assistant looked bewildered as Rebecca rushed off.

When she got to the end of the aisle, Joseph was nowhere to be seen. With panic setting in, she looked with ever-increasing desperation from aisle to aisle. There was no sign of him.

'Has anyone seen a dark-haired man, about this high?' Rebecca held her hand up above her head as she went from person to person. 'Joseph!' she called. 'Joseph, where are you?! Joseph!' She raced out of the shop and heard Joseph's cries coming from the right. Rushing along the street, she approached a group of youths who were huddled together looking down at the ground and laughing. Joseph's sobs could be heard over their voices.

'Get out of the way!' she shouted, pushing her way through. She found Joseph on the ground, crying and frightened. He'd wet himself. Rebecca bent down and brought him close to comfort him. He grabbed onto her, burying his face in her shoulder.

'It's all right, Joseph. I'm here,' she told him soothingly. 'I'm here now.'

She glared up at the young men who had begun to walk away, still cracking jokes at Joseph's expense.

'Oh, has poor little Joseph's mommy come to protect him,' one of the men said.

'I wouldn't mind getting a cuddle, too, mommy,' said another, smirking.

Rebecca said nothing as she didn't want to scare Joseph further. He wouldn't be able to distinguish between her being angry with them from being angry with him. She helped him to his feet after he had calmed down and brushed him off. His soft, light blue jogging bottoms had a big wet patch on them, which people stared at as they went past, making Joseph uncomfortable with the attention and Rebecca angry that his dignity had been compromised.

Looking around she guided Joseph to the only shop nearby that had trousers in the window. As they entered a bell jingled, announcing them to the shopkeeper, who stood behind the counter serving a man and a little boy. A sign indicated the trousers were located at the back of the store, which was stocked full of army surplus and military type clothing.

'No changing room,' Rebecca mumbled to herself. 'Wonderful.' After taking a quick glance around, Rebecca quickly slipped Joseph's trousers off, plucked a pair of camo trousers from a rack and redressed him, as he wriggled and writhed in protest. Standing back to admire him in his new attire, she was pleased as they were a near perfect fit. Joseph had always liked watching military parades on TV and as he looked around he caught sight of a poster of an officer saluting. He suddenly went bolt upright and mimicked the pose. A chuckle came from behind them, making Rebecca jump.

'He looks good in those, just the part,' the shopkeeper said.

Joseph giggled and relaxed back into his normal slouch. The man quickly covered his confusion at Joseph's childlike demeanour with a grin, recognising his apparent disability.

'Would sir like anything else from the store?' he asked Joseph, who was busy playing with the waist cord.

'I don't think so,' – Rebecca whipped up Joseph's wet attire from the floor – 'we just needed some pants. It was an emergency.'

'No need to be embarrassed,' the man said. 'My dear old mother, God rest her soul, had incontinence for years; I was forever changing her clothes. If only they'd had those adult diapers it would've saved me a lot of trouble and washing of hands!'

Rebecca laughed in spite of herself, relaxing in the jovial old man's company.

'Did you want me to put those in a bag for you?' He pointed to the clothing in her hand.

'Yes, please, that's very kind of you.'

'No problem at all,' he said, smiling, 'it's all part of the service.'

They followed the man back to the front of the shop where a young boy jumped out on them, making shooting noises with a toy gun.

'I'm sorry,' said the man accompanying him, 'he's got a bit excited.'

Joseph laughed and began making shooting noises back at the child, who gleefully chased him round and round a display cabinet.

'Don't worry,' Rebecca said. 'He looks very cute, your son.'

'Thanks, although he's not my son, he's my nephew. He just loves all things military.'

'Joseph loves the parades.'

'And guns, too, by the look of it,' the man said.

Rebecca looked round to see Joseph had picked up a replica machine gun and now chased after the boy with it.

'Joseph, no!' Rebecca said. 'Put that down!' She didn't want him getting used to holding, or to like holding, a gun. Mentally disabled people and weapons of any kind didn't mix.

The shopkeeper had come back with a bag and handed it to Rebecca. He made pistols of his hands and pointed them at Joseph, making *pow pow* noises. Joseph grinned and held up his hands, dropping the rifle to the floor.

'Oh, I'm so sorry.' Rebecca rushed to pick up the gun, but the shopkeeper got to it first.

'No harm done,' he said, smiling reassuringly at her as he stowed it behind the counter.

'Is it damaged?'

'It will cost about two hundred dollars to repair.'

'Oh dear.' Rebecca felt sick. 'I don't have that kind of money on me.'

'I'm only kidding,' the shopkeeper said, 'sorry, poor joke.'

Rebecca gave a nervous laugh, relieved as she didn't have two hundred dollars to spare, on her or otherwise.

'Right, I'll leave you to it,' said the man with his nephew. 'It was nice to meet you both.'

'Goodbye,' she said, 'nice to meet you, too.'

Joseph waved goodbye to the little boy, who waved back, the door ringing as they left. Rebecca paid for the trousers, thanked the man again for his help and bade him farewell.

On their way back home they passed a lamppost plastered with various information and warning flyers from Government and local agencies. One read:

IMPACT DAY PREPARATIONS
AFTER FEBRUARY 9th 2040
DAILY CURFEW
19:00
ENFORCED BY
NATIONAL GUARD &
LOCAL POLICE SERVICE

Another read:

IMPACT DAY PREPARATIONS
FOOD RATION CARDS
COLLECT FROM YOUR LOCAL
GOVERNMENT OFFICE

Another:

IMPACT DAY PREPARATIONS
RIOTERS AND LOOTERS
WILL BE SHOT ON SIGHT

Rebecca looked up at the sky. She couldn't see any sign of the meteor yet, but there was still two weeks to go. Supposedly in the days prior to impact it would be visible to the naked eye at different times of the day and night as its trajectory brought it closer to its final destination. She sent a silent prayer to God to give her the strength to protect those she cared for in the coming months and years, which would see day turned to night.

Rebecca sat watching the television after Joseph had been put to bed at the care home. She had a small apartment on the grounds, as did a few other carers who worked alongside her. It was convenient and cheap, which was lucky as her wages meant she struggled to pay her bills on a weekly basis. The news was filled with the same old stories of how governments were gearing up for the dust cloud, and images from Washington D.C. where the President issued yet more words about how the whole world was ready for the impending disaster and calling for calm.

She switched channels, but wherever she looked more of the same greeted her. The closer it got to Impact Day, more and more TV channels focused in on the event. Even fictional programmes had storylines based on it to add to their realism. She finally settled on a small local independent channel, and while it still covered Impact Day, it was more down to earth and realistic than the other channels, which sensationalised the whole thing almost beyond imagination.

The show's presenter had a couple of townspeople on and was asking them how they were being affected, discussing things like rubbish collections, postal deliveries and whether the lawn mower would be able to run on chip fat due to the ongoing fuel shortages.

'—well thank you, Margaret,' the presenter was saying, 'for that insight into how gasoline lawnmowers can be made to run on chip oil. And now let's speak to Dwain and Emma who are outside looking at how you can protect yourself against intruders and rioters who may target your home for wanton looting and mayhem.'

So much for not sensationalising things, Rebecca thought with a wry smile. The camera switched to a view of the outside where they had a mock-up of a house frontage, complete with door and windows.

'So, Emma, when the dust cloud sends people a bit ga ga and turns day into a thief's wonderland, what can you do to protect yourself and the ones you love?'

'Thank you, Dwain. Well, for a start you need to make sure you have your doors locked and windows shut and bolted even before the curfew has started. Remember daylight hours will no longer be light when the cloud is overhead so treat the day like you would the night. Be wary, as darkness is when criminals like to operate and a permanent twenty-four hour night will make their lives easier and yours more dangerous.'

Emma looked at the camera. 'But we can help you improve your chances of getting through the coming years in safety and with peace of mind.' She moved to the entrance of the fake house. 'First of all we have this super strong nano fibre door frame and brace. Simply fitting behind your door, it acts as an impenetrable barrier to your home if the door itself is breached.'

'And this will work for the windows as well?' Dwain said, impressed.

'Of course,' Emma replied, 'the company that produces these anti-intruder doors also provides a wide range of window fittings which do the same job if your window is smashed.'

'And the price?' Dwain asked her.

'It is reasonably cheap at three hundred dollars for the door and fifty to two hundred and fifty dollars per window, depending on aperture size.'

'Wow, that is reasonable! And we'll be showing the viewer where they can get these at the end of the programme. What else have you got to show us, Emma?'

'We have these powerful pepper sprays and high powered catapults for those that don't have access to guns. They can be very effective at deterring all but the most determined of unwanted visitors.'

'So what should someone do if they are confronted by a raging mob?'

'Stay inside and try and frighten them off by whatever means available. Of course there will be a strong military presence on the streets at all times, but there is a limit to how many places they can be at once. If in doubt, hide or run away. You can rebuild and repair a house, but you may not be able to repair yourself.'

'Wise words, Emma, thank you; and it's back to you in the studio.'

'Thank you, Dwain and Emma. We'll be broadcasting further sets on this topic every day this week, so tune in for more handy tips and tricks to help with your Impact Day preparations.'

Rebecca zoned the TV out and thought about how the care home could prevent getting embroiled in any such problems. The main building itself was secure, but it wouldn't withstand an assault. It was also in a bad position; it bordered on a large, poor, housing estate located a significant way away from the stores and more prosperous areas of the town. *Not the best place to be*, she thought. They'd had trouble anyway, even as recently as last week when some kids had pelted the building with rocks and bottles. The janitor had scared them off eventually, but some damage had been done and many of the residents had been scared, especially patients like Joseph, who had cried all the way through the incident. It had taken her the rest of the day to calm him back down again.

A beeper sounded in the kitchen, the noise bringing Rebecca back to the present, prompting her to go to the washing machine. She extracted Joseph's now clean jogging pants and hung them out to dry on an airer. She thought about his camouflage trousers and the nice man at the surplus store and had an idea as to how they might protect the home and the residents. *It will cost*, she reasoned, *but it should work*. She got up, put her coat on and went out, the television still droning on as the door swung shut behind her.

The military surplus shopkeeper, Darren, was shutting up shop. It was four in the afternoon, but with a seven o'clock curfew he needed to shut then in order to get home, get the shopping and do some house repairs. Just as he pulled down the last shutter on the door a pair of woman's shoes appeared.

'We're closing, sorry. Come back tomorrow.'

'Hello, it's me,' said a voice that sounded familiar.

He pulled the shutter back up and saw that it was the woman who'd been in his shop with the simple man earlier that day. 'Hello, did you forget something?' he asked her.

'No,' she said, her expression determined, 'but I really need your help.'

CHAPTER TEN

IT HAD TAKEN SARAH, Trish and Jason the whole day to get back to the Turkish town. Thankfully they had passed a small village on the way, enabling them to take on some much-needed water. Darkness had asserted itself by the time they got to a rundown hotel where Sarah got a room with the meagre amount of money that Carl, the turncoat cum infiltrator, had given her. They traipsed up the wooden stairs and opened the door to the sparse double room. The three of them went in and all but fell down onto the two beds, exhaling great groans of relief as aching muscles were soothed and relaxed.

Since they had worked all through the previous night, followed by the gruelling walk to the village, they all slept until ten the next day. After cleaning themselves up as best they could with zero supplies and only the amenities provided by the hotel, they sat on the beds and discussed their options as to what to do next.

'Well, I guess by now the site has been stripped clean or is still under guard,' Sarah said. 'We might be able to follow them at a safe distance, though, see where they go; maybe even retrieve the bones or some of the relics from the canister.'

'What,' Jason said, incredulous, 'are you thinking of going back there?'

'Err – yeah. It's the biggest find of my career, possibly in history,' Sarah said with real feeling, an edge of anger to her voice, 'you think I'm going to give it up? Not likely!'

The fact that these military types might be linked to her mother's death also meant Sarah now had a lead, whereas before she'd had none; it was a stroke of luck delivered within a poisoned chalice, but one she couldn't allow to slide. She couldn't help but blame herself for her mother's death, although she knew she hadn't pulled the trigger; *I just loaded the gun*, she thought with bitter remorse.

No, whoever had started that fire – ordered it and planned it – was as culpable as she, and Sarah would not rest until some semblance of justice prevailed; she owed her mother that much at least. Never one to come at something from a single angle, Sarah would also make it her mission in life to expose whoever attempted to cover up the existence of Homo gigantis, be that separate individuals, groups or one big organisation, and prove beyond doubt the existence of this ancient race to the world.

'All right, but look, Sazza,' Jason was saying as she refocused to the present, 'you said it yourself – the area will be stripped if you get back there and we'll have no kit, not to mention we now have virtually no money to buy any more. If they are still there, what are you going to do if they spot you – and they could well do – overpower them? I don't think so, somehow. Look what happened to me. These guys are military and top of the pile, by the look of their kit.'

'And what do you know about military hardware?' Trish said.

'I did a stint in the Territorial Army, didn't I? Besides which, I've seen films and programmes, and they looked well kitted out.'

'I thought the TA was only for a month and then they kicked you out?' Trish said in accusation. 'You said you didn't even get to hold a gun.'

'Well, yeah, but they had catalogues and stuff. Look, I know they were some kind of elite unit, alright? Cheap hired guns don't go zooming about in those types of vehicles and with that kind of get up; they had serious money behind them.'

'He's right,' Sarah said.

'Thank you!' Jason raised his hand aloft while looking at Trish, triumphant his deduction had been recognised and supported.

Trish ignored him.

'Did you see that bloke who was with them, that Italian in a suit?' Sarah asked them. 'They've got to be something to do with the Church.'

'Church? What church, St Bartholomew's near your flat?' Jason said, confused.

'Not the local church, you donkey,' Trish said. 'The Vatican.' She looked at Sarah for confirmation. 'You think they work for the Vatican, right?'

Sarah nodded. 'It ties in with what my group have been saying for years. They keep their eyes open for anyone undertaking small digs, or large ones for that matter, and intervene when necessary. That explains his Italian accent, and the money they'd have behind such a scheme would be huge. Do you know how rich they are?' Sarah said. She didn't wait for an answer. 'They've been around for over a thousand years. They've stockpiled precious art and artefacts. Destroyed books in their millions and waged war across continents. They predate the banks, stocks and companies themselves.

'Who do you think invested in the first companies when they began to become powerful? The rich of the day, which included monarchs and – most definitely – the Catholic Church. They probably own some of the big multinationals along with other massive private companies we know nothing about. If there was ever any organisation capable and motivated to cover up this kind of thing, it's them.' Sarah slumped onto the bed looking deflated and morose; everything was stacked against them.

'Perhaps they'll miss something,' Trish said. 'We could just go back and pick it up later when they've gone.'

Jason's snort of derision told her what he thought of that suggestion.

'Well, have you got a better idea, then?' Trish said angrily.

He bristled with defiance. 'I do, as a matter of fact.'

'And that is?' she said, as he paused and rummaged about in his trouser pocket.

'We could try and decipher this!' He held up a crumpled bit of paper.

'And what is that, a receipt for the dunce's hat you bought last week?' Trish said, her voice scathing.

Sarah sat up and looked at the piece of paper in Jason's hand. 'What's that?' she said, curious.

He crouched down at the foot of the bed and spread it out for them both to see.

Sarah couldn't believe it. Jason had somehow got hold of a map similar to those she had found all those years ago, before they had been lost in the fire. It had the same intricate symbols dotted over its surface, although this one portrayed a more localised area rather than covering whole continents. It depicted a coastal land mass which covered nearly half the page, and it looked familiar somehow, but she didn't know why.

'I've seen this before,' Jason said.

Sarah frowned. 'That's what I was just thinking. But I can't place it.'

Trish came over to take a look. 'I think I know why you both recognise it,' she told them, after studying it for a moment.

'Why?' Jason said.

'Because it's been on the TV now for what seems like forever.'

They both looked at her with blank expressions.

'It's the damn impact zone; it's the South African coastline, the eastern coast to be more precise.'

Sarah and Jason looked again. 'She's only flippin' right,' he said in amazement. 'It's South Africa!'

'What I want to know is how you got this out without them finding it?' Trish asked him. 'I saw them search you thoroughly; unless,' – her nose wrinkled in distaste – 'you stuck it somewhere I don't want to know about.'

Sarah moved her hands away from the map's surface.

Jason saw the movement and looked from Trish to Sarah and

back to Trish again. 'What? – NO!' he said. 'I didn't stick it up my arse. Blimey, I think they may have noticed me doing that when they turned up. Hang on, lads; turn around, will you, while I stick this ancient map up my bum hole.'

Trish made a face.

'So how did you spirit it out of there, then?' Sarah asked him.

'You know before they put us in the car I attacked Carl?'

'Yeah, when he kicked your arse, you mean,' Trish said.

Ignoring her, Jason continued. 'Well, I slipped it out of his pocket during the scuffle. That was my intention all along. It was worth it,' he said, rubbing his shoulder, 'just.'

'Oh, Jas, that's fantastic! I could kiss you. In fact, I will kiss you.' Sarah got up and planted one on his forehead.

Jason blushed and grinned foolishly while Trish looked on stony-faced. 'You got lucky,' she said. 'What if he notices it's missing? What then, smart arse?'

Jason's face dropped a little. 'He hasn't, so far, has he? Otherwise they'd be here, now, doing us over again.' He paused and then looked around, his eyes wary. 'Unless they're listening in on us right now ready to strike—'

Sarah and Trish looked at one another in alarm and then peered around the room as Jason tiptoed over to the door, opened it and peeked into the corridor.

'HOLY SHIT!' Terrified, he leapt back, making Trish scream and Sarah jump up from the bed.

But when no armed men came swarming into the room Jason shut the door, unable to keep up his pretence any longer. 'The look on both your faces!' He pointed at them, in fits of laughter. 'I almost pissed myself.'

'You fucking bastard,' Trish shouted at him and went over and punched him hard on the arm.

'Ow!' he said, scowling at her before looking at Sarah. 'That was a good one, though, wasn't it, Saz?'

Sarah grinned at him. 'Yes, very good. I'll have to get you back for it, though.'

'Don't encourage him,' Trish said, 'he's bad enough as it is.'

But Sarah wasn't listening; she'd gone back to studying the map.

Trish looked over her shoulder. 'What's that?' she said, and touched the larger pendant that hung in front of the smaller one around Sarah's neck.

Sarah had forgotten all about it after everything that had happened. She unclipped her new find and opened the end, then teased out the paper hidden inside. As she unfurled it she noticed it felt similar in texture to the map Jason had pick-pocketed from Carl. Incredibly, it spread out to a substantial size. It felt thick to the touch, but flexing it she could tell it was much thinner than normal paper. It was unlike anything she had felt before, including Jason's map.

'Where did you get that from?' Jason said in amazement. He picked up the pendant and examined it.

'I found it in a weird metal canister I discovered before we were hit by those goons. This was the only thing I had a good look at and luckily they didn't spot it.'

'They nearly did, though, didn't they?' Trish said, remembering.

'Yeah, it was a pretty close call. As soon as I saw all those cars I knew something was up, so I quickly clipped this new pendant on my chain and it settled nicely on top of my other one. Carl just assumed it was the one he'd seen me wearing before. I completely forgot about it until you just noticed it, I was so tired and exhausted during the walk it just left my mind.'

'I just thought it was odd,' Trish said. 'I looked over your shoulder and saw two pendants rather than just one.' Trish accepted the pendant from Jason for a closer inspection. 'Now I know what I'm looking at, I can see this new one is a bit bigger and it's got designs on it, too, plus this little compartment; intriguing.'

'Let's have a look then,' Jason said to Sarah, who was now staring at the new parchment intently. It appeared to be a page of text. She laid it out next to the map so they could all see.

'Has anyone noticed that these parchments are not faded or degraded in any way?' Trish said, feeling each one in turn. 'They look like they were made yesterday.'

She's right, Sarah thought to herself. The parchments, for want of a better word, had neither faded nor cracked. They looked brand new, although made of some light brown material that wasn't skin, paper or anything else she recognised. The quality of the printing, as that's almost what it looked like, was extremely high; however, the faint marks and flicks of the instrument that had created them could be seen, indicating they'd been drawn by hand. *Curious*, Sarah thought, utterly fascinated.

Three principal colours, grey, white and a light green, dominated the designs. The symbols were fine and intricate, similar to a modern alphabet, although there didn't seem to be a strict order to them.

'These can only be the work of Homo gigantis,' Sarah said, tracing the obscure script with a finger.

'You think?' Trish said.

'Why not? It stands to reason; they were found near the skeleton and at about the same depth. The map carries the same markings as the ones I found previously in roughly the same area. This text doesn't look like anything I have ever seen before, though. It's clearly an alphabetical system rather than pictogrammatical, which rules out ancient human civilisations; plus if this is handwritten, which it looks like it is, then look at the spacing and size of the letters – a large hand wrote this, don't you agree?'

'I suppose,' Trish said. 'Given what I've seen in the last few days I would be inclined to lean towards your theory.'

'Theory? How else can you explain it? The skeleton, maps, casket, pendant, the military intervention and cover up?'

'I can't, Sarah, but that doesn't mean you're right, it just means I can't think of an alternative reason; they're two different things entirely.'

Sarah didn't say anything as she knew Trish would play devil's advocate until the cows came home, but she was convinced. Add all this to the other historical evidence and accounts made by her friends, and it was just too conclusive.

'My pendants and past discoveries, and our first-hand experience of the skeleton, can only mean that Homo gigantis evolved hundreds of thousands of years ago,' Sarah said, unable to contain herself any longer, 'and all evidence of their existence has been swept under the carpet by the Catholic Church, and God knows who else, over the last millennium or more. Add to that these parchments and clearly they were extremely well advanced. They had an alphabet, they could cast metal objects with an accuracy that matches anything we can do today, and whatever these parchments are made of seems to be age resistant.'

'Skeletons,' Jason said.

Confused, Sarah just stared at him. 'What?'

'You said skeleton,' he told her, 'when there were two – so skeletons, plural.'

'What are you going on about?' Trish said, exasperated.

'I'm saying there were two fucking skeletons and not one, what do you think I'm saying?'

'Two, how did that happen? No one mentioned two before!' Sarah said, looking at Trish accusingly.

'Don't look at me, I didn't know, this is the first I've heard of it.'

'Just as the men were pulling up,' Jason said, 'me and prick face Carl had just unearthed the edge of another skull close to the feet of the first. I was going to take some pictures when everything went pear-shaped.'

'Why didn't you tell us before?' Trish asked him.

'I only just thought of it. We're not all perfect like you, are we?'

Trish gave him the finger.

'Hang on a minute,' Sarah said. 'Where did the map come from, then, the one you got from Carl?'

'Dunno. From your casket, maybe? I saw him look at it and then stuff it in his pocket, so I thought I'm gonna have that, you two-faced git.'

'One of the men that grabbed me must have passed it to him – the bastards,' Sarah said, before going back to studying the second parchment.

The ancient material measured about twice the size of an A4 piece of paper. A faint, indented circle sat in the top right corner. She looked at the map; that had one, too, the same size and in the same place. She felt it with her thumb and the page shimmered and the text changed.

She yanked her hand away in astonishment. 'What the—?'

Trish and Jason, who had been looking at the map, glanced up at her. 'What is it, Saz?' Trish said.

'Did you see that? It just changed. The text just altered!' She stared in shock at the page before her.

'What? What do you mean, changed?' Jason said, confused.

'I put my finger on that circle and it changed the text on the page.'

Jason reached out and touched it. Nothing happened. Seeing the same sunken circle on the map, he touched that too; still nothing. Trish did the same, to no avail.

Sarah touched the page once more in the same place and ... nothing.

'It moved, I'm not imagining it,' she said, seeing Trish and Jason exchange looks.

'Perhaps it was the sunlight making it look like the text changed,' Jason said.

'Or you blinked, or your eyes went blurry; mine do that sometimes when I'm tired,' Trish added.

'I'm not tired, I didn't blink and it wasn't the damn sun. I'm telling you the text changed when I touched it.'

'So why didn't it do it again?' Trish said, her tone soothing as she tried to calm Sarah's growing frustration.

Jason gestured at the parchment. 'Perhaps you pressed it harder the first time?'

Sarah pressed her thumb harder on the circle and again nothing happened. She rubbed it. Licked her finger and then pressed it, tapped it, scratched it, all to no avail. She threw her hands up in exasperation.

'What exactly were you doing when it happened?' Jason said. He made a face at Trish, whose expression indicated he shouldn't pursue it any further.

Sarah thought for a minute. 'I was just sitting here holding the parchment in one hand – no, wait, I was holding this pendant in one hand,' – she picked up the newly found pentagonal disc – 'and I touched the page with my thumb like this and—' The text on the page shimmered once more and a new set displayed in its place. 'It changed again! Did you see it?!'

'Bloody Ada, it did change, I saw it!' Jason said, flabbergasted.

Trish gaped at the page in sheer disbelief. 'Are you friggin' kidding me?'

Sarah pressed it again, and again, and each time what appeared to be a fresh page of text revealed itself.

'It's bloody magic,' Jason said in awe.

'More like a super sophisticated digital display,' Sarah said.

'But it's so thin,' Trish murmured.

'Perhaps it uses nano machines or something,' Jason said. 'They say the military have been using things like that for years.'

'Perhaps, but whatever it is, it's mind blowing.' Sarah couldn't take her eyes off it. 'Surely this proves they were advanced, and way beyond us, by the look of it. What do you think now, Trish?'

Trish nodded her head in agreement, dumbfounded by this new turn of events.

'Try it on the map,' Jason said, eager to see more.

Sarah pulled over the map and, holding the pendant in her left hand, she put her thumb on the circle. The map didn't move or alter in any way.

Disappointed, she put the pendant down.

'Perhaps the power's run out?' Jason said.

'Don't be stupid,' Trish told him.

'Why not? The other one only worked when Sarah held the pendant, perhaps that powers the paper?'

It's a fair point, Sarah thought. *The pendant might be some kind of sophisticated power source worn around a person's neck to enable them to activate all sorts of gizmos, including this display*. She wondered what other fantastical treasures had been contained in the casket. She made the writing change again, this time with her index finger, showing that the power – if that's what it was – still worked. *So why doesn't it work on the map?* she asked herself.

'Perhaps it's not a power source at all,' she said to them, turning the pentagonal pendant over in her hands, 'perhaps it uses our bioelectricity to activate the parchment. It makes sense; if it's only to channel the body's own electricity then the battery never runs out. It would be an amazing piece of tech, no?'

The two looked at her expectantly.

'So—' she continued, eager to keep the ideas flowing, 'if I was a very big person, I would have more electricity in my body and consequently I could power bigger and more complex things. How much would someone measuring eight and a half feet weigh, roughly?' she asked Trish, who was the maths wiz.

'If it was an average male, perhaps four to five hundred pounds? A female, anywhere from three-fifty to four hundred and fifty?'

'That would be one big woman,' Jason said, 'she'd be the size of a house!'

'She wouldn't be overweight,' Trish said, 'far from it, she'd be in perfect proportion for her species. It may sound excessive,' she continued, 'but eight and a half feet is massive. Think about it. She'd be three foot taller than your average woman, that's half as tall again. But unlike height, weight is effectively measuring three dimensional volume so even though the height is half as much the volume is magnitudes greater, about three times greater in this instance.'

Jason didn't look convinced.

Trish sighed. 'It's simple mechanics. The bigger the animal, the bigger and stronger the muscles required to support it. Think of an elephant and how big their limbs are; same principle. Homo gigantis may appear stockier than ourselves, granted, but not massively so. In fact, if their muscles were much denser than ours, like that of an ape, for instance, they might have body shapes resembling our own, just scaled up.'

Jason nodded, although Sarah thought he still looked confused. 'So let's say four-fifty on average, then,' she said. 'I weigh about one-forty-five. What are you, Trish, about one-thirty?'

Trish nodded. 'One three eight last time I checked.'

'Jas?'

'Bout one-eighty.'

'So in total we all weigh, what? Four hundred and sixty-three pounds, give or take? Just about right for a fully grown Homo gigantis!'

'And what does that prove?' Trish asked her.

'It means if we all join hands we might be able to power the map!' Jason said, looking at Sarah for confirmation.

'That's right,' Sarah said, and held out her palm with the pendant in.

Jason put his hand over hers and Trish put her two hands around them both. Sarah sent out a silent prayer and touched the circle on the map. It flickered and changed, showing an image that looked very similar to a satellite photo you'd find on the net.

'Oh, my God,' Trish murmured.

'What are those?' Jason peered at some markings that ran down the side of the image. Tentatively, he reached out and touched one. The image rotated. He touched another and the image zoomed in.

'This is just – wow!' Sarah said, goosebumps tingling on her arms. They grinned at one another, momentarily lost for words, caught in the moment only felt by those witnessing first hand an incredible discovery.

'I can't believe this, am I dreaming? – Ow!' Sarah jumped as Trish pinched her arm, causing her finger to jump off the circle. The image disappeared, leaving the original map showing once more.

'Sorry,' Trish said, 'just checking.'

After Trish and Jason bickered a bit, they tried again and this time they were able to zoom in on some kind of structure on the ground.

After half an hour they had managed to circle the front of an odd looking building which appeared to be made out of mud bricks and logs. Sarah thought this very strange; *they obviously had advanced technology*, she reasoned, *so why build a structure out of such basic materials? Unless*, she thought, *they didn't build it*. Which then begged the question, who did?

From what she could see, the rear of the building backed onto a low slung escarpment and various indigenous plants could also be seen growing all around it. It wasn't a photo as such, more a graphical representation; extremely detailed, but not real footage.

Jason experimented and pressed a combination of buttons and the screen went blank and returned to the plain map once again.

'Why did you do that?' Sarah said, annoyed.

'He was only testing it,' Trish said, defending him for once.

Jason looked as surprised at this as Sarah did.

'Well, he was,' Trish told her, 'we wouldn't have been able to see as much as we have if he hadn't messed about with it.'

Trish had a point, Sarah realised. The problem with this method of holding the pendant was that she couldn't access the functions herself, as her finger was always touching the circle.

'Hang on guys, I've got an idea.' Sarah removed her hand from theirs and hung the pendant back on her neck chain, resting it against her skin with the smaller one in front of it. Then she put her finger back on the map.

'Put your hands on my arm,' she told them.

As they did so, the map image changed once again and Sarah was now able to access the map with her spare hand.

'Nice one,' Jason said.

'You'd have thought if they were so advanced that you could power the DPD using just your touch anywhere on the page,' Trish said, 'rather than having to stick your finger on that circle all the time.'

Jason gave her a quizzical look. 'DPD?'

'Digital paper display.'

'Not bad, not bad at all,' Jason said, impressed.

Trish nodded an acceptance of the compliment, looking smug about her wordsmithing effort.

'Perhaps the ... DPD,' Sarah said, 'does work that way, but we just don't know how to activate it.'

'Also a valid point,' Jason said, leaving Trish looking peeved at his instant betrayal.

'Whatever this place is,' Sarah continued, zooming back in on the building again, 'it looks like a very solid structure, even if it is made out of mud and logs. If it was built by the same race who made these parchments, then it would be made to last. There might be something left of it in this area – and look, what's that?' She pointed at an object which had appeared inside the building as she'd moved the viewer in even closer.

'It looks like a large metal egg,' Jason said.

'It's a casket like the one I found at the site!'

'Are you sure?' Trish asked her.

'Definitely, it's exactly the same shape as the one I found. If it's still there and we can hide our tracks from those thieving bastards then maybe we can get some more artefacts. This could be huge!'

'That's two big ifs and an even larger maybe,' Trish said.

'But it would be worth it. We have to try, don't we?'

Jason looked uncertain.

'You do realise where that is, don't you?' Trish asked her. 'In the evacuation zone. No one's allowed in and those that are left behind are criminals and pirates trying to harvest what's left of the infrastructure, and even they will be getting out as it's ... what? Two weeks until Impact Day? There's no way we're getting down there and if we did I'd rather not be in the path of some mountainous rock travelling faster than a speeding bullet; how about you?'

'I don't care,' Sarah said. 'I'm going down there on my own, if need be. And as you say, there'll be some activity across the evac border even if it's not legal. It'll be a case of jumping in and jumping back out again. There won't be second chances after it hits, so you say goodbye to that canister for good. It's worth the risk and I'm going to take it.'

Jason raised a hand. 'I'm in.'

'We don't even know if anything's there!' Trish said, sounding desperate. 'Please, Sarah, we don't have to do this.'

Sarah hadn't mentioned to Trish her epiphany about the fire and her mother's death, so she couldn't explain her motivations to her without going into a deep conversation about it. Even now her mind shied away from the mere thought of talking about it with anyone else; to admit her guilt, to confront those emotions again – no, she couldn't, she wouldn't.

Sarah didn't answer and Trish glared at them both in turn as she realised neither was going to budge. 'Fine, I'll go, but I'll sort out the travel. I want to make sure we'll get in and out before we're vaporised.'

'Excellent!' Jason said exuberantly while Trish sat stiff and stony-faced as she stared at Sarah.

'We're going to need to know exactly where this place is, otherwise we'll be looking around aimlessly,' Trish continued. 'We need to get to it, dig it out if it's still there, and then get out. No messing about, we won't have time.'

'Okay.' Sarah stood up and looked out of the window in concentration. 'Jason, you get a detailed map of Africa off the net, there's a café down the road that'll have access. Here's some cash.' She passed him a few notes. 'I'll go to the embassy and get some more money using my passport, and Trish; you can arrange the flights to get there. Sound good?'

'Fine, I'll go with, Jas,' Trish said, 'and hook us up the flights there. Be careful, though, Sarah, we don't know if those people are following us or what.'

'I doubt it. They only knew we were there last time because Carl was some kind of mole. It'll just be us this time, no worries.'

'I hope you're right.'

'Trust me,' Sarah said, her confident tone belying her real feelings.

Sarah came back to the hotel loaded with bags full of new clothes, rucksacks, canteens, sat nav and a couple of computer phones, amongst other things. Trish had booked a flight from Van to Istanbul and then onto Gabon, the closest African country open to civilian aircraft so close to Impact Day, and one located right next to the evacuation zone's border.

According to the present day maps Jason had downloaded, the site they wanted to visit was just outside Johannesburg, right next to the Sterkfontein Caves; also known as the Cradle of Humanity, due to the plethora of fossils found there, some of which dated back many millions of years to Homo sapiens' earliest beginnings. This was an interesting development, although Sarah still couldn't believe that they had recognised the location on the gigantis map. *How lucky was that?* she marvelled. However, it was also incredibly unlucky that it was smack in the middle of the predicted meteorite impact zone. In less than a couple of weeks the land depicted on the parchment would be obliterated by shockwaves, fires and potential flooding; not to mention the threat of massive earthquakes triggered during the collision.

Using an application which triangulated major landmarks, they narrowed the area that hopefully still contained the ancient structure to a zone about four hundred feet square. Jason reckoned he could narrow that further once they were actually there on the ground. *Not bad*, Sarah reflected, *considering the Homo gigantis map is far beyond ancient in human terms*. For all they knew it might be over half a million years old; or to give it perspective, one hundred times older than the Egyptian pyramids or older than humanity itself!

Once they had packed up all the gear they needed and changed into new clothes, they left the hotel and caught a taxi to the city of Van. They all kept a careful watch for any suspicious vehicles following them on the way, but much to everyone's relief they seemed to be in the clear. They then caught the plane to Istanbul and the connecting flight to Gabon without much problem, which was mainly down to Trish's organisational skills.

The flight down to Gabon would be slow as it was only a jet plane rather than a Sabre craft, but it would still get them there in roughly nine hours. Sarah settled down in her window seat as the plane gained altitude and Turkey drifted away beneath the clouds. She hoped the risk they were taking paid off, and if it did fame and fortune followed; but far more importantly so would vindication and some kind of vengeance, irrefutable proof of an advanced pre-human race and civilisation. The pendant and parchments should be proof enough for most people, but for those who would accuse her of trickery and faking the finds – of whom there would undoubtedly be many – a canister full of artefacts would quell their objections and prove beyond doubt that Homo gigantis was no myth. Happy with that thought, she drifted off to sleep as the drone of the engines took them ever higher.

CHAPTER ELEVEN

THE PLANE TOUCHED down in Gabon in the early hours of the morning, and shortly after Sarah descended the aircraft steps into a beautiful sunrise that shimmered off the runway surface. A soothing breeze played in the nearby trees that surrounded the airport's terminal building. It was a truly magical place and supposedly – according to Trish – elephants, buffalo and hippos wandered along its beaches and even went into the sea itself. Unfortunately they weren't there to take in the atmosphere, soak up the sun and experience the sights, no, far from it. They were on a tight schedule and one they couldn't afford to dally on. Time was of the essence, now more than ever.

They quickly departed the Leon M'Ba International Airport and headed towards a remote airport in Tchibanga from where, Jason had heard from their taxi driver, illegal forays into the restricted evacuation zone were conducted. It took them the best part of the day to get to the tiny airport and when they arrived they were greeted by a desolate looking place containing a few buildings and a handful of small planes.

'There's no way we're getting to South Africa in one of those things,' Trish said in dismay.

The taxi driver, a large jolly Nigerian, laughed. 'Don't you worry, missy, the plane that will be taking you to South Africa is not here. You'll have to a wait a day or two for it to come in.'

'A day or two,' Trish said, 'are you kidding me? We can't afford that kind of delay!'

Trish was right, Sarah knew; they had to get going as soon as they could and hanging around for two days was not an option. She looked out of the window at the sky; no sign of the meteor yet, but it was getting nearer all the time. She pulled her phone out of her pocket; twelve days and five hours until impact. Two days off that, plus another for the journey to the destination, left just nine days. They'd then need to get a flight back out and get to Gabon's main airport with more than three days to go to Impact Day, when all flights would be grounded by the UN's Global Meteor Response Council, the GMRC. With the return journey taking another two days, that only left them a maximum of four days at the site – or just two if Trish had her way.

'I'm not waiting till the last minute to get out of there,' Trish had told them. Sarah was inclined to agree with her. Being in the immediate vicinity of a meteor strike, perhaps the largest one for sixty-five million years, was not the best idea in the world. In fact, everything screamed at her to stop and go back, everything apart from the voice that told her another find of a lifetime and definitive proof of her theories lay near the Cradle of Humankind.

They paid the taxi driver and then paid him double the amount on top to come back in six days' time and wait for up to another two days. Sarah told him they would then pay him four times that for the ride back to the capital city, Libreville.

'For that much, missy, I will wait for another four days!' the cabbie declared enthusiastically.

This excursion was costing Sarah a small fortune. She was lucky the money transfer system had been built into the latest international passports. You connected it to your bank account and then, via a series of security features, you could get cash out from any country in the world. Very handy; *especially when you've been robbed by some shadowy organisation bent on a worldwide cover up*, she thought wryly.

As the taxi departed they picked up their bags from the dusty earth and struggled into the main building. The majority of the weight was undoubtedly down to the two large pieces of kit being manhandled and pushed along by Jason. One was an SPVU, a directional ultrasonic Sediment Pulse Vibration Unit – expensive, but worth its weight in gold when it came to loosening and breaking down compacted earth and soft rock, it would enable them to excavate deep down in a fraction of the time. The downside was that it had a very limited battery life. The second and equally important piece of kit was a ground penetrating scanner. It was nothing like Sarah's top of the range handheld device – that had gone the way of all their other equipment – as it weighed ten times more and lacked the same accuracy, but it would do the job and beggars couldn't be choosers. They were both stolen, of that Sarah had no doubt, as the man she'd got them from made a banker look trustworthy, no mean feat.

The advantage of stolen kit, however, was that it wouldn't be flagged up, alerting anyone to their intentions. She'd been lucky to find them at all to be honest, but the price she'd had to pay for them both made her feel a little sick. She really was out on a limb, financially, morally and professionally. This had to pay off.

As luck had it, they only had to wait a day for their plane to arrive. It sported a twin jet engine design, very common, and thankfully – hopefully – reliable. If Sarah thought she'd paid a lot for the scanner, the fare for this was beyond the pale.

'How much?!' she screeched at the co-pilot who was going to take the money off her once they'd loaded up.

'Ten thousand.'

'But that's ridiculous, we can't pay that,' Trish said, backing her up.

'Then you're going nowhere,' the man told them bluntly.

'Fine,' Sarah said, and handed over the cash, despite Trish's protests. 'We've come this far, haven't we? A bit more won't make any odds.'

'A bit?' Trish said, choking on the words. 'You do realise it'll be the same coming back ...' She put her mouth to Sarah's ear and whispered, 'Or more!'

'What choice do we have?' Sarah murmured back.

Trish had no answer to that. How could she? They were all-in; there was no turning back now.

And so, with the extortionate fee paid, they settled in for the flight, which would take them two and a half thousand miles south east across the African continent. To reduce the risk of being caught by the patrols which flew irregular flights up and down the border's length, the pilot took off at dusk; apparently going out to sea first and coming back in an arc minimised contact with the Jian-10B Chinese-made multi-role fighters employed by the UN Task Force to patrol the skies.

An uneventful flight passed by relatively quickly and they were soon touching down on a disused airfield twenty miles out of Johannesburg. The place was pretty much deserted – as you would expect with a meteor on the way – and it was daylight as they left the plane behind after hiring a rusty old pickup from an equally aged local man who apparently refused to leave, declaring he'd rather die than abandon his home. Some people became dangerously attached to a location; something Sarah had a hard time comprehending.

During the drive Jason had time to forage around in their luggage and he found something which made him over the moon. 'Oh, my God, this is like Indiana Jones's hat!' he said, thrilled, and held up a distressed leather hat that Sarah had bought for him back in Turkey.

'Indiana who?' Trish said as he put it on.

He looked at her in amazement. 'You haven't seen those classic films with Harrison Ford?'

'No, should I have?'

'You haven't lived. Call yourself an archaeologist, I don't know. All I need now is a whip.'

'If you say so,' Trish said, amused.

'Philistine!' He nudged the brim higher, his mood undampened.

With Jason continuing to enthuse about his new headwear, the short road trip to the location he'd pinpointed for them was soon over, satellite navigation having led them to the exact spot they desired. Once there Jason, proudly wearing his new hat, triangulated their position again and narrowed down the area they had to search to a much smaller section of about forty feet square. Cracking on, they set up camp in double quick time and deployed the ground scanner as soon as they were able. Taking shifts over the next day they meticulously scanned the area, which proved frustratingly fruitless.

Jason couldn't understand why they couldn't locate anything. Utilising another application he attempted to locate the area depicted on the ancient map once more. The result came back the same.

'I don't understand it,' he said. 'This should be the place. No, this *is* the place.'

Sarah wiped sweat from her brow. 'So where is it, then?'

'Well, it means one of two things,' Trish said, as she came over to them both and handed them each a cup of steaming tea. 'One, the scanner isn't up to the job. Or much worse, two, the canister and building are no longer here.'

Sarah was crestfallen as she admitted to herself her worst fears.

'I'm sorry, Saz,' – Trish touched her arm – 'but that second option seems the most likely, doesn't it? If it's thousands of years since it was here, perhaps even hundreds of thousands of years, then it's probably long since gone.'

'We still have the maps, though,' Jason said, remaining optimistic. 'They're proof enough on their own, aren't they?'

Sarah didn't reply. *All that money, all the risk, for nothing.* She took a long draught of her tea, lost in her thoughts. *The other canister I found in Turkey must have been there for a similar amount of time*, she reasoned. *No, it must be here, it must!* The scanner wasn't great, but it was working; she'd tested it out and they'd been able to locate and unearth a tree root at a test horizontal depth of fifty feet.

She looked around at the barren scrubland surrounding them.

Hard compacted earth and rock littered the landscape. The escarpment shown in the digital map was barely visible as it cut across the landscape. *At least we can see it*, she thought, *that's something*. It meant the canister would be just in reach, some fifteen feet down; hopefully, anyway, as any further and it became too deep to excavate, even with the SPVU excavation machine, which was primarily a horizontal tunnel boring aide than a vertical excavation device.

She had been concerned that the landscape would be radically different than in the ancient digitised image on the map. Her hope had been that the location they now found themselves at, which she'd researched on her new phone, had been similar for tens of thousands of years or longer. It was a gamble, but one that had paid off; the top of the escarpment was testament to that fact. And then she had it. The answer to why they couldn't find the canister.

Sarah turned to them, her face lit up with excitement. 'We're looking in the wrong place!'

'We can't be. I've run different software packages multiple times,' Jason said, looking dejected. 'This is the place.'

'Long shore drift, sediment build up,' Sarah said, 'coastlines change all the time! Were you using the coastline as a reference point in your triangulations?'

Jason nodded.

'Then that's it then,' she said, 'run them again using another point and we'll have the location.'

Jason was already furiously tapping away at his computer, inputting the relevant data. Sarah paced around in agitation, waiting, her impatience tangible.

'Got it,' he said at last, and pointed westwards. 'It's about a mile in that direction.'

'We were way out. No wonder we couldn't find anything,' Trish said.

'All right, let's pack up and get to the new site. We don't want to be here any longer than need be.'

'I second that,' Trish said.

'Thirded,' Jason added.

'There's no such word!' Trish protested.

'There is now,' he replied impishly, a broad grin on his face again.

The hunt was back on.

They stowed all their gear and equipment in the vehicle and headed off at speed, dust and dirt shooting out from beneath the wheels as they sought to gain traction.

They soon reached the new location; however, it was quickly apparent they had a big problem. The low bluff which had just been visible at the previous site was now nowhere to be seen.

Sarah looked back the way they had come to see the top of the promontory dip below the surface about half a mile away. Over time dirt and rocks had built up beyond thirty feet, that or earthquakes had caused uplift. If they were able to locate the canister with the scanner it would be too deep to retrieve, something Jason had noticed, too.

'There's much more sediment build-up here. We can adjust the scanner with some software tweaks to scan more deeply, but if we find anything we won't be able to get to it.'

'He's right, Sarah, this is going to be pointless.'

'Let's just find the damn thing first,' Sarah said. 'Jas, map out the area, I'll sort out the scanner and we'll get imaging. If we find it we'll have to hope it's moved nearer to the surface.'

Jason and Trish moved off to unload and Sarah overheard them talking about the futility of what they were doing. *Perhaps they're right*, she thought. In fact, she knew they were right. Although even if they couldn't get to it, it would be some kind of success to locate it. They'd come this far, they might as well get some closure and finish the job.

She looked at her phone, eight days until impact. Glancing up, she searched the sky for the telltale glint of light that signalled the approaching asteroid. Was that something near the horizon? She squinted, trying to focus on it, but the haze disrupted her vision. *It's probably Venus or a star, you fool*, she berated herself. *Get your mind on the job in hand.*

Another day passed by as they painstakingly scanned the area. The greater the depth of a scan, the slower the scanner could be moved, and it was late in the day, as the sun shimmered on its downward curve against a bright blue sky, that their breakthrough came.

A shout went up from Trish, who had taken on the current scanning shift. 'I've found something!'

Jason popped his head out of the pickup truck's passenger window and Sarah did likewise from the driver's side. They both jumped out, the doors slamming shut as they ran over to where Trish bent over the scanner's display screen.

'What is it, is it the canister?' Sarah asked her.

'I don't think so. It looks like a hollow space. Have a look.'

Sarah moved to the display and shielded it against the sun's glare. The screen's image portrayed its results mainly in bright pinks and black. Dense metallic objects showed up in green, ceramics and bone in yellow, but neither green nor yellow were present. The pink areas in shifting shades indicated ground density and the black areas voids. Approximately thirty-five feet below them, a large black blotch was clearly evident on the screen.

Jason leaned in to have a look. 'Perhaps it's just a space created by boulders?'

'I don't think so.' Sarah adjusted a couple of the dials slightly to expand and rotate the image. 'No, look, it has straight sides. That is definitely not a natural formation.'

'Could it be that building we saw in that DPD?' Trish said.

Jason frowned. 'What was DPD again?'

'Digital paper display, idiot,' Trish said impudently. 'Keep up.'

Jason swore under his breath.

'What was that?' Trish asked him.

'Nothing, just clearing my throat.'

'Hmm,' Trish said, sounding unconvinced.

Sarah moved the scanner to one side and took another scan.

'That is a big void down there. I think you're right, Trish, it could well be a building, perhaps even the one on the map.'

'We can't get to it, though,' Jason said.

Trish tutted. 'She knows that, numpty head.'

Jason made a face at her.

'BOLLOCKS!' Sarah shouted at the top of her voice. 'So bloody close, yet so bloody far.'

'At least we found something,' Trish said, trying to console her.

'I'll search this area for a bit,' Sarah told them, 'get a complete picture of the structure.'

Jason and Trish left her to it. They could tell she was not in the mood for company as her face had that determined, taut look to it, the *don't talk to me or be near me* face they knew well.

Sarah took scans for the best part of half a day, getting a clear overview of the chamber. At one point the device sent back a weak signal on a deeper pass, alluding to the presence of metal; subsequent scans, however, failed to find it again. This was perhaps the most frustrating time of her life and at the same time, the most exciting. Almost within touching distance, the possibility of an actual building which might be unthinkably old, something that would make Stonehenge seem like a twenty-first century new build.

Once she had finished she transferred the information to her phone and plodded back to the truck, feeling depressed. Trish and Jason were nowhere to be seen. Now that she thought about it, they had shouted something over to her, but she had been so engrossed in the scanner's display she'd barely heard them, let alone paid attention to what they were saying. She now wondered where they'd got to. The landscape had gradual undulations, so they must have walked off a fair way. Not wanting to wander about aimlessly looking for them, she settled down in the pickup's passenger seat to rest and wait for their return.

Sarah woke with a start; dusk had crept up on her and she felt groggy and cold. Rubbing her arms warm she looked about; still no sign of them. *Odd*, she thought. Picking up her phone she dialled Jason's new number. A buzzing sounded next to her; she looked across to the driver's door pocket to see a bright screen with the message *incoming call* on it. *Bloody hell, Jason, why did you leave it here?* Just as her concern mounted, a loud bang came from the rear of the truck. She jumped in shock. Whirling around, she jumped again and yelped as a face peered in the back window at her, eyes staring wide accompanied by a hideously stupid grin.

'Jason, you friggin' twathead, you scared the shit out of me!' Sarah shouted.

Jason laughed uproariously, waved at her and jumped down onto the ground next to Trish, who was grinning at her through the window.

'Sorry, Saz, he persuaded me into letting him do it.'

'That's two I owe you now,' Sarah told him, laughing in relief.

'I thought you were going to crap yourself,' Jason said gleefully.

'I nearly did,' she said, making him laugh again.

'Forget that,' Trish told her, 'we've found something that'll perk you up a bit.'

'What's that?' she asked curiously.

'Grab a torch and come and see,' Jason told her, clearly upbeat about something.

Wondering what they were both going on about, she got out, stretched and picked up a large flashlight.

The sun dipped below the horizon as night closed in and the three friends trooped across the hard-packed earth, each with a beam of light bobbing in front of them. Their boots crunched along as they made their way down a slope and around an outcrop of rock.

Sarah followed behind them both when Jason suddenly disappeared into the rock. As she neared the spot, Trish also vanished from view. In fact, they had passed into a cave mouth nigh on impossible to see in daylight, let alone at night. To enter you had to squeeze past a dense bush that broke up the entrance, and Sarah knew the likelihood of anyone knowing it was there was slim to none. She switched her torch to a higher setting with a click and ducked inside.

The ground sloped down a little, enabling her to stand upright. The smooth walls reminded her of the caves at the World Heritage Site not far from their location, where remains had been found of humanity's earliest ancestors.

A few animal bones lay strewn across the floor as she followed Jason and Trish deeper inside. It wasn't a system of caves, just one winding, contracting and expanding tunnel. Not like the caves at Sterkfontein which were extensive and went deep into the earth.

At sixty feet in, they came to a dead end.

'So, what do you think?' Jason asked her.

'I think it's amazing. How did you find it?'

'We got bored so we went for a walk, we did tell you,' Trish said, 'and then faceache here wanted to go to the loo—'

'And I found this little beauty.' He held his arms outspread, showing off the cave they now stood in.

'And you're thinking what I'm thinking?' Sarah asked them.

They both grinned. 'Yep,' Jason said, 'if we scan in here we can use the ultrasonic doodah to punch a horizontal hole into Trish's void.'

'So why are we still standing around jabbering?' Sarah said, a smile creeping onto her face. 'Let's get to it."

'All-nighter!' they all said in unison, laughing as they picked their way back out of the cave.

CHAPTER TWELVE

IT WAS hard work getting the tools and equipment into the narrow chamber, but they managed to in the end after much grunting and swearing. Night was not the best time to set up a dig, especially when you had minimal lighting.

Once everything was in place Sarah scanned the walls of the cave to try and find the chamber she had mapped so extensively earlier in the day. It didn't take her long until she found it again, however she was unable to locate the elusive canister signal she'd momentarily glimpsed from the surface.

Marking a spot on the rock wall some ten feet from the end of the cave, they withdrew the scanner; all three of them then manhandled the ultrasonic unit into position. They each donned goggles, dust masks and ear defenders and Jason started up the machine. A loud roar echoed round the cave and out into the cold night air. Inside, the noise was deafening even with ear defenders on. It wasn't the ultrasonic waves that made it so loud, but the machine that produced them; to project the sound waves deep into the soft limestone and earth required immense power, hence the machine's limited usage.

Dust kicked up by the cooling fans swirled around them as vortices spiralled down the tunnel.

'I'm moving it closer!' Jason shouted to them. 'Move back!'

'What?' Sarah yelled, putting a hand to an ear indicating she hadn't heard what he'd said.

'Move away!' he said again, motioning them backwards.

Sarah gave him the thumbs up and they moved back a bit as Jason edged the machine nearer to the wall, increasing the resonance and noise even further; small stones torn from the wall ricocheted around them, forcing them to retreat a few more paces. After twenty ear-ringing minutes, Jason powered it down enabling everyone to remove their protective gear. The rock and dirt that had been between them and the void had been turned into a heavy granulated dust. A uniform hole, as straight as a die, had been punched through the earth and into the underground chamber ahead, which itself was buried forty feet below the surface. The newly created tunnel lay half-filled with dusty, pulverised rock and so, replacing their masks, they picked up shovels and began the arduous task of clearing it out.

By morning light they had completely emptied Jason's creation, depositing the spoil throughout the length of the cave. Sarah was the first to go inside, followed by Trish, with Jason bringing up the rear. Sarah squeezed out of the crawl space and into the void, now able to stand upright. The air smelt dry and stale inside, which was unsurprising as it may have been trapped there for untold millennia. As a precaution they wore their dust masks, but with added filters to help prevent against harmful microbes and any other unseen nasties that might lurk within.

Sarah shone her torch around the structure realising she could very well be the first person to ever set foot inside it; *the first human person, anyway*, she told herself, soaking up the moment.

She walked forwards with care; it was definitely not a natural void, as it had straight sided walls, mirroring the scans made from the surface. The ancient map had depicted some kind of log construction, but there was no sign of that inside, although there wasn't any guarantee this place was the same as the graphical representation. It might have been rebuilt many times over for all they knew. The ceiling looked to be about ten to twelve feet high, cracked in many places and seeping dirt and old roots.

Even with the filters, the air tasted dry and stale; Sarah moistened her lips with her tongue.

Ten feet away, on either side, the walls gradually diverged, opening the area up further.

Sarah heard Trish making her way in behind her. *What's that?!* she thought, catching a glimpse of movement ahead; looking again, she saw it was just her own shadow cast on the far wall by Trish's torchlight. Relieved, Sarah smiled to herself, then she suddenly had an idea. Peering back, she saw Jason had reached the end of the tunnel and was about to step inside. Seizing the opportunity Sarah momentarily removed her mask, dropped her torch with a clatter and shrieked in pure terror. A scream and a commotion came from behind. She picked up her torch and turned round to see Jason disappearing back down the hole as fast as he could. Trish, initially looking terrified, laughed as she put her torch onto Sarah who was now wetting herself, doubled over. Some moments later a small voice came down the tunnel to them.

'You cow!'

'Frightened, were we?' Sarah called back.

'I just needed some fresh air,' Jason said, trying to deepen his voice manfully, but failing dismally.

'Oh, Sarah, that was priceless,' Trish said, still chuckling.

'I don't think I can scream that high!' Sarah said down the tunnel.

Jason's curses came back at her as he clambered back towards them, and he looked suitably sheepish when he dropped inside the void once more. 'Even?' he asked Sarah, looking hopeful.

'Maybe,' she said, enjoying herself, 'I'll let you know.'

Jason laughed, although she thought he still sounded a little strung out. Still smiling to herself, Sarah began a search of the area again while Trish logged the surroundings on her computer. Back in the zone, Sarah quickly noticed a dark shadow near the centre of the floor. The scans hadn't shown this feature up, which was strange. As she approached, she saw it was a hole, framed by a ragged edge hewn out of the rock; it measured about eight feet long. The rest of what was clearly a single chamber lay empty and lacked any other obvious features.

'What's that?' Trish said, coming up to stand beside Sarah.

'A big deep black hole by the look of it,' Jason said, as he too came alongside to peer down into it. 'I can just see the bottom if I focus the beam.'

He was right; Sarah could just make it out as he stretched out to highlight it with his torch.

'How far down would you say that was, seventy feet?' she asked them.

'Give or take,' Trish said.

Sarah weighed up their options. 'We'll need a rope.'

'You're not going down there, are you?' Trish said in concern. 'It could be dangerous.'

Sarah looked at her friend and raised her eyebrows in surprise. 'Trish, I've spent a fortune getting here, we've spent weeks to get to this point and, last but no means least, we're in the immediate path of the largest asteroid to hit the planet in sixty-five million years; a little more danger ain't gonna make much difference.'

'Good points, I'll go get it,' Trish said, and zoomed off back down the tunnel.

'Nothing like being reminded you're about to be squished by a multi-trillion tonne space rock to motivate you,' Jason said wryly, as he watched Trish go.

A short while later, with Trish having returned, it wasn't long before Sarah slowly descended into the earth, supported by Jason and Trish above. Fortunately the width of the hole was narrow enough that she could brace herself on the way down; this meant Trish and Jason didn't have to take her full weight on the descent.

Light in hand, she could see the bottom drawing ever closer. 'You're going to have to take my full weight now,' she said, her voice still muffled slightly by her mask. 'I'm dropping down into another chamber of some kind.'

The rope tightened as Jason and Trish took the strain, and the rock face on either side disappeared as Sarah entered the larger void. Dangling on the end of the rope, her feet finally touched down onto a surface strewn with loose rock.

'I'm down!' she called up to them.

'Leave the rope attached,' Trish shouted back. 'You don't know what's down there.'

'Will do,' she replied. It was sound advice; it might be dangerous already, but there was no need to increase the risk even further.

Sarah had been expecting to find herself in cramped quarters, but shining the torch around she saw she stood in the middle of a substantial cavern, by the look of it a natural formation. The cave walls loomed at the edges of the torchlight. Large boulders had fallen down randomly, standing tall and immobile on the floor like sentries guarding a forbidden temple.

Sarah fed out some more of the rope still attached to her small waist harness to enable her to move with more freedom.

She walked past a particularly large rock, caressing its surface with a hand as she went, her fingers brushing off small particles of rock and dust which cascaded to the ground.

Switching to a wider beam, she increased the torch's power output and was greeted with a fabulous sight. Twenty feet away, two stone pillars stood either side of a massive stone plinth of a circular design. Approaching it, her excitement peaked as she caught sight of the glint of metal. Taking the torch, she extended its small built-in tripod, positioning it on the floor, and then turned on her head torch. On closer inspection the stonework was smooth and well crafted, yet disappointingly lacking any kind of detailing.

Unable to see on top of the circular plinth due to its height, Sarah stepped back a few paces and then ran and jumped up, placing her hands on the flat surface above and hauling herself upwards and onto her knees. The sudden movement sent more dust swirling and dancing around her in the ice-blue glow of the torchlight that now bathed the area.

As the dust settled, it became clear what she'd glimpsed moments before. In the centre of the platform sat a large metallic ovoid canister, much like the one in Turkey, but with a couple of differences, the main one being it had a deep dark red hue.

'Oh, my God,' she said, unable to believe her luck. Taking out her computer, she took some video.

'Are you okay, Sarah?!' Trish called out, her voice sounding distant.

Sarah looked back over her shoulder. 'Yes, I'm fine!'

Trish's interruption made Sarah remember time was still a scarce commodity; she couldn't afford to stand and gawp. Rolling the artefact onto its side with a dull thud, she lugged it back to the bottom of the shaft.

Not wanting to stand underneath as Trish and Jason hauled it up, Sarah had time for a quick sweep of the rest of the cave. It consisted of various natural features, but the one that caught her eye was a large mass of debris that had collapsed in from the ceiling. Her light revealed a deep black void hidden behind the fallen rock. On approach, Sarah noticed a carved stone column still stood on one side of the opening. This was no natural formation; it was a purpose built tunnel.

Now free of the rope, Sarah's instinct was to investigate so she climbed up the rubble pile and pushed her way through a tight gap, sending small rocks and gravel clattering and slithering down the slope behind her.

Inside, the tunnel petered out after thirty yards, completely sealed by another huge landslip. As she was about to turn back something caught her eye. Clambering over a couple of the larger boulders she dropped down between them into a small clearing. Almost beneath her feet the unmistakable forms of bone protruded through a layer of loose sediment. Bending down, she lifted her mask and blew hard at the surfaces. Dirt parted and a thick dust eddied upwards, uncovering a small group of bones, not animal but humanoid. Her heart beat faster.

The bones appeared odd, thin and elongated. She touched one and moved her hand along its length. It was a bone from an arm, a humerus. Standing up and adjusting her head torch, she withdrew her computer to take some in situ photos. As always, she had a ten pound coin to hand to add scale to the image.

After visually analysing them further she deduced the remains belonged to a single individual, probably taller than seven feet but nowhere near the size of the bones they'd found previously. Also, there was no skull, only bones from one arm, a hand and some other fragments. Sarah surveyed the scene and wondered if this creature – whoever, or whatever, it was – had been killed by the falling rocks during an earthquake. It seemed a likely scenario considering the precarious nature of the surrounding terrain.

Returning to the present, she had to remind herself she wasn't dreaming. She couldn't believe it, not only had she found a canister but bones, too. *These remains might even be from another monster-sized species of hominid*, she thought, *perhaps a relative of Homo gigantis, or a sub species*. It was incredible, was her luck changing? *At the moment it is*, she told herself, giddy with sweet success. With her spirits soaring, she carefully collected up the bones and deposited them into her rucksack.

As she squeezed back out into the main chamber, her bag, now fuller, caught on one of the rocks above. Twisting to help it through, her shoulder dislodged a piece of crumbling earth, which in turn shifted the rocks around her. Without warning a large stone directly above dropped a few inches, smashing the light on her head and plunging her into darkness. As her eyes adjusted to the faint light emanating from her larger torch, which rested beneath the shaft some way away, Sarah could tell she had a problem before even looking. Her leg was trapped.

'Shit,' she said, struggling to free herself. The rock wouldn't budge; she was held tight. 'Fucking hell!' she said, a sense of panic upon her. She leaned back, bracing her free foot against another boulder, and pushed with all her might, grunting in exertion. Held fast, she paused as Jason called out to her, his voice faint.

'Sarah, where are you? The rope's ready for you!'

Sarah didn't reply; taking a few deep breaths, she gathered herself. Lifting her foot up higher, she sought and found better purchase with her hands, then pushed out with as much strength as she could muster. She cried out as she strained every sinew, fought with every breath, and then – suddenly – she was free and tumbling backwards, before landing heavily on one side and bruising a shoulder.

In pain, but awash with relief, Sarah scrambled to her feet and checked the bag to make sure the bones hadn't been damaged in the fall. Thankfully they seemed to be okay.

Moving back to the shaft, she looked up to see the small silhouettes of Trish and Jason above. 'I'm here,' she said, as she picked up the torch and hooked herself onto the waiting rope, 'lift me up, already!'

Once Sarah was safely back up top, the three friends turned their attention to their discoveries. To Sarah, the ancient metallic relic looked smaller than the previous one from the Turkish plains; *in fact*, she thought, *that's probably why I was able to lug it about so easily*.

'This is friggin' unbelievable,' Jason said, tentatively touching the canister. 'This might be one of the oldest objects ever unearthed; we could sell this for hundreds of thousands, maybe even hundreds of millions!'

Trish snorted. 'And who's going to buy it, the British Museum? Gimme a break, they wouldn't believe us when we told them where we found it, or our theories behind it. Besides, those bastards who mugged us before would probably do so again, but this time they'd make sure we didn't find anything else. *We'd* end up being buried, to be unearthed thousands of years later, I can hear it now "*—three mysterious bodies were found today; according to archaeologists, they are a twenty-first century people who met with a brutal and violent end.*"'

Jason looked crestfallen as his dreams of riches turned to dust. 'It's a nice colour, though,' he said somewhat lamely to Sarah. 'Wasn't the other one silver?'

'Yeah, this one is a little smaller too.'

'I like it,' Jason said, perking himself up again, 'it looks like a giant Easter egg.'

Trish looked at Sarah and rolled her eyes heavenward. Sarah

smiled at her friend's expression, and then, remembering she had something else to show them, pulled off her backpack and removed a couple of the bones.

'Seriously, I can't believe this,' Trish said after Sarah had explained her new find to them. 'More bones, incredible.'

'It's a shame we can't dig about further down there,' Jason said.

Sarah packed the bones away again. 'I don't think we'd find too much. Besides, let's not get greedy, we've got a haul better than we could have wished for. Not as good as back in Turkey, but a very close second, don't you think?'

'It's certainly paid off,' Trish said, giving Sarah a congratulatory hug.

'Group hug!' Jason said, joining in by squeezing them both together.

Trish struggled against his grasp. 'Ow, geroff, you big oaf!'

After some more banter and the patting of backs they made their way out into the fresh air. Sarah checked her phone. Six days left until impact. She looked anxiously up at the sky; *perhaps this is how an ant feels*, she thought, *when a human's foot slowly descends on it from above*. A tiny speck about to be obliterated; it wasn't a pleasant feeling.

'Let's get the fuck out of here,' Trish said as she saw 'six days' displayed on Sarah's phone.

'Hell, yes,' Jason agreed fervently, also looking skyward.

Packing everything up as best they could, Sarah was torn as to whether to leave the ultrasonic excavation machine behind. It was very expensive to just dump, but time was now of the absolute essence and the struggle they'd face to get it back to the vehicle was not worth risking their lives for. Also, it would be hard to sell or cost a ridiculous amount to ship with them out of Gabon. *No, it's dead weight*, she told herself. *It's done the job and we have our reward. It's getting left behind, end of.*

In short order they leapt in the pickup and drove, bumping and skidding across the bush, heading back to the abandoned landing strip they had come in on. Having dropped off all their gear, Sarah and Jason then went to return the pickup to its owner, leaving Trish behind to guard their possessions. As they pulled up the man came out to meet them.

'That was bad timing,' he said as they got out.

'How so?' Jason asked him.

'Your plane's been and gone.'

'What?!' Sarah said in shocked disbelief. 'What are you talking about? It's supposed to be coming in and waiting until tomorrow!'

'Well, they came and they went. I told them you hadn't got back yet and they didn't seem to care. I'm sorry.'

Sarah felt physically sick. They had to catch that plane. They had to get out of the country or they'd be killed in the blast. She doubted a car could escape the devastation zone in time, especially considering fuel pumps would be dry and one tank would not get them far enough away.

'Oh, my God.' Jason held his head in despair. 'We're fucked, we are truly fucked!'

'You're welcome to stay with me,' the man said, trying to comfort them.

'What, to wait to die?' Jason said. 'Thanks, but no thanks, old timer.'

Sarah slumped to the floor. 'What are we going to do?'

The old man, seeing her discomfort, disappeared inside and came back out with a glass of water, which she accepted numbly without a word.

A minute of silence passed before he said, 'I might be able to help you.'

Sarah and Jason looked up at him with a fearful expectancy.

'I was only staying as I've lived in this house all my life. I'm old and if I'm going to die I wanted it to be here, but seeing as you folks are in trouble I can probably help you get to safety.'

'How?' Sarah said. 'You won't have enough fuel in your car and the distance is too great.'

'I didn't say I'd drive you out of here, did I?' he said with a smile.

They looked at him in confusion.

'We'll fly out,' he said.

'You can fly?' Jason asked him.

'Of course, I've been flying since before you'd even drawn breath as a babe.'

'You're forgetting one thing,' said Sarah, 'a plane?'

'Ah.' The man tapped the side of his nose and disappeared back into his house.

'What does that mean?' Jason asked Sarah, who shrugged. 'I think he's lost the plot, the silly old—'

Jason clammed up as the man came back with a coat and small bag in hand.

'Shall we get going, then?' he said with a grin.

'What's going on?' Trish asked when they arrived back with the old man in tow.

'Change of plan,' Sarah said.

'What? Why?'

'Looks like we missed our flight,' Jason said. 'Those idiots came on the wrong day or got cold feet or something.'

'How do you know that?'

'Frank here told us. Frank, Trish. Trish, Frank,' Sarah said by way of introduction

'So what are we going to do?' Trish said, looking terrified.

'Don't worry, miss,' Frank told her. 'Old Frank's here to save the day. Or your bacon,' he added jovially, his chuckles quickly turning to wheezing, followed by uncontrollable coughing.

Trish didn't look reassured and looked to Sarah, pleadingly.

'He knows a place where they left some planes before the evacuation. We should be able to fuel them up and get the hell out of Dodge.'

'Should!?'

'Will,' Sarah said quickly. She and Jason had thought they were as good as dead, but this lifeline had buoyed them considerably. Trish, however, was going from thinking they were getting picked up safely to *may* be getting flown out, a big difference in perspective. Jason took her to one side, speaking to her in low comforting tones while Sarah helped Frank put their kit back into the pickup.

It took them half a day to get to the small private airfield Frank had told them about. When they arrived it was deserted, much like everywhere else they had passed on the way. They entered a hangar and Frank selected one of the planes. Sarah and Jason then went about siphoning out fuel from the other aircraft, after getting instructions from Frank, while Trish helped the old man get their kit on board.

A few hours later they'd managed to fill up the plane's tanks. It wasn't a jet, but a small twin-engined propeller passenger plane used for excursions and parachute diving. Supposedly they needed to stop off once to refuel and then they could make it to Gabon and meet up with their taxi driver on schedule. The plan seemed okay, apart from the refuelling, which sounded more than a little dodgy to Sarah. There were no guarantees they'd find extra fuel on the way up. Still, what other choice did they have? None.

As the plane taxied out of the hangar, Sarah looked up out of the cockpit window. A bright object, too big to be a star or planet, flickered in the sky high above. The meteor had finally arrived and they were leaving in the nick of time. *We cut this way too close*, she thought, but then remembered their prizes, nestling at the back of the plane, and knew it had been worth it.

They slept fitfully during the first leg of the flight. Touching down in the south of Angola, they refuelled, thankfully with little problem, once again siphoning out gasoline from abandoned light aircraft. During the next leg, Sarah decided it was an opportune time to investigate the red casket, which turned out to be harder to lever open than the one she'd found on the Turkish plains, as she didn't have the finer chisels to hand; however, after some pounding and brute force from Jason they managed to prise off the lid. Once again a handle presented itself inside and it pulled out smoothly with the same satisfying suction release.

Anticipation building, they peered inside.

A single piece of folded parchment rested tantalisingly at the bottom.

More than a little disappointed at the lack of other objects contained within, Sarah carefully removed the solitary item. Unlike the others, this had no map or text on it. It was blank apart from the usual indented disc at the top. As before, Sarah put her finger on the circle and Trish and Jason held her arm, boosting the bio electricity needed to power the digital paper display.

This time an image materialised on the page. Sarah zoomed in on it after the appearance of the familiar control symbols down one side. It appeared to be some kind of super-detailed schematic or blueprint. She couldn't easily make out what she was seeing as the sheer amount of data embedded in the graphic was immense.

A mass of symbols flowed over the page as she rotated the view and moved in and out.

'Go back a second,' Jason said.

She zoomed out a bit to the previous location.

He motioned with a finger. 'Rotate thirty degrees.'

She moved the view to roughly thirty degrees from the previous location.

'And now zoom in.'

She did so.

'More,' he told her, 'more. Keep going.'

The ancient display flashed and the schematic melted away to be replaced with a vista that took their breath away. Golden trees surrounded a lush meadow as light shone down from the sky above. In the distance what looked like poles jutted up out of the ground. She zoomed in further and they skimmed across the surface of the grasses. The view shifted again and they were rising up higher and higher. The poles transformed before their eyes. They were not poles at all, but spires, hundreds of spires. The image rose higher still until they floated over a spectacle that was awe inspiring. A city; no, a super city! It was astounding, mesmerising.

They soaked up what they saw, but as suddenly as it had appeared, the screen dimmed and faded. They cried out in protest but couldn't retrieve the image. Again and again they tried, but only the original schematic presented itself, along with its streams of unintelligible data. Frustrating was not the word, it was perhaps comparable to glimpsing nirvana and then being sucked back out into drab mundania.

'Did you see that place?' Trish murmured, wiping a tear from her eye. 'It was beautiful – so beautiful.'

'I can't believe how big it was,' Jason said. 'Those towers … do you think it existed?'

Sarah glanced at him before returning her attention to the parchment. 'I don't know. It was magnificent. I haven't seen anything like it – ever. It makes even our biggest cities look crude, small and dirty in comparison.'

Jason sighed. 'I don't think I've wanted to see anything again so much in my whole life.'

'Why can't we get the image back?' Trish said, sounding cross.

'I'm not sure. Perhaps it needed an outside power source to run it,' Sarah said. 'It was such vibrant footage, compared to the graphical nature of all the other parchment images we've looked at so far. And I agree with you, Jas, I wanna see it again so badly it hurts.'

'If that city did exist, then where did it go?' Jason looked from Trish to Sarah. 'Something that large would have been found by now.'

'It might be under the Antarctic ice sheet,' Sarah said. 'Although with the new satellite system sent up specifically for archaeological surveys, it surely would have shown up on the scans, something that big?'

'Unless it was destroyed somehow and only its remains are left,' Trish said, 'or it's on a sea or lake bed somewhere.'

Sarah thought for a moment. 'Or it never existed at all and it was a simulation or just a plan that never reached fruition.'

Trish frowned. 'That's a depressing thought.'

'Or it's on another planet,' Jason said seriously.

Sarah laughed. 'Ha, and I'm the Queen of Sheba and my uncle's E.T..'

'E.T.?' said Trish.

'A little brown alien with big eyes and a glowing finger,' Sarah told her.

'Man, you really haven't watched any films, have you?' Jason said, laughing.

'Not rubbish ones, I haven't,' Trish said, riled.

Sarah smiled. 'I kinda liked it, he was cute, too, in a wrinkly, brown, hairless way,'

'It sounds delightful,' Trish said. 'Give me a romcom and I'm there, but smelly small aliens? Leave me out.'

Sarah and Jason screwed up their faces in a sign of disgust and this time Trish laughed.

Jason grunted and leaned over to Sarah, who pulled back as he reached his hand out to her neck. 'What are you doing?' she said, feeling uncomfortable and putting her hand to her neck protectively.

'Sorry,' he said. 'I just noticed your new pendant and I recognise a symbol on it. It was on the first map we looked at and now that I think about, it also cropped up on the new parchment from our red friend here.' He patted the open metal casket next to him. 'Can I have a closer look?'

'Sure.' Sarah unclipped the pentagonal pendant and passed it to him.

He examined it carefully. 'I think I've seen some of these other symbols on here, too.'

'As soon as we get the chance we should copy out all the letters in the parchments,' Sarah said, 'assuming that's what they are, and run them through a language deciphering and recognition programme to see what it spits out. You never know, we might get lucky.'

'Can I look at the original map again?' he asked Sarah.

'Course you can.' She withdrew it from her zipped pocket and passed it to him.

He looked surprised.

'It's as much yours and Trish's find as mine,' she told him, 'you drive and we'll power it.'

Jason, now looking like the cat that got the cream, brought up the map image, while Trish and Sarah held onto his arm.

'There,' – he pointed a finger at the parchment – 'that's the same symbol as on your pendant – and that one, too.' He continued to analyse the map. 'They seem to coincide with some kind of key down the side of the map.'

'Like co-ordinates?' Trish said.

'No, more general, like longitudinal lines which portray time zones on a globe.'

'So what are you saying?'

'I'm not sure. Let's have a look at the new parchment again.'

Sarah handed him the now blank looking piece of light brown paper they'd found in the red canister. Powering it up, he manipulated the image with another symbol they hadn't tried before. The image changed and a familiar small building appeared. It looked like it was made out of mud bricks and logs, almost exactly the same as the one they had seen on the other parchment they'd just been looking at. On closer inspection it wasn't identical, it was more rectangular, but it did show up a new type of object: a large, flat square on the base of the building's interior floor.

Touching another symbol with a finger, in conjunction with one they had used previously, Jason brought up a new view altogether, a view they all instantly recognised.

It was the Earth.

Trish and Sarah gasped while Jason sat open-mouthed staring at the near perfect image of the planet floating on the page before them.

A pulsating shape indicated where the small building was located: Central America.

Sarah leaned in closer. 'Where's that? Panama?'

'No, that's further down,' Jason said. 'Costa Rica, maybe?'

'No, that's only just above Panama,' Trish told them. 'That symbol is where Honduras is today.'

Jason gave a shake of his head in disbelief. 'Bloody hell, how many more places are we going to find?'

Sarah flashed him a broad grin. 'We've opened Pandora's Box, now there's no going back.'

'So it looks like we're going to Honduras, then?' Jason asked her.

'Looks that way.'

'I suppose muggins here will have to arrange it all,' Trish said.

'Thanks, hun,' – Sarah stood before bending down to give her a hug – 'you're a star.'

Leaving Trish and Jason talking excitedly about their new discoveries, Sarah moved along the narrow seating aisle to the front of the plane to see how Frank was doing.

Entering the cockpit, she sat down in the co-pilot's seat as the clouds below them glided by and the twin engines droned away outside.

'How are you kids doing?' Frank said, glancing in her direction.

'We're fine, thanks. How are you, though?'

'So so, it's been a while since I've flown this far. My back's giving me a bit of gip,'

'Is there anything I can do?' she said, not thinking there would be.

'You could take the wheel for a bit.'

Sarah looked at him to see if he was jesting, but he didn't appear to be. 'What? I can't fly the plane!'

'Of course you can. It won't be like you're trying to take off or land it. Just point and shoot, sort of thing, easy.'

Frank got up and Sarah reluctantly slid over to sit in his warmed chair.

'Oh, that's good,' he said, as he stretched himself out and massaged his arms, 'just keep the wheel steady and that's pretty much it.'

Sarah gripped the wheel tight, her knuckles going white.

'Relax, now, there's no need to hold it so hard. That's it.'

The plane nosed down slightly.

'Not that relaxed, though,' he said quickly, guiding the wheel back up with one hand as she held on firmly yet not too grimly, as per his instructions.

'That's it. Perfect. I'll just go back to the others and you give me a shout when you want to swap.'

'What!' she said, her voice going up a couple of octaves.

He laughed, his eyes alight with mirth. 'Only joking, I'll just sit here next to you and have a little doze. Just keep your eye on the horizon, and keep the wings straight and level on the white line of the artificial horizon dial.' Frank tapped a gauge with a finger. 'Shout if you need help,' he said, and sat down and shut his eyes.

Sarah didn't think she could be that trusting if she was in his position. She grasped the wheel tighter, but caught herself and relaxed her grip again.

After a while, with her initial anxiety calmed, she actually began to enjoy it. The view was great. The beautiful rolling landscape below crept along like a giant slow-moving travelator, while their plane soared high above it through clear skies.

It was a dreamlike experience, flying, with the world laid out beneath you, and it was also one Sarah knew she could get used to if given the opportunity.

The dream, however, wasn't to last as what seemed like moments later, but in actuality was an hour, Frank woke up and took back control, thanking her for her help.

In a buoyant mood, Sarah made her way back down the cabin to where the others rested.

'If I'd known you were flying, I'd have jumped out, parachute or no,' Jason said, after she'd told them what she'd been doing.

'Ooh, I want a go,' Trish said, and went forward to ask Frank if she could.

A minute or two later the plane jerked upwards and then dived down sharply and a shriek echoed down to them.

'I think I preferred your flying,' Jason told Sarah, looking a little green as the plane levelled out.

Sarah gave a nervous laugh. 'Me too.'

The rest of the journey passed relatively uneventfully. Trish documented their latest discoveries by taking photos, plus some video footage where Sarah described the canister and parchment to camera. They then tried accessing new parts of the parchments, but it proved more complicated than they thought it was going to be. Also, three people could only stay in physical contact with each other for so long before someone got irritated or stiff and moved their hand away. Jason suggested putting his feet on their legs while they rested, but neither of them liked the idea of that, much to Jason's consternation.

'Why the hell not?' he'd said.

'There is absolutely no way I'm letting your grotty feet touch me anywhere,' Trish had told him adamantly, crossing her arms to emphasise the point. 'And that's final.'

With the remainder of the flight interspersed with quiet conversation and sleep, their plane approached the border zone just as the sun sank below the horizon. In the distance a deep rumbling alerted them to the presence of a patrolling fighter jet as they swung out over the sea, but thankfully it must have been much higher up and a few miles away as they flew on unimpeded.

Soon after, they were touching down in Gabon and the plane's landing lights could be seen illuminating a familiar looking taxi that waited for them in a nearby car park, as arranged.

They thanked Frank profusely for his lifesaving intervention and Sarah insisted he take some money, which he accepted after some heated persuasion. Jason then asked him if he was going back to South Africa.

'I might as well live out my days here as any other place,' he said. 'This little adventure has given me a new lease of life. I may even be able to get some work flying after the initial debris has settled down in the lower atmosphere.'

Wishing one another luck, they parted ways. Trish and Sarah gave Frank a hug and a kiss goodbye, and Jason shook his hand, and then they were off in the cab heading back to Gabon's capital city. Using Sarah's computer, Trish had managed to arrange a flight while they travelled in the cab. She wasn't able to get one to Honduras, but El Salvador was the next best thing.

When the taxi driver deposited them at their destination Sarah reluctantly handed over another thick wadge of cash in payment for service rendered. They then loaded up a couple of airport trolleys and made their way to departures, which brimmed full to bursting as people made use of the last opportunity to get away before all civilian flights were grounded. Sarah wasn't gone on the fact that their precious finds were going into the hold, most likely to be chucked about by underpaid and overworked baggage handlers. She had little choice, however, and they'd packed them well in heavy duty crates, which eased her mind somewhat.

The taxi journey had taken a whole day and the wait for the flight a further ten hours. Sarah didn't need to check her phone now for the time left until impact. It was displayed everywhere they went, especially in the airport, which also showed real-time footage as the meteor drew nearer and grew ever bigger in the sky above. Three days and eight hours. They couldn't have timed it any closer, as this had been virtually the last flight to the Americas out of the airport. Sarah imagined the mass exodus from the continent as people fled the approaching asteroid in what some still saw as the end of days, regardless of what their governments and international bodies told them. Perhaps more than most, the African populace was a superstitious one and that tended to make people more unpredictable and volatile. Not the best personality traits when calm and patience were required. *Although*, Sarah thought, *how would other peoples react if the impact was on their doorstep? Badly*, she decided.

With the waiting over and boarding complete, their plane took off in good time and they all grabbed the opportunity to get a good sleep, recouping spent energy and soothing frayed nerves after their whirlwind tour of the African continent. They also needed to preserve energy for the work to come. The impact might be on the horizon, but Sarah's quest for the truth wouldn't stop. She would accumulate what she could and present it to one of the leading institutes in China. Europe and the U.S. could prove to be too risky, considering their encounter in Turkey, and any country where Catholicism had a strong influence now made her very wary. No, China was the place to get her finds recognised, and hopefully that could be achieved without further incident.

Sarah knew, however, that despite her optimism she still had to plan her moves very carefully, with contingencies in place to prevent any untoward intervention pushing her off course.

After jotting down some of her ideas, she secured her pen back inside her wallet, but rather than returning the fabric case to her pocket she unfolded a compartment to reveal a photo of herself and her mother standing at the edge of a mountain plateau near Angel Falls in Venezuela. She remembered that day vividly; the view had been spectacular, the waterfall magnificent, but it was the precious moments she'd shared with her mother that she most cherished. 'I won't let them beat me, Mum,' she whispered, with an ache in her heart. 'I promise.'

CHAPTER THIRTEEN

THE SUN BEAT down on the state of New Mexico. In its centre the city of Albuquerque sprawled, straddling the Rio Grande River, which slunk its way south through the hot arid desert. The resident populace went about its business as usual, people and vehicles on the move in every quarter. Rebecca, the mental health worker, reclined on a couch in her apartment, watching the television. Outside a dust-cart could be heard through an open window collecting the week's trash. Joseph sat at the table, drawing contentedly.

Picking up the remote Rebecca switched channels to the BBC. The show she had been waiting to watch from England was her favourite, as it gave a better world view than normal U.S. programmes. It had also become the most watched news stream in the world. She turned up the volume as the intro faded and the main studio came into focus.

'Good evening, I'm Jessica Klein and this is the BBC's Worldwide News Service transmitting to you live from our dedicated Impact Day studio in Broadcasting House, London, England.

'It has been twenty-nine years since the asteroid 2011 AG5 was first discovered by the Mount Lemmon Survey on the 8th January, 2011.

And this formidable interstellar traveller is now due to arrive off the South African east coast in less than six hours' time.

'Joining me tonight for this historic moment are a special panel of experts from various fields, who will help guide us through these final hours and give us an idea of what we can expect in the days ahead.

'We have Professor Guraj Singh from the Indian Institute of Astrophysics, and to his right, Michael Bailey from the United States Department of Homeland Security. On my left, his grace Dr. Mowberry, the Lord Archbishop of Canterbury from the United Kingdom, and to his left Mariana Lima from the Global Meteor Response Council.

'Firstly, welcome to you all, and thank you for providing us with your valuable time and expertise during this most momentous of events. I am sure the public will agree with me when I say that everyone is on tenterhooks right now. The build-up in the media has been almost endless since the threat and potential consequences were first disclosed to the wider public in the summer of 2022. There are a lot of inaccuracies and urban myths that have built up over the years with regard to the meteorite and its impact, so I will first go to Professor Guraj Singh for a breakdown of the most pertinent facts and figures available to us at this time. Professor?'

The camera shot moved onto a small man who carried a little too much weight, had a receding hairline and a long sleeved shirt in need of an iron. 'Thank you,' Professor Singh said, while nervously adjusting his small red bow tie. '2011 AG5 measures four point two miles in length and one point nine miles in diameter. It is travelling at thirty-six thousand miles an hour. To give this some perspective, a bullet from a forty-five calibre handgun travels at around six hundred miles an hour. This tells us that AG5 is moving at approximately sixty times faster than a bullet from a semi-automatic handgun.

'The speed, of course, isn't the only factor that makes AG5 such a threat to this planet. The mass of a forty-five calibre bullet is on average fifteen grams, whereas the mass of AG5 is one point two four multiplied by ten to the power fourteen kilograms, or approximately one hundred and twenty-four trillion metric tonnes. This figure is estimated, as the actual density and composition of the asteroid is unknown; in actuality it may be much less or significantly greater, although this is considered unlikely. Such variables will determine the size of the blast produced on impact, the size of the devastation zone and the power and duration of the predicted ensuing after-effects. Mathematical modelling software and forecasters have striven to predict the fallout on our beloved planet since AG5's discovery in 2011.'

'So what type of blast and after-effects can we expect, Professor Singh?' Jessica Klein said.

Gaining momentum, Professor Singh continued with more assurance. 'The impact will result in an explosion of two multiplied by ten to the power of seven megatons of TNT, or twenty million megatons. This is equivalent to four hundred thousand 50-megaton nuclear bombs. The crater will measure close to one hundred miles wide.

'As AG5 hits, two hundred miles due east of Durban in the Indian Ocean, a procession of mega tsunamis will expand from the site. Initial tsunamis will measure around one mile in height close to the impact zone to approximately a quarter of a mile high two thousand miles from the impact zone, decreasing in height until they hit landfall, where they will rear up once more. After the first wave ripple a train of smaller tsunamis of varying heights will be caused by the steam uplift produced by sea water entering the white hot meteor crater; further tsunamis will also be produced by shifting of the Earth's crust resulting from the initial impact and detonation.'

The camera turned once more to the host, who nodded in understanding. 'I see. Will these tsunamis affect only South Africa or will they spread around the whole world?'

'No on both counts,' Professor Singh said. 'Thankfully Antarctica will take the brunt of the tsunamis; however, the various nations surrounding the Indian Ocean will experience significant mega tsunami strikes. The countries of eastern Africa, Madagascar, Yemen,

Oman, Pakistan and India will all be badly hit and mass evacuations have been underway for many years to minimise casualties.'

'We are led to believe that a kind of nuclear winter will follow the impact; is that correct?' Jessica Klein asked him.

'It isn't a nuclear winter, rather an impact winter, but yes after the impact dust, steam and gases will be ejected into the upper atmosphere. The Earth will slowly become enveloped in a dense dust structure that will pervade skylines the world over.'

'One last question, Professor,' she said, 'if I may?'

Professor Singh nodded his consent.

'It was first publicised in 2011 that AG5 would impact the Earth in 2040 and that it was a mere few hundred feet in size. This prediction was then reversed soon after, with scientists informing us that it would only come close to Earth, passing half a million miles away. Nearly a decade later we were told that the meteorite would indeed be colliding with the Earth in 2040, and a couple of years after that it was revealed that the size of the meteor was much greater than previously thought. My question is, was this slow revelation of the truth a way to soften the blow to the public and to prevent panic and fear, or was it incompetence on the part of NASA and other international space agencies?'

Showing discomfort, the professor shifted in his chair as the rest of the panel and millions of viewers around the world looked on. He cleared his throat. 'I think I speak for all astronomers when I say that we were in no way involved in the initial reports fed to the media.'

'Some call it a deception,' Jessica Klein said.

'The course of action taken was agreed upon by the international community and the UN Security Council,' he told her. 'Although, personally, I think people could have dealt with the reality better if they had been told the truth from the beginning.' He paused to gather his thoughts. 'Were the initial reports that it would not hit us a deliberate deception? I don't know, perhaps. If so, I can understand their reasons for it even if I do not agree with them myself.' Looking a little shaken after having to fend off such probing questions, Professor Singh took a sip of water as the camera cut back to Jessica

Klein. 'Thank you, Professor Singh, for your candour and for the comprehensive breakdown of the facts and figures surrounding the meteor and the impact itself—'

'There is one point I would like to add,' the professor said, cutting in.

'Of course,' Jessica replied as the camera shifted back onto the man from India.

'It is a common misconception that AG5 is a meteor or meteorite. Technically it should only be referred to as an asteroid; the three terms are not interchangeable. Once it enters our atmosphere AG5 can be classed as a meteor and once it has been confirmed it survived impact, it can be called a meteorite.'

'Thank you, Professor. That was actually a question I wanted to ask you later in the programme. I have to say, though, I prefer the term meteorite rather than asteroid. I think it's been referred to as such for so long that it's almost altered its meaning.'

The professor didn't appear overly enamoured with the newsreader's assertion, but Jessica Klein had already continued. 'Moving on, I'll now ask our U.S. panellist, Michael Bailey from Homeland Security, a few questions.'

The camera cut to a powerful looking man in a crisp grey suit.

'Michael, what can we expect from governments around the world in response to this disaster? How have countries prepared for the coming events and what will the future hold for us all?'

'Jessica, this event will affect the populations of every nation on the planet, of that there is no doubt. We will all experience significant disruption to our lives for many years to come, perhaps lasting a lifetime and beyond. Most of us have already had our lives altered on a daily basis due to measures introduced by UN resolutions, and by governments looking to ensure civilisation and economies continue to function at the highest levels possible during this biggest of transitional periods in human history. The challenges we will face individually and collectively will be great and spread across all aspects of our lives and work.'

'What sort of economic challenges do we have to overcome or adapt to?' Jessica asked him.

'Good question. They will almost be limitless; however, the main issues will include adaptation to minimal or zero continental and long distance flights due to the dust in the atmosphere. Coupled with zero sunlight, this will have a catastrophic effect on the tourism market.

'Farmers have had to adopt genetically modified grasses and crops to ensure the worldwide population does not starve. Satellites we have depended upon for what seems like an eternity, floating unseen above us, will be made virtually redundant due to the all-encompassing dust cloud set to encase the world. As a result significant fiscal stimulus has been injected into the global economy to switch to more robust surface-based networks.

'Adapting to events that may or may not happen are perhaps the most challenging, it is not known whether we will experience acid rain, for instance. Still, this ambiguity has not prevented some companies from producing and marketing acid resistant clothing and umbrellas to protect us.'

'So what are some of the more major disruptions we can expect in the years to come?'

'If the ozone is damaged beyond predictions,' Michael Bailey continued, 'the human race may have to take on a twilight existence, going outdoors only after dark.'

'That will be once the dust cloud has cleared, I take it?' she said.

'Well, it will be hard to distinguish between night and day in most places; however, during the daytime, if you can't see the sun it will be possible to go outside since even intense UV rays will not be able to penetrate the dense particulates in the air. In answer to your question, yes, once the dust cloud has cleared, direct sunlight may be off limits. UV light without the ozone protecting us will bring about cancer and many other health issues, not just for us, but for all plant and animal life.'

'Is that why many governments have daytime curfew redundancy procedures in place in case of such an event?'

'It is. There are a whole raft of counter measures in place in the event of varying side effects caused by the meteor strike.'

'Thank you, Michael. We will go into these issues in further detail later in the programme. I'd now like to speak to the Archbishop, if I may?'

The Archbishop of Canterbury, a greying, bearded man dressed in simple unassuming robes, nodded his head in acceptance.

'Dr. Mowberry, I think now more than at any other time in human history, the church, religion and spirituality in general is something many of us will turn to in this, perhaps our darkest hour. Do you have any words of comfort that you can bestow upon our many viewers and listeners around the world?'

'Well, first I'd like to say that you don't have to be religious to believe in God, or gods, if you wish. Everyone has a right to believe in what they want, when they want and wherever they want. I believe in my faith, Christianity, but you can also have faith in whatever you choose. Faith will give you strength and comfort and prevent you from becoming too fearful. Negative emotions such as hate, fear and anger will corrupt your decision making processes, leading to a spiralling, self-perpetuating circle of negativity. Faith will protect you, be that faith in God, Christianity, family or friendship. The power of light will help keep the soul bright even under the darkest of clouds.

'Spirituality is not the jurisdiction of just one religion or one group; it is for all races, colours and creeds to adopt as they so wish. This standpoint, of course, has not always been preached by my predecessors, but with enlightenment comes responsibility for the past and for the future. Without addressing past wrongs, the future will always be clouded and shrouded by old deeds. Repentance begins at home for individuals and religions alike. The result of the asteroid which God has decided to test us with has been difficult for faiths. Our commitment and resolve has been tested and our ways challenged. It has forced us to address our failings on a grander scale, to relinquish power to those that do not seek it, rather than to those that do, to instigate real transparency and to prevent hidden factions from subverting the decisions and actions of others; something, perhaps, that companies and governments may also do well to adopt in these changing times.

'God created us all and it is his will that this meteor is set to change all our lives. I pray for people to stay true to the light and not to embrace the darkness that may try to engulf them during the difficult times ahead. God tests us all, every day of our lives, and the coming days and years will be no different. Stay strong in your beliefs and pray to God for all our salvation, be that physical or spiritual.'

'Thank you, Dr. Mowberry, they were wise words indeed and I think such a change of perspective and stance by the Church of England has seen your attendances surge to unprecedented highs over the last few years; quite a turnaround from the lows seen earlier in the century.'

The camera flicked to a wide angle view of the whole panel and then focused on to Jessica Klein once more. 'We'll now hear from our last guest, Mariana Lima from the Global Meteor Response Council, or as we all know it, the GMRC. Thank you for joining us today, Ms. Lima. What kind of organised response can we expect from governments across the world?'

A camera homed in on a smallish olive-skinned woman with jet black hair and an open face. 'Jessica, it is a pleasure to be on your show and I hope I can help some of your audience understand how the GMRC operates and how it has prepared for Impact Day and beyond. Never before has humanity pulled together its collective resources and skills for one common goal, preparing for the arrival of AG5 and what is, without doubt, the most significant event in the history of the human race; and the most significant for our whole planet since the meteorite that wiped out the dinosaurs sixty-five million years ago.

'The GMRC has had unilateral support for the last ten years and we have accomplished much in this time. The education of the populace, the analysis of forecast data, the preparing of protocols and processes to be actioned by governments and the UN, in accordance with our modus operandi, which was defined and voted for unanimously by every government on Earth.

'The main protocols governments the world over will be enforcing include curfews, National Guard deployment, food rationing and water monitoring stations. Curfews will be fully adaptable to side effects of the impact and will ensure civilisation does not collapse due to panic and fear. Governments have been advised that heavy handed tactics have to be utilised for the benefit of all. National Guard and police forces have been trained to enforce curfews and prevent civil unrest, which includes rioting and looting. We all know that rioting occurs from time to time in societies; however, this event may cause mass hysteria on an unprecedented scale. To prevent this from happening, all necessary force can be undertaken by a government to ensure peace is maintained within its borders.'

'And will this include lethal force?' Jessica said.

'It will,' Mariana Lima replied matter-of-factly. 'To prevent the breakdown of our way of life it must be upheld by the strictest of laws and lethal force will be the biggest deterrent, and perhaps the only deterrent, for those that may lose a grip on their sanity in the days and years to come.'

'I think everyone is already used to food rationing,' Jessica Klein said, 'but please explain to us why it is necessary and how long will it go on for?'

'Food rationing is critical in our response to AG5's strike; without it certain nations may starve and in a worst case scenario we may all become severely malnourished; especially those with an influx of peoples evacuated from the African countries and those in and around the Indian Ocean. Food shortages also result in civil unrest, which is almost a greater threat than the asteroid itself. As I have already iterated, our way of life must be preserved and order cannot give way to chaos. We have many protestors and opponents, as toes have been squarely trodden on in many instances; this, however, cannot weaken our resolve.'

'What would you say to theorists and people that accuse the GMRC of pushing through a programme of control and governance that is tantamount to the instigation and groundwork for an all-powerful global government and police force?' Jessica Klein asked the GMRC representative.

The camera zoomed in further on Mariana Lima, highlighting the importance and gravity of the question posed to her. 'These concerns are very real; however, we have a dissolution programme which has been agreed upon by all but the most stubborn of governments. We will slowly give up our powers and as a new dawn emerges from the shadows we will become just another organisation to be wound up and shelved.'

'And how long will it be until this new dawn you mention?'

'Ask me that question in a year and I'd be able to give you a more precise answer. My answer now would be ten years, once the dust cloud has settled and when rebuilding work is well underway and a sense of normality has returned to all our lives.'

'Thank you, Ms. Lima, that has been a nice taster for what is to come on the rest of the programme. We'll now switch to the Telemetry Team for some real-time information. James, over to you.'

The image shifted to an adjoining studio where a young suited man stood next to a large screen which had multiple pictures and graphs on it. 'Thanks, Jessica, and good day to you all. It's that time of the show where we update you on the meteorite's latest data ... sorry, asteroid, and on ground reports from all over the world.'

James touched the screen and enlarged a shot of the asteroid itself as it slowly rotated on a skewed axis. With a flick of his hand the image became holographic, floating in the air beside him. 'Breaking news,' he said, 'apparently gravitational pull from the close pass to the moon has altered AG5's trajectory very slightly. Data now suggests it will be striking one hundred and fifty miles due south of previous predictions. This may affect a few penguins down in the South Pole, but the rest of us not so much.

'AG5's speed hasn't changed, although images from tracking systems tell us it has shed more ice from its surface along with a chunk of rock a couple of hundred feet in diameter. This new piece of debris heading our way,' – he flicked his finger and brought up another image, this time showing the reverse side of AG5 – 'has been imaginatively entitled AG5 Minor and it may prove to be an anomaly which was unforeseen by many of the world's scientists. The reason for this occurrence is that the composition of AG5 Minor is theorised to be less dense than its bigger brother. Another explanation is that it has been slowly detaching for thousands of years and the recent shift in gravity finally enabled it to break free.

'We will be running a poll later to rename AG5 Minor, so please utilise your chosen media port to send us your ideas. I'd like to call it Ernie as it's quite cute compared to AG5, which I like to refer to as Bert. As you may have guessed, I'm a big Sesame Street fan.' James grinned at the camera before moving to another image frame and expanding it to reveal live footage of an ocean – off to the left hand side a land mass could be seen, South Africa. 'Here is ground zero looking nice and quiet, although give it a few hours and this stream will become the most watched film ever; eclipsing even that of the famous moon landings of the 1960s.

'When the super-condensed frame rate is viewed a millisecond at a time, we will be able to analyse the impact of a meteorite like never before, or indeed, perhaps ever again; no, doomsayers,' he said with a roll of his eyes, 'that's not because we'll all be dead, but because this may be the only meteorite we will ever be able to track and predict its impact site accurately due to its size, predictability and the resources we have put into tracking it – oh, I'm sorry, everyone, my producer is telling me that I didn't tell you all where Ernie is going to land. Well, according to our friends at the GMRC, AG5 Minor, aka Ernie, will be landing somewhere in ... hang on, is that right? Sorry, folks, bear with me.' He put a couple of fingers to his right ear for a moment, listening. His face grew grave. 'Apparently AG5 Minor will be impacting in India, near the town of Agra. Evacuations have already begun. They believe they can get most of the area clear before ... oh, God. I'm sorry; this is difficult news to disclose live. Current estimates have the population of Agra at three million people.

'The GMRC emergency unit was mobilised as soon as they

received confirmation of AG5 Minor's strike zone, twenty hours ago. They already have seventy per cent of the devastation zone cleared and a further thirteen per cent will be achieved before the time of impact, which is going to be nearly identical to that of AG5 itself. Up-to-date prognosis is that loss of life will be half a million—' The presenter looked stunned, staring blankly into the camera as he comprehended the news he had just delivered.

The camera switched view to Jessica Klein, who hastily moved some paperwork to one side. 'This is truly devastating news and our thoughts and prayers go out to those people whose families' lives are going to be cut cruelly short. We'll revisit the progress of AG5 and AG5 Minor later on in the programme. Now we'll take a look at the worldwide weather forecast, which will include details of how climate and weather patterns are predicted to change after impact.'

Rebecca turned off the television. *All those poor people*, she thought, feeling quite emotional and helpless. She sent out a silent prayer to them, they who wouldn't see out the next day, asking God to protect their souls. She looked over to Joseph who was happily colouring in a pop-up fire station. He caught her looking and gave her a loving smile, and then turned his attention back to the job in hand, his face screwed up in concentration as he fought to keep within the lines of the image. After she had tidied up some of Joseph's toys, she poured herself a drink and settled back on the sofa, her mug of cocoa steaming between her hands. She turned the TV back on.

'—yes, I can hear you; this is terrible news, do you know when it started and what is happening right now?' Jessica Klein was asking a reporter who appeared to be in a crowded city somewhere.

'It started recently, word got out about the new threat and panic has swept through the country, it's absolute carnage here. Thousands are being shot by the army and police, but this is happening across the whole of India. News of AG5 Minor has brought terror to the streets of the capital!' he said, raising his voice as automatic gunfire cracked nearby. People in the background screamed and shouted in fear as armed men could be seen advancing on them.

'I have to relocate, the use of deadly force is indiscriminate!' He ducked down as bullets rained around him. The camera angle shifted to the ground and began jerking up and down as the cameraman sprinted behind his colleague for safety.

'I can't get in anywhere!' the reporter shouted, terror clear in his voice as the camera angle glanced past his legs. Gunfire roared out and chilling screams streamed over the feed, which continued to transmit before fuzzing out.

The TV went dark for about ten seconds before Jessica Klein reappeared on screen looking distraught. 'That was a live report from Martin Johansson in New Delhi. We don't know if Martin or his cameraman sustained any injuries as the stream has gone down; the Indian government has locked down communications to try to stifle further unrest. We can only pray they made it to safety in time. We're now switching to a report coming in from here in London. Keira, can you hear me?'

'I can, Jessica. This is Keira Jones on the streets of London. The already deployed Territorial Army are being bolstered by regular troops. Tanks are rolling menacingly down The Mall and Typhoon fighters have been scrambled as the UK government seeks to deter any mass hysteria similar to that seen in India. Live rounds have been authorised, we have been told, so I advise anyone in the street to go indoors and to stay put until things have calmed down.

'This unexpected turn of events is having major repercussions, but the GMRC has told me that there are protocols in place for occurrences such as these. I just hope they won't result in the further bloodshed of civilians like the scenes we just witnessed on the streets of New Delhi; back to you in the studio.'

'Thank you, Keira. We're now going straight to another location in Saudi Arabia. Clare, can you hear me?'

'I can, Jessica,' replied a middle-aged woman wearing a head scarf. 'Something strange is going on here; people are rioting, but the Saudi government isn't doing anything in response. I think they may be waiting for it to burn itself out, but that doesn't appear to be happening. Wait ... I can hear something, a deep humming noise. It's a helicopter, I think – no, wait – yes! It's helicopters and they're broadcasting from a speaker system around the city telling people to go back inside, but it doesn't appear to be working. They're Apache Gunships. Wait, they're opening fire! Oh, my God, they're not stopping, can you see this?! They're committing mass murder!!'

The camera zoomed in on the military helicopters which fired off rapid bursts into the crowds of rioters and looters.

'This is horrendous! I don't think we can show any more right now—'

The television picture went back to the studio and Jessica Klein. 'That was Clare Andrews reporting from Saudi Arabia. We're getting reports of other full scale military deployments all around the world, thankfully no other scenes like those we've just witnessed, but since the meteorite hasn't even hit yet we may be in for a very bumpy ride. Actually, we're temporarily suspending this programme as we bring you a Global Alert Warning from the GMRC's media platform.' The screen went black once more and a familiar emblem displayed.

GMRC

The screen dissolved into a shade of red, and white letters appeared.

THIS IS A GMRC EMERGENCY BROADCAST
DO NOT ADJUST YOUR MEDIA PLAYER
THIS IS A CRITICAL ALERT
PROTOCOL ONE DELTA:

AN EMERGENCY WORLDWIDE CURFEW
WILL COMMENCE IN TWELVE HOURS
PROCEED CALMLY TO YOUR HOME
OR A PLACE OF REFUGE UNTIL

FURTHER NOTICE

LETHAL FORCE WILL BE UTILISED
TO PRESERVE THE PEACE
THIS IS EMERGENCY
PROTOCOL ONE DELTA

THIS IS NOT A DRILL

The GMRC logo displayed again and then the message repeated itself. Rebecca's phone sounded an alarm and she picked it up. It was the same message from the GMRC. Full curfew was going into effect already; her buried fears suddenly rose to the surface and her pulse quickened. A knock on the door made her jump. She went over and opened it.

Julie, her co-worker, stood in the hallway looking nervous. 'We're all in the main lounge; do you want to come and join us?'

Rebecca saw Julie was scared, so she nodded. 'I'll just get Joseph and I'll be right with you.'

'Come on, Joseph, let's go to the playroom!' she enthused to him.

Beaming away, Joseph packed up his pencils and crayons and folded away his pop-up book. 'Later,' he said.

'Yes, you can finish it later; let's go now with Julie to see the others.' She took Joseph's hand and went out into the corridor.

'Have you seen the news?' Julie said. 'It's so awful. All those people killed. I've got the janitor to lock up the building. Do you want a cup of tea or anything?' she asked Rebecca, her voice shaking.

Joseph shuffled into the lounge, but Rebecca stopped and held onto Julie's arm. 'Julie, we have to be strong for them, if they think we're scared they will get scared.' She looked into Julie's eyes to see if she could find the girl's reason. 'Okay?'

'Okay,' Julie said, giving her a weak smile.

They followed Joseph in to find all the other residents, carers and patients alike, gathered in the room in two groups. The mentally handicapped were off entertaining themselves on a rug and Joseph had already gone and joined them. The carers had huddled round the TV and spoke in raised, agitated tones.

Rebecca headed towards the TV to see the news ran in one image while another displayed the GMRC's alert message. She went straight up to it and switched it off.

'We were watching that!' an older woman said to her. She was one of the second tier carers who helped manage the building and admin, normally issuing duties and rosters to Rebecca, Julie and the part timers.

'We know what's going on,' Rebecca replied coolly, 'so instead of feeding your own fear and passing it around, I think it would be better for us all to concentrate on our wards; we should focus on them rather than a situation we cannot control.'

'But we need to know what's going on,' said the older woman as she leaned around Rebecca to turn the TV back on.

Rebecca moved so she couldn't reach the switch. 'Maria, we have our phones for GMRC and local news updates,' she said, her expression stern, 'we do not need the TV on in here any longer.'

Maria squared up to her trying to stare her down, but Rebecca held firm, her face set. She raised her eyebrows and Maria relented.

'So what do you propose?' Maria grumbled, her defiance deflated but not gone.

'I say we look after them and act as normally as we can. In the meantime, Julie, come with me, I need your help.'

'With what?' Julie said.

'Just some clothing I got recently,' she told her. Rebecca left the room and led Julie back to her apartment. On entering, she quickly turned on the TV, hooked up her phone and scanned the local information feeds. Thankfully, much to her relief, no disturbances had been reported. Switching it off, she went over to a cupboard and opened it up to reveal two large bulging black sacks.

'Help me with these, will you?' she asked her friend as she passed a heavy sack to her.

'This weighs a ton what have you got in here?'

Rebecca tapped her nose mysteriously and winked which eased the tension in Julie's face.

'Just some supplies in case things get a little ugly.'

'Like what?'

'Wait and see,' Rebecca said, as she hefted her own bag down and shut the cupboard door.

CHAPTER FOURTEEN

IMPACT DAY

SPACE, a cold deep expanse, an endless void interspersed by spherical bodies of matter and energy so large they defied comprehension. And within this cosmic eternity the solar system continued to perform its majestic dance without pause. Sunlight glinted off the surfaces of Earth's oceans as the Sun edged out from behind its silhouette. Wispy white cloud structures slipped across a new dawn as a dark shape loomed large above, still distant but closing impossibly fast.

Barely noticeable on the very limit of the planet's gravitational field, bisecting Earth and the blackness of space, a small craft manoeuvred into position. Rays reflected off its white casing and small irregular jets of gas vented out into the vacuum surrounding it.

'This is Orbiter One, we are prepped and a go for live feed, Houston.'

'Orbiter One, we are reading you five by five. Live feed is a go.'

'We are tracking two targets, Houston, as expected. Velocities and trajectories are following observational data and impact sites will be unchanged. I repeat, impact sites will be unchanged, Houston.'

'Roger that, that's a visual and confirmed telemetry check, thank you, Orbiter One. Please ensure all secondary and tertiary recording systems are activated and data transmission is shielded as per simulations.'

'We read you, Houston. We are proceeding as directed, Orbiter One out.'

'Copy, Orbiter One.'

Tyler Magnusson shifted his seat one hundred and eighty degrees to take in the view from the nano fabricated observational window on the U.S.S.S. Orbiter One. His fellow astronaut, Ivan Sikorsky, sat beside him for what was going to be the biggest show on Earth ever witnessed. At the flick of a few switches and tapping of buttons Tyler dialled in the telescopic digital head-up display and brought up the tracking window. The asteroid had reached the final transition towards Earth's atmosphere.

'This is it then,' he said to Ivan.

'These glasses will protect us from the flash, won't they?' Ivan asked him as he fidgeted nervously with them.

'So they tell me,' Tyler said. 'If in doubt just don't look.'

'What, and miss the greatest ever event in history? I don't think so.'

Tyler twisted a couple of dials overhead, their tiny cams clicking for each notch moved, and then checked the countdown timer. It read one minute five seconds.

'Here we go,' Tyler said and they both pulled down their visor glasses to block out the blinding light of the impact that was about to occur. 'All camera video streams are recording across the board, let's enjoy the show.'

The two men gazed out into deep space with the shining light of Earth on their left.

AG5 2011 hurtled towards them, now clearly visible with the naked eye. In a heartbeat it was past, shooting through the thin layer of gas surrounding the planet. Moving at nine miles a second, the asteroid cut like a burning comet through the sky below. A brilliant flash of white light eclipsed their field of vision, momentarily blinding them despite their protective glasses. A yellow dome erupted from the centre of the light, ever climbing and widening as the impact explosion shattered everything in its path. The first tsunami streaked out like a ripple on a pond, except this ripple was a mile high and travelling at one thousand miles an hour. A smaller trail of smoke indicated the course of AG5 Minor, which had impacted in India at roughly the same instant as the main strike off the South African coastline.

A dark cloud rose up from the primary impact zone, and a haze from a great plume of steam expanded alongside it as water rushed back into the massive crater left by the asteroid.

'I hope they managed to get everyone out of the way of the smaller one in time,' Ivan said.

Tyler nodded in solemn agreement. Houston had told them the people were being evacuated, and that was some time ago, so hopefully casualties had been minimal. He flicked a switch as the show below still unfolded in what looked like slow motion from so far away, but which in actuality occurred at frightening speed on the surface.

'Houston, are you getting this?'

'Copy, Orbiter One, we have one hundred per cent data conversion down here, not a packet lost, good job.'

'Tyler?' Ivan said.

Tyler looked over at his colleague, who still looked intently at the planet.

Ivan pointed far off to the horizon, thousands of miles away from the impact zone. 'What are they?'

Tyler looked back down following the path of Ivan's finger. He squinted, trying to make sense of what he was seeing. About a dozen small trails were arcing up from the surface in unison. At the tip of each trail a small bright light pulsated, a pinpoint from their distant vantage point.

'They look like rocket trails, don't they?'

Ivan was right; that's exactly what they were. Another wave had launched behind the first, perhaps twenty more. Tyler brought the reserve camera online and positioned it on the area. 'Houston, this is Orbiter One. I'm sending you an additional feed. There appears to be some ballistic activity over China.'

A silent pause hung in the air as he waited for a response.

'Copy, Orbiter One, we're receiving your new signal. Decrypting.'

Tyler watched the trails drop back to the surface, where small domed lights sprang up as each one struck, and it dawned on him what he was seeing. A nuclear attack!

'Houston, we have confirmed multiple detonations, over.'

'Copy, Orbiter One, we see them too. Utilising one of our satellites it seems the Chinese have launched a full blown nuclear strike on Japan and South Korea.'

'Dear God,' Ivan said.

'Copy that, Houston,' Tyler said, watching in horror as rockets lifted off in a return volley from Japan. 'And may God protect us.'

Rebecca sat in her room, resting, while checking the BBC news show on her TV display. She had witnessed the image of the meteorite hitting the Indian Ocean and multi-image videos informed viewers about the progress of each wave, fire, earthquake and dust cloud from the main site. She brought up another channel; the same images played out. She tried another and another, and another three after that. All showed the same pictures.

At last the inexorable wait was over and it felt liberating. The veil had been lifted and life could now push ahead and brace for the future instead of concentrating on one single point in time. She checked the data feeds again. The National Guard had been bolstered by the army, but tensions ran high as people were herded like cattle to prevent disorder. *This is going too far*, she thought, the images she'd witnessed earlier still strong in her mind's eye. She switched back to the BBC. Jessica Klein was still on air.

'—according to reports,' the newsreader was saying, 'the dust cloud is travelling across the upper reaches of the sky much quicker than had been predicted. The whole of Africa is already in darkness and it is only a few hours since AG5 hit. You can see from these military satellites, which are still operational, the coverage is spreading at an alarming rate.'

Rebecca watched as a dark smear gradually swallowed up the continent of Africa.

'What had been estimated to take six to twelve months seems like it is only going to take a few days. The resolve of governments will be tested to the limit as already nervous populations may be overwhelmed by this new turn of events. As I mentioned earlier, we will now be going live to New York for an address from the United Nations Secretary General, Enitan Owusu.'

A tall African man stood in front of a rostrum, with a slim black microphone in front of him and the United Nations' logo emblazoned on a hoarding behind. 'People of the world,' said the Secretary General in a deep and measured voice, 'the asteroid has impacted and the predicted after-effects are playing out as we envisaged. Yet there is one small factor that seems to have been miscalculated, and that is the dust cloud. The unexpected speed of the cloud's expansion is an anomaly; however, preparing for and dealing with unforeseen repercussions has been an element of GMRC protocol responses for many years. Every one of us has long been aware that such scenarios were possible, thanks to the teachings of the GMRC's global education programme.

'Every nation's government is fully prepared for every eventuality, including this one, and there is absolutely no need for panic. Please stay in your homes and remain calm. Governments have bolstered National Guards with regular military personnel all around the world to ensure you are protected and kept safe during this period of transition. Please remember looting and rioting will not be tolerated on any level and people who do so will be dealt with swiftly and effectively. There is no need for alarm as these measures have been in place for many years and are for your protection.

'Once the dust cloud has completed its coverage of the

atmosphere, normality will resume as quickly as possible. It will take time to get used to living beneath the cloud, but the restricted daytime curfew tests which have been undertaken by each nation's government in the last six months will stand us all in good stead for what is to come. GMRC reports and updates will be issued on the hour, every hour, for the next month and bi-hourly thereafter. This message will be repeated every hour on all media platforms and translated into all languages for seven days. You will now receive messages from your respective leaders. Thank you for your time.'

The studio view came back on screen and Jessica Klein was once more centre stage, her red outfit complementing the blue and white of the studio set. 'We are now going straight to an address by your country's leader, depending on your location.'

An animated BBC graphic displayed briefly and then the President of the United States of America was at his desk in the Oval Office. 'My fellow Americans, and to all our military personnel stationed around the world, the difficulties we will face in the days ahead will be challenging but not insurmountable. Due to unforeseen fallout resulting from the meteorite's impact, the dust cloud predicted to reach the east coast of the United States in a few months' time is now likely to arrive in three days. I have deployed U.S. Army troops onto our streets to bolster the National Guard, already positioned throughout the country—'

Rebecca listened intently as the president outlined the people's responsibility to remain calm and optimistic during what was a minor setback to planned proceedings. Rebecca wasn't convinced by his rhetoric, most of which just reiterated what the Secretary General of the UN had already said. The dust cloud was spreading quicker than expected and after listening to the speeches she felt an increased anxiety rather than the calm they were supposed to induce. She'd prepared herself for a specific timeframe and now that had gone out of the window everything was up in the air, literally. With a wry smile slipping from her face as quickly as it had appeared, she left her small apartment to rejoin the others.

In the lounge, the TV was back on.

Rebecca sighed and went to turn it off, but Maria caught her hand in an iron grip.

'What are you doing?' Rebecca said, twisting herself free and looking at the others, who avoided her gaze. 'We agreed to keep this off.'

'While you were gone we decided that things had calmed down a bit and we could put it back on without upsetting them,' Maria told her smugly.

Yourselves, without upsetting yourselves, is what Rebecca wanted to retort, but unfortunately Maria was right, all the carers seemed much more composed and they sat quietly showing little sign of agitation, although most still looked pale and worried.

'Fine, just make sure it stays that way,' Rebecca said, sitting down next to Julie and a very old woman whom Julie looked after on a regular basis.

'Hello, Edna, how are you keeping?' Rebecca asked the woman loudly.

'I'm fine, dear. I don't like this film, though,' – Edna indicated the news channel on the screen – 'it seems to keep repeating itself.'

'I didn't correct her,' Julie whispered to Rebecca. 'No point scaring her.'

'Good idea,' Rebecca said, as she started watching.

'—we now have some breaking news, so we're going directly to our Chinese correspondent, Simon MacDonald, in Beijing,' Jessica Klein was saying.

The studio shot slipped to one side of the screen and in a digital frame a reporter with a graphic of the Beijing city skyline behind him appeared. 'Thank you, Jessica. Only moments ago rockets heading out towards the east coast passed overhead in what can only be a military attack by China on its closest neighbour, Japan. Other reports are also coming in from the north of missiles being launched in the direction of South Korea, although this is currently unverified.'

'Was there any warning this was going to happen?' Jessica asked him.

'None, although there have been steadily disintegrating tensions in the area for the last decade. China has been growing ever stronger while South Korea and Japan have waned, both economically and militarily.'

'Surely they know the rest of the world won't let this action go unpunished?' Jessica said.

'They obviously don't care,' Simon replied. 'With their economy the major force in the world and their military might unrivalled, who can stand against them? There is only the United States and their resources are massively overstretched due to AG5 and its fallout; likewise with the EU and other powerful nations.'

'What about the UN?'

'The UN is in China's pocket these days,' he said. 'Sadly, this is something we should have seen coming.'

'Shouldn't you be getting to some kind of shelter?'

'We're already in a basement office. We'll be going down to a lower level car park after this broadcast.'

'Are there any reports of retaliation from the Japanese or South Koreans?'

'The South Koreans no longer have nuclear weapons due to a decommissioning pact with North Korea five years ago. Japan has some, but China has been investing heavily in its missile shield defence system for some time and it's unlikely anything the Japanese fire at them will get through.'

'Is this something the Chinese have been planning for a long time, then?'

'That may well be the case. What better time to launch an attack than when the rest of the world is looking elsewhere?'

'I can't see the U.S. standing by and letting this happen to two of their allies,' Jessica said. 'Surely they will react?'

'I don't know about that, but I do know that many people will have just died and many more will continue to die in the most terrible of ways imaginable.'

The window showing the BBC's Chinese correspondent faded

from view and Jessica Klein once more filled the whole screen, with multiple news tickers flagging up the latest reports from around the world. 'We have just received a statement issued by the White House of the United States,' Jessica continued, 'which reads as follows:

"'*Such a blatant attack on our allies will not be tolerated, now or ever. We will be sending in negotiators to both sides to try to resolve the issue before any further blood is shed. U.S. and NATO forces are on high alert and UN diplomats are also on their way to speak to the governments concerned. Rest assured that this incident will not bring about a world war during a time when upheaval is already upon us. Further updates will be made via the White House when and where necessary. End of statement."*

'Going back to our panel of guests; Michael, if I may speak to you first, it seems your government is not willing to back up its allies with force. This is an extremely surprising statement, isn't it?'

The image zoomed out slightly and then focused in on Michael Bailey from the U.S. Department of Homeland Security. 'I don't think so, Jessica, as the White House administration has stated quite clearly our position is clear. The United States will ensure that peace is quickly brought about and by any means available to us.'

'And does that include the use of force?' she said, pressing him for an answer.

Michael Bailey sat up straighter, his body language defensive. 'Until I have been properly briefed I am not in a position to comment further.'

Jessica Klein looked a little incredulous at his response. 'Dr. Mowberry, you have had experience with international affairs; how do you see this military non-intervention policy by the United States?'

'I think it's too early to speculate, but considering the arrival of AG5 the U.S. is obviously more concerned with ensuring stability at home than wading into a war with arguably the most powerful nation on the planet. We also don't know the reason for the aggression and which side is accountable for instigating initial hostilities. Perhaps we should get some clear facts before calling for further action by a third party.'

The newsreader nodded her head as she took in the Archbishop's answer. 'I think they are very valid points; however, such an apparently weak statement from the White House is almost unheard of. Am I missing something here? The use of nuclear weapons is a declaration of war, and since it is a declaration of war on America's allies then it is a declaration of war on America itself, and yet the statement released by the White House is virtually as toothless as those issued by the UN on a regular basis when military action is called for—' Jessica put her finger to her ear as she took instructions from her producer and nodded. 'My apologies, we're going to have to suspend this discussion as we're shifting to a live report coming out of South Korea where we have footage of the aftermath of one of the bombs. The images you are about to see are from a remote camera and may be disturbing.'

The studio scene once again shrank to one side of the screen and another frame enlarged. Smoke billowed ominously in the initial image and then it cleared to reveal a decimated landscape that had once been a great city.

A reporter, Andrew Stapleton according to the graphic, described what was being shown. 'This complete annihilation of an urban area laid out below us is the remnants of South Korea's capital city, Seoul. Untold numbers of people are dead and that figure will only rise, considering many other bombs have ravaged the nation, bringing it to its knees. The bodies you can clearly see lying sprawled out on the street are—'

Rebecca got up and walked to the window, not wanting to see or hear any more of the report. She looked over to where Joseph sat sleeping in a chair after his day's exertions. She went over to him and gently moved his hair out of his eyes. He looked so peaceful, and as she had before on occasion she envied his innocence. To have such a free mind, albeit one mentally challenged, was perhaps a gift in some respects. Not fearing or worrying about your own mortality or having to concern yourself with the rights and wrongs and evil deeds of others; soon forgetting any stress that you did experience, allowing happiness to once more exert its powerful spell of safety and contentment; life could be so cruel and yet so kind at the same time.

Rebecca sat down next to him to watch him breathe while attempting to forget what she'd just witnessed by thinking of happier times; for a while it helped to ease her mind and soul, when both were weary.

CHAPTER FIFTEEN

LONDON, ENGLAND.

Mark swayed at the bar. Stumbling backwards, he bumped into a couple as they tried to pass behind him without spilling their drinks; he promptly gave them the finger for their efforts. The tall young man, who now found half his pint on the floor, stopped and turned back to give Mark a hard stare. Becoming aggressive, Mark picked up his bottle threateningly. 'And what?' he said, speech slurred.

The man, pulled back by his girlfriend, walked away, still angered but relinquishing to common sense.

Mark watched them go before turning back to the bar and calling for another drink.

He'd hit the booze on a nightly basis ever since Sarah had left him to go treasure hunting in Turkey. Tonight he'd had more than usual and in a state of lairiness he'd already insulted a group of women sitting at a nearby table, a barmaid, and a colleague, who'd left in disgust. Some of his other remaining work mates were equally as drunk, but seemed slightly more restrained.

Impact Day was upon them and many in central London got in a drink before the curfew saw them scurrying back to their homes. Some office workers, of which Mark was one, had decided that

Impact Day should be celebrated much like any other notable day, such as the New Year, or Friday.

'Mark, where's your lovely girlfriend tonight?' one of his friends asked him.

'Who? Oh, her. I dumped her; she was getting too clingy and needy. To be honest, she was a pretty weak person; I'm better off without her.'

'She was a looker, though, and no mistake. Sarah, wasn't it?'

'Yeah. She wasn't that good-looking though; you should have seen her in the morning, well rough!'

'Whatever you say, buddy. Have you got her phone number? I might give her a call since you're done with her.'

Mark laughed loudly. 'I wouldn't touch her, mate. I think she gave me crabs or something. Pretty rotten. I'd stay clear, if I were you.'

'Really? That's nasty that a girl like that could be diseased. Hey, Charlie, did you know Sarah gave Mark VD?!' the man shouted to his mate further up the bar.

Charlie made a face and then went back to talking to someone next to him. Mark noticed something going on outside. He pushed past a young couple who gave him dirty looks which he ignored as he lurched to the open door.

Police walked down the road on either side, shadowing a mass of people who chanted slogans as they marched along the street with placards and banners.

'GMRC OUT!'

'Unelected government!'

'GM—RC unelected mon—keys! GM—RC unelected Na—zis!'

He took another swig from his bottle and belched while considering the scene before him. He had been saying for years the GMRC had too much power. What had he told people for years? The GMRC had too much power. They weren't even elected!

Struggling back to the bar, he downed the rest of his drink, slammed the empty bottle down on the counter and put on his jacket. Not bothering to say goodbye to anyone he ambled out into the street, stepped between two parked cars and fell into step with the marchers.

'Where are you heading?' he shouted to a man walking next to him.

'Parliament Square!'

'I didn't think you were allowed to protest outside Parliament these days,' Mark said, as he dodged the wing mirror of a parked van.

'You're not, but what kind of a democracy prevents you from protesting when and where you want?'

'A shit one!' Mark said angrily.

'You got that right.' The man held his hand up for a high five, which Mark duly delivered with a resounding smack.

'Protesting never does much good though,' Mark told him. 'The bastards just ignore you and do what they want anyway. The people don't matter, only the corporations matter these days.'

'It depends on the sort of protest you do,' the man said.

'What do you mean?'

'I mean we're into affirmative action, not this pussy footing about shouting and waving banners.'

'Isn't that what you're doing now?' Mark said.

'Now, yes, but when we get to where we want to be, it's going be a whole different story.'

'Affirmative action? What, violence?'

'What other type is there? Violence is the only way to get noticed or to get anything done. It worked for Nelson Mandela and the ANC in the name of freedom and it also worked in Northern Ireland. Christ, Nelson Mandela is hailed all over the world and at one time he was deemed one of the biggest terrorists going. There's even a statue of him in Parliament Square, you'll see it soon if you stick with us.'

Mark considered the man next to him. He had a dirty, unshaven face with multiple piercings, and tattoos all over; a typical anarchist type. But then what he said made sense and he was all for affirmative action. Yes, violence was the key to change. He liked the sound of it. 'You can count me in!' he yelled as the chanting swelled again.

The man grinned and gave him the thumbs up as he joined in with the crowd once more.

After twenty minutes the protestors had merged with many others who had prearranged a route on the way to the square. Usually the police would have blocked off their entry using an illegal but effective technique called *kettling*. This tactic essentially hemmed crowds of people in to a specific area and then held them there for hours and hours until they had burnt themselves out.

The Met had used the tactic for decades, while breaking their own laws in the process, but no one in the establishment cared much as long as the protesters couldn't put pressure on the politicians in their ivory towers.

These days, however, the ever-present shadow of Impact Day had stretched police resources to the limit. Combine that with the major cuts in government budgets due to the never ending deficit and it seemed the protestors had chosen the right day to voice their opinions. The military would be out to enforce curfew, but that was still some time away and it enabled the protest to go unchallenged, for now anyway.

More and more people filtered into Parliament Square where at last a sizeable police presence had gathered, ensuring access to the Palace of Westminster itself was completely barred. Mark glanced back to see fresh reinforcements of police moving in behind them, preventing their escape; the kettling had begun. Mark already needed to relieve himself, but he knew the police wouldn't allow anyone out regardless of their plight.

Darkness descended as the sun went down, and Mark's new friend had disappeared somewhere. Looking about for a place to drain the lizard, he was pushed hard from behind and staggered into the people in front of him. The crowd compressed, its cohesion buckling as the police moved in to segregate the masses, enabling them to prevent any kind of unified resistance or breakaway. Mark had seen this tactic many times on TV; its use meant that protests were easily broken down and dispersed as the police saw fit. A sudden horn blast sounded off to one side followed by three more all around them. Cheers went up and people slid their placards down their support shafts, turning them into shields. Many also pulled out small visors and large flick extension sticks which they'd had concealed inside their jackets. Peaceful protestors had now transformed themselves into a makeshift army with equipment rivalling the riot gear used by the police themselves. The majority of the constabulary, however, weren't riot ready; most wore standard uniforms and were armed only with their small batons.

The horns sounded again and various people in the crowd shouted out orders for people to converge and move into a specific formation. Jostled and shoved from place to place, Mark struggled to keep his feet as the protestors positioned themselves according to the ringleader's instructions. Grim faces surrounded him; feeling vulnerable, Mark snatched a wicked looking stick from someone as they pushed past him. The crowd heaved once more as the police tried to manoeuvre them further, mounted officers using their horses to corral the dissidents like a herd of cattle.

A megaphone rang out behind them. 'Shields up!' came the order and as one the protestors' makeshift banner shields were presented to the police, forming a solid, impenetrable wall. 'Advance!' came the cry from the megaphone and the protestors slowly moved forwards.

Mark eyed the front line of the police, who struggled to maintain their ground as the organised anarchists exerted pressure on them. The megaphone rattled out instructions and then settled into a chant. 'Push! Push! Push!'

The protestors continued their advance and the police line bowed ominously and then finally broke. The crowd roared and surged forwards, hurling the enemy aside, trampling many underfoot. Mark, swept along with them, managed to get in a lucky strike on a policewoman as she knelt dazed on the ground. Struck hard on the temple, she went down without a sound. Mark's blood was pumping and the people around him broke apart as they entered an empty street and picked up speed. Shop windows were shattered and smashed, and cars overturned; mayhem raged on the streets of London as one hundred thousand men and women baying for blood erupted into Regent Street.

Mark launched himself at windows, swinging his pole with all his might as bystanders fled into buildings to escape the carnage that had suddenly engulfed them. He neared the front of the protesters now and raised his arm in the air, roaring his comrades forwards. They rounded a corner and were brought up short by the sight before them: a military blockade made up of armoured vehicles and soldiers.

A brief moment passed as the two sides eyed each other and then a bellow of defiance echoed from the howling mass, they raised their weapons and threw themselves forwards once more, shields raised.

Time slowed down for Mark as he charged at the people blocking his way. He was thirty paces away and then twenty. The soldiers in the blockade raised their rifles, taking aim. Mark saw one gun aiming straight at him; he slowed as realisation hit him as to what was about to happen, but it was too late – a flash of fire and a deafening crack of gunfire blasted out and he fell backwards, knocked from his feet.

As he lay on the ground, Mark felt the pole slip from his hand as screams of terror surrounded him. A terrible pain lanced through his stomach and he cried out for someone to help him. He was unable to move even though he dearly wanted to, as he heard the sound of a large mechanical clanking getting nearer and nearer. He looked up to see the street lights becoming obscured as a massive tank track crushed down upon him.

CHAPTER SIXTEEN

'BECCA,' a voice said from behind, making her turn. Julie stood nearby, beckoning her over. Standing up, Rebecca moved away from the slumbering Joseph to speak with her friend.

'What is it?' she said, noticing that Julie looked very worried again.

'Some of the girls have gone to the church round the corner,' Julie told her.

Rebecca gasped. 'What?! What are they thinking? The curfew is coming up.'

'I know. I couldn't stop them. Maria wanted to go and she convinced a couple of the others to go, too.'

'How long since they went?'

'A few minutes.'

Rebecca swore. She led Julie out of the door into the hall. 'I'm going to go and see if I convince them to come back; their patients need them now more than ever and if they're out after curfew they'll be stuck there. What is that woman thinking?' she said, referring to Maria.

'I don't think she was. She's scared, Becca. We all are, aren't you?'

'Of course, but I don't matter,' Rebecca said as Julie held out her coat for her. 'Joseph and the others *do*, and we have to be here for them no matter what.' She slipped her arms into the sleeves and pulled the coat tight about her as a chill embittered the air; darkness had already arrived.

Julie unbolted and deactivated the electric security lock on the side door located near to Rebecca's apartment. Rebecca opened the door and turned to Julie. 'Look after Joseph for me, will you? If he wakes, tell him I'm cooking dinner and I'll be back shortly.'

'I will, he'll be fine. I'm more worried about you walking around out there on your own.'

'Don't be,' Rebecca said confidently. 'It's only a short walk. I'll be back soon.' She gave her friend a quick hug and set off into the night. Julie went back inside, the door shutting and then locking behind her. Rebecca looked up at the stars. It wouldn't be long until they would be stripped from the sky as the dust cloud raced across the Atlantic Ocean towards the Americas. No Sun, Moon or stars; a frightening prospect. She imagined the sheer terror those people in remote locations would feel as their world turned upside down in less than a few hours.

The GMRC's education programme had its limitations, even in 2040. Aboriginal tribes surviving deep in the remotest forests had little to no contact with the outside world. They wouldn't understand what was happening any more than the animals they lived alongside. They'd only know that the light had gone, the animals died and the plants withered. Efforts by the GMRC had been made to reach these types of people, but looking for them had been deemed too time-consuming and a poor use of funds, given the mountain of work they had to address in so many other areas. No, those poor people would be alone and very vulnerable. Predictions indicated many in the north of Africa might also perish due to ongoing mundane issues such as famine, poverty and disease, which made them more susceptible to the side effects of the meteorite's arrival.

Rebecca hurried along the sidewalk, then ran across the road and onto the other side. Few people ventured out at this time and those that did moved quickly along, heads down, occupied with their own thoughts as the curfew loomed.

She checked her phone; one hour to go. *Damn that woman!*

Turning a corner, she saw the church in the distance. It was lit up by floodlights, an illuminated sign sitting near the outermost border of its large front lawn. As she drew closer a National Guard vehicle cruised past down the empty street, the sound of its petrol engine unusually loud compared to the noise made by civilian electric cars.

Rebecca followed an old man and his wife into the church, holding the door open for another man who was close behind her. He thanked her and moved past to take a seat towards the front of the congregation, of which there were surprisingly many; it seemed quite a few people had been drawn to the church that evening.

She noticed a board to her right which read:

IMPACT DAY SERVICE
ALL WELCOME
CURFEW BEDS AVAILABLE

That was why so many people had gathered, they didn't have to get back before the streets became off limits. Rolls of bedding and sleeping bags lined the rear of the church and tables were laid out with water jugs, glasses and mugs. Rebecca looked about to see if she could locate Maria and the other carers who had gone with her. She spotted them two rows from the back in the middle of a long pew. Rebecca squeezed past some other parishioners as she made her way along to her quarry.

'What are you doing?' Rebecca said angrily to Maria and her cohorts. Luckily any sermons had yet to begin and the general murmuring of the waiting crowd helped to cover their conversation.

'What does it look like we're doing?' Maria said sarcastically.

'You do know you have people to look after back at the home, don't you? They're relying on you during this terrible time and you've left them behind!'

The other two women looked suitably guilty, but Maria remained as defiant as ever. 'We're allowed a break, aren't we? Anyway, who died and made you in charge?'

Rebecca gave her a withering look just as a muffled noise came over the speakers in the hall. Rebecca looked up to see a portly, middle-aged man at the microphone.

'We're very sorry, ladies and gentlemen. A small electrical fire has broken out in one of the back rooms and we're going to have to evacuate the building as a precautionary measure. If you would like to make your way slowly outside we will wait for a firefighter to give us the all clear to come back in; once they get here, that is. Thank you.'

Chairs ground backwards on wooden floorboards and people stood and began streaming out of the church and into the grounds outside. Rebecca and the others were amongst some of the first out, given they'd been at the rear of the hall.

People chatted animatedly to one another as the area in front of the church filled up with a thousand people, the unexpected disturbance adding fuel to the stressful situation they'd all been trying to flee.

After a while a fire truck turned up, horns blaring and red lights flashing, the beams bouncing off the buildings and trees around them. Everyone had vacated the church now, but as Rebecca looked on wisps of smoke drifted up into the night sky from the rear of the building. The firefighters, clad in their gear, shouted instructions and moved the crowd of people into the street and surrounding area.

People had come out of their houses to see what was going on, and a couple of police cars arrived on the scene as fire rose above the church, tongues of orange and red flame licking up against the bell tower. More and more people gathered as another fire truck arrived, utilising short honking blasts to help dispel the people who milled about in its path. The fire crews unfurled their hoses in double quick time and began dousing the flames, which now raged through the building and the house next door.

A discordant chirruping all around them made people look to their computer phones.

Rebecca withdrew hers, but she already knew what it said. Curfew was now in effect.

As the fire raged, more police cars turned up and another fire truck. At the edge of the area a patrol of armoured National Guard vehicles also arrived at the now chaotic scene.

Loudspeakers rang out. 'This is the National Guard citizens are to proceed to their homes immediately!'

Some people shouted back at them. 'We were here to stay the night, we live too far away!'

'We have nowhere else to go!'

'We won't be able to get back home, there are no more buses!'

'Curfew is in effect,' came the response from the megaphone. 'Please disperse or we will be forced to detain you!'

Rebecca and the carers were buffeted as the scene turned ugly; troops had started breaking up groups of people as they sought to assert control. The police tried to calm the situation down. Some officers argued with the National Guard commander on behalf of the displaced church goers and local residents who had come out of their houses; the firefighters had evacuated many in fear of a gas explosion.

A soldier stood nervously off to one side on the back of one of the National Guard's flatbed trucks, armed with a large machine gun mounted on a tripod. As a matter of course, he had his weapon trained on the crowd, as he'd been taught. Unbeknownst even to himself his finger had strayed onto the trigger and at that moment a big explosion from behind the church lit up the night sky. The violent noise and resulting fireball made the soldier flinch and the trigger compressed. In the blink of an eye gunfire burst into the crowd. People fell and screams resounded all around as everyone ran in all directions.

Terrified, Rebecca grabbed one of the girls who had been with Maria and sprinted for cover. Looking around from relative safety Rebecca saw bodies lying on the ground. One moved weakly. Steeling herself, she ran back into the now deserted road and hunkered down over a little girl; blood seeped out from a gunshot wound in the centre of her chest. The infant looked into Rebecca's eyes, small hand gripping her fingers. As a soft groan escaped through her parted lips, the light faded from the child's eyes and the fingers that had grasped Rebecca's own went limp.

The crowd was gathering once more and building in greater numbers. Outrage surged through them as they turned on the National Guard, who had struck down innocents in cold blood. Unprepared for the backlash the soldiers, reluctant to fire at civilians, were quickly overcome and then the rioting began.

It took half an hour for Rebecca, Maria and the two young carers to make their way back to the home. Cars and buildings burned, set alight during the carnage that had ensued.

Inside, they bolted the doors and Julie came to meet them. 'What's happening out there? It sounds like Armageddon!'

Rebecca was still in shock and she just shook her head, trying to dispel the sight of the young child who had died in her arms. Tears rolled down her cheeks and Julie took her into her apartment to help her get cleaned up. After a few minutes Julie went out of the room and brought Joseph back with her. Seeing Rebecca's distress, he sat down next to her and cuddled into her. She fought back more tears as she stroked his hair, the familiar sensation comforting in its regularity.

The rioting in the streets still raged and Julie turned on the TV to see what the local news had to report about it all.

Helicopter footage showed the extent of the problem faced by the National Guard and police force.

'—half the city of Albuquerque, normally quiet under strict curfew conditions, is in turmoil tonight as a freak incident resulting in the deaths of six civilians sparked angry protests and rioting,' a newsreader was saying. 'Police and the National Guard have been forced to leave the area in order to prevent further bloodshed. Meanwhile looting has become rife as lawlessness is brought to the streets.

'We asked the authorities to comment on the decision to set up a perimeter around the poorer parts of town, but they refused to respond, preferring instead to issue this statement, and I quote—

'"The National Guard and City Police have decided to pull back in the best interests of the civilian population. The lack of support by the U.S. Army in the downtown section of the city has meant that order cannot be maintained by force at this time. We advise all residents in the zones marked out on this map,"' – an image appeared on screen which mapped out sectors covering half the city – '"to remain indoors. You are advised to lock your doors and windows and to defend yourself and property, by force, if necessary. Order will be restored as quickly as possible as we redirect troops to your location from other parts of the state. End of statement."'

Julie switched channels.

'Put the BBC on,' Rebecca said. 'Channel forty two.'

Julie switched it over.

'—these pictures,' Jessica Klein said as video footage played on screen, 'were captured as AG5 Minor struck in India near the city of Agra. A TV crew had left remote cameras near the Taj Mahal before they were evacuated to safety.'

At the top left of the video a small white light appeared in the sky, moving impossibly fast. The light expanded, growing ever brighter into a shimmering ball of fire which lanced through the atmosphere leaving a large trail of smoke in its wake. As the meteor hit a massive explosion ruptured the silence. The percussion of the expanding shockwave raced outwards and the once magnificent white marble mausoleum was obliterated, the great dome exploding into a million pieces, along with the towers that surrounded it. The debris rushed towards the camera in a wall of dust and stone and then the screen went black.

Jessica Klein reappeared on camera. 'Yet another great monument destroyed,' she said, saddened, 'and one which joins the long list of many other important sites lost in the countries directly affected by AG5 itself.'

A gunshot in the distance brought Rebecca back to her senses.

Giving Joseph a quick hug she gently moved him out of the way and went over to the black sacks. 'I'd hoped these wouldn't be needed,' she told Julie as she bent down and upended one of the bags. Military clothing tumbled onto the floor. She picked up the other one and emptied that, too; more clothes spilled out, but along with them guns and knives tumbled down, hitting the ground with dull thuds.

Julie stared in shock at the arsenal of weapons strewn on the floor. 'Oh, my God, Becca, where did you get those from?'

'They're not real, silly,' Rebecca said. 'They're those airsoft replicas; they fire little plastic BBs.'

'So why did you get them, then?'

'In case there was rioting or anything.'

Shouts echoed out as people ran past the building.

Rebecca looked back from the window to the pile of fake guns and army clothing lying on the floor. 'And right now, I'm pretty glad I did.'

'So what do you expect us to do with it all?'

'Help me pull these orange tips off the barrels and then they'll look like the real thing, a deterrent to anyone who thinks about breaking in. It's the only thing I could think of at the time.'

'Why did you think of it at all?' Julie said, as she gingerly picked up a small revolver and attempted to prise off its brightly coloured plug.

'I saw a TV show, it was selling products to protect against intruders in case of civil unrest after the meteor hit. It gave me the idea that we needed to do something just in case. A kind man I recently met let me have all this on loan; he said it wasn't really in saleable condition anyway, so he was happy to lend it out to me.'

'Nice guy,' Julie said, as she moved on to tackle an assault rifle.

After they had made all the guns look more realistic, they sorted through the clothing. They kitted out Joseph in a flak jacket and, along with his camos, some black boots and a balaclava; he looked extremely imposing.

'I've been teaching him to cock this pretend shotgun,' Rebecca said to Julie, as she handed Joseph the weapon. He pumped it on cue and a blue and metal shell popped out of the ejection port. His grin shone though the balaclava's mouth opening. 'He looks intimidating, doesn't he?' Rebecca said, surveying her handiwork.

'You could say that,' Julie said, watching Joseph walk about parading his shotgun and doing a little dance. 'I'm not sure that the dance will scare anyone, though.'

Rebecca smiled despite the situation they found themselves in.

'I didn't think you liked him to get into that sort of thing?' Julie said. 'Guns and stuff.'

'I don't ... or I didn't, anyway. I realised, though, that this meteorite was going to change the world we live in more than I'd really wanted to admit to myself. Times are changing and in most cases not for the better; if this helps to protect us all then I can live with it.'

They sorted through more of the clothing and Rebecca selected a small yet heavy black vest, lined with some kind of metal plate. Desert coloured trousers rolled up at the hems and wrist guards completed her ensemble.

Julie, garbed in a similar fashion, pulled on her balaclava. 'How do I look?' she said, doing a little twirl.

'Not bad; pick up the rifle.'

Julie picked it up and slung it around her neck with the strap.

'Excellent, you look quite the terrorist. I wouldn't want to mess with you.' Rebecca was relatively pleased, although Julie didn't appear as frightening as she'd hoped she would. Instead she looked like a small woman in outsized clothing. The gun, however, was the one bit of the costume that would make anyone think twice; that was the plan, anyway.

They de-masked and Rebecca went to tell the others they would guard the front entrance. Maria, unsurprisingly, voiced the loudest criticism of the plan, which Rebecca duly ignored before rejoining Julie and Joseph, who now occupied the main lobby overlooking the street. It was a little quieter now, the mob having moved on to pastures new, and they sat for some time, playing I spy to while away the boredom. Joseph had taken his colouring book along to keep him occupied, but he still wore his mask, which he'd grown attached to.

Julie had tried to take it off him at one point, but he'd got angry so she'd let him be. Tired now, the three comrades in arms got comfortable and, one by one ... drifted off to sleep.

Rebecca woke some time later. The lights were off and she discerned the slow breathing of Julie and Joseph close by. She wondered what time it was, and then she heard it – a quiet clicking noise, click, click ... click. The sound stopped, and then, after a while, started again. Click, click ... click echoed in the silence, and Rebecca, her ears out on stalks, strove to make out what it was.

It came from the door.

Why are the lights out? she wondered, as she stretched and gave a stifled yawn. Julie must have turned them off after I dropped off, she decided.

A dark room, however, didn't show off their array of fake firepower; not much of a deterrent to potential looters and rioters. She got up and felt her way to the light switch. As she pressed the button the light came on, but at almost the same moment the main door swung silently inwards.

Rebecca froze. In the doorway stood two men looking as startled as she must have done as the now-illuminated lobby laid all bare. One of the men held a pistol in his right hand; the other, a crowbar and a small multi-tool. Rebecca didn't understand why they weren't moving. The man in front looked down to the floor near where she'd been asleep; Rebecca followed his gaze, her eyes settling on her replica AK-47 BB gun. Julie stirred in her slumber, her own fake assault rifle on the floor at her feet.

Rebecca's mind raced. The two men were obviously breaking in and the sound she'd heard, which had probably been what woke her up, had been one of them picking the locks. They, on the other hand, were greeted by a disturbing scene: three people in a now brightly lit room. Two were asleep and one was staring right at them. Perhaps most worrying for them, was that all three were heavily armed.

Counter to this fact, the formidable weapons rested on the floor, all except for the one held by the sleeping Joseph who cradled the pretend shotgun like a babe in his arms. The second man, meanwhile, had his own gun firmly in the palm of his hand.

Obviously deciding it was worth the risk despite the threat, the two men advanced, the pistol now aimed at a terrified Rebecca. The second man put a finger to his lips telling Rebecca to keep silent as they approached Joseph. Just as the first man extended his hand to take Joseph's shotgun, a loud bang outside followed by a scream came from close by. Julie, always the deep sleeper, moved in her sleep once more and didn't waken. Joseph, however, was instantly awake, his wide eyes studying the intruder as he leaned in towards him. With a little giggle Joseph jumped up. Rebecca had forgotten how tall he was. With his imposing balaclava still covering his face, he cocked his shotgun and laughed at the men in front of him. Believing they were in mortal danger from a masked lunatic, they turned tail and fled.

'No, Joseph!' Rebecca cried out, as he went to chase them thinking it a game.

Joseph looked round at her in confusion and Rebecca rushed to the door and slammed it shut.

Julie woke with a start. 'What's going on?'

Rebecca shook her head in disbelief and slumped to the floor, letting out a massive sigh of relief.

A few hours later sirens sounded close by the care home, and soon after that a fire truck drew up outside. Rebecca, now fully alert due to their previous encounter, looked out of the window to see firefighters piling out of their vehicle and rushing to unpack the hoses.

Leaning forwards she pressed her face to the glass to glimpse a deep red glow emanating out onto the front yard of the house next door.

Wisps of ash drifted past the window and she sniffed the air. Smoke, and it wasn't coming from outside as the windows were shut tight. Going over to the wall she turned the butt of her rifle round and smashed the fire alarm, sending a deafening noise ringing throughout the care home. She grabbed Joseph, who had reawakened, chucked his shotgun to one side and threw away his mask, opened the door and went out into the night.

CHAPTER SEVENTEEN

To say Malcolm Joiner was displeased was an understatement. His plan had gone mostly as envisaged – Steiner was held under lock and key, Darklight positions had been retaken and the majority of Steadfast's population were tucked up where they belonged – and yet one major problem remained: Goodwin. He'd evaded him, along with a large Darklight contingent and many thousands of civilians. According to base surveillance they had all relocated to the surface via elevators and exit points which had been somehow jammed open via the computer system. This left Joiner with a few problems.

First, Goodwin had to be prevented from leaving the vicinity. Now that Steiner was taken care of it meant the threat Goodwin posed was reduced, but it was still a threat nonetheless, especially considering Steiner may have passed him sensitive information. If Joiner had any luck, Goodwin would have been detained by the U.S. military, topside, but a second problem had presented itself; since the impact things had changed on the surface drastically, beyond what he'd expected.

Significant worldwide unrest due to the dust cloud spreading much faster than predicted, coupled with China's bold attack on its neighbours, had meant that the United States government had been forced to redistribute troops far and wide in order to defend its borders and citizens. This left Joiner with only a token force on the ground to block and curtail Goodwin's movements. So far this hadn't proved too much of an issue as the evacuees had holed up in a nearby Darklight facility. Joiner wasn't sure what Goodwin intended to do up there, but as long as he stayed put that was fine by him.

What he had been able to do was to cut hard lines and jam wireless communications to Goodwin's new home. The problem had been contained for now which, considering the circumstances, was the best he could hope for.

Joiner's time and work at Steadfast was nearly complete, but he had a few other loose ends to tie up first. He swivelled round in his chair and took in the scene around him, a dense and verdant rainforest, which he guessed was located in South America. *Goodwin's office is plush*, he thought, *and this screen is something else*; he decided he would have it disassembled and shipped to Sanctuary before he left. The real time footage would be pointless, however, since he already saw in the distance the long grasping fingers of the dust cloud, which would soon encompass the blue skies above.

The Darklight base pulsated with a hive of activity as the contractors and civilians sought to prepare themselves for the journey ahead. Two massive multi-tiered personnel carriers, their engines roaring, manoeuvred into position in the complex's vast hangar. Shifting nearly thirty thousand people more than a thousand miles was a logistics nightmare at the best of times, but that combined with the recent global events and people's lack of provisions ensured the situation was chaotic at best.

Goodwin stepped out of the barracks side door and jumped back as a futuristic all-terrain vehicle sped past, belatedly honking its horn. Steadying himself after his near miss he set forth for the security complex on the far side, making sure he stuck to the red-lined pedestrian pathways as he crossed the hangar's expanse. Soldiers in various garbs and units passed by and he had to make another evasive manoeuvre as a small cargo loader trundled past on what he had wrongly assumed was a safe zone for walking. He shouted a half-hearted rebuke at the disappearing rear of the loader; the driver stuck up his hand in apology and carried on to a massive twenty wheel transporter which must have stood some thirty feet in height.

Goodwin knew some private security firms were well equipped, but seeing the resources available at this base was a big eye opener. A small army had assembled itself here, complete with top of the range high spec hardware of almost every description. Having been around U.S.S.B. Steadfast for a number of years he had grown accustomed to military equipment, so he knew high end gear when he saw it. He wouldn't have a clue how to use any of it, of course, as he'd never even fired a gun, let alone one of the high powered beam weapons he'd seen some of the soldiers lugging about.

Finally, and still in one piece, Goodwin reached the facility's main building, where a guard recognised him and waved him through. He now found himself in a large atrium that housed a sweeping reception desk, behind which a huge, polished, stainless steel Darklight emblem hung on the central wall.

Goodwin found this cross over between corporate offices and heavily armed personnel a kind of unnatural oddity; he knew he would never get used to seeing it. In any normal office you saw people walking about in suits or smart casual wear; here, however, he was greeted by a woman wearing heavy armour with a sidearm at her waist and a wicked looking knife strapped to one side of her chest.

'Ah, Director Goodwin, the commander has been expecting you,' she said, giving him a broad smile. 'Take elevator seven to the eighth level, then turn left down to the Canyon Suite.'

Thanking her, Goodwin made his way across a tiled floor which looked like some kind of exotic marble, his crisp footfalls clip-clopping across its unforgiving surface. Inlaid red and silver streaks wove their way sublimely across the expensive substrate, guiding him to the elevator where he pressed a button and waited. Soon after, the polished metal doors slid to one side. Goodwin stepped to his left in order to let out a soldier who was pushing a wheeled crate marked with various hazard symbols. The main one that caught his eye read:

THERMAL SWORD
HANDLE WITH EXTREME CAUTION

He hadn't heard of such a weapon before and he peered at the label on the lid, which showed a technical diagram of the device.

The man noticed him looking. 'They're brand new stock. Came in a few months ago; I don't think they've even been taken out of the crate yet.'

'What are they for?' Goodwin said, curious.

'Apart from carving up the enemy in close quarter combat, they cut through metals; not the harder types, but steel, aluminium, stuff like that. Hot knife through butter,' the man said with a grin on his face.

Goodwin gave him a nervous smile. Some people got very excited over weapons; *I suppose that's why they joined an outfit like Darklight*, he thought.

'Right, better get on. This little lot is getting dispersed to some lucky officers. They get all the cool stuff,' the soldier said as he moved off, allowing Goodwin to get into the elevator and hit the number eight button.

The doors closed and a low hum sounded as the express elevator delivered him to his floor. Following the signs, Goodwin located the Canyon Suite, and as he entered he saw that it lived up to its name; it was decorated with a complete static surround image of the Grand Canyon, showing it off in all its majesty.

Hilt sat at one end of a jet black rectangular desk, poring over some maps that were laid out in front of him. His rifle hung on the back of his chair and his body armour on the rear of another.

He looked up as Goodwin approached.

'Sir, take a seat,' he said.

'Commander,' Goodwin replied. 'Please feel free to call me Richard if you like.' He was never one for too much formality.

Hilt didn't seem to hear as he slid a map round to show him. 'I've been plotting a course into Mexico. Unfortunately our location doesn't afford us too many options.'

'How so?' Goodwin said.

'The closest and quickest point to cross the border is here.' Hilt pointed at a spot on the map.

'El Paso,' Goodwin read aloud. 'Looks good to me.'

'You would think. However, here,' – Hilt pointed a short distance away – 'is the U.S. Army's second largest installation, Fort Bliss, home to 1AD, the 1st Armoured Division.'

'Ah,' Goodwin said, 'not good.'

'No,' Hilt replied, his voice grave. 'What's worse, Fort Bliss is also home to various 1AD support regiments along with the 32nd Army Air and Missile Defense Command.'

'I'm not sure what that is,' Goodwin said.

'It's a special one off asset that the Army utilises to accomplish all types of missions which require short notice deployment anywhere in the world. Over the last few years the Biggs Army Airfield at Bliss has been overhauled and they now operate highly classified aircraft and drones which police the skies over the Americas and beyond. If we want to get over the border, then passing Fort Bliss would be like running the gauntlet; we'd have to pray the national emergency ensured eyes were looking elsewhere rather than at local roads. Since federal intelligence also has a strong presence at Bliss, Joiner would have direct command channels in place, perhaps resulting in the whole base operating under his control, whether directly or through the Joint Chiefs, which he apparently has significant leverage over.'

'What route do you suggest we take, then?' Goodwin said.

'This one.' The commander ran his finger down the map.

'It looks a lot slower.'

'That's because it is,' Hilt said, 'but not as suicidal as going past Bliss. It has its own share of risks, however. We'd be taking smaller roads, meaning we would be spread out further, making us more vulnerable to any attack; in such an instance having our force split into two or more groups would be a real possibility.'

'How would we cross the border?'

'We'd pass through Big Bend National Park and create a hole where we see fit. I imagine about here.' He pointed at the map once more. 'Satellite imagery will tell me more.'

'Won't the Mexican military or Border Control notice such a large breach into their territory? We're not exactly going to be inconspicuous, looking at the size of some of the machinery you've got out there.'

'They'll hopefully have their hands full with their own population control to be looking at such a little used section of the border. We'll also have one big advantage, regardless of where we cross.'

'And that is?' Goodwin said.

'Cloud cover. According to reports, AG5's dust cloud will be hitting the East Coast of the United States in,' – he looked at his watch – 'a few hours' time.'

'And that will help how?'

'People will be disorientated and preoccupied. Also, all our vehicles are equipped with Blackout Systems, enabling us to drive without any lights. We'll go dark. Add to that the sudden lack of real-time satellite imagery that militaries the world over rely heavily on to monitor ground movements, and we have a fair chance of getting through.'

'Undetected?'

'Unlikely. Resign yourself to the fact that we will encounter resistance to our relocation from either U.S. or Mexican forces at some point. If things go our way casualties should be minimal on both sides.'

'It sounds like you've thought of everything, Commander,' Goodwin said, trying to ignore the fact that further bloodshed might be unavoidable. 'Good job.'

'Thank you, sir.'

Goodwin sat back. 'I have to say, I'm impressed by this base and its equipment. I didn't realise Darklight had such resources available to it.'

Hilt smiled. 'You should see our North American headquarters up in Washington State.'

'Big?' Goodwin said.

'Perhaps ten times the size of this one.'

Goodwin whistled. 'I bet the Government doesn't like that on their soil.'

'You'd think, but security is big business. Besides, we're contracted out to many of America's largest companies on a regular basis. The government itself also uses us for covert black ops unable to be carried out by their own forces.'

Goodwin didn't like to ask what kind of operations they were hired for; in fact, he felt he'd rather not know. Private security was a highly secretive business and one didn't pry into it too deeply. He believed Darklight operated mostly under the GMRC remit, which meant they weren't sent into controversial secret wars – as far as he knew, anyway.

'Sir, may I ask you some questions?' the commander said.

'Of course.'

'As you told me, we're heading to U.S.S.B. Sanctuary, and the coordinates you gave me are as Professor Steiner indicated.'

Goodwin nodded.

'The location is approximately two hundred miles north of Mexico's capital city,' Hilt continued. 'The area we will pass into is in the south of the Sierra Madre Oriental mountain range and the exact location is about five thousand feet above sea level.'

'Will this prove a problem for the vehicles?' Goodwin asked.

'It shouldn't as they're designed for all terrains and such an elevation is well within their capability.'

'Regardless of the type of access roads to the site?' Goodwin said.

'The roads may prove a problem, but we have the necessary equipment and skill sets to negotiate any tricky passes we may encounter.'

'So what's the problem?'

'When we get to this *back door* that will take us into the base, will it be under surveillance? I would guess almost certainly. Will it be guarded? Perhaps; but most importantly, will it be locked? Most assuredly. How then are we going to get in? You told me we would discuss this matter at a later date and it is now a later date. I need to know your plan.'

'I'm sorry, Commander, I should have brought this up first.'

'Not a problem, sir. I just think that we are going into the unknown. I need to know all there is to know to make the most informed decision to ensure the safety of those under my command. We are heading into the lion's den, so to speak. We are looking to evade the U.S. military, although we may perhaps engage them further, and yet we are heading towards one of their strongholds, a place of which we know very little. If I may be blunt, it seems a little insane.'

'All valid points, Commander, and your fears are ones that I share. The professor was very clear, however; we must get to Sanctuary, even though it seems counterintuitive to do so. I trust the man with my life and with the lives of those under my care. The entrance we're to exploit is rarely used, according to the professor, and he should know as he helped design all U.S. subterranean bases, including Sanctuary. If anyone knows the best way in, it will be him. The professor also supplied me with a piece of software, more like code actually, that will ensure we can get at least part way inside.'

'Part way?'

'The code itself looks very similar to that used at Steadfast's entrances,' Goodwin said. 'Once we breach Sanctuary's surface facility I will then get in touch with a contact on the inside who will help gain us full access to the elevator shafts.'

'The contact is a reliable one?'

'I hope so. It's a General Ellwood. Have you heard of him?'

The commander shook his head.

'Neither have I. Well, by the sound of it, he owes Professor Steiner some kind of favour.'

'A favour?' Hilt said with concern. 'I hope it's a big one.'

'So do I, but that's all we've got.'

'And this general will let thousands of refugees and heavily armed contractors into his base?'

'I didn't get the impression Ellwood was in charge of the base, but he's high enough up to be able to help us. The professor did say that we wouldn't be able to let the general know how many of us there are, otherwise he would baulk. I'll tell him it's twenty or so people and we'll have to hope our approach is unseen.'

'Is that going to be possible?' Hilt asked. 'Our convoy will be extensive.'

'You said it yourself, satellite imagery will be down, cloud cover will be overhead and your vehicles can operate with stealth. Besides, if Sanctuary is operating on the same protocols as Steadfast, then it will be sealed tight so there will be no need for the base to be looking groundward.'

Hilt seemed satisfied with Goodwin's answers. *He'll have to be*, Goodwin thought, *it's all I've got*. 'Moving on to transportation,' Goodwin continued, 'will there be enough room for everyone? It took scores of trips to get us this far, and that's just twenty kilometres, with some people walking part of the way. Surely even this base isn't prepared to relocate the mass of people we've brought with us?'

'You forget,' Hilt said, 'Darklight has helped relocate millions of people from the African states. We're geared up for large scale evacuations, it's what we do.' The Darklight leader walked to the nearest wall and pressed a button, which sent one side of the room's Grand Canyon frieze rolling up into the ceiling.

Goodwin joined the commander at the newly revealed window and looked down into another section of the compound, previously hidden from view. This second hangar, albeit two-thirds empty, contained another two dozen enormous multi-tiered personnel carriers, machines with a capacity ten times that of civilian coaches. Alongside these, other types of smaller transporters had been assembled, all of which were being prepped for departure.

'Impressive,' Goodwin said, 'but it still doesn't look enough, not by half.'

'If we were at full capacity then it wouldn't be an issue,' Hilt said, 'but no, you're right; at the moment we aren't geared for such large scale movement of personnel. Twenty-five thousand civilians plus five thousand Darklight contractors, that's a lot of bodies.'

'Enough to fill a small sports stadium,' Goodwin agreed.

'We're going to have to overload the troop carriers,' Hilt said, 'and every other vehicle for that matter, perhaps by over seventy-five per cent.'

'That sounds excessive.'

'It's the only option we have. It'll be tight and uncomfortable, but it'll do.'

'I suppose comfortable travel is not really our highest concern at the moment,' Goodwin said, with little humour.

'No,' Hilt agreed. 'What is our concern is the DEFCON level; it was already high due to the meteorite, but since China's nuclear attack on our allies SAC is at DEFCON 1 and the pistol is cocked.'

'SAC?'

'Strategic Air Command. The rest of the armed forces are at DEFCON 2.'

'DEFCON 1? That's unprecedented, isn't it?'

Hilt nodded, his expression solemn. 'Even during the Cuban missile crisis, the highest level reached was two.'

'And I take it that's bad for us?'

'It will mean all U.S. military divisions will have their fingers on or near the trigger. Tensions will be running high. Add to this fact the dust cloud and satellite blindness and you've got a powder keg. We do have some good news, however. I've called in a Darklight aircraft carrier, the Phoenix, to assist us. It has full air support capability, although high altitude missions are off limits due to the cloud's particulates.'

'Won't it take some time to get here?' Goodwin said, knowing that ships moved relatively slowly.

'Ordinarily yes, but Professor Steiner told me to activate our top assets when he called Darklight into Steadfast, so the ship is already positioned in the Gulf of Mexico.'

Thank you, Professor, Goodwin thought, *your foresight is helping even now.* 'Have you got anything else up your sleeve?' Goodwin asked Hilt hopefully.

The commander smiled. 'That's pretty much it, although we do have helicopter gunships at this base. We won't make them airborne to avoid attracting attention, but they can be deployed from their transporters while on the move.'

'Nice,' said Goodwin. 'We obviously want to avoid any kind of battles though; the people we're going to come up against aren't our enemy.'

'Tell that to Malcolm Joiner,' Hilt said. 'We're trying to save lives and anyone in our way will try to prevent us with deadly force; that makes them an enemy in my book. Every soldier knows the risks of their duty. Sometimes they will find themselves on the wrong side, depending on perspective, that's just part of the job. It's what we sign up for.'

Goodwin still felt concerned and it must have shown.

'We will obviously try to avoid engaging anyone, be they American or Mexican,' Hilt told him, 'but, as I said before, it will be a miracle if we get to the co-ordinates without any casualties. I think the question you must ask yourself is, do you believe what we are doing is the right option?'

'The professor does and that's good enough for me.'

'Then we must stay the course.'

Goodwin nodded, more confident now. 'They are wise words, Commander, and I thank you for them. It won't stop me from praying for that miracle, though.'

'Amen to that, sir,' Hilt said. 'Amen to that.'

Goodwin was resting in his temporary quarters at the compound when a sharp knock came on the door. 'Come in,' he said, sitting up on the edge of his bed.

The door opened to reveal a civilian aide. 'It's happening, sir.'

'Right.' Goodwin got to his feet, donned his coat and followed the man into the corridor, where many others also hurried towards the exit.

Outside, the stars shone brightly in the crisp, cold night air, while a full moon cast subtle shadows on the ground, its silken light gleaming in the dark. Thousands of people gathered en masse, Darklight contractors and civilians alike, all eyes turned upwards to the heavens.

Some people pointed off to the east and a low chatter rippled through the crowd as expectations grew. And then Goodwin saw it, or rather its effects. Stars in the distance disappeared one by one as though snuffed out by a great hand, like a flame on a candle. The sky behind it appeared as black as death's cold void. The stars directly above them were reached as the dust cloud continued its unstoppable advance, their eternal light extinguished in the blink of an eye. The Moon came next, allowing the cloud to be glimpsed directly as it moved ominously past.

After what seemed like only seconds the night sky had turned pitch-black.

Eternal night was finally upon them.

A few hours later Hilt informed Goodwin that the forces Joiner must have sent to block their escape had been taken care of. According to the commander, they had been overcome with relative ease since they consisted of regulars and were short on numbers. They would be detained and then released at a later date.

Dawn broke with an empty promise when they moved out an hour or so later. No sunrise greeted them, only more of the dense, pervading darkness. The mood of the civilians mirrored that of the sky above and the soldiers were grim-faced and melancholy. To top off the darkness outside all vehicles operated under low interior lighting and zero external lights due to the order to utilise Blackout Systems. To any external witness the convoy, despite its size, would meld into the background of the New Mexico scrubland, the only clue as to its location the roar of the large personnel carriers moving at the core of the procession.

Heading towards Santa Fe, they were quickly on to one of the main trunk roads. The curfew, still in effect, ensured easy passage although they did go by two National Guard units which must have noticed the two hundred plus vehicles as they shot past them at a rate of knots. They were not pursued, however, and why would they be? Such a large armed contingent must be government-run – at least that's what Goodwin hoped any onlookers would assume.

Goodwin rode in the lead personnel carrier, seated on the edge of an aisle seat next to Kara Vandervoort. Conditions were predictably cramped and the air was thick with warmth, the results of a few hundred people confined in the space meant for nearly half their number. The blacked out windows provided no view of the outside and even if they had, the darkness would have shown them little on the open roads.

The door to the driver's cab opened in front of Goodwin and a soldier poked his head out. 'Can you come up front, sir, the commander is on the com.'

Goodwin nodded, gave Kara a comforting smile and followed the man into the vehicle's cockpit. Three men sat up front with an array of screens, buttons and dials surrounding them, the ice-blue lights of the consoles glowing against the low-lit red illumination the soldiers operated under. A head-up display on the main arching window portrayed a green image of the road ahead. From the personnel carrier's elevated vantage point they could see nearly to the front of the mechanised caravan, where Goodwin knew Hilt was located in the lead vehicle.

'Put this on, Director.' A soldier passed him a small, one-sided headset.

Goodwin held the device up to his ear. 'Commander?'

'Sir, we're coming up to a police checkpoint in the centre of the city,' Hilt said. 'We're going to be stopping while I secure us passage. I'll keep you apprised.'

'We're in Santa Fe, I didn't realise?'

'Yes, sir.'

Goodwin looked at the edges of the display, now able to make out the street lighting and buildings around them, each a varying shade of green. 'Do you need any help?'

'No, it should be fine. If you stay on the radio I'll open the mic up so you can hear the exchange.'

'Very good, Commander.'

'We're stopping now,' Hilt said. 'Stand by.'

The military trucks ahead slowed, then pulled up, and Goodwin's personnel carrier lurched as it came to a halt behind them.

'Sorry, sir,' the soldier driving said, in apology for the jerky stop. 'The vehicle's not designed to carry this kind of load.'

'No need to apologise,' Goodwin told him as he listened in on the radio to Hilt ordering two of his men to accompany him.

A muffled rustling sound indicated the Darklight officer had exited from his transport.

'Safeties off,' Goodwin heard the commander say as he made his way to the police ahead of him.

'I'm patching through the feed from the commander's head camera,' the driver told Goodwin, tapping away on some keys.

A full colour screen powered up just above the windscreen displaying an image of a large, permanent checkpoint installation around which a few police officers loitered. With the floodlights blazing down, an officer advanced to meet the Darklight commander as he approached. Goodwin heard the footfalls of the men cease as they stopped in front of each other.

'I don't recognise your unit, soldier,' the policeman said in a confrontational tone.

'We're covert ops,' Hilt said with authority. 'Lower your barriers so we can pass through. We're on a tight schedule.'

'We can't do that, I'm afraid, sir,' a second police officer told him. 'We have an itinerary of all military movements in this area and you're not on the list.'

Goodwin cursed, but Hilt remained as calm as ever.

'I understand your predicament,' Hilt said, 'but in light of recent events the schedule has changed. We're on DEFCON 1; do you know what that means?'

'That we're on high alert?' the first officer said.

His colleague shook his head. 'No, five is the highest alert, idiot.'

'DEFCON 1 is the highest,' Hilt said, correcting him. 'And that means I can pretty much do what I want, so if you don't get that barrier down, I'll tear it down.'

The police officers looked at Hilt for a moment, then at each other, before moving away a few paces where they entered into a heated discussion. A few seconds later the first man walked off, while the second turned back to Hilt.

'We'll just get confirmation from Fort Bliss; it won't take long.'

The view from Hilt's camera swung ninety degrees. 'Jam communications, Lieutenant,' Hilt said under his breath, apparently to a Darklight officer who was also listening in. 'Prepare to pacify. Wound only, no kill shots.'

Goodwin suddenly had a thought. 'Commander, can you hear me?'

'Go ahead, sir.'

'There is an emergency command code that gives me the authority in extreme circumstances to override civilian authorities, including the police.'

'Belay my last,' Hilt told his men. 'Do you have the code, sir?' he asked Goodwin.

'I have it on my phone, hang on.' Goodwin took out his computer phone and unfolded its larger display. He navigated to his Steadfast control file and bored into subfolders until he found what he was searching for. 'I have it, Commander, civilian override GMRC protocol nine five sigma. Code five eight nine seven six dash X-ray X-ray Quebec eight Kilo. They will need to confirm by contacting GMRC dispatch, but it should work.'

'As long as Joiner hasn't deactivated your clearance,' Hilt said.

Goodwin hadn't thought of that. 'Let's hope he hasn't had time.'

Hilt turned back to the policeman who waited for his superior to return. 'Officer, I have a GMRC code for you to verify.'

The man took the code and radioed it through to his sergeant, while Hilt told his men to cease jamming and waited for a response. Goodwin held onto the back of a chair, his fingers digging into the cloth as the tension rose.

Finally the first officer reappeared and waved them through as the hydraulic metal barriers slowly lowered.

'Good job, sir,' Hilt told him as he made his way back to the convoy.

'Thanks,' Goodwin said in relief, his grip relaxing, 'that was touch and go.'

'Indeed. Let's roll out,' Hilt said, as he swung back into his seat and slammed the door shut.

Goodwin's video feed was cut and their personnel carrier's massive engines roared back to life.

It wasn't long before they had regained speed and ploughed ahead into the darkness once more, heading east along I-25. They weren't on the interstate for long before they turned right onto a smaller road heading due south. Goodwin put down his headset and moved back to his seat, but before he could get there they slowed again and came to a sharp stop, forcing him to grab onto an armrest in order to maintain his footing.

'You better put this back on, sir,' a Darklight operative told him, holding out the communication device Goodwin had just discarded.

'Commander?' Goodwin said into the microphone as he returned to the driver's cab.

'Yes, sir,' Hilt replied through the earpiece. 'We've been scanning the area ahead to ensure we don't run into any more unexpected obstacles. It was just as well we did, as there is sizable force coming up a few junctions away.'

'Military?' Goodwin said.

'U.S. Army, by the looks of it. We could take them out, but I know you want to avoid such a confrontation.'

'What do you propose we do?'

'We're not sure if they're even trying to intercept us,' Hilt said. 'They could just be on their way to any number of locales in the southern states. If we turn around and cut west we can take the I-40 and rejoin the I-25 south for a distance. We can then take a left towards Roswell, hopefully bypassing the Army, and carry on our way towards the national park. The only problem is that this will take us much closer to Fort Bliss than I would like.'

'I suppose we don't have much of a choice, do we?

'Not really, sir.'

'That would also mean we'd have to pass through another city, wouldn't it?'

'Albuquerque, yes, sir.'

Goodwin paused trying to think of alternatives, but he had none. 'Do it, Commander.'

'Very good, sir.'

Two hundred plus vehicles carried out a one hundred and eighty degree turn.

As they picked up speed again, the lead vehicles shot past them as Hilt took point once more.

'Keep me updated, Commander,' Goodwin told him.

'Of course, sir.'

Goodwin passed back the headset to the soldier and made his way out of the cabin to rejoin the other civilians. He sat down next to a quizzical Kara.

'Problems?' she asked.

'Nothing major,' he said. There wasn't any point in worrying her or the rest of the people onboard any more than they already had been. He settled back into his chair and made a silent prayer for some better fortune as the convoy rattled on into the gloom.

CHAPTER EIGHTEEN

THE GENERALS of U.S.S.B. Steadfast had been called to the Command Centre for an emergency meeting by the Intelligence Director, Malcolm Joiner. Following the infiltration by the Darklight private security firm, the Joint Chiefs had ordered a military intervention. As ever, Malcolm Joiner had stuck his nose into the operation, utilising his own operatives to run parts of the campaign. The generals disliked the power the Intelligence Director had over them, but they were more concerned by the control he apparently exerted over the Joint Chiefs themselves. Virtually anything he wanted was sanctioned, and now that he had Professor Steiner under arrest on spurious grounds, effectively relieving him of his command, and Richard Goodwin had fled the base, the man was in an unassailable position.

They were discussing their options when Joiner came into the room, flanked by one of his agents. The tall, greying Director sat down at one end of the table, away from the military men who had gradually fallen silent at his arrival.

'What is the meaning of this meeting, Director?' General Shultz demanded. 'You've had us waiting around for an hour and now you turn up without any hint of an apology or even an excuse.'

Joiner ignored him and held out his hand to the man who now stood to one side and slightly behind his superior. The operative pulled out a folder from a satchel and passed it forwards. Joiner took it and placed it on the table in front of him. Smoothing the front cover down with his palm, he opened the document and put on his spectacles. He appeared to read for a moment and then closed the folder again, removed his glasses and tucked them back into his front pocket.

'It seems, gentlemen,' Joiner said, in his nasal voice, 'that you will all be relocating to U.S.S.B. Sanctuary.' He paused to let his words sink in. 'With immediate effect.'

The generals were instantly up in arms. A couple stood up, unable to contain their anger, as they all voiced their outrage at such a move. Joiner merely sat and watched them with no sign of emotion or reaction. They fell silent one by one when it became apparent that Joiner wouldn't respond until he had their full attention once again.

'Finished?' he asked them insolently. 'Excellent. This command has come from the Joint Chiefs.' He took a sheet of paper from the folder and passed it to his armed aide, who handed it to General Shultz. The general read it and then threw it in disgust to his colleague sitting next to him.

'How did you swing this?' Shultz said, incredulous. 'You can't leave the base without military leaders and the Joint Chiefs would not give this kind of order unless they had been forced into it.'

'Sadly, the request was not from me in this instance,' Joiner said. 'I would rather let you all stay here to rot, but it seems you all have friends in higher places and in order to keep the peace I am ensuring the Joint Chiefs get what they want.'

'Not dancing to your tune for once, eh?' another general said with venom.

'Oh, they'll follow my direction, as well you all know, but even I must make the occasional concession and it turns out that you're it. You will be travelling under my control and without any of your forces. You may pack the bare essentials and your families are being rounded up as we speak.'

'You better treat my children with care, Joiner,' another general said, standing up menacingly, 'or I'll throttle your scraggy little neck!'

The intelligence operative's hand went to his sidearm, but Joiner gestured to his man to stand down. 'Your *get* are being well looked after, General,' Joiner said, his emotionless eyes boring into him.

The general held his gaze until Joiner, unfazed, looked around at the others in the room. He stood. 'My agents will ensure you are ready to depart at twelve hundred hours. Good day, gentlemen.' Joiner left without another word, his bodyguard opening the door for him and then swiftly following the Director out of the room. The doors to the room swung shut and the generals were left alone once more, the unusual sensation of impotency upon them.

CIA Special Operations Agent Myers was waiting for Malcolm Joiner as he came out of his brief meeting with Steadfast's generals.

'Sir, reporting as ordered,' Myers said, as he fell into step with his boss.

'We're leaving Steadfast at twelve hundred hours and the generals and their families will be joining us,' Joiner told him.

'We, sir?'

'The whole intelligence division at this base.'

'Everyone, sir?'

Joiner strode along the corridor of the Command Centre, which still bore the extensive scars inflicted by the firefight a few days before. 'You heard me, Agent.'

'Can I ask where we are relocating to, sir?'

'Sanctuary,' Joiner said in distraction. 'I want you to gather together computer and structural engineers and welders from the civilian workforce and the army. I want them topside in an hour.'

'Will they be coming to Sanctuary as well?' Myers said.

'Yes.'

'And their families too?'

Joiner scowled. 'If they must.'

'Sir?'

'Yes. Gather up their families and then we can get out of this godforsaken hole.'

'Very good, sir.'

Joiner slowed his walk as his thoughts returned to the source of his disquiet. 'What is the situation with Goodwin on the surface?'

'As far as we're aware he's still at the Darklight base,' Myers said. 'The army's monitoring the situation; do you want me to send in some agents to keep an eye on things?'

Joiner considered the question for a moment. 'No,' he said at last, 'just keep me apprised of any developments.'

Myers nodded and turned to walk off to carry out his orders.

'Oh, and Myers.'

'Yes, sir?'

'Get a couple of workers to take down the screen in Goodwin's office, along with the tech that powers it. I want it boxed up and shipped with us.'

'Certainly, sir,' Myers said, as he withdrew his phone to make the necessary arrangements.

A few hours later a group of black SUVs had assembled at the main surface entrance to U.S.S.B. Steadfast. Joiner had been waiting for Agent Myers, who was inside the topside complex overseeing the final preparations before their departure. Unfortunately he was failing to perform his designated tasks, as he'd called in Joiner to speak to one of the engineers who was apparently giving him grief.

'What is the problem here, why isn't work underway?' Joiner said, approaching a man who was arguing fiercely with Myers.

'This idiot expects me to cross weld the exits and disable the elevator mechanisms,' the engineer told Joiner. 'He's lost his mind!'

Myers looked exasperated and he stepped to one side, enabling his Director to take the lead.

'I want these exits sealed and the elevators permanently decommissioned,' Joiner said, 'it's a matter of great importance.'

'I won't do it,' the engineer said.

'Then I'll get someone who will.'

The man blinked a few times as he computed that information. 'No one will do what you want,' the engineer said, outraged at the suggestion he might be replaced.

Two other engineers who were present voiced their agreement.

'I don't understand why you would want to prevent anyone from Steadfast getting to the surface,' the main engineer continued. 'It doesn't make any sense and it also condemns hundreds of thousands of people to virtual imprisonment.'

'My reasons are none of your concern, and you are here to complete tasks as ordered, not to question them,' Joiner told him, and then considered the man for a moment. 'If you must know, there is an outbreak of a potentially deadly virus which has to be prevented from reaching the surface,' he said, hoping his lie would be accepted. He was to be disappointed, however.

'A virus, you expect me to believe that?' the engineer scoffed. 'There's no virus down there, we'd have been issued with quarantine protocols if there was.'

Joiner's agitation spiked and he moved in close to the man's face. 'I'll give you one last chance to reconsider your position,' he said with barely concealed anger. 'Things will not go well for you if you don't comply.'

'Comply, what kind of talk is that? I don't respond well to threats, so you can take your orders and stuff them where the sun don't shine.'

Joiner had had enough. He turned to Myers, who stood close by. 'Make an example of this man, Agent,' Joiner said.

Agent Myers acknowledged Joiner's order and understood its connotations. He moved past his superior, pulled out his silenced gun and shot the engineer once in the head. The man slumped to the ground, stone dead.

The remaining two senior engineers cried out in terror at what had just transpired. One leaned against a wall and retched while the other looked to be in shock as he stared wide-eyed at the body prone at his feet.

Joiner waited in calm disinterest until the two men had regained some of their senses. 'Now, I want those exits and elevators sealed and disabled within the day. Agent Myers will oversee your work; make sure it meets his requirements otherwise you'll be facing the same fate as your friend here.' He indicated the body on the floor.

The two men stared at him, uncomprehending.

'DO YOU UNDERSTAND?!' Myers shouted at them, stepping forwards, his hand once more on the grip of his firearm.

The engineers nodded woodenly.

'Do your job and keep quiet about this incident,' Joiner told them, 'and you and your families will be rewarded with top class accommodation at U.S.S.B. Sanctuary.' He walked away, beckoning Myers alongside. 'Get rid of that body.'

'Yes, sir. What about his family?'

'Drop them off in the nearest town.'

'What should I tell them?'

'I don't know,' Joiner said in annoyance. 'Make something up. When the workmen have finished their jobs, round them up and dispose of them.'

'Sir?'

'You heard me. The elevator shaft would be an appropriate place for an accident, don't you think?'

'Yes, sir,' Myers said, his face deadpan. 'And *their* families?'

Joiner glared at him. 'Do I have to think of everything? Drop them off with the others. Tell them they will be relocated and reunited with their loved ones in a few weeks' time.'

'Yes, sir, very good.'

Joiner strode off leaving Myers behind to clear up the mess. The two remaining engineers stood forlornly next to their dead colleague, unaware that their fate was already set in stone.

Colonel Samson had been receiving phone calls from all over Steadfast. Since the evacuation of about five per cent of the civilian population – many of whom ran the command centre – and the battle between the army and Darklight forces, unrest and panic had spread throughout the base. This was to be expected, of course; however, he was now getting calls from military personnel who were unable to get in touch with any of the base's generals. Word had reached him that a meeting had been seen taking place earlier in the day between Intelligence Director Joiner and the top brass. Since then there had been no sign of them and Samson had got that uneasy feeling that things were far from right.

Other colonels operated on the base, but due to his position on Special Forces he was looked upon as more of a leader than the rest. His phone bleeped again. Taking it out, he hit *reject call*. He'd had enough of this. Striding along a corridor and down a flight of stairs, he flung open some double doors and moved into a loading bay. Off to one side crouched a man working on the bodywork of a small, open-top military truck. Without breaking stride Samson hopped onto the back of the vehicle and jumped into the driver's seat. Starting it up, he sped off, heading for the Command Centre and leaving a startled looking mechanic in his wake.

Ten minutes later Samson arrived at the large plaza, which was still littered with signs of the carnage that had taken place during the assault. He cut the engine and vaulted out onto the paving stones, his boots crunching down onto shattered glass that had been missed in the clear up. Stalking through the main entrance and up an escalator, he took a flight of stairs up to the next floor, where he found an elevator still in operation. A short time later he was barging open the doors to the main control room, where Nathan Bryant had been installed by Joiner to temporarily control the base.

'Colonel, to what do I owe the pleasure of your company?' Bryant said, his tone scathing.

'What are you playing at?' Samson said. 'This base is a complete mess. Systems are failing all over the place and some barracks are without any power.'

'What do you expect to happen when most of the people who have the expertise to analyse and control this place are forced to evacuate by you and your cronies?'

Samson suppressed a snarl. 'Joiner is no friend of mine.'

'Then why are you carrying out his orders like some little errand boy?'

'Careful, Bryant,' Samson said, his expression darkening, 'don't push me.'

Nathan laughed at him. 'What do I care what you do to me? I've betrayed my friend, resulting in his imprisonment and the deaths of innocent civilians. I'm past caring, so why don't you just fuck off and leave me alone.'

Samson's blood boiled over and his hand strayed to his rifle.

'Go on, then!' Bryant said, goading him. 'You love to kill don't you? Why not me? Add me to your ever growing list.'

Samson realised the man wasn't in his right mind and his fury dissipated. Out of habit he removed one of his pills, which he chewed before swallowing.

'If you'd care to let out the professor,' Nathan continued, 'then things may go our way a bit. I'm not sure if you've noticed, but Joiner and your beloved generals have left you in the lurch.'

'What do you mean?' Samson said as his calm returned.

'One of the systems indicated a malfunction with the elevator shafts; I had some computer specialists check it out. It seems they've been completely disabled from the surface.'

'That doesn't matter,' Samson said, 'we're under lockdown anyway. The meteor hit, didn't it?'

'Of course it hit, but if we're in lockdown why has Joiner left, along with the generals and his whole Intelligence team? Lockdown is lockdown, no ifs and buts, and yet he's high-tailed it out of here, along with Goodwin and Darklight. Seems to me everyone's leaving but us.' Nathan's eyes went distant and his voice grew quiet. 'We're up shit creek in more ways than you could know.'

'What did you say?' Samson said, but Bryant didn't reply. Samson had to agree the man had a point. *Perhaps I should let the professor out*, he thought. *Fuck! I hate these damn people and their politics.* He gave a growl of frustration and left Bryant in the Control Centre, and headed back downstairs. A few floors down he emerged from a stairwell and met up with two of his Terra Force team outside Steiner's makeshift cell.

'Open it up,' he said.

One of the men produced a key card and unlocked the door.

Samson entered to find Steiner sitting in his chair eating some food.

'Ah, Colonel, joining me for a spot of lunch?' the professor said, his manner far too jovial for Samson's liking.

He gritted his teeth. 'Get up and get out.'

'I don't think it's time for my walk yet, that's normally in a few hours' time. If you'd care to wait awhile, I'd be happy for you to join me.'

'Get up,' Samson said, struggling to contain his irritation. 'You're free to go.'

Steiner looked at him for a moment, perhaps to see if he was being serious. If Steiner had known him at all, he would have known that Samson never joked. Not bothering to wait any longer in the man's company, he walked back out of the room. 'Men, on me,' Samson said as he passed the soldiers, who followed him away from Steiner's room, now open and unguarded.

Professor Steiner sat looking at the open door. He'd been a prisoner since the Command Centre had been overrun by the military, acting on Joiner's orders. He'd been fed and allowed out for the occasional walk, but he'd been denied access to any communication devices and he had no idea what the status of the base was or how the impact had affected the planet. Since he had been preparing for the impact for the last twenty-nine years, it was extremely frustrating, to say the least, that he'd missed the event and also been unable to help the GMRC respond to it. Still, the bulk of his work had long since been finalised, so he felt confident that the global community would have reacted appropriately.

What concerned him was Goodwin and his evacuees, and the hundreds of thousands of people left behind in Steadfast. He was also confused about being let out. What was Joiner up to now? Why lock him up for days on end and then suddenly let him go? It made no sense. *If you stay sitting here, you old fool*, he thought to himself, *you'll never find out*. He finished off his meal and drank the rest of his water, then got up and walked out into freedom; his first port of call the Control Centre. He was soon walking through the doors to find Nathan overseeing a chaotic scene. Warning lights flashed on displays all over the room and telephones rang off the hook. A full contingent of staff occupied the workstations, but apparently none of them knew what they were doing.

'Where is that air system failing?!' Nathan shouted to a man over the far side of the room.

'I don't know, the power grid sensors for that section are down!'

Nathan threw his hands up in disgust.

'Problems?' Steiner said mildly.

Nathan looked round to see his friend standing behind him. 'Professor!' He strode over and embraced him. 'Am I glad to see you! Samson let you out, then?'

'He did. I take it this mess is the reason why?'

'Yes, it seems we're suffering power failures all over the base and critical systems are beginning to switch to backups. I don't know why it's all happening, but it started getting bad in the last twelve hours or so.'

'You haven't been able to rectify any of it?'

'With this lot and me in charge? Not a chance. Most of the people here have been brought in from other divisions; they don't have the expertise. Perhaps if the system was stable, we'd be just about okay, but time is not on our side right now.'

Steiner took off his jacket and hung it on the back of a nearby chair. He rolled up his sleeves, interlaced his fingers and stretched them out with the satisfying sound of cracking joints. 'Let's see what we can do.'

Nathan moved to one side, enabling Steiner to access the main command console. He tapped away at the keys. Windows and data sprang onto the screen at dizzying speed as he discarded the graphical user interface and drilled down into the code itself.

It seemed to Steiner that the elevators and exits had been deliberately tampered with. Chunks of data were missing and command lines erased from the system. Shaking his head, he put on a finger circlet and moved to the Control Centre's large wall display. He grabbed a virtual schematics folder and opened an elevator shaft diagram, which he then merged with a live electrical field map. As the two came together, he saw that power supply trunk lines had been cut. He checked the other elevator mechanisms, which showed the same problem.

'It seems when they disabled the elevators they also cut into power lines, quite a few of them.'

'Can't we switch to internal power? The reactors should easily be able to provide us with what we need.'

'Usually, yes, but whoever did this has executed system overrides and massive amounts of computer command structure is just gone. Backups are online, but it's only a matter of time before they start to fail, too.'

'So they've not just trapped us down here, they're trying to slowly kill us by catastrophic system failure?'

'Perhaps,' Steiner said.

'Joiner?' Nathan asked him.

'Who else?'

'He's a piece of work,' someone said from nearby.

Steiner and Nathan looked round to see Colonel Samson standing behind them. The fearsome officer moved past them to look around at the room's array of screens, and said nothing more.

Steiner and Nathan looked at one another, Nathan's eyebrows raised in mock shock that Samson had deigned to join them.

'Did you want something, Colonel?' Steiner said.

'Just trying to find out what's going on and when we can expect normal service to resume.'

'Not yet, awhile, but your presence is actually quite timely.'

Samson turned to face him. 'How so?'

'We need to physically redirect power from non-critical systems. We'll need some technicians, electricians and engineers. I need them rounded up and in a meeting room in less than half hour, can you do that?'

Samson nodded. 'I'll need a list and location for these people.'

'Nathan will help you with that,' Steiner said.

Nathan didn't look too enamoured at the thought of working with the colonel, *but then who would?* Steiner reflected.

With the decision made, the two men left the room while Steiner worked on at the job in hand.

Ten minutes later, Nathan returned to the Control Centre. 'All done?' Steiner asked him.

'Samson's on it,' Nathan said. 'I don't get that man, he's seething with anger one minute and acting like nothing has happened the next.'

'He's a conflicted soul, of that there's no doubt.' Steiner continued to work on Steadfast's systems for a moment before he glanced in Nathan's direction. 'So,' he said, 'what's been happening during my confinement?'

'Goodwin got out with the majority of the Darklight forces.'

'How many civilians did he take with him?' Steiner said, already knowing the answer.

'We're thinking around thirty thousand, but that's a guesstimate, really.'

'Joiner must have acted swiftly to head off my evacuation command.'

Nathan nodded. 'AG5 hit as scheduled,' he continued, 'but there have been some complications.'

Steiner raised a quizzical eyebrow and Nathan went on tell him about AG5 Minor and its impact in India, along with the dust cloud's rapid spread across the upper atmosphere.

'The incident in India is tragic,' Steiner said, 'although there was always a risk that break up might occur during its final transition towards Earth. To be honest, it could have been a lot worse; some had predicted mass impacts, so just one is almost a good result. I can say, though, that the speed of the dust cloud's expansion is extremely unexpected. We had protocols in place to cover such an occurrence, but even so, the GMRC and governments would have been unprepared for it. There must have been some unrest as a consequence?'

'You're not wrong,' Nathan replied, 'some governments didn't show much restraint when it came to enforcing curfews and populations were in turmoil in many countries. To be honest, though, that transition wasn't the biggest problem. The Chinese, in their infinite wisdom, decided the asteroid's arrival was an opportune time to launch a full scale nuclear assault on South Korea and Japan.'

Steiner felt stunned. He knew the Chinese always had a hidden agenda; what government didn't, these days? But to launch an attack when the world was at its most vulnerable was insane. 'I can't believe it,' he said. 'Are they out of their minds?'

'You'd think, but on reflection it was perhaps a predictable move on their part. When better to strike than when everyone else is looking elsewhere? The Chinese have got the biggest budgets and manpower, so they could afford to prepare for both preservation from the meteor, and offensive planning and manoeuvring, at the same time. Given our government's response, I think the Chinese, in their view, made the right choice.'

'We haven't retaliated, then?' Steiner said.

'No, some wishy washy statement was aired, but that was about it. We're at DEFCON 1, mind you.'

'Didn't Japan and South Korea fight back?'

'They did, but the effectiveness of China's missile shield left them virtually unscathed.'

'My God, what's happening now?'

'The last we heard China had moved in ground forces to secure the two countries. What's left of them, anyway. Most of the major cities have been destroyed. Apparently some of the bombs weren't nuclear; they were some kind of new device with mass destruction and zero residual fallout in the form of radiation. The People's Republic of China has expanded into an empire almost overnight.'

Steiner processed all the information he'd just received and then put it to one side to digest later. More pressing matters had to be addressed, like getting out of Steadfast. 'We have another problem,' Steiner told Nathan.

'What now?'

'Communications have been disrupted: cut and jammed.'

'He certainly doesn't want anyone else getting out of here, does he?'

'The man's paranoia is working overtime,' Steiner said. 'Add to this fact that he cares nothing for the lives of those around him and you've got a very dangerous mix, especially when it's someone with his resources.'

'Professor, I don't want to state the obvious,' Nathan said, keeping his voice low to ensure he wasn't overheard, 'but we really can't afford to be down here if what you found is accurate.'

'We have some time on our side,' Steiner told him.

'Will it be enough?'

'We shall see.'

'Should we inform the rest of the base?' Nathan said. 'They all have a right to know.'

Steiner pondered the question, and then shook his head. 'It would be unwise to cause further panic. It would push people over the edge. We must galvanise the workforce and military, not divide them. No, what we know must stay between us.'

Nathan didn't look convinced at this course of action, but Steiner knew it was the right decision to make. He considered their options for a moment. 'Nathan, I think it would be an idea for you to arrange the relocation of all personnel to the lower chambers.'

'Won't that arouse suspicion?'

'Not if there is something to validate the move.'

'Such as?' Nathan said.

'Critical systems failure in upper level chambers. I'll issue a base-wide alert.'

'That should work,' Nathan agreed, and then paused for a moment, clearly torn as to what to say next. 'Professor?' he said at last.

Steiner arched a brow.

'Professor, I betrayed your trust. I'm so sorry.'

Steiner looked at Nathan with sympathy. 'The Director can be a persuasive man.'

'You knew?' Nathan said in shock.

Steiner nodded. 'I was cooped up for days with little to occupy my mind. I realised someone close to me must have informed Joiner of my plans and you were the only one I'd confided in. It wasn't hard to put two and two together.'

'I am so very sorry, Professor. I only told him about your plans for Darklight, nothing else, I swear. I don't know what else to say.'

'You've already said it and I accept.'

'Don't you want to know why?' Nathan said, full of sorrow.

'I don't need to know the reasons, Nathan. You're a good man, but a good man can be corrupted, like any other.'

'You wouldn't be,' Nathan said.

Steiner shook his head. 'None of us can know what we would do if extenuating circumstances were arrayed against us. I am no different. Whatever Joiner's hold on you was, or is, I don't need to know right now. Perhaps in future when things are less—'

'Fubared?' Nathan suggested.

Steiner smiled. 'Yes, I think that turn of phrase describes our position quite succinctly,' he said, patting Nathan on the shoulder as they turned back to the screens and chaos that was U.S.S.B. Steadfast.

CHAPTER NINETEEN

The small tropical Central American country of El Salvador lies on the western rim of the Pacific Basin, sandwiched between the rolling waves of Earth's greatest ocean, with Guatemala to the north and Honduras to the east and south. Known as a surfer's paradise, the hot and humid Spanish speaking nation consisted of small towns and cities with their fair share of squalid deprivation and corrupt bureaucratic oversight. Outside these urban oases the pristine beaches and rolling landscapes reasserted the natural untouched beauty that drew in travellers from the world over.

Dotted with volcanic craters, often doubling as great lakes, a high central plateau dominated El Salvador's interior, framed by parallel mountain ranges and separated from the seas by a narrow coastal plain. Located on this strip of lowland, and south of the capital city of San Salvador, sprawled the runways of Comalapa International Airport, where an hour before Sarah, Trish and Jason had safely arrived, fleeing the imminent arrival of the long awaited asteroid. Transported alongside them were Sarah's crates containing the bones and red canister they'd unearthed in South Africa, the same bulky loads that had been testing Jason's resolve ever since they'd collected them from the revolving baggage carousel.

'We can't lug this lot around with us all the time,' Jason said to Sarah, stopping to rest the heaviest container on the floor. 'Why can't we leave it all at airport storage?'

'Seriously,' Sarah said, 'you expect me to trust airport security in El Salvador? My previous finds have been swiped from a secure vault, so some tinpot storage facility isn't going to protect it very well. No, the finds stay with us at all times.'

'We're going to have to repack them in smaller containers, then,' Jason told her, 'otherwise they'll slow us down big time.'

'Fine, get some strong plastic postal tubes. Most of the bones will fit inside and we can wrap them, too. That should make them light enough to carry about between the three of us, attached to our backpacks. The canister can go in with the scanner and our other equipment, but there's no getting away from it. They go where we go.'

With their course set, they caught a bus to the city of San Salvador, where they arrived a few hours later. Once they'd disembarked, Jason went off to source the tubing while Trish, left at a cafe with all the luggage, was tasked with organising passage into Honduras by computer phone. Sarah, in the meantime, was out looking for an ultrasonic vibration unit like the one they'd abandoned back at the cave site. Some time later she had found her way back to Trish, who'd been joined by Jason. The hustle and bustle of the city flowed past them as they sat in the shade with a couple of iced drinks. Sarah flumped down into an empty chair and called over a waitress to order her own beverage.

'Any luck?' Jason asked her.

'None,' Sarah said glumly. 'I have to say, I'm not totally surprised. I thought I'd be able to find a smaller unit, though, but there's nothing and I traipsed round all over the city.'

The waitress came back with Sarah's cola and she took a long drink, the ice cold liquid quenching her thirst with its refreshing flow. She relaxed back into her seat and let out a satisfied groan as her sore back muscles gained some light relief.

'That puts the kibosh on excavating anything we find on the scanner, doesn't it,' Trish said, also a little downcast.

Sarah nodded, her sullen expression saying it all.

'I've got some good news,' Jason told Sarah. 'After I sorted out the bones I looked at where we need to go – exactly.'

'Excellent, you used the photos of the parchment's map Trish took on the plane, right?'

'Yep,' said Jason, looking very pleased with himself. 'Using the same software I used before, I've been able to pinpoint the position of the building the parchment showed us.'

'Where is it, then?' Sarah said, annoyed, as Jason just sat there beaming at her.

'You won't believe it,' Trish told her.

Sarah glared at them both, in no mood for games after her failed shopping mission.

Jason laughed, unable to keep her in suspense any longer. 'It's smack in the middle of the Ruins of Copán,' he said, his face expectant as he waited for her reaction.

'Oh – really?' Sarah said, unimpressed.

Trish and Jason looked disappointed at her lack of enthusiasm.

'The fifth century ancient Mayan site, you don't think that's pretty weird?' Trish asked her.

'There could be some connection between ancient human civilisations and Homo gigantis!' Jason said, excited by the discovery. 'It's pretty mind-blowing, don't you think? We thought so, anyway.'

Trish nodded in agreement, but Sarah remained unenthused.

'Just because it's in the same location doesn't mean they have anything to do with each other,' she told them. 'That super ancient site we found on the parchment might be ... what? Half a million years older than the Mayan site? Considering the number of human settlements in the world it seems only logical that some may tally up with any dwellings made by Homo gigantis.'

'We didn't think of that,' Jason said, disheartened by the observation.

'Don't get me wrong, there could be a connection,' she said, trying to bolster them a little. 'I'm just saying, keep an open mind. In my opinion it just seems unlikely.'

'Is it still worth going there, then?' Trish said.

They gave her an odd look.

'I'm just saying, since you couldn't find the excavation device, is there any point in wasting our time? Especially with the meteor strike less than three days away and considering everything we've already found.'

Sarah contemplated the question. 'No, I definitely think we should check it out. We've come all this way and now Jas has found the exact spot; you never know, we might get lucky again. We can still scan the area, so if we find anything we can come back at a later date.'

'I suppose you're right,' Trish said.

'Of course I'm right, I'm always right!' Sarah said with good humour.

'Even when you said Carl, the Vatican mole, was a nice chap?' Trish asked.

Sarah grimaced. 'Well, nearly always right.'

'You're nearly there,' Jason said.

'Where?' Sarah was confused.

'You're nearly at my level.'

'Level? What are you going on about?' Sarah said, totally bewildered now.

He grinned. 'Being perfect.'

'Ha, perfect!' Trish said, while Sarah laughed. 'I've seen dog turds that are more perfect than you.'

'Dog turds!' Jason said in complaint.

Trish and Sarah cracked up as Jason sulked, then the waitress returned and the three friends decided to order some lunch.

After they'd sated their hunger, Trish proceeded to inform them about their travel plans. 'I've booked us on the express train from here to Santa Rosa de Copán in Honduras. It shouldn't take us too long, although there has been some activity in the region from an anti-government militia who operate in the area. They've been fighting the government for years against what they see as state murder of civilians who speak up against them.'

'How will that affect the train?' Jason asked her.

‘They’ve been known to hijack them, rob the passengers and extract any goods onboard.’

‘Ah,’ he said, ‘not good then.’

‘No, not really. Still, there’s nothing else we can really do. The bus services are being locked down across the borders due to curfews and road traffic has also been prohibited. I’d say catch a light aircraft, but even they are being strictly controlled, so foreigners booking with little notice are not going to get a flight; that’s according to the local British Embassy, anyway.’

‘Looks like it’s the train then,’ Sarah said. ‘When is it leaving?

‘Tomorrow, noon,’ Trish told her.

Sarah nodded and sipped her drink, content in the knowledge they’d soon be heading off to the location depicted in the ancient parchment. They stayed at the café a while longer, letting their meal settle, and then found a couple of cheap hotel rooms to stay in for the night. Waking early the following morning, the companions gathered their possessions and struck out for the train station. After making their connection, the locomotive departed the platform, a heat shimmer rising from the tracks ahead. Another clear blue sky and bright sunshine accompanied them, the countryside speeding past as the train reached maximum velocity.

Sarah looked out the window expecting to see the meteorite in the sky, although it supposedly wasn’t visible during the day on this side of the Atlantic. The great ocean and its massive expanse was a welcome barrier between her and the impact zone which, until very recently, had been far too close for comfort. Resting her eyes, she settled down once more, another journey and adventure within her sights. The freedom she felt was all encompassing and invigorating, especially compared to her dull existence back home with Mark in London. She might have more important matters to attend to, but this was definitely the life for her; this is what she had been missing. She’d found herself again, her purpose in life, and it felt like home. Her head lolled to one side as she dozed off to the drone and rattle of the express train as it surged onwards.

Santa Rosa de Copán in Honduras wasn't a large place, perhaps home to one hundred thousand people. A small city, but located in a beautiful setting, with friendly welcoming locals. The centre of town looked as striking as the scenery surrounding it. Neoclassical buildings lined the cobblestoned streets and if it hadn't been for the GMRC curfews it would have been pulsating with tourists. People usually flocked to explore the city and the surrounding areas, which included the Ruins of Copán and the Celaque National Park, with its subtropical cloud forest featuring mountainous elevations from four to nearly ten thousand feet.

As usual, sightseeing was off the menu for the team of three and they had already arranged transport to the ruins. A small bus regularly ferried locals and tourists alike to the Mayan site and they had lucked out, as a driver who took the route was a relative of the owner of their base of operations in town, a modest bed and breakfast run by a lovely old couple. According to the timetable, the bus departed in twenty-three hours and Sarah's phone told her the impact was due to occur in less than twenty.

The following day they ate breakfast with the couple and then returned to their room to watch the television. Sarah flicked it onto a Honduran English speaking news channel and sat back to watch. They didn't have to wait too long before the stunning, yet disturbing images of the meteorite's final flight and impact were aired. The three watched in silence, punctuated by the occasional gasp from Trish and swear word from Jason, as the newsreaders covered and discussed the fallout.

Trish gave a shake of her head. 'To think we were only there just a few days ago.'

'That's a sobering thought,' Jason said, unusually sombre.

Perhaps even more worrying than the impact was the breaking news that China had launched some kind of attack on as yet unconfirmed countries. It may have even been nuclear. They watched the scenes of worldwide panic unfold and then a GMRC warning interrupted the programme. The organisation's logo flashed up with a message. The phones that all three now had also chirruped as video text alerts came through.

'It's the same message as on TV,' Sarah said, as she read the screen.

THIS IS A GMRC EMERGENCY BROADCAST
DO NOT ADJUST YOUR MEDIA PLAYER
THIS IS A CRITICAL ALERT
PROTOCOL ONE DELTA:

AN EMERGENCY WORLDWIDE CURFEW
WILL COMMENCE IN TWELVE HOURS
PROCEED CALMLY TO YOUR HOME
OR A PLACE OF REFUGE UNTIL
FURTHER NOTICE

LETHAL FORCE WILL BE UTILISED
TO PRESERVE THE PEACE
THIS IS EMERGENCY PROTOCOL ONE DELTA
THIS IS NOT A DRILL

'Fuckin' hell,' Jason said. 'This is going to screw us right up.'

'I don't think so; the bus leaves in a few hours,' Sarah said. 'We'll be out before the curfew and when we're in the wilderness, there won't be any patrols to worry about.'

'We won't be far away from Copán Ruinas, the small town,' Jason said, 'so it'll hardly be a wilderness.'

Sarah chose to ignore him.

'What about coming back?' Trish asked her.

'We'll speak to – what was his name, the driver?'

'Javier,' said Trish.

'We'll speak to him. I'm sure he'll come back for us if the price is right.'

Jason looked unconvinced. 'Not if a total curfew is in effect, he won't.'

'I suppose,' Sarah said. 'It depends how strict they are round here, they're quite lax on most things so perhaps this will be no different.' Trish and Jason looked at her with deep scepticism. 'Anyway,' she continued unperturbed, 'they can only keep people holed up for so long. As soon as things calm down, the normal curfew times will be reinstated. Come on, it'll be fine, stop being a couple of wusses.'

Trish and Jason muttered some choice words, but after some heated debate they eventually saw things Sarah's way.

Not long after, they made their way outside the bed and breakfast, where Javier picked them up and their ride to the ruins began.

'How close will you be able to get us, Javier, to the co-ordinates we gave you?' Sarah said.

'Pretty close. You'll only have a short walk. I don't think the locals will let you do any digging or scanning; they can be pretty touchy about that sort of thing.'

Sarah exchanged meaningful glances with Trish and Jason. The locals might not want them to scan, but Sarah wasn't prepared to abide to silly rules and regulations at this point. Their groundbreaking discoveries had put her well on her way to proving her theories and she wasn't going to slow down now.

The bus, which was empty apart from them and a few locals, wound its way higher into the mountainous region. Creaking and groaning, the vehicle's suspension buckled and dropped over the uneven road surface as the jungle slid by. As Sarah bumped around in her seat, she pondered the situation in China. Going there now to validate her finds would not be a good idea. International tensions would be at breaking point, or past it, and foreigners looked upon warily or with outright hostility. *Where else can I go?* she thought. *Canada, perhaps, or France; Brazil, maybe?* She needed to discuss things with the others at a later date before any firm plans could be made.

Sarah swayed in her seat as the bus came to an abrupt halt, bringing her out of her reverie. She peered out the front window to see a group of men with guns looking at the vehicle. Javier turned the engine off and got up.

'*Quédate aquí voy a averiguar qué está sucediendo*,' he said to the locals. 'Wait here,' he told the three companions in English and then he got off.

'What's going on?' Trish said, worry etched on her face.

Jason looked similarly concerned. 'I think they're those rebel militia you told us about.'

'They don't look like government troops,' Sarah said, 'no uniforms.'

Javier had reached the rebels and now spoke to two of the men. Hands were waving and gestures being made on both sides. After what seemed an age Javier walked back to the bus and climbed back on, shutting the doors behind him.

'They're letting us through, I know one of the men from when I was a child. You three better stay down, though, or avert your faces. If they see outsiders, they might change their minds.'

He started up the engine and they pulled off at a sedate pace. Trish had sunk so far down in her seat she was hardly visible, while Jason had gone one further and sat on the floor. Sarah looked around and saw an old woman looking at her, so she got up and made her way along the aisle towards her.

'What are you doing?' Trish said, sounding scared. 'Get down!'

'They're not blind,' Sarah said. 'Those men saw how many of us were on here. It'll look suss if three suddenly vanish into thin air.' She stopped in front of the woman. '*¿Me prestas tu sombrero*?'

The woman gave Sarah a blank look.

'What's disguise in Spanish?' Sarah asked Trish.

'*Disfrazar*.'

'Sarah, we're nearly on top of them!' Jason said.

'*Disfrazar*,' Sarah said to the woman a note of urgency in her voice. '*¿Por favor*?'

The old woman smiled, removed her large hat and passed it to Sarah, who quickly sat down, placed it on her head and looked down at the floor. Out of the corner of her eye she glimpsed the militia on either side of them, assault rifles held loosely in their hands as they looked at the passengers as they drove by. Sarah held her breath and then they were past and picking up speed again.

Heaving a sigh, she took off the hat and handed it back to the woman. '*Muchas gracias, señora.*'

The woman smiled again and nodded in acknowledgement.

After their scare they made quick progress, although they did pass a couple of vehicles carrying more armed men on the way.

'Aren't there any government forces around here?' Sarah asked Javier as they passed another one.

Javier shook his head. 'No, señorita, they do not operate out here any more. It's too dangerous for them.'

'Does that mean there is no curfew in these parts?'

'Yes and no,' he said, 'the rebels want to appear in control in the area, so they act like they are the government and try to protect the people as they would. They aren't as strict, though, and they are more likely to just reprimand you rather than lock you up or worse.'

'Good to know,' Jason said from nearby.

Half an hour or so later they pulled up at a stop just outside of a small town. The locals got off first and then Sarah, Trish and Jason followed suit.

'Will you be going back from here tomorrow?' Trish asked Javier.

'Yes. When I was speaking to the men in the road I asked them if I could keep running my service even after the GMRC alert. They said I could, although I may have to pay some kind of toll for the privilege.'

'That's great,' Sarah said, 'does that mean you'll be travelling as normal throughout the week?'

'I hope so,' he replied.

That was excellent news, as Sarah was unsure how long they would be there for. Thanking Javier for the ride and bidding him farewell, they picked up their gear and made towards the location Jason had brought up on his phone.

He pointed due west. 'It's about three hundred yards that way.'

They stood near the top of a valley and the view was stunning. Tobacco farms dominated the lush, green and fertile landscape. A variety of animals and birds made their presence known in and around them as their squawks and calls drifted along on the light breeze, the tall trees set against a clear blue sky. A river could be seen in the distance, weaving its way through the landscape, glistening like crystal clear diamonds.

'Have either of you ever been here before?' Sarah said, taking a deep breath and filling her lungs with the fresh sweet smelling air

'No, but I've seen pictures,' Trish replied.

'I know someone who's been here,' Jason said, 'they told me it was breathtaking in the height of summer and the Mayan ruins are something else.'

It looks pretty idyllic now, Sarah thought as they made their way down through some sparse trees and plants which had been cultivated in order to provide easy access to the complex.

The ruins appeared deserted; tourists had stayed away for obvious reasons and the local workers had apparently thought likewise. The meteor had its advantages after all, it seemed, as digging about in a world heritage site without authorisation was a sure way to get arrested.

As they moved towards the interior of the long abandoned city, Jason carried the scanner and pulled other gear – including the precious canister – behind him in a small trolley. Sarah and Trish had the tubing on their backs containing the bones, plus they also bore food and camping supplies. Their bulky clothes and other non-essentials for the search had been stowed back at the bed and breakfast accommodation.

Approaching a clearing, Sarah was able to make out a large stone structure through the trees.

Trish let out a shriek. 'What the hell is that!' she said, pointing into the undergrowth.

Sarah squinted into the shadows to see what had terrified her friend and then she saw it, a large black shape moved in the bushes. She took a step back as it headed towards them.

Jason laughed when a pig-like creature came ambling into view. 'Oooo scary,' he said.

Sarah grinned in relief and Trish gave him the finger as he continued to chuckle.

With the less than frightening creature snuffling its way back into its habitat, they forged ahead once more. As they bypassed a large monument, the view gave way to reveal low slung pyramids, and a massive stepped building with a huge tower reaching towards the skies.

'Wow, that's pretty spectacular,' Trish said.

Sarah had to agree, it was a marvel to behold. She paused for a moment, taking it in, and then reinstalled the reason for them being there in the forefront of her mind. 'Jason, where now?'

'Err—' he murmured, as he pointed his phone around in front of him, 'there,' he said, at last getting a fix. He now pointed at a large temple right next to the imposing tower.

Sarah glanced up at the sun pulsating directly overhead. 'Let's get going then.' She gestured at a smaller enclosed temple off to one side. 'Trish, you set up camp inside there. Jason, dump your stuff and get the scanner ready.'

He saluted her. 'Yes, ma'am.'

'Very good, soldier,' she said with mock gravity.

Sarah dropped off her burden and joined Jason as he made his way to the scan site. They calculated exactly where the search area would be, marked it out with some tape and sticks, and then got underway. It was quite a large grid to cover so they took it in turns to carry the heavy scanner.

Many hours had passed by the time Trish called them for dinner and the two trudged back to the camp looking as weary as they felt.

'Any luck?' Trish asked them.

'None so far,' Sarah said. 'We've nearly covered the area, but we've only been scanning at one level due to having to penetrate the dense rock of the temple. We'll have to go over the site a few times at various depths to make sure we don't miss anything.'

The next day came and went and then on the third, Jason found what they were looking for – a telltale void deep underground. This time, though, there was no cave and no excavation machine. They mapped it out and then transferred the data to Sarah's computer phone. Unfolding a larger screen, she brought up and analysed the new image.

'It looks bigger than the other one we found,' Jason said, looking over her shoulder.

'You're right. Do you see this section?' Sarah pointed to the right hand side of the void. 'It looks like there might be another, larger, structure further down, and not a natural formation, either, like the cave in South Africa.'

'That's pretty wild. I wonder what's down there?' Trish said, when they showed it to her. 'Perhaps the one back in South Africa had extra chambers, too; that tunnel had to lead somewhere, the one that had collapsed.'

'Maybe, we'll never know now.' Distracted, Sarah rotated the image in a manner almost akin to the ancient parchments they'd found.

'Whatever's buried under these Mayan ruins, we're not going to be able to get at it, either,' Trish said in glum realisation as Sarah passed the image to her so she could take a closer look. 'Even if we had the equipment, no one is going to allow us to disturb this site.'

'Unless there's a secret door or something we've missed,' Jason said.

Sarah smiled at the thought while Trish gave a despairing sigh at his naive optimism.

'What? There could have been,' he said defensively, noting the two women's scepticism.

'Now that you mention it,' Trish said, trying to keep a straight face, 'I did see an ancient jewel in the wall; perhaps if we'd turned it anti-clockwise, it would have opened the secret passage to Narnia.'

'Very funny,' Jason said, lacking his usual retort.

Sarah experienced a sense of achievement at the find, but utter frustration that they could do nothing with it. If a chamber, or even a whole complex, existed down there, who knew what treasures might lie waiting to be discovered? It was too much to bear; she jumped up and went outside to walk off the gnawing irritation that sought to drive her mad.

The day drew to a close as she moved amongst the ancient ruins. Exotic birds sang sweet music in the dusk, deep shadows casting themselves across her path as the sun dipped and hid behind monuments and trees alike. As she walked, her mind wandered along with her body. She passed a stepped pyramid and a few stelae, narrow stone structures rising up out of the ground, perhaps five metres in height and one in width. On one side the stelae consisted of intricate relief carvings of a deity or king and on the flat reverse, or other three sides, detailed hieroglyphic text adorned the surfaces. Each one was a wonderful work of art and yet also acted as an ancient record of events over a thousand years past.

As she moved back the way she had come she passed close to a stela near to the area they'd been scanning. This one had a lot more detail than the others she'd seen and the limestone had been carved more in the round, too, a high relief. An imposing image of a man with a huge feathered headdress threatened to leap out from the substrate itself, such was the craftsmanship. And then she saw it, a lone symbol. She stopped dead in her tracks and took a backwards step. Peering up at the figure, she saw a familiar form, one she had seen recently. And based on her limited knowledge of the subject, it was not Mayan – at least as far as she knew it wasn't. She held out the larger of her two pendants; the top symbol was identical to the one on the statue before her. The Mayan had no alphabet and so the symbol she was looking at could not be there by chance. She walked around the stela, delving into its detail with her eyes. No other unusual markings appeared evident on the front, so she moved around the other three faces which brimmed with hieroglyphs.

It was a few minutes before she spotted another anomaly amongst the norm, a shape she recognised this time from the parchments they had been using. The location of this letter, if that's indeed what the symbols were, was lower down than the other, close enough to reach. She touched it with her fingers, tracing its outline. What did it mean? Did the earliest Mayans have direct contact with Homo gigantis? Surely not. What was more likely was that they knew of their existence. Perhaps they had found or accessed the chamber that even now sat undisturbed below them.

Eyes straining in the fading light, she reached the final side, on which something much more amazing greeted her. Yet another familiar symbol, but below it a shape embedded deep in the stone. It would have looked innocuous to anyone else, but Sarah knew this shape and its size well, very well. It was pentagonal and seemingly identical in size to the large pendant that even now hung around her neck. Hers fingertips caressed its features as her other hand instinctively went to her chest to touch the metal artefact.

Unclipping it, she looked at it and then at the hole. She then slowly but purposefully sank the pendant into the stone. Nothing happened except for the arrival of her disappointment. What did she expect; the statue to light up and open out to reveal a hidden staircase? Well, yes, that really was what she'd been hoping for in the deep recesses of her mind. This, however, was real life and things were never that easy or convenient. Their recent successes had woven a sense of fantasy into her life and she'd begun to ride its heady wave. *Stop daydreaming, you fool*, she admonished herself. Taking the pendant back out, she clipped it back onto the chain. Then she had an idea and she hurried back to camp to collect the scanner.

'Doing another sweep?' Jason said as she came in.

'Something like that.'

'I'm doing a cup of tea in a while, do you want one?'

'Sure,' she said, her mind elsewhere, and disappeared back outside again.

Back at the stela she heaved the scanner upright after adjusting its settings and started a sweep of the stone. Due to its weight and the position in which she held the machine, the screen wasn't visible, so she made one complete three hundred and sixty degree pass and then put it down to inspect the results. Disappointingly most of the interior appeared to be plain limestone, but directly behind the statue's front face, twelve inches in from the surface, was a dense metal object. To make sure this wasn't a normal occurrence within these stelae, she quickly scanned three more which stood close by. After looking at the results and seeing no such objects buried underneath these surfaces she concluded it highly likely the first one was unique and worth investigating further; especially considering the gigantis symbols weren't apparent on any of the other stelae, either.

She returned once more to the camp and dropped off the scanner, telling Jason to download its data onto her computer.

'What have you found now?' Trish said.

'I'm not sure; I'll let you know.' Sarah grabbed a small pick and some hand tools from one of the packs, along with a torch, and departed out the front of the temple once more.

Intrigued, Trish got up and followed her.

When they reached the stela, Sarah passed Trish the light. 'Can you point that on the carving, please?' She indicated the face of the Mayan king.

Trish powered up the beam and shone it on the location, as instructed. 'Sarah, what's going on? What have you found?'

Sarah didn't reply, too wrapped up as she was in concentration and purpose. Dropping the hand tools to the ground, she grasped the pick and swung it with full force at the statue's face. The point bit deep and the light Trish provided jerked to one side.

'Are you mad?!' Trish screamed at her. 'You can't do that, it's a priceless relic!'

'*That*,' Sarah said, emphasising the word and pointing at the stela, 'is not ancient. *This*,' – she grabbed her large pendant and brandished it at Trish – 'is. Now, put the damn light back on it, will you? There's something in there that doesn't belong.'

'Like what?' Trish said, still fuming.

Jason sauntered up to join them. 'Like a metal plate of some description.'

'I don't care what it is,' Trish said, outraged. 'You can't go around desecrating ancient monuments. I don't care what else we've found, this is humanity's history, we can't destroy it!'

'Trish, look, I have to dig this thing out,' Sarah said in a conciliatory tone. 'You've got to understand, this is huge, it may even link early human civilisation to Homo gigantis.'

Trish wasn't having it, however. 'I don't care; I won't let you do it.'

'*Won't* let me?' Sarah said, each word loaded with defiant incredulity.

Jason couldn't help but notice the tone of the discussion had taken an ominous turn. 'Look, it won't hurt, will it, Trish? There's loads more of these things and what we're discovering is almost out of this world. I'm sure we can dig out the stone and then replace it again, right, Sarah?' he said, almost pleadingly.

Sarah didn't say anything as she locked eyes with her friend.

'Fine, take her side as usual!' Trish shouted at him. 'I'm having no part of this.' She switched her light off and walked back to camp without another word.

'I don't always take your side, do I?' Jason said, watching Trish storm off.

Sarah ignored him. 'Put your light back on here, will you?' She collected the pick, drew it back, and then sent a shuddering blow thumping into the stone carving.

This time a large chunk fell away at her feet.

More strikes rained in as she went to work, breaking into the interior of the statue.

'I don't think we'll be able to repair that,' Jason said looking at the mess on the ground.

Sarah didn't hear him as she'd swung once more; this time a metallic impact was heard as the pick end struck a different type of material. Breathing hard now, she swapped over to a flat-ended mallet, which she used to beat the area at varying intensities for a few more minutes until most of the metal was revealed. She then discarded that tool and took up a hammer and chisel.

As dusk turned to night, Sarah finally managed to pry out the object she'd seen revealed on the scanner. With care she pulled it clear, limestone dust and debris falling off its surface as it came. Jason brought the light in nearer so they could get a better look.

Measuring just under a foot wide and nearly the same in height, it felt quite heavy as Sarah hefted it. The metal, as that's clearly what it was, had a matte, almost beaten, look. Its thickness was about the width of Sarah's finger, which accounted for its weight. She stroked its coarse un-worked surface, before turning it over to inspect the smooth reverse which had been etched with fine lines. Tilting it, indistinct markings glinted in the torchlight. No circle or letter-like symbols adorned it; however, dusting it off further revealed hieroglyphs surrounding a single line.

'This isn't like the other things we've found,' Jason said at last.

'No,' – Sarah continued examining it – 'it's a Mayan design, although I don't think I've heard of anything like this being found before, have you?'

Jason shook his head.

'I felt sure it was going to be something like our other finds,' she said, disheartened.

'Me too; but perhaps it's still linked to them in some way. The symbols on this statue and this metal plate must be connected somehow; it can't be coincidence, surely.'

'Can you read it?' Sarah said, suddenly hopeful.

'No, but Trish should be able to.'

Sarah sighed. 'That's if she's still talking to me.'

It soon became apparent that Trish wasn't talking to either of them, although after many apologies and much pleading she eventually came around.

'Give it here, then,' she said irritably, holding out a hand.

Sarah passed the metal plate to her and, under the powerful glow of a lamp, Trish angled the object so she could read the glyphs.

The seconds ticked by as she analysed it and Sarah felt her impatience grow.

'I'm not an expert in these by any means,' Trish told them.

'Just tell us what you can,' Sarah said.

Trish assessed it for a while longer and then laid a finger near the start of the line. 'These hieroglyphs stand for Oxwitik, which is probably what the Maya called Copán. These ones here,' – she pointed further along the line – 'are the place name for Holtún, the lost city discovered late in the twentieth century in Guatemala. These I'm not so sure about.' She indicated inscriptions higher up. 'But I think one might be El Zotz, another Mayan city. It's some kind of map, yet operating in a linear format rather than a typical two dimensional one. At the end of the line there is something quite interesting. These glyphs appear to represent the words *large peoples* or perhaps a better translation would be—'

'Giants,' Sarah said in hushed excitement.

Trish looked down at the mysterious relic which gleamed in the half-light. 'Yes,' she said, unable to contain her wonder, 'giants.'

CHAPTER TWENTY

A BRIGHT NEW glistening morning greeted Sarah the next day, and while their search hadn't found any primary evidence of Homo gigantis, the metal plate with its obscure reference to giants was perhaps the next best thing. It also posed a number of interesting questions, both about ancient human civilisation and that of Homo gigantis. With modern day technology moving archaeology into a new golden age, ground-breaking discoveries were being made across the world in many fields. Sarah's own breakthrough in the last few weeks, however, might prove to be the greatest in human history.

She inhaled a deep breath of fresh mountain air, soaking in the mystical vision that was the Copán Ruins at dawn. Rays of sunlight glittered on tiny water droplets that had accumulated on surfaces overnight, while sluggish mists slowly eddied around the Mayan buildings and caressed the statues, stelae and carvings that adorned and surrounded them.

It had been decided the previous night that further exploration of the site would prove fruitless, given the tools and manpower available to them and not forgetting that they didn't even have permission to be there in the first place. No, it would be wise to move on to pastures new and to determine the location at the end of the map depicted on the metal Mayan tablet. The underground chamber that lay so tantalisingly close would have to be recorded and investigated at a later date through proper channels.

They had attempted to repair the stela that Sarah had literally defaced, but without the expertise of a stonemason it had been an impossible task. Instead, they'd put the interior debris into one box and the pieces containing the artistic detail in another. Sarah was confident the surface of the carving could be restored to its former glory, although she had to admit it would be a painstaking job. Using her computer, Trish had found the location of the visitor centre for the ruins, due north of their camp and a short walk away, and she'd personally taken the boxes to the building and deposited them outside the main entrance, along with a note of apology.

With reparations complete, their attention returned to the mysterious final location on the metal tablet, but before they could find it they needed to translate all the hieroglyphs. Trish had suggested they visit the renowned Mayan university in San Benito, Guatemala; however, after some research on her computer, they deduced that no rail lines ran north across the Honduran-Guatemalan border. Traffic crossings had been blocked by the Guatemalan government to prevent the Honduran rebels entering their territory, and taking a boat ride from the Honduran Atlantic coast to enter Guatemala was also restricted, by coastguards from both nations carrying out GMRC control orders.

That left them with one of two options: travel on foot for five miles across unforgiving mountainous jungle terrain and then catch some form of transport within Guatemala's borders to cover the extra two hundred miles to San Benito – a journey they simply weren't geared to tackle – or alternatively, take a plane. The choice was an easy one. Trish had quickly found that Santa Rosa de Copán, where they were staying, had an airport. Although it resembled a field more than anything else it suited their needs, as all they wanted was a small plane to take them across the border and on to San Benito and the university.

With a plan in place, they stowed their kit and made their way back to the bus stop they'd arrived at a few days earlier; making sure to stay back from the road itself in order to hide their presence from any rebel patrols. As they waited for their transport a handful of hours came and went, and they spent their time chatting and sitting in quiet contemplation until Javier arrived in his bus. No local townsfolk waited to be picked up, but quite a few disembarked when the coach finally came to a halt nearby.

'Did you find what you were looking for?' Javier asked them when they boarded.

'We did,' Sarah said, 'but we weren't able to get to it. We'll have to come back another time, I think.'

'That's a pity,' he said with genuine sympathy.

'You live in such a beautiful place, Javier, you're very lucky,' Trish said, a tad sycophantically; most likely out of guilt that they'd just defaced a priceless local monument, Sarah assumed, her own shame lying heavily upon her.

He smiled. 'Thank you. It is nice, but like anything you get used to it and if you've grown up with it you know no difference. It is home, though, and I try to appreciate its good points over the bad.'

Once they got back to the town they quickly packed up their belongings, paid their dues, and asked Javier if he could take them to the airport. After boarding the bus once more, a short five minute journey to the airstrip had the three explorers ready for the next leg. They thanked Javier once again, gave him something extra for his troubles despite his protestations, and went into the small airport office to arrange a flight.

Due to the rebels not enforcing some GMRC protocols, air services were still operating, and even flights across the border were available, albeit for a much greater fee.

After Sarah had handed over the money, the universally accepted U.S. dollar, she realised her finances had finally run short.

'We've got a serious cash flow problem, guys. We'll need to get some more in San Benito.'

'Do they have a British Embassy there?' Jason asked her.

'I doubt it, but they should have a local office, and they'll hopefully be able to see us right until we reach a bigger city.'

The plane they waited for – a tiny single propellered craft – was due to depart in an hour. As the time neared they organised themselves and their baggage, putting most of it onto a couple of trolleys. All was calm until a speeding car approached outside the departure room. They heard it skid to a stop on the loose gravel and moments later Javier burst in, a look of desperation on his face.

'You must leave right now!' he shouted at them.

'We were just going to get onto the plane,' Jason said in surprise, 'what's the rush?'

'*Los rebeldes están llegando*!' he yelled, lapsing into his native tongue.

They looked at him blankly.

'The rebels,' he said, 'they're coming!'

'Coming for who – us?' Trish said.

'*Si, si!* They found the statue you smashed. They are coming! You must go, NOW!'

'Jesus Christ!' Jason looked like he was going to be sick.

'I told you we shouldn't have touched it,' Trish wailed.

'Now's not the time!' Sarah said, as they grabbed their things and rammed them in the trolleys.

Rushing outside, all three ran as fast as possible towards their plane, the trolleys bouncing and rattling over the uneven grass. At the front of the craft the pilot was running some final checks.

'Start the plane!' Jason shouted at the man as they drew closer.

Startled the pilot looked up to see the stampeding wild-eyed foreigners bearing down on him. 'We depart in five minutes, waiting for clearance, okay?' he said, nonplussed at their frenetic state.

'No time for that,' Jason said, as they careered to a halt next to the plane, 'we have to go right now!'

'*Peligro, la milicia*!' Trish screamed at him as she threw their belongings into the plane.

Sarah heard a noise behind them; she looked back in horror to see in the distance three militia-laden pickup trucks tearing down the road towards the airport.

'Hurry up!' she said.

'Start the damn plane!!' Jason bellowed at the pilot.

Eyes widening at the sight of the rebels' vehicles, comprehension dawned and he traced the lines of a cross on his chest, swore, and ran to the front of his plane. With a couple of powerful pulls he got the propeller going. Jason and Trish scrambled into the plane alongside their gear and slammed the door shut. The pilot ran to his side and Sarah to hers, both jumping in.

Sarah looked back. The cars were onto the airstrip, now, and had stopped at the buildings. Armed men swarmed inside.

The small plane was positioned at the correct end of the landing strip for take-off, and the pilot had hardly lined it up when the rebels reappeared outside. Sarah watched as one of the men pointed in their direction. Guns were raised and shots fired into the air.

'I think I'm going to throw up,' Trish said, as fear increased its grip and squeezed.

'I think they want us to stop, no?' the pilot said, clearly terrified. The plane, which had been accelerating, slowed as his hand dropped back on the throttle.

'That's not an option.' Sarah grabbed his hand in a vice-like grip and whacked the lever full ahead. The plane's faltering engine note surged into a high-pitched whine. Some of the militia had seen that they weren't stopping. Two vehicles cut across to block their escape. The plane remained glued to the runway as it struggled to get airborne and Trish cried out as the cars slid to a halt in their path. The aircraft, its speed, now too great for it to stop, ploughed onwards. The flight yoke inched backwards as the pilot wrestled with it. Cars loomed large before them. The rebels dived to safety on either side just as the aircraft lifted from the ground. Sarah shut her eyes tight, waiting for the inevitable impact. Shouts and cries of fear came from inside and out. Two loud bangs reverberated through the fuselage and then ... nothing.

Sarah cracked open an eye; they were airborne, soaring into the sky above! Looking back she saw the rebels getting up off the ground and looking after them as they flew off into the distance. She half-expected to see their landing gear embedded in the cars, but the sound must have been the tyres impacting on the vehicles' rooves as they scraped over them. She let out a deep sigh. Jason whooped in joy and Trish had her head in her hands.

The pilot looked shaken.

'*Muchas gracias, señor*, thank you,' Sarah said, patting him on the back.

He didn't look at her, but nodded his head in acceptance, clearly distressed at their close shave. She looked down below. Already high up, the Ruins of Copán slid past beneath as they picked up speed and gained altitude. *Next stop Guatemala*, she thought as the plane flew onwards.

Two hundred miles of dense jungle terrain separated them from San Benito. They had already crossed the border into Guatemalan airspace and the midday sun gave the passengers a perfect view of the forests below. Cruising at a few hundred feet made it possible to see far into the distance, while also being able to pick out a lot of detail on the ground, and it was perhaps this perspective that prompted Jason to break the silence.

'Is it me or is it getting a bit dark?' he said from his seat behind Sarah.

Sarah looked outside; the sky seemed to be clear of any clouds, but Jason was right, it was definitely getting darker.

'I thought it was just me,' Trish said. 'Thought I was just tired or something.'

'There are no clouds,' the pilot said, also sounding unsure.

Sarah looked out of the window behind her to see a disturbing sight. The sky and land in the distance wasn't just dark, but pitch-black.

'What is that?' Trish asked, as she also looked behind, 'a thunderstorm?'

'An eclipse?' Jason suggested.

The skies around them grew darker and darker, as if the sun was setting at five times its normal speed, the problem being it was not dusk but noon.

'I don't think it's either,' Sarah said. 'Look up.'

They all craned their necks to look upwards. Directly above them a dark cloud raced across the sky. But this was no ordinary cloud, as it stretched from horizon to horizon and everything behind succumbed to its embrace, devoured by the most dense and blackest of nights.

'Que Dios nos proteja,' the pilot said.

Jason looked nervously out at the strange phenomena. 'What did he say?'

'May God protect us, I think,' Trish said.

The cloud had passed them now, eating up the blue sky above like a dense plague of locusts. Light had turned to dark and they hung suspended in the air, literally between night and day. The jungle disappeared into darkness below them, and the pilot flicked a few switches and the plane's lights came on inside and out.

'It's got to be the meteor,' Sarah said.

'That can't be the dust cloud, it wasn't supposed to hit here for at least a few months,' Trish said in complaint, 'if not a year.'

'I can't help that, I'm sure that's what it is. In fact, it can only be that. They must have got it wrong.'

'I'll check.' Trish turned on her computer. 'It's not working,' she told them after a while. 'I can't get a signal.'

'That confirms it, then,' Sarah said, 'the satellites are out. Change to a land-based station.'

'I would not bother,' the pilot told her, 'Guatemalan, Honduran and Belize governments haven't invested in the system; it was said to be too expensive.'

'Wonderful.' Trish switched the computer off.

After half an hour had passed, they found themselves in total darkness, the only sign of the Sun far off in the distance; a bright shining light fighting a losing battle against the great cloud, which sought to devour it in its gaping, all-consuming maw. According to media reports and GMRC informational broadcasts – that had been issued with greater frequency leading up to the impact – once the cloud had dispersed the sun would not be visible again for a number of years, perhaps for as many as ten. A sobering thought. Being told that something was going to happen never prepared you for the actuality of the event itself. *No more sunlight*, Sarah thought. *No more sunrises. No more sunsets. Just endless night.*

'I can't believe they got it this wrong,' Jason said at last.

'Well, they did,' Trish said, her voice stressed, 'deal with it.'

'You're all heart, you are.'

'It's part of my charm.'

'I'd call it something else,' he said moodily.

The two bickered for a while and Sarah tuned out, as she normally did when her friends descended into mindless tit for tat.

With the remainder of the journey dragging by, she took the time to contemplate the new turn of events and its implications for their mission.

Eventually, as she stared off into the distance, the lights of a large urban area appeared as they cleared a high ridge: San Benito. They landed soon after, and checking in through customs they were advised to find a hotel quickly, before curfew came into effect.

People had fled indoors when the dust cloud had hit and the streets of the city echoed to an eerie silence. Rather than bother with finding the embassy office they checked into a large, more expensive hotel with the capability to issue money via their passports. Sarah waited at reception while the manager went away to verify her bio signature and the digital encoding embedded in the passport. She'd decided to withdraw another ten thousand pounds and have it converted into U.S. dollars.

The manager returned and handed back her documents. 'I'm sorry, your request has been refused,' the woman told her.

'What – why?' Sarah said, confused.

'There appears to be no money in your account, madam.'

'No money? I don't understand. There should be another twenty thousand in there!'

'I'm sorry,' the woman said, and left to serve another customer.

'No money?' Jason said when Sarah went upstairs to tell them. 'I thought you had loads left?'

'Not loads, but enough.' She massaged her eyes, her mind in turmoil.

'Then where's it gone?' he asked her.

'Mark?' Trish said.

Sarah groaned. She'd forgotten; Mark did have access to her account, he'd needed to deposit some money while they were out once and she'd lent him her details so he could use it temporarily. She'd transferred the money into his account soon after, but he must have kept the information. The look on Sarah's face confirmed Trish's suspicions.

'That two-faced bastard!' she said. 'He not only hit you, he stole your money, too!'

'He hit you?' Jason said, dismayed.

Sarah sank onto a bed and covered her face with her hands.

Trish came over and placed a comforting arm around her. 'Don't worry, Saz, he'll get his in the end, those types always do.'

'I've got some money,' Jason said, sitting down next to her, 'and Trish is loaded, so she can put some in, too.'

'I'm not loaded, just comfortable, thank you,' Trish said, still with an arm around Sarah, 'but yes, I can put some in too.'

'Thanks, guys, I don't know what I'd do without you two.'

'You'd get lost,' – Trish gave her a squeeze – 'a lot.'

'And be bored,' Jason said.

'Be less popular,' Trish added.

'Be smellier,' Jason said, laughing as Sarah chucked a pillow at him, a smile stealing across her face.

With her friends continuing to lighten her mood, Sarah let the sounds of joviality wash over her and some time later, after Jason and Trish had collected their money, they surfed the net to locate someone at the Mayan university who might be able to help them.

Trish pointed at a picture of one of the lecturers. 'He looks like a good bet.'

'Yochi Cayut,' Jason said, reading the text underneath. 'Funny name.'

'It's Mayan,' Trish told him. 'Looking at his credentials he'll be ideal to translate the rest of the map. Plus, this site tells you in real time if they're on campus and he's got a green dot next to his profile, so he should be there right now.'

Sarah got to her feet. 'Let's go and see him then.'

'We'd have to move quickly to beat the curfew,' Trish said.

'All the more reason to hurry, then.' Sarah picked up her coat and zoomed out the door. Trish cursed and quickly followed, with Jason trailing along behind.

It seemed spooky out on the empty streets. The lights had been turned on, but everyone had apparently sought the comfort and security of their homes.

When they traversed any unlit areas, the sky above was pitch-black. No sign of the Sun, the stars or Moon. It was uncanny, even more so since it should have been broad daylight. Hastened by the ghostly surroundings and a sudden nip in the air, it didn't take them long to reach the university, located on the edge of town. As with most campuses, they were able to saunter in unchallenged and, using a printout they'd got at the hotel, they soon found the lecturer's department and then his office.

Sarah knocked on the door.

'*¡Está abierta!*' a voice called out.

Sarah looked at Trish for confirmation.

'Go in,' she said.

They walked inside to find a small, middle-aged man with dark skin and jet black hair sitting behind a desk. Books, folders and paperwork loaded the shelves and, by the look of it, all other available surfaces, too.

'Señor Yochi Cayut?' Sarah said.

He studied their appearance with curiosity. '*Si*.'

'We're sorry to intrude, señor,' Sarah said, 'but we urgently need your help to translate some Mayan hieroglyphs for us.'

For a moment Yochi looked intrigued, but he quickly became distracted. 'I don't really think this is the time,' he said in a strong local accent. He looked out of the window. 'There are things going on greater than research right now. Come back in a few days and I will take a look at it then for you.'

Sarah took the metal tablet out of her coat and placed it on the desk in front of him. Due to its weight it made a satisfying thump as she let it go.

'Please, señor, it's very important.'

Yochi glanced down at the Mayan relic before him. The ancient patina and unusual nature of the piece must have piqued his interest, as he picked it up, noted its weight and then angled his desk lamp to highlight the inscriptions in more detail. He looked up in astonishment. 'Where does this come from?'

'The Ruins of Copán,' Jason said.

Yochi turned it over in his hands, feeling the surfaces. 'It is fascinating,' he said, turning it again to look at the inscriptions. Nothing further was said for a minute or so as he examined it.

'We need you to decipher it for us,' Sarah said at last.

'Of course,' he said, without looking up. He grabbed a blank piece of paper, drew a line and then wrote on it, referring back to the artefact every now and then for guidance.

'It is a map,' Yochi said once he had finished.

'We guessed that part,' Trish said. 'I was able to identify Copán, Holtún and El Zotz, but the rest I couldn't translate.'

Yochi looked up again at the three people standing in his room, suddenly realising they weren't just students or tourists. 'You are archaeologists?'

Sarah nodded. 'Yes, from England.'

'And Wales,' Jason said.

'I see. You are quite correct in your initial deductions. The ones you were missing are here.' He indicated the piece of paper and handed it to Sarah.

Trish and Jason moved in closer to see that Yochi Cayut had copied out the line and added to it the names of the places he had just translated.

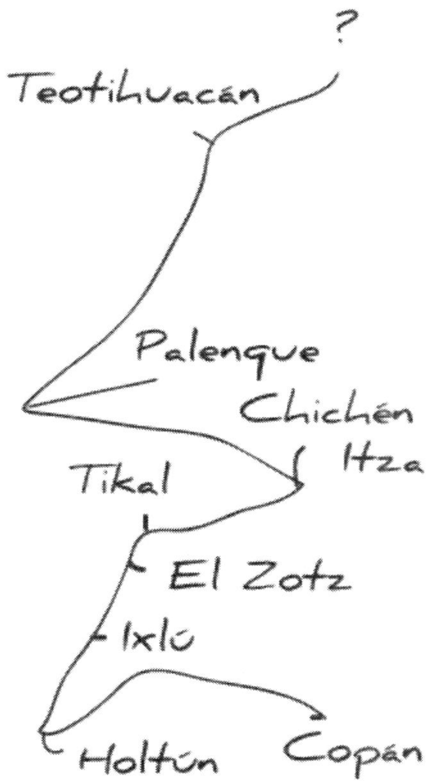

'Perhaps the most interesting thing is the inclusion of Teotihuacán,' Yochi said. 'It reinforces other finds linking the great city of the north to the Mayan civilisation in the south. I really must know how you came to have this piece. Did you discover it on the site or acquire it from another source?'

'We bought it from a dealer,' Jason said. 'It's authentic, though,' he added quickly, thinking on his feet. 'It came with a wooden case which we had carbon dated; it's over a thousand years old.'

Sarah was thankful Jason was on the ball. If they'd told him they'd unearthed it then he would no doubt have insisted they turn it over to the relevant authorities or Mayan Institute. The fact that they had acquired it financially made its ownership a much greyer area.

'You've left a question mark at the top,' Sarah said, pointing to it.

'Yes, I don't recognise it. It's definitely not a Mayan name. I think you will need to visit an authority on Mexican Mesoamerica.' He fumbled around on his desk. 'I should have a card here somewhere.'

'What about the other hieroglyphs?' Trish said. 'The ones at the very top.'

'Yes, I did see them. They aren't a place, more a description. I guess it means *bear men* or more literally *beast men*.'

'It doesn't mean giants, then?' Jason said.

'I suppose it could be interpreted that way,' he conceded, smiling a little at the suggestion. 'There are many references in ancient Maya records to bears that walk like men. It's a normal occurrence in cultures all over the world where bears, especially grizzly bears, are located.'

Yochi Cayut picked up the artefact and examined it again. 'Would you mind if I took a photo of this?'

'Go for it,' Sarah said.

He placed the metal plate back on his desk and used his phone to take a couple of pictures. He then came round the desk, holding the relic in both hands, and carefully passed it back to Sarah. As he was quite small, the top of his head barely reached Sarah's chin, and it was probably for this reason that he noticed something.

'What is that?' He pointed to Sarah's chest.

Automatically wondering if her bra was showing, she looked down in embarrassment, only to realise he meant her pendant. *Idiot!* she chided herself, *of course he meant the pendant*. 'It's a piece I found on a dig in Turkey,' she said.

'I've seen those symbols before. May I?' He held out his hand.

'Sure.' Sarah took off the larger of the two pendants and handed it to him.

'You have another one, too,' he said, as the smaller metal pentagon was revealed beneath.

'Yeah, I found this one near to that one. You said you recognised the symbols?'

'Most definitely. I can't quite believe what I am seeing, to be honest. Only a year ago some artefacts were discovered under the Pirámide del Sol at Teotihuacán. I'm not sure if you are aware, but there is a manmade tunnel underneath the pyramid which leads to a cave. Initially it was theorised the underground chamber was used as a royal burial tomb, an assumption that persisted for decades, right up until last year.'

'What changed their minds?' Jason said.

'The artefacts recovered are clay tablets. It looks like the cave was used as some kind of library. The interesting thing is, they don't have any hieroglyphics on them. They contain symbols, akin to an alphabet, and some of them are identical to these.' He held up her pendant.

'You've seen the tablets, then?' Trish said.

'No, not first hand, anyway. A friend of mine showed me some photos he had printed out. I studied them with him for a bit, but we couldn't make head nor tail out of them. He was supposed to meet up with me again so we could continue our work, but I haven't heard from him since and he's not answering my calls or emails.'

Sarah exchanged a meaningful look with Trish that spoke volumes.

'Do you know where we can find this friend of yours?' Jason said.

'I do if I can find his card.' Yochi rummaged about on his desk again. 'Ah ha!' he said triumphantly, and waved a small business card in the air which he then passed to Jason.

'Victor Fernandez. *Conservación Científico y Filólogo. Museo Nacional de Antropología*,' Jason read aloud, then passed it to Trish who then gave it to Sarah.

'He will be able to help you, I'm sure – if you can reach him, that is. If not, someone else in his department will be able to help you.' Yochi handed the pendant back to Sarah. 'I would ask a favour of you though, if I may?'

'Of course,' Sarah said, only too happy to help.

'Once you track Victor down, can you tell him to call or email me? Also, if you find out anything to do with those symbols and your map, I would be very interested to know. Actually,' – he withdrew a wallet and passed his business card to Sarah – 'all my details are on there.'

'Not a problem, I'll be sure to do so. Thank you so much for your time,' Sarah said, shaking his hand, 'you've been extremely helpful.'

After more pleasantries were exchanged, they made their way back out into the depressing darkness of the day, where they hurried back towards the hotel through the deserted streets of San Benito.

'That was a pretty successful trip,' Jason said, as they crossed another empty road.

'You're telling me. We've got to get a look at those tablets,' Sarah said, bristling with enthusiasm. 'God knows what they would reveal if they could be deciphered.'

'I don't think we should even try and find out,' Trish said.

Jason and Sarah looked at her in disbelief.

'You heard what he told us,' Trish said in answer to their expressions, 'he hadn't heard from his mate in ages. Bit of a coincidence, don't you think? After they find tablets with symbols we believe are proof of Homo gigantis?'

She has a point, Sarah thought. Had she learnt nothing from her past experiences? She'd got so caught up in their successes she'd almost forgotten the precarious nature of their position. 'We don't have to see the actual tablets themselves, do we,' Sarah said, 'we just need to get hold of those photos. If it seems too dodgy we can just ask searching questions without being too obvious. At the very least we can find out what the place is called on the map.'

'I don't like it.' Trish turned to Jason. 'Surely you must agree with me?'

'You'll just accuse me of taking sides again,' he said despairingly.

'Ah, so you do agree with her, then!'

Jason threw his hands up in disgust.

'Trish, it will be fine,' Sarah said. 'Look, we'll go up there, I'll go on my own to see this bloke and you two can stay back with all the gear and protect our finds. I'll be less conspicuous on my own.'

'What, a tall, leggy blonde in Mexico? I'm sure you'll blend right in,' Trish said, her voice dripping with sarcasm.

'There are such things as hats and trousers, you know,' Sarah said, giving her friend a playful nudge with her arm. Trish glared at her, but Sarah put on a pout and tried to look pathetic.

Trish smirked and then laughed. 'Bloody hell, you're really annoying, do you know that?'

'You love me really,' Sarah said, laughing with her.

'Group hug!' Jason said, and squidged them all together.

'Jason, get off you idiot!' Trish said, trying to be angry but unable to keep the smile from her face.

'Mexico, baby!' Jason said as he released them. 'Can we go to Cancún for a stop off? I need a bit of R and R.'

'If you fancy sunbathing in the dark, you can,' Sarah told him.

Jason looked up at the black sky.

'Oh, yeah, I forgot about that,' he said, his mood lowering.

They continued their journey back to the hotel, their momentary elation quelled, but not extinguished. When they arrived some time later Trish prepared yet more reservations via the establishment's in-house internet service, and with nothing else to do but wait, they settled down for the night.

Eight hours of restless sleep faded into memory, ushering in a difficult next day as they adjusted to the absence of sunlight. Many people in the hotel also had strained looks on their faces as the realisation of a new type of existence dawned on them, in more ways than one.

By mid-morning they'd returned to San Benito's airport and they were airborne again hours later, the three explorers leaving the city behind ablaze with artificial lighting, the next leg of their quest beckoning them onwards.

CHAPTER TWENTY-ONE

SHROUDED dense and sinister blackness hung over the city of Albuquerque. It should have been daylight and yet no sun had risen. *The dust cloud must have passed over in the night*, Rebecca concluded, as she huddled close to Joseph in the ruins of the burnt-out care home. It had been days since the fire and yet half the city was still being left to fend for itself by the authorities. The rioting had died out seventy-two hours after it had begun; looting and destruction had now taken precedence.

It was amazing to think how fragile civilisation actually was. People complained about the police and government but without them society's darker side asserted its control. Gangs and criminals, usually below most people's radar, thrust to the surface. The cold reality of life without law and order exerted its unyielding grip on the district; taking a walk down the street was now a very dangerous proposition, triply so if you went unarmed or alone.

The rain had been beating down for the last two days straight, which was extremely unusual in New Mexico. Rebecca assumed weather patterns must have been disrupted, as predicted and discussed on a few TV shows prior to the impact. Ordinarily this wouldn't have posed too great a problem, but they now found themselves crowded into a couple of rooms, the only two which still had a roof over them. Thankfully one was a small kitchen so they'd been able to get a steady supply of food as they waited for help to come. Help had not come, however; only the pervasive darkness and a keen drop in temperature.

Every now and then gunshots rang out and the occasional scream shattered the oppressive silence that closed in around them. Only three of the carers remained now; Julie, Rebecca and a young timid girl who was about as much help as those they looked after. Joseph had been very quiet since the fire crew had left the scene to attend a blaze in another part of the city. He wasn't alone, though; the home catered for twelve mentally disabled people of various ages. One in particular was of great concern; Edna was in her nineties and had come down with a chill two nights before.

'How is she?' Rebecca asked Julie as she came over to where the old woman had been covered up on one of the beds they'd been able to salvage.

'Not good,' Julie said, concern etched deep on her face. 'I don't think she has much time left.'

Rebecca didn't know what else to say. She put her hand on Julie's shoulder and gave it a squeeze before she went round the other patients to feed and comfort them and to make sure they had enough to drink. The other carers had slowly disappeared when it became apparent that they had been left to fend for themselves. Maria had, of course, been the first to go; she'd claimed to be going to get help, but Rebecca had seen an unbridled fear in her eyes indicating that the only one she cared about was number one. Her job was just that, a job, whereas to Rebecca it had been a calling and a profession. She found it very hard to understand how someone could leave such vulnerable people to fend for themselves. In fact, she didn't care what their reasons were; it was just unadulterated selfishness and a lack of compassion, sadly an attitude that seemed to have grown quite prevalent in modern society.

A while later, after completing her rounds, Rebecca moved over to Julie as she rooted through the stores. 'Everything okay?' she asked her.

'We're running out of fresh food,' Julie said, without turning round.

Rebecca looked into the cupboard over her shoulder. Only a few cans remained, along with some long life milk and a couple of boxes of cereal. The main kitchen that provided for the patients had burnt to the ground along with the rest of the rooms. 'We're going to have to restock,' Rebecca said.

'Where from?' Julie asked, her voice quavering. 'We can't go walking around out there, it isn't safe.'

'Have you got any other ideas?'

'We could try asking at some of the houses down the street. It would be better than going near a shop. I think that would be too dangerous.'

'Good idea,' Rebecca said. 'They might not want to open their doors, though.'

'When they see it's just a woman they will though, won't they?'

'Would you?'

Julie looked on the verge of tears. 'What else can we do?'

'No, you're right,' Rebecca said with a conviction she didn't really feel. 'I'll go and see what I can get. You stay here and look after everyone, I'll be as quick as I can.'

Julie nodded her head and Rebecca picked up the black vest she'd worn to scare off intruders; without hesitation, she inserted the heavy metal plate into it, too. She was only going down the street, but its presence supplied her with some semblance of comfort and protection. Picking up one of the two torches, she looked about at the pitiful scene of their forlorn group as they huddled around a small fire in the middle of the room. Without another word she climbed over some fallen debris and made her way out into the darkness.

There was movement some distance away but all was quiet nearby as she shone the light in front of her. The first house she came to had its front door ajar. Furniture and clothes littered the ground outside. She considered entering, but only briefly. *Don't be stupid*, she thought, *anyone could be in there*. Moving on, the next house also lurked in darkness, but it didn't show any signs of having been disturbed. She crossed the front yard, knocked and waited. No response. She tried again; still nothing.

Returning to the sidewalk, she started to cross the road, but raised voices approaching from her right stopped her in her tracks. Quickly deciding that being hungry was preferable to any kind of confrontation and that discretion was the better part of valour, she beat a hasty retreat, walking quickly back to the remnants of the care home. As she neared safety, a shadowy figure emerged from behind a tree. Heart pounding in her chest, she stopped and shone the torch in its direction. The light revealed a large dishevelled man; a deep cut had lacerated the skin on one cheek and his eyes gleamed with a disturbing oddity.

'Can I help you?' Rebecca said, trying to keep the fear out of her voice.

The man said nothing, but moved closer. She took a step backwards and bumped into something. Jumping forwards, she swung round. Another man stood there.

'A pretty girl like you shouldn't be out here alone,' the second man said, an ugly smile distorting his face.

Rebecca dropped the torch and ran towards the home. The first man reacted quickly, cutting off her escape. Cruel fingers dug into her flesh, dragging her backwards and she kicked and screamed as the second man closed in from the front. The sound of other voices closing in on them made her scream out.

'Help! HELP ME!!'

Torchlight appeared as she struggled to free herself. 'Found yourself some new game?' a gruff voice said as more men came into view.

To her horror Rebecca realised they were friends of the two that now held her.

'Leave her alone!' a familiar female voice shouted out.

'Julie!' Rebecca wanted to tell her to run, but a hand had clamped down over her mouth.

'See who else is inside and bring them out,' the third man said, clearly in charge.

Rebecca continued to struggle, but the person who held her tightened his grip and she began to find it hard to breathe. Her captor stood up straighter and her feet lifted off the ground, her toes just brushing the pavement. She heard Julie scream and then she glimpsed Joseph and the others being herded out into the fractured torchlight.

Joseph, who walked with his head bowed, looked up and caught sight of Rebecca. Crying out in anguish, he rushed towards her and her eyes widened in shock as one of the men kicked away his legs. Others waded in and blows and kicks rained down on him as he curled into a ball on the ground. Rebecca bit hard into the hand holding her mouth and the grip that held her released, sending her sprawling to the sidewalk. She scrambled up to reach Joseph, but someone grasped her from behind. A vicious blow exploded against her head, knocking her from her feet once more. Crawling forwards, she reached out a despairing hand to Joseph, but she was grabbed again and thrown onto her back. A punch slammed into her temple and light flashed before her eyes. Rough hands pulled off her trousers and spread her legs while others held down her arms. She screamed out as a man's face bent over her own, his dead eyes staring into hers. As a tear rolled down her cheek she heard the sound of vehicles passing by. *Why aren't they stopping?* she asked herself, shutting her eyes as time slowed and her mind shrank away from her body.

Moments later a bright light shone through her eyelids. Blinking, she opened them in time to see the large man on top of her being yanked backwards like a rag doll. He appeared to float in mid-air for a moment and then disappeared from view. A second after the grips on her arms also vanished.

Shouting and blinding light was everywhere now. Huge arms encircled Rebecca's shoulders and legs, and she was picked up off the ground and carefully placed on her feet. Disorientated, she swayed slightly as she stared around her.

Someone gently tugged her trousers back up, but she hardly noticed as armed, black-clad soldiers swarmed everywhere. The men who had attacked them lay bound, face down on the ground; most struggled against their bonds while a few lay unnaturally still.

'It's all right, miss, it's over now,' her rescuer said in a deep powerful voice. 'I want this area secured and cleared in three,' he told a passing soldier. 'We can't afford to stop for long,'

'Yes, Commander.' The man saluted and moved off, issuing orders.

Rebecca looked for Joseph and the others. Then she saw them next to a large armoured vehicle. The officer who'd saved her guided her over to her group. 'Will you be okay, miss?' he said, but she didn't really hear him.

She bent down to Joseph who was being tended by a woman with a medikit. 'How is he?' she asked her.

The woman gave her a reassuring smile. 'He'll live,' she said in a strong South African accent. 'It's lucky he was wearing this flak jacket otherwise he might have sustained serious injury.'

Rebecca felt dizzy and the ground lurched beneath her.

Someone caught her from behind. 'I think you need to sit down,' a new voice told her as they lowered her down next to Joseph.

'Thank you,' she said as a sob escaped her lips, sparked by the compassionate tone in the man's voice; it had been a long time since she'd been cared for. As her tears flowed, Joseph cuddled into her and she clung onto him as he held her close.

Goodwin left the young weeping woman in the arms of her friend and made his way over to Hilt.

'Good job, Commander. What are you going to do with those?' He pointed at the men who had been bound and placed face down on the roadside.

'There are a few things I'd like to do with them, but this is still the

United States and unfortunately on the spot capital punishment is not an option.'

'What about them?' Goodwin indicated the three dead bodies of the rapists.

'Casualties of circumstance; they made their choice and paid for it. I'm a soldier, sir, not a politician. I act as required.'

'I can live with that,' Goodwin said.

Hilt looked over at the small group of people they had gathered together. 'Are we taking them with us?'

'We can't leave them out here now. This part of the city is a free-for-all. No, we can squeeze them in.'

'They may be better off here,' Hilt said.

Goodwin considered the traumatised woman. 'Given what they've just gone through, I think they might disagree.'

'It's your party, sir, although we better get moving again. There don't appear to be any military or police in this sector, but we shouldn't hang around to find out.'

'Good idea, let's get going.'

'Let's move out!' Hilt shouted to his soldiers.

The gang of men, still prone and restrained on the ground, cried out as the Darklight forces departed.

'You can't leave us like this!'

'Untie us, you bastards!'

'Where are you going?! I'm innocent!!'

The calls fell on deaf ears as doors slammed and engines roared to life once more. Goodwin climbed back into the multi-wheeled transport, soldiers and civilians alike retaking their previous positions.

The Darklight convoy rolled out, quickly regaining speed, and flew through downtown Albuquerque after its pit stop.

Goodwin was satisfied with his decision to get involved. He'd been watching a stream from one of the lead vehicles and noticed the incident taking place on the pavement. Hilt had wanted to press on, but Goodwin had insisted. The commander had returned to the site and had taken charge of the situation personally. Goodwin knew the man was a trained killer, but he could tell Hilt was happy to have intervened. He might be a gun for hire, but under Goodwin's command he intended to show him his skills could be used more positively.

Having worked his way back to his seat near the front of the personnel carrier, Goodwin looked round as Kara Vandervoort came up to join him after helping the new additions to settle in.

'How are they?' he said, as she sat down next to him.

'Most of them are fine. They are all mentally handicapped to various degrees, except for the three women with them, who are their carers. The woman who was raped, Rebecca, is still in shock. Joseph, her dependent, has suffered a cracked cheekbone and extensive bruising, but he will make a full recovery. The old woman we found on the bed has been made comfortable, but I fear she won't be with us for much longer.'

Goodwin nodded, looking pensive.

'You made the right decision, Richard.' Kara placed a reassuring hand on his knee. 'You're a good man.'

'Thanks,' he said, suddenly feeling self-conscious. 'I try my best, but sometimes it's difficult when you have so many people relying on you to make the right call. I just hope stopping hasn't compromised our position.'

'A few minutes won't have made any difference. Besides, the commander knows his stuff; he'll get us through to Sanctuary.'

'Sir.' The door of the cab had opened and a soldier motioned to Goodwin. 'You're wanted on the com.'

'I hope so,' Goodwin said to Kara. Getting up, he followed the Darklight operative into the vehicle's control cockpit. He accepted the proffered headset and put it on. 'Commander?'

'Sir,' Hilt said, 'we have a problem.'

'Another one? What is it this time?'

'The army detachment we avoided has been redirected. They are closing in on our position from behind.'

'We can just outrun them, can't we?'

'We could if there wasn't a second, much larger force approaching from the east.'

'So what do we do?'

'They're coming at us from the north and east. We could head west, but that would make any border crossing virtually impossible as we would be run down by the time we reached a viable location. That leaves us with only one option; south.'

'Past Fort Bliss?' Goodwin said, knowing the answer.

'Yes, we have to cross at El Paso. The sooner we get into Mexico the better.'

'Am I missing something? Surely they're pushing us south intentionally; won't we be playing right into their hands?'

'That is a possibility, but I don't think so. If they had the manpower at Bliss then they would be coming at us from the south, but they aren't – why? I think the majority of units at the Fort had already been deployed prior to our departure. Once we were on the move Joiner, or whoever is tasked with restricting our movements, called in any available assets to close on our position.'

'But you can't be sure?' Goodwin said.

'It is only a theory, but we don't have much else to go on and our alternatives are rapidly disappearing. We must act now, sir. The final decision is yours. El Paso or full engagement?'

'What would our chances be if we were to tackle this new threat to the east?'

'We would take heavy casualties as we would be hit from two sides and effectively crushed in a vice.'

'We head south then, Commander, and pray your theory is correct.'

'Yes, sir. I advise you stay in direct communication with me for the duration. Quick decisions may need to be made. I'll stream a live video feed to your vehicle from mine so you can get eyes on from my perspective.'

'Good idea,' Goodwin said, as a soldier offered him his seat so he could view the screen in comfort. Goodwin nodded his head in thanks and sat down in a tight yet well-supported chair surrounded by a plethora of dials, switches and buttons.

'Sir,' Hilt continued, 'I'll need you to put your microphone on mute unless we're talking as I'll need a clean line during operations.'

'Of course, Commander, I'll switch it off now.'

'Thank you, sir. To ensure you can hear all my commands and the feedback from my men, I've patched you into to my audio.'

'Excellent, Commander,' Goodwin said, 'I'm going silent now.' Goodwin pushed a button on his headset. With the confab over he settled in to watch and listen to the Darklight officer as he followed out his order.

'Lieutenant,' Hilt said, 'increase our speed to ninety-five miles per hour. I want to pass Bliss as quickly as possible.'

It wasn't long before Goodwin's transporter also picked up speed to match the lead vehicle, the roar of its massive engines increasing as it did so.

The convoy was really shifting now. The roadside flashed by on the edges of the green head-up display a Darklight operative was utilising to drive the vehicle. Goodwin hoped they didn't encounter any civilian traffic on the road; at this speed and with such a large train of vehicles any accident might well prove disastrous.

'Sir, the army are closing on us at the rear,' Goodwin heard a soldier tell Hilt.

'Distance, Major?'

'Less than a mile. They have some high-speed light armoured Humvees.'

'Tell the rear units to drive three abreast and block their path. Prepare the gunships for launch at my command.'

'Being actioned, sir,' the major told his superior. After some moments he came back on the com. 'Rolling blockade is in place and all helicopter launch bays are open.'

'We have movement up ahead, Commander,' Hilt's lieutenant said, 'air radar indicates multiple targets converging on our location. They're on the deck, sir, altitude one hundred feet. Speed, nine hundred knots. Bearing zero fife seven point two six!'

'Drones?' Hilt asked.

'Hard to tell, sir.'

'Launch the gunships,' Hilt said, 'defence pattern niner bravo eight, and get me the Phoenix.'

'Yes, sir, patching you through.'

'Captain, this is Commander Hilt. I need some low altitude air cover a-sap at my location.'

'Commander, this is Captain Takahashi of the aircraft carrier Phoenix; we can send you two Sabre interceptors; they'll be with you in five.'

'Copy that, Phoenix, Hilt out.'

'We have inbound, sir, secondary single high-speed bogey.'

'Position?'

'Crossing over us now, east to west pass.'

As Goodwin listened in on Hilt's conversation an ear splitting thunderclap shattered the silence and sent vibrations shuddering through his seat. On instinct he looked out of the blackened window and glimpsed the receding glow of an afterburner searing into the black sky.

'This is gunship Sigma Two; we have a confirmed sighting of a reconnaissance drone circling our position, over.'

'That is an affirmative,' said the lieutenant, 'confirmed drone, manoeuvring for another pass on our six.'

Goodwin got a feedback whistle through his headset as Hilt forwarded a message over the vehicle's intercom and throughout the convoy.

'This is Hilt, deploy all weapons systems and activate window shielding. We are under protocol eight six two, we are a go for engagement. Hostiles closing on our position. I repeat, we are a go for engagement.'

Goodwin felt helpless and vulnerable as a clanking noise indicated shutter shields were being lowered over the transporters windows. The crew of three around him activated various systems as per Hilt's orders. The man behind him pulled down a bulky instrument which looked like a giant helmet, inside which twin screens shone brightly. The soldier positioned the optics close to his eyes and switched on its tracking and targeting technology.

'We're passing Bliss, sir,' Hilt's driver said.

Goodwin's tension rose higher as he saw an imposing fence on their left via the HUD signifying their proximity to the U.S. Army's base. He could also hear the rotors of one of the Darklight helicopters as it patrolled their moving airspace.

'Our air support won't reach us in time, Commander.'

'Copy that, Lieutenant,' Hilt said, his voice grim.

A thumping explosion detonated nearby, followed by another, even closer, which rocked the transporter and sent it into a violent skid. The driver grappled with the wheel as the overladen personnel carrier veered across three lanes and then back again, only its bulk keeping it from turning over. Goodwin gripped onto the dashboard in front of him as the vehicle swerved again and finally regained its previous course.

Another ear splitting roar shot past overhead and then another. Two more followed in quick succession.

'Four bogeys, Commander,' someone told Hilt. 'All drones.'

'Report,' Hilt said.

'Two gunships are down and three trucks have been destroyed,' the lieutenant said. 'Our weapons are ineffective against such low targets. They're coming about.'

Hilt's radio crackled and then a muffled voice came through. 'This is Sabre Delta Phoenix Niner, we have your bogeys in sight and are in pursuit, over.'

'Copy that, Delta Niner,' Hilt said to the pilot in the skies above.

A deep rumbling, whooshing noise streaked past overhead, followed by another, indicating the Sabre fighters deployed by Phoenix had entered the fray.

'Commander, we've engaged ground forces at our six. They've been repelled and their path blocked by surface percussion mines. They won't be able to follow us any further.'

'Good job, Major,' Hilt said.

'Sir, we're approaching El Paso,' Hilt's driver informed him.

Goodwin looked at the screen in front of him to see a mass of blazing lights less than half a mile away.

'Sir, there are two class four tanks situated on the border crossing bridges.'

'Thank you, Lieutenant,' Hilt said. 'I see them. Move the gunships in to clear the way.'

'Roger that,' the lieutenant replied as he got on the com.

Goodwin watched on his screen as the helicopters advanced on the tanks blocking their path. Multiple rockets fired and a blaze of light filled the image.

'Targets neutralised,' the lieutenant told Hilt. 'There's still the gates themselves, sir, shall we take them out?'

'Do it.'

More rockets wove through the air to obliterate the massive border gates.

Hilt came back on the internal speaker system throughout the convoy. 'Inform our civilian passengers we will be experiencing some rough terrain and they will need to brace themselves for possible impact. Darklight personnel, as we cross into Mexico we will be engaged by hostiles. Do not return fire on civilian guards on either side. I repeat, do not fire upon civilian targets.'

Shortly afterwards, the convoy smashed through the remains of the tanks and then barrelled on through the debris of the gates. The huge transporter heaved and rolled as it caught the sides of the narrow passageway as it shouldered its way through. Bullets whizzed all around them, raining down on the armoured skin of the vehicle as the border guards opened fire on both sides.

Federali patrol cars barricaded the Mexican side of the crossing. Goodwin saw men running out of the way as the Darklight train broke through, sending the bodies of mangled cars high into the air. And then they were through, the United States behind them and what was hopefully the relative safety of Mexico ahead.

Goodwin turned his mic back on. 'Well done, Commander, that was – very frightening. But excellent work, you got us through.'

'We took some casualties, but they were less than I had feared.'

'Let's hope we can make it to Sanctuary without any further incidents,' Goodwin said.

'I fear your hope may be misplaced,' Hilt told him. 'We have incoming contacts from the air.'

Goodwin looked heavenward. *Can't we get any breaks?* he pleaded silently.

CHAPTER TWENTY-TWO

'TARGETS ARE CLOSING on our position, Commander,' Hilt's lieutenant said.

Hilt accessed the convoy's intercom, this time speaking to the passenger compartments, too. 'We have inbound hostiles; brace for impact.'

Goodwin heard screams and shouts of terror and despair emanating from behind him in the main compartment of his personnel carrier as the Darklight officer's warning came through.

Goodwin looked at a screen to his left; it showed multiple red dots bearing down on a central white mark, which he knew represented their particular vehicle. Preparing himself for the inevitable air strike, his body tensed and his fingers clenched into his perspiring palms. Digital warning indicators flashed and beeped as the imminent threat bore down on them – and then the dots shot past, accompanied by the sound of multiple jet engines roaring through the dark daytime sky above.

'Commander, we haven't been fired upon or even targeted; they're Mexican F22s out of Santa Gertrudis!'

'Lieutenant, get our gunships to dock. I want them out of the air, NOW!'

'Yes, sir!'

'The Mexican Raptors must have been scrambled to protect the border,' Hilt said. 'The U.S. Army's drones and our Sabres from the Phoenix must have triggered a threat protocol.'

Goodwin adjusted his headset's microphone. 'I think our border crossing might have thrown up some red flags, too.'

'Without a doubt,' Hilt said. 'The supersonic aerial threat will overshadow our entry, however; their priority will be to protect their airspace. The attack may have played into our hands a little.'

'There's no pursuit by Mexican forces from the border, sir,' the lieutenant said, 'and the U.S. drones are bugging out.'

'Delta Niner, this is Black Leader; return to the Phoenix. Targets are no longer a threat. I repeat, disengage and return to base.'

'Copy that, Black leader. Delta Niner out.'

'Perhaps our luck is finally turning?' Goodwin said.

'Perhaps,' Hilt replied.

Goodwin got the impression the Darklight officer wasn't one to believe in luck. 'Good fortune shouldn't be underestimated, Commander,' Goodwin said encouragingly. 'Don't look a gift horse in the mouth and all that.'

'I admire your optimism, sir, but I'll only relax once our mission is complete.'

Goodwin knew Hilt was right. A lot still had to be accomplished before they were safely ensconced in Sanctuary. It was six hundred miles to the co-ordinates Professor Steiner had sent to his phone during their evacuation from U.S.S.B. Steadfast. Hilt believed it would take two days to reach the location and predicted a slower final leg due to the elevation they had to climb. Goodwin signed off from his coms exchange with the commander and took his turn to talk to the convoy at large. After he'd hopefully calmed some frayed nerves, he took a seat back next to Kara in the main compartment.

'You look a little pale,' he said as he sat down.

'You don't look the essence of calm yourself,' Kara said, taking the sting out of her words with a smile.

Goodwin grinned as some of his tension left him. 'It's certainly not the dullest ride in history, I'll give it that.'

Kara leant over and gave him a peck on the cheek. His heart began beating faster again and this time it wasn't due to fear, which made a pleasant change. 'What was that for?' he said, mollified.

'Just a thank you for your efforts, I think we're all very grateful to have you in charge.' She gave him a smile that could have disarmed a legion. '*I'm* very grateful.'

Goodwin swallowed nervously. *Is she coming on to me?* She was very attractive, of that there was no doubt. *So what's the problem?* he asked himself. 'I'll just go and see how our new guests are coping. I think I need to explain our situation to them a little better.'

Kara was still smiling at him knowingly as he moved off down the corridor with a sense of confusion. Shaking off the feeling, he put it to one side as he reached the stairs and made his way down to the next level. 'Where are the people we picked up in Albuquerque?' he asked a soldier who sorted through an armaments cabinet.

'Next level down, near the middle,' she told him.

Thanking her, he carried on down the stairs to the lowest floor. The noise of the transporter increased as he reached the bottom. The engines were situated beneath his feet and as he squeezed past some people sitting on the floor, the vibrations of the combustion process pulsed through his legs, an alien experience to that of normal civilian electric transport, and a lot louder, too. The noise, however, was perhaps a good thing as it should have masked the sounds of the gunfight and the explosions occurring outside; Goodwin hoped so, anyway, as their guests had been through enough already.

He spotted the young woman he'd met briefly on the roadside; she was surrounded by her group. The young disabled man who sat next to her was looking the worse for wear, but he seemed happy enough.

Goodwin moved closer and she turned, noticing his presence. 'Hi, there,' he said, 'I hope you're settling in okay. Have you been offered any drink or food?'

'We have, thank you,' she said. 'The soldiers' ration packs aren't the tastiest, but they're better than nothing.'

'I'm Richard Goodwin, by the way; I don't know if you remember, I was with you briefly back in the city?'

A pained expression flitted across her face at the memory and Goodwin instantly regretted the reference.

'Vaguely,' she said, getting up and indicating they should talk elsewhere.

Understanding, he led the way back to the relative space of the staircase; she sat down on the third step and held out her hand. 'I'm Rebecca,' she said. 'Are you in charge?'

'At the moment I am,' he said, shaking her hand. 'I think I need to explain our situation to you a little. I fear I may have placed you in more danger than you were in previously.'

'Even if that were the case, I would take here over there any day. You've provided us with shelter, food, water and medical assistance. I – we – can't thank you enough.'

'You may have noticed we have been through some scrapes and that we have been—' He tapered off as he struggled to define their situation.

'Under attack?' she said.

'Exactly, thank you. I'm sorry, I'm not really cut out for this kind of military excursion, if that's what you would call it. I'm a civilian, I work for the GMRC.'

'I see. I originally thought you were part of the city's authorities and were regaining control, but you're not, are you?' she said, more as a statement than a question.

'No. We're not National Guard or U.S. military. Darklight are a private security contractor that we use to carry out certain tasks.'

'By "we" you mean the GMRC?'

'Correct. I'm actually in charge of a more covert side of the GMRC, but I can't really tell you any more until I know whether you will be staying with us.'

'Are you planning on getting rid of us, then?' she said with some concern.

'No! No, of course not, but I'd like to give you a choice. We're heading to a facility in Mexico which requires the highest security clearance and I can't disclose anything further until I know if you will be joining us or not.'

'Can you drop us off somewhere?'

'We can and that is the alternative to staying with us.'

'I don't know where we could go. Perhaps to another home somewhere ... they might take care of us until we are relocated.'

'That is certainly an option, but there is a small problem.'

Rebecca gave him a questioning look.

'We're in Mexico.'

'Mexico? Is that what all the fighting was about, we were crossing the border?'

Goodwin nodded. The woman looked a little shocked, but she was taking it all better than he'd expected. She was a tough one and no mistake.

'And you can't turn round?' she said perceptively.

'No. I'm afraid not.'

'Then I think that seals it; we'll have to go with you. I don't speak Spanish and I wouldn't be able to take care of myself, let alone a whole group of people.'

Goodwin wanted to apologise again, but it wasn't really appropriate in the circumstances. 'I'd like to be able to say I can guarantee your safety,' he said instead, 'but I don't think I can.'

'Considering what's going on out there at the moment I don't think anyone can guarantee anyone else's safety anywhere.'

'I think we are through the worst of the danger,' Goodwin said, hoping to reassure her.

'Then that will have to do,' she replied with finality.

'All right then.' Goodwin clasped his hands together in thought. 'I'll try to explain our situation a little better.' He hesitated before continuing. 'I work in an underground facility in Dulce; its purpose is to protect our way of life against the effects of the meteor and other events which threaten the United States and this planet.'

'Such as?'

'Solar flares, super volcanoes, nuclear war – things like that. The facility we were in was evacuated due to ... well, I'm not exactly sure why, but we were evacuated and told to relocate to a second underground base in Mexico. The problem is, we may have trouble getting into this new facility as we may not be welcome. I can't really go into any more detail right now, but that about sums it up.' Goodwin thought his explanation sounded lame, but Rebecca didn't seem to agree.

'I understand, Mr. Goodwin.'

'Richard, please.'

'Richard,' she said. 'I understand you can't tell me everything, especially if it's all top secret. You've taken good care of us so far and I'm happy to put my faith in you; I just didn't expect the meteor to affect everything so much, so fast; it's a little overwhelming. I suppose you're more used to this sort of thing.'

'You'd think,' Goodwin said, 'but to be honest, the dust cloud has taken everyone by surprise. An event of such magnitude can never be fully predicted and the best laid plans can always go awry. It's our job to adapt; I think that's what life is all about really, adaptation to circumstance. That's certainly been my experience, anyway, and it's been especially true over these last few days.'

'I suppose the real test is how you adapt, positively or negatively,' Rebecca said.

Goodwin smiled. 'Ah, now that's the trick, isn't it? We either embrace the light or let in the dark and then deal with that decision and its consequences.'

Rebecca smiled politely in response and stood up. 'I'd better get back to Joseph and the others,' she said, looking tired.

'Oh, there is one final thing; wait here for a moment.' He went up the stairs to find the Darklight contractor he'd spoken to on his way down. He found her still checking through bits of kit. 'Have you got any spare armour I can borrow?' he asked her. 'It doesn't need to be anything special.'

'Sure.' The woman delved around in a compartment. 'Here you go.' She passed a heavy armour-plated helmet to him.

‘Perfect, thanks,’ he said, and returned back downstairs, where he handed the helmet to Rebecca. ‘Here, your friend might like this to play with; it should go well with his jacket.’

‘His name is Joseph and he’ll love it, thank you.’

Goodwin bid Rebecca farewell and went back upstairs a lot happier now that he knew she was up to speed on their position, and that she and her group were now officially under his care. He eased along the rows to his seat, where Kara chatted to someone next to her. She flashed him a smile as he sat down and he returned it, still unsure whether she was flirting with him and wondering what to do about it if she was. Feeling tired himself, he decided to get some shut-eye while things were relatively calm. It had been an exhausting day and it wasn’t over yet.

It seemed mere moments since Goodwin had closed his eyes when he awoke with a start. Kara was asleep next to him, as were many others, he noted, as he looked around. Disorientated, he sat for a moment gathering his thoughts. He looked at his watch: it was 3.30 a.m.; he must have needed his sleep and the fact he got it also meant that they hadn’t experienced any further problems; otherwise someone would have woken him. Realising he wasn’t getting back to sleep again anytime soon, he got up and stretched out his back. A satisfying cracking sound in his vertebrae was perceptible as he twisted from right to left. Taking a couple of steps to the door of the cab, he knocked and entered.

‘Good morning, Director,’ the driver said to him as he appeared.

‘Morning,’ Goodwin said, yawning.

‘Drink, sir?’ a woman asked him, holding out a bottle of water.

‘I don’t suppose you have any coffee?’

‘Fraid not,’ she said, looking gloomy.

‘Then yes, I’d love one, thank you.’ He accepted the bottle, unscrewed the cap and took a long draught. Remaining standing, he noticed they now drove with the headlights on rather than using the head-up display system. The back of a supply truck glided along the road in front of them and further ahead he could make out the lead vehicles, their lights also ablaze.

'No stealth system?' he said to the driver.

'No, sir, the Commander decided we were out of immediate danger and tired eyes function better under real lighting.

'I can take over for you if you like,' Goodwin said. 'I have a commercial driver's licence.'

'Really?' the man said, sounding surprised.

Goodwin laughed good-naturedly. 'Yes; my first management post had me looking after a supply depot for the GMRC. I thought it a good idea to know the ins and outs of the job, so I signed up for lessons.'

'It's a nice offer, sir, but a CDL isn't appropriate for something this large. We have to take a specialised training course; it's quite a beast of a machine. Besides, we're taking it in turns to drive and rest.' He indicated the woman next to him.

Goodwin finished the rest of his bottle of water and took his leave of the two drivers to see if he could get back to sleep. Although deep sleep evaded him, he dozed in his chair for some time until someone touched his left shoulder.

'Director, are you awake?'

He opened one eye to see a civilian looking at him. 'I am now.'

'Sorry, sir. I'm Dean Ward, a medic. I've been caring for Edna, the old woman we took onboard?'

'Yes, I remember her,' Goodwin said, stretching out his arms.

The man hesitated and Goodwin waited for him to continue.

'I'm afraid she's passed away. I thought I'd better inform you.'

Goodwin sighed; *far too many people are dying*, he thought as he stood up. This one was slightly less tragic, due to the person's age, but it was still sad and would come as a blow to Rebecca and the other carers.

'Lead on,' Goodwin told the man and they moved down to the second level where two soldiers placed the corpse into a body bag.

Rebecca, already there, held another young woman who started sobbing as the bag was zipped up. Goodwin waited as Rebecca led her friend back downstairs before speaking to the soldiers. 'Do you have anywhere to put her?'

'We can temporarily place the body in a supply cupboard and then transfer it to a field ambulance when we reach our destination.'

'A cupboard,' he said with some chagrin, 'it's not very dignified. Isn't there anything else more appropriate?'

'Not really, sir, sorry.'

'Do it then, but make sure it's locked. I don't want her falling out, people are freaked out enough as it is.'

'Very good, sir, it'll be secure.'

Goodwin left the soldiers to the grim task and decided to go back up front with the drivers for a change of scene. Some hours later, as they neared what should have been a bright new dawn, Hilt came back on the radio.

'Sir, we have a military checkpoint up ahead. I think it'll be best for the convoy to stop here while we go and speak to them.'

'We?' Goodwin said.

'Yes, sir, I think you need to use your GMRC credentials again and see if you can get us a pass.'

'Very well, Commander, let's get on with it.'

The long procession of Darklight vehicles came to a stop half a mile away from the checkpoint. Hilt then picked Goodwin up in his lead command truck and took him to meet the Mexicans.

They pulled up twenty feet away and Goodwin and Hilt exited, then walked towards the soldiers who barred their path. Goodwin shrugged on a GMRC jacket, emblazoned front and back with the organisation's logo, and zipped it up as they approached. '*¿Hola como estas*?' Goodwin said in as pleasant a tone as he could muster.

The officer in command held out his hand for paperwork, his expression bland. '*Buenos días*.'

Goodwin handed him his GMRC ID card. Both he and Hilt gambled on the fact that their unofficial presence in Mexico hadn't been disseminated throughout the country. The Mexican army had been notorious over the last decade for its inefficiency and lack of administration, due to large scale government cuts enforced by an almost totalitarian Mexican president.

Apparently satisfied with Goodwin's credentials, the soldier then took some time looking at Hilt's Darklight temporary GMRC ID card. Obviously unsure of letting through such a large armed force, he called over another officer to confer.

Goodwin's nervousness grew as the two men looked at the card, intermittently glancing up to look at him, the commander and the distant stationary convoy. As they conversed in low tones Hilt produced some actual paperwork, which one of the officers examined in a manner Goodwin perceived as deep suspicion. Hilt shifted next to him and Goodwin glanced down and caught site of the commander's hand unclipping his sidearm. Goodwin quickly looked away, adrenalin kicking in. One of the Mexicans looked up at the sudden movement and studied Goodwin, and then Hilt, before resuming his conversation with his colleague.

After more excruciating moments of tension crept by, the soldiers finally came to a decision on something and handed everything back.

'*Todo parece estar en orden*,' the officer said. 'Everything is in order. You are free to go past.'

Relief washed over Goodwin as they thanked the men and returned to their transport.

Without delay, Hilt ordered the expedition forward and they were soon underway again, driving deeper into the unusually cold Chihuahuan Desert, the dust cloud's ever-present cast causing temperatures to plummet.

Thankfully they weren't presented with any further patrols or checkpoints to hinder their progress and, driving virtually non-stop, they had neared their destination by the end of the day. The Sierra Madre Oriental, a range of mountains, ran down the east side of Mexico spanning over a thousand kilometres north to south. The entrance to U.S.S.B. Sanctuary Professor Steiner had told them to use was located on the western face of Cerro El Potosí, at over twelve thousand feet the highest peak in the range.

Unable to see the mountain due to the lack of discernable light,

Goodwin observed the peak via one of the displays in the transporter's cab; its great bulk rearing up ever larger on the screen as they approached its western slope. Their ascent slowed to a crawl as the roads progressively narrowed, until one section became so constricted the convoy came to a dead stop.

Goodwin radioed ahead. 'Are we stuck, Commander?'

'We aren't yet, but the transporters won't be able to get any further,' Hilt said. 'We've scouted a mile ahead and even our smaller vehicles will not be able to negotiate the route.'

'So what do we do?' Goodwin asked him. 'Go back and find another way up?'

'This is the only road up, sir. No, we're going to have to abandon the transport and move on foot.'

Goodwin frowned. 'Really? How far is it?'

'A few miles as the crow flies, six on the road. It should take us three hours max, allowing for the slowest of walkers.'

'What about the convoy and all your kit?'

'We can take the essentials with us. My troops are trained to carry large back packs so we should be fine in that regard. The convoy will have to be parked up further back. If we get inside, we can then order them to redeploy or potentially gain them access at another entrance. Alternatively, if we can't get in, they can come back up to pick us up.'

'Sounds like we don't have any other options,' Goodwin said.

'Not really, sir, no.'

'Then let's do it, Commander.'

With Hilt acknowledging the order, it wasn't long before twenty-five thousand civilians and the five thousand strong Darklight contingent had disembarked to begin their trek up the mountainside. Behind them the convoy's lights picked out the terrain as it wound its way back down the steep incline.

Due to the effects of the impact winter and altitude, the temperature presented a problem to many of those now travelling on foot, although as ever Hilt had prepared for such a scenario. The convoy had included numerous supply trucks and he'd crammed some full of thick clothing.

Some civilians already wore a couple of layers due to the cool temperatures experienced in some areas of Steadfast; many more now sported various military jackets, coats and body warmers. This extra protection soon proved its worth when it took Hilt and his teams a little longer to locate the entrance than predicted; but just as Goodwin's patience was wearing thin, Hilt's lieutenant returned after yet another scouting foray.

'I've found it, sir. It's half a click over that rise,' he said, pointing behind him.

Hilt pulled his visual spectrum enhancement goggles down onto his eyes and then passed another pair to Goodwin. The crystal clear grey image clearly showed the area the lieutenant had indicated. It was a welcome feeling to actually see where they were as the darkness surrounding them was complete. There was no artificial urban glow anywhere near to aid them in this remote location.

Hilt motioned his recon team forward and Goodwin watched as they spread out, guns raised and locked into their shoulders as they moved as one, gliding effortlessly over the terrain. Negotiating the last few hundred metres, Hilt and Goodwin followed and they were soon looking down a shallow ravine at a substantial metal door. To one side a small building had been constructed. Cracks of light seeped out from within this tiny military installation; not U.S. military, however, but Mexican, according to the markings on the outside. This wasn't a surprise to Goodwin as Professor Steiner had told him that the Mexican government had troops guarding the surface of the base alongside their U.S. counterparts.

Hilt scanned the area with another bit of kit that hung around his neck. 'I count five X-rays, recon leader,' Hilt said into his radio.

'Copy that, Commander, I see them,' came the response. 'We are going dark, out.'

Goodwin watched as the elite Darklight team moved in on their unsuspecting targets. They reached the building and one man moved forward to place a charge on the door, then retreated a safe distance. A powerful explosion shattered the quiet and echoed through the mountains like a thunderclap as the Darklight soldiers swarmed into the outpost. A flurry of muffled gunshots rang out before silence fell, and then the operative came back on the radio.

'Area secure. Zero casualties.'

'Good work, Captain,' Hilt said.

Goodwin was pleased; he hadn't wanted any unnecessary deaths and had insisted on the use of non-lethal force to take control of the entrance, and the use of tranquilisers had obviously worked just as effectively as bullets would have done.

Now that the area had been made safe, with Hilt and Goodwin at their head, the mass of people moved into the ravine and towards the entrance of U.S.S.B. Sanctuary.

CHAPTER TWENTY-THREE

INSIDE THE BUILDING Darklight had just captured from the Mexican soldiers, Goodwin sat down at a computer terminal to access their system while Hilt's team finished tying up the prone forms of the tranquilised men. Goodwin knew Sanctuary would be in isolation, as the lockdown protocols would have been actioned prior to the meteor's strike. This would make their job slightly easier on the surface, since personnel should be minimal or non-existent once they breached the outer gates.

Taking out his phone, Goodwin uploaded the access programme Professor Steiner had provided onto the system. He activated a subroutine and sat back as various windows popped up and programming code executed numerous tasks. Multiple warning and *Access Denied* dialogue boxes came and went until finally a static window appeared with letters flashing in bold green, *Access Granted*. He was in.

Working quickly, Goodwin entered the gateway override protocols, which were virtually identical to those of U.S.S.B. Steadfast. He was surprised to see the surface access map of the base as it was much larger than he'd imagined, far exceeding Steadfast's footprint.

He studied the schematic, scanning through gate designations until he reached one on the outskirts of the diagram, designated *Kappa Sigma Two: Auxiliary Access.*

'Commander?' Goodwin said, calling over the Darklight officer. 'Can one of your men find and verify any markings or signs found on the gate itself?'

'Of course,' Hilt said, getting on his radio.

It wasn't long before a reply came back. 'Kappa Sigma Two,' could be heard over the com.

'Did you get that?' Hilt asked.

'Yep,' Goodwin said, already dialling into the gate's command structure. Quickly finding the appropriate programme he initialised the opening sequence, being careful to disable any alert procedures built into the system. Getting up, he rejoined everyone else outside.

Large mechanisms shifted as bolts and locks disturbed from their sealed positions clunked, clanked and groaned.

In eerie silence the giant metal door slowly swung inwards to reveal a dark expanse against which the dim beams of personal torches proved useless. But this issue was resolved moments later when huge illumination rails flashed on in quick succession, the light cascading down a tunnel that was revealed in a brilliant glare.

Squinting at this new light source, Goodwin held back as the Darklight recon team took point, rifles once again at the ready as they moved inside. With Hilt accompanying him, Goodwin followed at a safe distance, having decided it best that everyone else remain out of sight at the entrance while he attempted to coerce the help of General Ellwood, as per the professor's instructions.

Goodwin found the tunnel extended much further than he had expected, as he strode along its yawning length, and after about a mile they reached another small building, which fortunately lacked any human occupation.

To the right of the small control room stood another large reinforced steel door, the imposing structure barring their way. This one was emblazoned with various warning signs, and one in particular stood out from the rest.

U.S.S.B. SANCTUARY

ELEVATOR SHAFT ACCESS
PRIMARY SUBTERRANEAN DESCENT
ELEVATOR SYSTEM ALPHA FIVE

'This is what we need,' Goodwin said, slowly wringing his hands together, partly against the cold and partly in anxious anticipation. They were nearly there.

'Do we need to get the general to open up this door?' Hilt said, his deep voice echoing in the tunnel.

'No, I should be able to get us in. It's the elevator system we'll need Ellwood to activate, otherwise we won't have a chance of getting down into the base.'

Goodwin tried the handle on the office door and to his surprise it opened. *No need to lock it inside a secure compound, I suppose*, he thought. He entered and took a seat at a terminal similar to the one he'd just used outside. Going through the same process as before, access was again eventually granted although this time it took a little longer, as he had to disable many more security protocols in order that they could avoid detection.

The second entrance swung open as smoothly as the first and the Darklight team ghosted inside to secure the area. When the all clear came, Goodwin and Hilt followed them in. Proceeding up two flights of stairs and right along a corridor, they found themselves in a huge, dimly lit loading area. On the far side big safety barriers prevented vehicular and pedestrian access to the deep blackness of the surface-to-base elevator shaft behind. The layout appeared similar to Steadfast's elevator configuration, only larger. He looked around the vast chamber, trying to locate an access panel.

Hilt must have noticed his difficulty. 'Try these.' The commander indicated the visual spectrum enhancement goggles which hung round Goodwin's neck.

'Good idea,' Goodwin said, feeling slightly stupid. Using the bit of Darklight kit, he quickly found what he searched for. He strode over to one side of the barriers, unclipped four large industrial-sized clasps and, with some difficulty, prised off a heavy panel. He went to place it on the floor, but the panel's weight caused it to slip out of his grasp and it fell onto his foot with a painful thud. He swore in shock, the word echoing into the distant corridors. Hilt stepped in, picked it up and effortlessly moved it out of his way; Goodwin could have sworn he saw a small smile on the commander's face.

Putting his dented pride to one side, he got on with the job in hand. A bright orange rubberised communications handset was what he was after. He slid back and opened a few panels until he found it nestling inside an alcove. Extracting the handset, he switched it on, its buttons and screen glowing in the half-light. He then removed his goggles and tapped in a few commands to activate the base's internal telephone system. Taking out his own phone, he scrolled to his contacts list and found General Ellwood's number, thoughtfully provided by Professor Steiner. Now they were in the base and he'd accessed Sanctuary's communications structure, any call he placed would appear to be an internal one; well, that was the plan, anyway.

Making a final prayer that the General owed the professor big time, Goodwin dialled the number and hit the call button. The line connected and began to ring. His initial nerves turned to annoyance as the tone rang and rang. *Perhaps he isn't in his office?* he thought, but just as he was considering hanging up someone answered.

'Ellwood,' a man said.

Taken by surprise Goodwin hesitated.

'Hello?' the general said, as Goodwin calmed himself.

'General, this is Richard Goodwin. I'm the GMRC Subterranean Base Director of U.S.S.B. Steadfast. I've been relocated to Sanctuary and require your assistance in entering the base.'

'Goodwin? Yes, I have heard of you, but I wasn't aware of your transfer.'

'It was a last minute decision by the council, something about civilian oversight, you know how it is.'

'Mr. Goodwin, you are aware we're in lockdown? We can't grant you access, I'm sorry.'

'I have Level 9 Alpha clearance,' Goodwin said, trying a different tack. 'I'm able to override the lockdown in an emergency.'

'I think you'll find Level 10 Alpha clearance is required for that protocol,' General Ellwood said. 'Besides, according to my computer you're already inside the base.'

'I am, but I'm at the surface. Look, General, I've come a long way. Me and my team are happy to submit to a decontamination programme to allay any fears of contagion from the meteor strike, which, by the way, we all know is an extremely remote threat.'

Hilt touched Goodwin's arm, shook his head furiously and mouthed no to him. What is he going on about? Goodwin wondered. Perhaps he's worried about the decontamination suggestion? I suppose they'll send a military unit to escort us and that would not be a good idea. Shit. Too late!

'Your team? How many of you are there?' the general was asking him as Goodwin shrugged to Hilt and mouthed an apology.

'What? Oh yes, there's only a few of us,' he said, lying through his teeth, knowing full well nearly thirty thousand of them waited outside. 'Ten in total.'

Ellwood paused for a moment as he considered the proposal. 'No, I'm sorry, Director, I can't go against protocol; you'll have to return to Steadfast.'

Goodwin's heart sank. He'd hoped not to force the man's hand, but he'd run out of options.

'General, I was sent by Professor Steiner and he told me you owed him a favour.'

Silence – and then the phone went dead.

'Crap!' he said in despair.

'What happened?' Hilt asked him, as calm as ever.

'He hung up on me!'

'Then call him back.'

'Right – yes – good idea,' Goodwin said, feeling confused. He redialled the number and listened to the call tone once more.

'Ellwood,' the General said.

'General, don't hang up! Please, I don't know what is going on between you and the professor, but he told me you owe him one last favour that's all, just one and then no more.'

'No more?' Ellwood said, his angry voice taut with stress.

'Yes, one more and then nothing else – *ever*,' Goodwin said, stressing the finality of whatever deal they had going.

The general didn't say anything for a while as he considered his options. 'Fine,' he said at last. 'But if I hear anything more of this, I won't be held responsible for my actions, do you hear me? I don't respond well to blackmail.'

'Of course, you have my word and the professor's,' Goodwin said. *Blackmail*, he thought, appalled, *what on earth is the professor up to!?*

'Where are you?'

'Alpha Five,' Goodwin said, trying to ensure the relief he felt wasn't transferred to his voice.

'I'll send it up. The decontamination team will be assembled during your descent and then you'll submit to quarantine procedure.'

'Thank you, General.'

Ellwood didn't respond, choosing to hang up once more.

'We're a go,' Goodwin told Hilt, who nodded.

'Major, we have an affirmative on entry,' Hilt said into his radio, 'bring them in.'

Over three hours later they were still loading civilians onto the multi-tiered elevator. At first Goodwin had started to wonder whether Ellwood had actually sent the elevator, as it was an hour and a half after he had made his call before it reached the surface. But now, as the last people moved onto the final level, Darklight took up their positions to ensure they would be the first into the base proper. This would enable them to take the decontamination team waiting for them below by surprise.

Goodwin and Hilt, the last to board, took a quick look around to make sure no stragglers remained. Satisfied, they made their way to the control booth and Goodwin launched the engine start command. The multiple turbines positioned throughout the elevator came to life, the intense whine increasing in pitch as they reached maximum velocity. Checking all safety protocols had been adhered to, he flicked up a small transparent cover and pressed a large red button. Clamps holding the massive elevator in place sprung away in succession. Red and yellow lights flashed and then, with a jolt, they moved downwards into the deep.

After an hour they were still descending into the Earth's crust and Hilt turned to Goodwin and said, 'Shouldn't we have reached the bottom by now?'

'I would have thought so. Steadfast's drop takes about half an hour, forty minutes max, and we're not showing any signs of stopping yet. Sanctuary must be a lot deeper down.'

After another half an hour, they slowed, and Goodwin moved aside as two Darklight units took point. They wore full battle armour, MX4s and beam weapons at the fore. They weren't messing around; Ellwood may have sent a large force if he'd caught wind of their numbers. Hilt had also donned the same kit and hefted a large assault rifle; a curiously shaped shield and a thick black scabbard hung on his back. Goodwin recognised the design; it was a thermal sword, the type he'd caught a glimpse of back at the Darklight facility.

'Stay back until we're secure,' Hilt said, as he lowered a slit-eyed visor down over his face. Pressing a button on the side of the helmet, he turned on a combat screen inside; the blue glow emanating out resembled slanted, rectangular glowing eyes. The effect, whether by design or otherwise, was an intimidating one.

After a few moments the opening to the underground base came into view. As the elevator shuddered to a halt the barriers came up and a disembarking platform sloped outwards, leading into the base proper. Hilt took the lead, mounting the large metal ramp as it swung downwards. With a loud metallic boom the platform hit the ground. Goodwin glimpsed a group of armed men in full decontamination suits waiting for them. Their weapons weren't raised and the Darklight force quickly surrounded them. With shouts and commands emanating from both sides, Hilt soon asserted his authority and the U.S. military personnel relinquished their weapons and submitted to restraint.

Hilt approached Goodwin, raising his visor.

'What now?' he asked.

Goodwin wasn't sure. He'd been concentrating so much on gaining entry that he hadn't really considered the options once they'd achieved their aim. Taking his time before answering, he quickly assimilated their position and the most credible courses of action they might take. Going through them one more time in his head, he felt satisfied his decision was the right one to take.

'We move into the base and secure an area, then negotiate terms with whoever's in charge down here. The professor seemed to think they wouldn't eject us, but I'm not so sure. In fact, as soon as Joiner gets wind of our presence here, it's almost a certainty he will try to relocate us.'

'That would mean we'll be throwing ourselves on the mercy of those who won't want us here,' Hilt said, not pleased at the prospect.

'Hence we build and defend a perimeter to guarantee we cannot be forcibly removed. It's not the greatest plan, but there are few alternatives.'

'There's always an alternative,' the Darklight commander said.

'Well, as far as I can see there are three other options, all of which leave us even more vulnerable. One, we leave the civilians here and Darklight returns to the surface.'

'There would be nothing stopping the military from just expelling you all again,' Hilt said, instantly finding the fault in that idea.

'Correct. The same would be true for alternative option two; Darklight personnel remain and surrender arms. Again, they could simply send us back to the surface. That leaves just alternative option three, which is to storm the base and try and take control of the Command Centre, which would be—'

'Suicide,' Hilt said, his face grim.

'That leaves us with my first suggestion. Nothing else makes sense.'

'I'm not happy with it,' Hilt said, 'but I have to agree it's the only viable option if we want to maximise the chances of the civilians remaining inside the base. We thought getting here would be the hard part, but it seems staying here will be much more difficult. We'll have to try and make the best of a bad situation.'

'Well said, Commander.' Goodwin contemplated patting the man on his considerable shoulder, but thought better of it. 'I don't think we should stay here too long,' Goodwin said, looking round at their captives. 'The general will get suspicious when his men don't report back.'

'You're right, I was thinking the same thing,' Hilt said, and called over two officers, his lieutenant and the major. 'We're moving out. Sweep pattern Delta Six. Recon only. As soon as anyone gets eyes on, I want an immediate sitrep.'

The two men saluted and got to work organising their men.

As the Darklight recon team headed off, the rest of Hilt's forces, the captured U.S. soldiers and the civilians formed up and followed behind. But after half an hour's march, they had a dilemma. Four tunnel entrances branched off from the one they'd been following and only one was signposted, the far left, which had the name *U.S.S.B. Sanctuary* above it.

Goodwin rubbed the side of his face, unsure what to do.

'If we want to remain undetected or to secure a defendable position,' Hilt said, 'preferably with supplies, then walking straight into the base is not an option.'

'What do you propose?' Goodwin said, valuing the commander's tactical nous far above his own.

'Interrogate the prisoners and find out the lay of the land.'

Goodwin didn't like the implications of that idea. 'We'll ask them what they know,' he said, his voice firm. 'If they're forthcoming, then all well and good, but we will not force information out of them; they are not the enemy, Commander.'

Hilt's expression remained as neutral as ever. 'Yes, sir, but it will prevent us from gaining a tactical advantage over our – opposition.'

'Duly noted, Commander.'

Goodwin spoke to the U.S. Army decontamination team himself, thinking a civilian presented a less intimidating front. Unfortunately his GMRC position didn't hold much weight here and the soldiers clammed up and revealed nothing but their name, rank and service number. He couldn't really blame them since the Darklight contractors represented a hostile force.

'Any other ideas?' Goodwin asked the commander after he came back empty handed.

'We explore the other three tunnels and assess their value for improving the success of our objective.'

Simple but effective, Goodwin liked the plan and the recon team had soon split into three units to recce the three other tunnels. But, as the minutes passed, a growing sense of unease worked its way to the forefront of Goodwin's mind. *What if we're caught in here by Sanctuary's military?* he thought. *We'd be sitting ducks. And would they stop at detaining and ejecting us, or see us as a hostile threat to be eliminated on sight?* Just as Goodwin decided to tell Hilt to call back his men, a team returned reporting the way ahead was blocked due to a recent cave-in.

The second unit took a little longer to come back, arriving some time after the first.

'There's another elevator shaft down there, sir,' an officer said. 'It doesn't appear to have been in use for quite a while. I doubt it's even operational.'

'And there's no way past it?' Hilt asked him.

'No, sir.'

Disappointed, they waited for the final group.

Another five minutes ticked by before the commander's radio crackled into life. 'Commander, we passed a few side tunnels and we've now entered a section which appears to be a naturally occurring cave formation. It's large and extensive. Some ways are blocked due to fallen boulders and rock. We haven't been able to locate an end to it yet.'

'Copy that, Recon Three. Have you seen any entrances into the base itself?'

'No, sir, although we are feeling a draught coming through the caves. There must be an air generation plant or circulation system further on.'

'Copy that,' Hilt said, and then looked at Goodwin. 'What do you think?'

'Sounds better than here.'

Hilt nodded and got back on the radio. 'Okay, stay put, Recon Three, we're following you in.'

'Copy, Commander; out,' Hilt's radio said, crackling due to interference caused by the tunnels.

Another half an hour passed and they had all reached the caves, the system sloping ever downwards. Goodwin had expected them to find something soon after that, but sixty more minutes came and went and still they hadn't reached an entrance to the base or seen any sign of human habitation.

Hilt called a halt to the group's advance.

'We're not getting anywhere fast,' he said to Goodwin.

'Shall we go back?'

'It's certainly an option. I thought we'd have exited into the base chamber system by now, but these caves, do they look odd to you?'

Goodwin glanced up at the distant ceiling, its rocky surface glinting in their torchlight. 'How do you mean?'

'I thought they were natural, but they seem too uniform. I don't remember seeing anything like this in Steadfast, or any other base I've been to for that matter.'

A deep rumbling noise made everyone pause, and then a powerful tremor ripped through the rocks under their feet.

'Earthquake!' someone shouted.

People screamed and ran in all directions as terror gripped them. The ground shook harder, dislodging chunks of rock which dropped from the ceiling high above to smash and shatter in clouds of debris. Unable to keep his feet, Goodwin dropped to one knee and held onto the floor with one hand while the other protected his head. A primeval fear of being buried alive consumed his mind as stone and dust cascaded down around him in a reverberating blur. The tremors continued for what seemed an eternity and then they petered out, their power waning until … finally … they stopped altogether.

The cries and moans of the injured filled the ensuing silence and Goodwin clambered to his feet, as many others did likewise.

After minutes of upheaval and organised chaos, Goodwin managed to ascertain that fifty-five people had been hurt during the incident, although miraculously no one had received serious injury.

But just when he thought things were settling down again an aftershock rippled through the bedrock. It was much weaker than the main quake, but it still sent people scattering for safety, and as Goodwin was wondering what else might go wrong, Hilt provided him with the disturbing answer.

'Are you sure?' he asked the commander, moving to one side so they couldn't be overheard.

'Quite sure; my team has surveyed the whole area to the rear and there is no mistake – the tunnel has collapsed behind us. We're trapped down here.'

Goodwin let out a string of expletives while the Darklight officer looked on, his impassive demeanour unchanged.

'Can we dig our way out?' Goodwin said, after regaining his composure.

'Not according to the report; the boulders are too large, even with the manpower we have available. I'll double check, but my operatives are very thorough.'

'Well, we'll just have to pray that this cave leads somewhere, then.'

'Indeed. There is one other option: we could use charges to break up the boulders, although that might well prove even more catastrophic and bring down the rest of the roof on us.'

'I think we'll leave that as a last resort,' Goodwin said.

Hilt gave a solemn nod.

With the unwelcome excitement over, the shaken company gathered together and began its slow march once more, the Darklight reconnaissance teams as ever in the lead as they travelled deeper and deeper into the depths of the Earth.

CHAPTER TWENTY-FOUR

The Hostel Mexico DF was a picturesque little place right near Mexico City Airport. The accommodation was cheap, but it had the big advantage of being off the grid. And since Sarah wanted to stay under the radar of any nefarious organisations, it was an ideal stop-off while she sought to determine the final destination on their Mayan map with the help of the elusive friend of Yochi Cayut, one Victor Fernandez.

Before they could do anything, though, they needed supplies, and this time Jason stayed at their base of operations while Sarah and Trish went on a shopping expedition. They were looking for batteries and more powerful hand torches to aid in future site searches; the dust cloud's arrival had changed the game and they had to adapt. They also needed warmer clothing; ambient temperatures had shot down as the predicted impact winter flexed its considerable muscles.

As Sarah and Trish traipsed through the city's dark and near deserted streets, it became clear the lack of usual daytime activity gave the metropolis a sinister air. Many people had obviously decided to stay indoors rather than venture out or go to work as the endless night brought with it a sense of foreboding and a tangible undercurrent of fear and tension. This widespread agoraphobia, however, was proving a boon to Sarah and Trish as the goods they sought were in plentiful supply. But give it a day or so and the panic buying would commence when people realised the new must-haves were thick jumpers, coats and personal torches.

Having kept a low profile and acting with haste, the two women soon arrived back at the hostel with bulging bags. They already sported new puffer coats, although Jason wasn't overly taken with Trish's choice of outer garment.

'Pink, really?' he said with incredulity.

'You like?' Trish did a little twirl for him.

'Not especially; you look like a tumble-dried flamingo.'

'Well, I like it, and you shouldn't complain, I've got you one in the same colour.'

He snorted. 'You better not have.'

'And matching gloves and hat,' Sarah said.

'You'll be pretty in pink,' Trish said, laughing, as Jason gave her the finger.

After they'd dispersed all their wares and presented Jason with his non-pink garments, he showed them the profile and picture of Victor Fernandez he'd found on the net. Sarah then transferred the data to her computer and donned a thick, woolly bobble hat.

'Very sexy,' Jason said, as she adjusted its position.

'I'm going for the blonde Scandinavian look,' she said, grinning.

Leaving Trish and Jason in the relative warmth of their room, Sarah headed out, the metal Mayan tablet and its map inscription weighing her down as it nestled in her back pack.

Victor Fernandez, a philologist and the man Sarah now sought, studied ancient languages, and one of his main duties was to ascertain the meaning of records and texts as they were designated by their creators. As his friend, Yochi Cayut, had told them, he was the perfect person to help them translate – and thus find – the final location on the Mayan map.

Sarah looked at her computer. The Museo Nacional de Antropología was located on the west side of the city in the Bosque de Chapultepec, the largest park in the western hemisphere.

Taking the Mexico City Metro Linea 1, she soon reached Chapultepec Station. The National Museum of Anthropology was a kilometre's walk through the floodlit park and her long strides quickly ate up the ground. She had always wanted to visit this museum to see the wonderful and mystical treasures it contained, such as the magnificent Stone of the Sun, Mayan murals, Aztec codices and many other wonders from Mesoamerica, including those of the ancient Olmec civilisation. Sadly, on this occasion she wouldn't get the chance to enjoy it.

Emerging from an avenue lined with trees, she was relieved to see the museum had its doors open to visitors, which made her job a lot easier as gaining access to the building was a simple case of walking through the entrance.

Knowing the academic offices would be off limits to the public, and that the Department of Linguistics would be no exception, she tracked down a comprehensive map of the building, pinpointed where she needed to go and headed off in the appropriate direction.

Since she didn't want to attract any attention, Sarah kept her hat on to ensure her blonde locks remained hidden. But as she passed through the various exhibits, she was acutely aware of the museum's handful of visitors and staff when they looked in her direction. Considering what Yochi had told them back in Guatemala about Victor's lack of contact since they had found the mysterious tablets under the Pyramid of the Sun in Teotihuacán, this was not surprising. Couple this with her own experiences and she felt extremely exposed.

Catching a couple of elevators and an escalator, she caught sight of a sign which read *Departamento de Lingüístic*. Following the arrow down a darkened corridor, she passed a few doors with varying plaques on them but not the one she wanted. Finally, the last on the right had Victor Fernandez's name on it. No lights shone inside, but she knocked anyway. No answer. *Surprise surprise*, she thought to herself. She tried the handle. *Unlocked, result!* Opening the door, she felt about for a light switch on either side of the opening. Finding one, she flicked it on. Light panels buzzed to life overhead and she was greeted with a nice tidy room, far too neat and tidy for an academic. No folders or paperwork of any kind broke up the clean lines of the furniture and shelving. Approaching the desk, no computer workstation was revealed, just some disconnected cables, and drawers devoid of anything of note.

The place had been picked clean – only a few books remained; her paranoia taking hold, Sarah left quickly, feeling more furtive than ever. *What to do, what to do?* she thought to herself as she paced around aimlessly at the other end of the hallway. She needed to find this man but she couldn't risk asking for anyone else's help as she'd have no idea who they were or who else they might tip off. If *they* tracked her down, then she, Trish and Jason could lose all their precious artefacts. No, it was far too big a risk to take with so much at stake.

But just when she had decided to give up she spotted another sign on the wall: *Departamento de Personal.* A personnel office kept employee records, including home addresses. *Sod it, it's worth a shot,* she thought and she strode off again with purpose.

Arriving at Human Resources, Sarah saw these offices were also unlit. However, the door this time had been securely locked. *This part of the building is pretty deserted*, she reasoned, and taking a look around the adjoining corridors confirmed her assumption. Returning to the office door, she tested it again and then took a step back and kicked out hard with the heel of her foot. It caught the door right next to the lock, splintering the wood and crashing it open with a loud BANG! She froze for a second, wondering about her own sanity, and then dived inside and closed the door behind her. Her heart thumped hard in her chest as she switched on the lighting. This office was well used; on the many desks that lined the walls paperwork had been piled high and filed in numerous trays. Cabinets off to her left drew her attention and she went straight to the first and pulled it open. It was full of various documents, none of which seemed useful. Shutting it, she decided to use her brain and check the tags on the outside of each of the drawers. They were in Spanish but she knew enough to get by.

Scanning through them she caught sight of a few with the same title: *Registros de los Empleados*. She didn't know the Spanish term, but it was close enough to English to decipher – Records of the Employees. Selecting the A – F range she tugged at the drawer. It didn't open and she muttered a curse.

Reasoning that since she'd already come this far she might as well go the whole way, she searched about for a tool. A free-standing coat rack by the door caught her eye. The top of the chrome armature was chamfered to a chiselled edge. Picking it up, she rotated it and advanced on the cabinet. Raising her arms high, she rammed the end into the top of the drawer and then, using her full weight, levered it forwards. Something cracked and gave way and the drawer slid open, revealing the files inside.

Putting the coat rack back, she rifled through the papers searching for Fernandez. There were three files bearing the name, the last being Fernandez, Victor! Yanking it out, she walked to a desk and opened it up. Victor's face and details, including his address, were on the first page. She folded the A4 sheet up and stuffed it into her pocket.

'Wait!' she said out loud. 'What are you doing?' Grumbling away to herself she took the paper back out, moved to a photocopier and turned it on. She tapped her foot in impatience while she waited for it to warm up, then copied the document, returned the original to its folder and returned that to the cabinet. *That should cover my tracks a little*, she thought happily. It was strange, she was really enjoying herself. *Perhaps I'm an adrenalin junky?* she reasoned. She really enjoyed rock climbing and had tried on occasion free climbing, in which ropes were only used to prevent falls, so perhaps this was an extension of that kind of thrill seeking.

Discarding such thoughts and fearing she might be stopped by security at any moment, she made her way back out to the park, where she finally relaxed. Blowing out her breath she found it hard to keep a grin from her face. *That was definitely exhilarating*, she concluded, as she took out her prize and checked it to ascertain Victor's home address. The area she needed was called La Condesa.

A quick check on her phone verified the exact position of his house. There didn't appear to be a train station close by, so once outside the park she hailed one of the few cabs that were running and jumped in.

It took about twenty minutes to reach his home, an apartment in an average-looking tower block. Soon at his door, she rang the bell. After getting no response, she banged a few times and then gave it a kick out of sheer frustration. Opening the letterbox she peered in. 'Victor Fernandez!' she called through the flap. 'I'm a friend of Yochi Cayut, are you in there?'

No answer.

'Damn it!' she said, turned and walked disconsolately back the way she'd come. As she plodded down the stairs, her head bowed, she passed a man coming up the other way. Looking up belatedly she caught a glimpse of his face and spun round. 'Victor Fernandez?' she asked the man, who was now a flight of steps above her. He stopped and looked down at her. It was him! His expression of surprise at hearing his own name turned to shock, then fear.

He bolted.

Cursing again Sarah chased after him, taking the stairs two at a time. He fled the stairwell, racing onto the nearest floor.

Kicking open the door which swung shut behind him, Sarah called out to the fleeing back of Fernandez as he pelted down the corridor. 'Wait!'

He didn't stop, merely disappeared down another stairwell. Sarah followed, rattling down the stairs behind him. She burst onto the street looking left, then right. *There he is! Damn, he's fast.* She went in pursuit, picking up speed. Her hat slowly inched loose before falling off, her blonde hair now streaming behind her as she ran. Her fitness and height told and she gained on him as they crossed a road and ran into yet another street. As they rounded a corner, she was within touching distance and managed to catch the rear of his flailing jacket; with a heave she dragged him to a stop. He was breathing heavily, as was she.

He backed away, his hands in the air. '*¡Por favor, no me hagas daño!*' he said, pleading with her.

'I don't understand what you're saying,' she told him as she gasped for breath, bent over with her hands on her knees.

'Please do not hurt me!' he said in English.

'Hurt you? I'm not going to hurt you; I only want to ask you a few questions.'

'I know nothing else. Please, I beg you, leave me alone!'

That was obviously the wrong thing to say, she thought. 'Look, Victor, I'm not here to hurt you, I just have something I want you to look at.' She removed her back pack, extracted the heavy metallic map and showed it to him.

He backed up further against the wall, his eyes still wide with terror.

Who got to this man? she wondered. Whoever it was, they terrified the life out of him.

'Look, I know Yochi Cayut, your friend. He told me to talk to you. He wants you to call him, he's worried about you.'

'I won't speak to Yochi, you told me not to. I won't speak to anyone, I promise. Please don't hurt me.'

Bloody hell, this isn't getting me anywhere, she thought, realising she had to shock him out of his hysteria. She took a look around; there didn't appear to be anyone in the vicinity. She took off her coat. *Here goes nothing*, she thought to herself, then pulled down her trousers and lifted up her top. Victor looked at her in astonishment, a near naked woman now standing before him. Sarah waited for a moment until she had his full attention and then dropped her top and pulled her trousers back up.

She moved closer. 'Now,' she told him firmly, 'I am not here to hurt you. I am not going to interrogate you. I am merely an archaeologist looking for some information. Do you understand me?'

He looked at her for a moment and then nodded, a bead of sweat trickling down the side of his face. 'You know Yochi?' he said in a small voice.

'Yes, I saw him a few days ago. He's worried about you and with good reason, apparently. Look, all I need is for you to look at this map and to tell me where this last place is.' She pointed at the last hieroglyphs on the line.

He looked down at the map in her hands and then at the glyphs. 'That is the City of Tancama.'

'And where is that?'

He looked around him realising they were outside. 'Perhaps it will be better to discuss this in private.'

She nodded in agreement and they made their way back to his home. Once inside he became calmer. Making some green tea, he passed a cup to Sarah who accepted it gratefully.

'So what can you tell me about this city?' she said between sips of her drink.

'Tancama? Well, it was a city built by the Huastecs circa 700 AD, it means *fire hill* in their language. It is theorised the Huastecs were a remnant of a northern Mayan tribe, left to their own devices as other Mayans relocated back to the south.'

'Is it near here?'

He held up his hand and disappeared into another room, before reappearing moments later brandishing a paper map, which he laid out on the table. 'It's about here,' he said, placing a finger on the map, 'about fifteen minutes' drive away from Jalpan de Serra, a small town in the state of Querétaro.'

'Victor, can I ask why you were so scared? What happened to you?'

He looked at her, worry seeping into his features once more.

'Was it to do with the tablets you found under the Pyramid of the Sun?' she asked him.

He took a long drink of his tea then put down the cup and inhaled deeply, steadying his nerves. 'You know about the tablets?'

'Yes, Yochi told me about them.'

'I see.' He took another sip, staring off to one side. 'At first the find was a revelation,' he said, beginning his tale. 'The cave had never been scanned with new technology due to the Mexican Antiquities Committee preventing its use in order to preserve it. When it was finally accepted that deep scanning didn't affect the composition and integrity of monuments and stone, it was given the green light.'

'This was a year ago?'

Victor nodded. 'The scans revealed a large cavity behind one of the cave walls. When we excavated it, we found hundreds of clay tablets. The amazing thing was they didn't contain hieroglyphics, but some kind of alphabetic system. Upon analysis they were found to be seven thousand years old, predating anything produced in the Middle East and Persia by a big margin. The find may turn the origins of writing, and indeed civilisation, on its head and undermine the current accepted historical timeline in so many ways it's mind boggling.'

'What happened then?' Sarah said, as he paused in contemplation once more.

'When my colleagues published some preliminary papers, we received interest from around the world. That is when things began to go wrong. Pressure was exerted on us from within our own government to stop our investigations. This was followed by claims from a couple of influential international organisations that our evidence had been falsified, thus discrediting our work. As the political intensity increased, the site was shut down and our funding cut, even the budget for the Museum itself was threatened. Just when we thought everyone was against us, we were contacted by a group calling themselves a collective of wealthy philanthropists. They wanted to get involved and provide financial support to our project. Of course, by this point, we were only too pleased to get any kind of backing, and with the help of their lawyers we had the site reopened. Their one request was that they got to send in their own teams to help with further exploration of the site and the process of deciphering the tablets. My superiors weren't overly enamoured of this demand, but we had no alternative save to agree.

'That was when things went from bad to worse. Soon after their arrival artefacts started to go missing and then even more disturbingly people did too. Many vanished without warning, leaving behind careers and families. Then the very people who said they were there to help us stormed our offices and confiscated all our work. Everything!' he said, throwing his hands up in despair.

Regaining some composure, Victor continued. 'My office was cleared; they gave me no reasons for it and it turned out security had been told not to stop them. All my work was taken. I saw this one man who looked like he was in charge and I started complaining to him. That was a mistake. They took me to an empty room and questioned me for hours, threatening me with violence; I've never been so terrified in my life.'

Sarah had a sinking feeling in the pit of her stomach. 'This man, was he wearing a suit and did he have an Italian accent?'

Victor Fernandez looked at her in shock. 'Yes! How did you know?'

'I've met him, briefly. He took things from me as well. Look, Victor, these people are very dangerous; why don't you move somewhere else if you're that frightened?'

'I would, but I grew up here, my whole life is here. I won't let them take that from me. Besides, they haven't been around for quite a while now. When I saw you, a foreigner in my building, I feared the worst and panicked, and when you chased me—'

'I'm sorry, not just for scaring you, but for what you've been through,' she said with heartfelt sympathy; his plight resembled her own.

They chatted some more and Victor revealed to her that other discoveries had been made at the site, besides the tablets.

'What sort of discoveries?' she said, intrigued. She wondered if there might have been bones or canisters like the ones they'd found.

'I didn't see them as they were confiscated along with everything else, but according to a highly respectable and credible colleague of mine who was at the site at the time the artefacts that were discovered were, and I quote, *"Not of this world"*.'

'Not of this world; what ... alien?' Sarah said, trying to keep the scepticism out of her voice.

'I suppose that's what he meant. What else could it be?'

Sarah considered the question. Perhaps it was an ancient device made by Homo gigantis, she thought, technology that advanced might appear alien when in fact it was terrestrial in origin. Whatever it was, it must have been some find and it was now in the hands of God knows who never to be seen again. Finishing on that frustrating note, Sarah took her leave of Victor, thanking him for his help, and made her way back to the hostel to report back to Trish and Jason on her mission.

'You did what?' Trish said, flabbergasted, as Sarah told them how she had got Victor's attention.

'I can't wait until I get hysterical,' Jason said with a broad grin, 'actually, I'm feeling a bit mad right now; perhaps you could—'

Sarah laughed and Trish punched him hard.

'Ow! Calm down, I was only kidding,' he said, rubbing his arm and scowling at her.

Sarah then went on to mention the other discoveries Victor's colleague had said were *not of this world*.

'Ha, I told you, aliens!' Jason said, jubilant in his vindication.

When Sarah pointed out it was probably some piece of ancient technology which appeared alien to modern eyes but was, in fact, very terrestrial Jason seemed disappointed. 'I still think it's aliens,' he said, sounding grumpy, 'it's always aliens.'

Sarah wasn't listening, as now that they had the final location on the map, they knew where they had to go next in search of further gigantis artefacts and treasures. To find anything else on top of what they had already uncovered would be the proverbial cherry on the cake, and Sarah would be satisfied she had left no stone unturned and would happily publish a paper after their finds had been documented and analysed.

She knew the risks involved, however, if any such outcomes were to reach fruition. If a national museum found it impossible to declare such artefacts, then how could she hope to do so? That's where her group came in. Circulation on the Internet, self-published books and independent media broadcasts would all help her to garner the support of a government segregated from the West – China. Desperate times called for desperate measures. They might have just started a war, but there was no one else. The Chinese cared nothing for the Vatican, and the Church's influence – if indeed the Church was to blame for any cover up – would be less there than anywhere else. She had to tell the world the truth and she'd go to any lengths necessary to do so. Too long this truth had been hidden from humanity. These people thought they could manipulate and hide history itself, they thought they could kill and rob the innocent at will; they thought they could kill her mother and get away with it. She would make sure this history would never again be left in the hands of those who sought to alter it to fit their own agendas.

With her resolve and purpose cemented in her mind, she headed to the City of Tancama with a determination she had never felt before. She felt like an unstoppable force had possessed her, driving her forwards. Her mind was an arrow and her discoveries the bow with which to launch it.

The next day the oppressive, sunless sky sought to dampen the spirits of the three explorers as they homed in on the City of Tancama. Victor Fernandez had provided Sarah with a detailed map of the site and directions to get there, something that in the dark would prove very handy indeed. They took with them, as ever, the finds from the other sites, along with the bare essentials for their trade, including the all-important scanner.

A taxi cab they'd requisitioned mid-morning dropped them off next to a small visitor centre and, collecting their gear, they switched on their torches and struggled into the unfenced historical city. Utilising a pop up tent they created a base camp and then assessed the map Victor had supplied. Tancama consisted of three main squares, El Mirador, Santiago and La Promesa. The drawings indicated most of the structures were round and the largest square, El Mirador, contained the majority of them, thirteen in all.

'We'll start here.' Sarah pointed at El Mirador.

'What are we looking for, exactly?' Jason said.

'More of the same, really, anything that has symbols on it that resemble the ones on my pendant or those in the parchments.'

'Surely Fernandez would have known that?' Trish said.

'I don't think so. He only deals with the language side of things, he wouldn't normally visit locations and he would have mentioned to me if he'd been here himself. Besides, they only first saw the gigantis symbols a year ago and most of the people who saw them are no longer around.'

'Which makes our brush with those guys in Turkey even more frightening,' Trish said. 'We were lucky they released us instead of—' She made a face and left the implication hanging.

'I was wondering about that,' Jason said. 'I think our off the grid exploration was what saved us; we were too inconsequential to bother about, whereas the Museum was too well-respected to be let alone.'

Sarah adjusted the beam on her torch. 'Or whatever they found at Teotihuacán was far beyond anything we recovered.'

'Hmm. Makes you wonder,' Jason said. 'Those bastards, they have their hands on all this stuff we can only dream of. I wonder where they keep it all?'

'God knows, some huge vault somewhere,' Sarah said. 'Right, let's stop talking about this, it's making me angry. So, we're looking for symbols but we also need to scan the site for any chambers, like those we've found previously. Alternatively, we may find some more bones, or, if we're lucky, another canister. Sound good?'

Trish nodded. 'Yep.'

'Baggsy scanner,' Jason said quickly.

'What?' Trish frowned in annoyance. 'It's my turn first.'

'You snooze, you lose,' Jason told her triumphantly, slinging the scanner's carry strap over his shoulder before she could react.

'Fine,' she said, relenting, 'but you can make the dinner.'

Jason grinned. 'Excellent. Sarah, we'll be eating decent food tonight ... for once.'

Sarah laughed and Trish made a swipe at him.

'Git!' she called after him as he fled from her with his scanner in tow.

Sometime later, with the three friends each searching different sections of the site, progress was slow as Jason had to prioritise where he scanned. At over four hectares and with no specific locus to target they had their work cut out.

Sarah walked around her third edifice, the light of her powerful hand torch skimming over rocks and stone. The monuments were primarily constructed out of large stone slabs and so far the city didn't seem to contain any carvings or internal rooms that she could see.

A few more hours passed and if the dust cloud hadn't been encircling the Earth the sun would've been starting to set. Sarah wondered how the area looked in sunlight; pretty glorious, she decided sadly. As she walked back to the camp, she heard a distant shout that sounded like Trish had found something. Being careful not to trip up in the dark, she trotted along, her beam bobbing along in front of her to guide her way.

Not long after she found Trish standing alone at the top of a huge mound, which had been encased in thousands of stone blocks. Unlike the others this building was square. Trish shone her light in Sarah's direction, blinding her as she climbed up to meet her friend. Sarah held up her hand to shield her eyes, but Trish had already switched it back to illuminate something at her feet.

'What have you got?' Sarah said, tense with excitement.

'It's difficult to say,' Trish replied. 'This is my fourth building and I've seen nothing resembling symbols, carvings, hieroglyphs or anything like that until I got here.'

Sarah looked down at the patch of ground lit up by Trish's torch.

Sunk into the earth and surrounded by grass was a single stone, measuring a metre in length and half that in width. Something might have been carved onto its surface, but hundreds of years of wear had taken its toll.

'I think they might be the symbols we're looking for,' Trish said. 'What do you think?'

Sarah wasn't sure what she thought. The erosion on the stone was great and the marks so indistinct that it was impossible to tell if they were even man-made, let alone the symbols they searched for. 'It's hard to tell,' she said finally.

'What about these two here?' Trish crouched down and traced two large marks with her hand.

'They might be, you're right, but equally they could be any number of things.'

'What could be what?' Jason said, puffing as he reached their sides with the scanner in his arms.

Trish pointed out the possible carved symbols to him.

'Well, I've just been scanning for hours and found diddly-squat, and this is the only place with any kind of marks on that I've seen so I'll fire this baby up and have a butcher's. Stand back, ladies!' he said with an ostentatious wave of his arm.

Trish rolled her eyes at Sarah, who smiled in return.

The scanner buzzed to life and Jason scoured the ground under and around the stone slab. He found nothing until he tried a different setting.

'I think there's something under this,' he said at last, showing Sarah and Trish the scanner's display screen.

'Another chamber?' Sarah asked him as she peered over his shoulder for a look.

'No, I'm not sure what it is. The setting it's on identifies ceramics, so it's not metal or bone.'

'It's relatively close to the surface,' Sarah said, 'a few feet down. I'll go grab some tools.'

Rushing off, she was soon back laden with a couple of shovels and some smaller hand tools, plus a lamp, which she placed on the ground atop a small tripod for elevation.

After excavating the stone, which didn't take long, they lifted it up and moved it to one side; it was heavy, but between the three of them they were able to manhandle it well enough.

A few hours of digging eventually revealed a dense mosaic of interlocking stones. Tightly wedged against each other, the blocks had been adorned with deeply carved hieroglyphs akin to the stelae back in Copán, with a single distinct image formed in their centre.

'Is it me or does that look like the Aztec calendar stone to you?' Jason said, as they looked down on their discovery.

'Pretty much,' Sarah said, 'albeit on a smaller scale.'

'So what's it doing here made up of Mayan markings?'

'They're not Mayan,' Trish told him, 'they're Olmec, and by the look of them they could be well over three thousand years old. The fact that they resemble the Aztec design is,' – she paused, her brow furrowing – 'disturbing.'

'How so?' Jason asked her.

'The Olmecs predated the Aztecs by a good two thousand years; for this design to appear here throws up some problematic questions about how the Mesoamerican civilisations interacted with one another.'

Sarah wasn't interested in the historical human connotations; she wanted evidence of a far older origin. 'I think this might be a tomb,' she said. 'This looks like a cover stone, don't you think?'

'Maybe,' Jason said, 'but if it is, they weren't very tall, definitely not of gigantis proportions, anyway.'

'Unless they were curled up in a foetal position,' Trish suggested.

He looked sceptical. 'Hmm, even then—'

Bending down, Sarah withdrew her trowel. 'Only one way to find out,' she said, and placed its blade between a couple of edging stones, before forcing it down with a few strikes from a hammer in an attempt to prise one out. They were well lodged in, however, and refused to budge, but after inserting another trowel, she managed to loosen one. Levering it out with care, she noted its thickness and weight, just under a foot and a good fifteen kilos, a substantial covering by anyone's book.

'There's something odd under here,' Sarah said, as she probed the dirt beneath with her fingers. Using a soft brush she dusted off the loose earth, revealing a shiny substrate. 'Help me get the rest of these off,' she said, moving to the next piece.

It took some time to remove all the blocks and, when the task was finally completed, they retreated from the trench to admire their labour. Below them rested a strange, perfectly smooth, oblong slab. It certainly wasn't stone, as it had an opalescent sheen to it almost resembling glass, the faint reflection from the branches of a nearby tree just discernable on its surface.

'Not a tomb, then,' Trish said.

'Well, this explains the signal I got from the scanner,' Jason said, 'although it doesn't look like any ceramic I've ever seen before.'

Sarah dropped back down to run her palm across it. 'It's completely uniform – absolutely flat.'

'What the hell is it?' Jason said, joining her as he too bent down to feel the odd-looking substrate.

Trish moved to dig around one end to try and expose the bottom edge. 'Guys, there's another section here,' she said, as her trowel met with resistance.

They worked on the new area for a further half an hour until it was free of soil. 'It looks like some kind of platform,' Jason said, looking down at it.

Sarah had to agree. The new section sat a foot lower than the main object, although the two were clearly connected and of the same material. Their latest discovery was also perfectly square; however, one faultless feature stood out from all the rest – a large sunken circle, positioned in its centre.

CHAPTER TWENTY-FIVE

SARAH LOOKED at the unearthed circle and instinctively knew what she had to do. Taking off her jacket and laying it on the ground, she sat down on it and removed her shoes and socks.

'What are you doing?' Trish asked her, curious.

'There's no hysterical people round here, you know,' Jason said, also intrigued by her actions.

'It's a circle,' she told them by way of explanation.

'Yeah, so what?' Jason said, clearly not realising her intention.

She stood up and wiggled her toes in the cold air, a ticklish breeze flowing over them. 'Where have we seen circles before?'

'The parchments, of course!' Trish said, catching on.

'You think this is a big version?' Jason said.

Sarah grinned at him and stepped onto the circle. The surface felt surprisingly cold on her skin and she padded about on it for a moment as her feet adjusted to the temperature. When she stood in one place she thought she could feel a tingling sensation on the soles of her feet, but it could just have been excitement flushing through her system. Rolling up her sleeves, she then released the smaller pendant from her neck chain and secured it in a zipped trouser pocket, allowing the larger pendant to touch the skin on her chest without interference. 'Hold my arms,' she told them.

Jason took off his left glove and placed his hand on her right arm.

'Trish?' Sarah said, looking to her friend.

'Are you sure about this?' Trish looked at the object they had unearthed with trepidation. 'We don't know what it does.'

'There's only one way to find out,' Sarah said. 'Come on, it'll be fine.' She gave her friend an encouraging nudge with an elbow. Trish took off her gloves and reluctantly put her right hand on Sarah's left arm, but as soon as she did so a sensation swept past beneath Sarah's feet, making her jump.

Trish snatched her hand away. 'What's wrong!?' she said in alarm.

'Sorry.' Sarah looked down at the platform. 'It got warm.'

'What did, the circle?' Jason asked her.

'No – yes,' she said in surprise, 'both, in fact, the circle and the pendant.' She touched the now cold metal pentagonal disc at her neck. 'Come on, let's try again.'

They put their hands back on her arms and again Sarah felt the pendant and circle heat up. Nothing else happened at first, but as the warmth slowly increased an indistinct glow began to emanate from the larger slab in front of them, gradually increasing in intensity. The three friends looked on mesmerised as the surface shimmered and shifted, and faint colours crept to the fore, swirling and writhing in a myriad of intertwining patterns. Darker shades formed to coalesce in its centre, while light now poured out from the edges. Sarah felt Trish's fingers slipping off her arm and she caught them with her right hand, keeping them firmly in place. The light show continued to build, then vanished, plunging them into darkness, and a great rush of air blew past them into the sky.

As their eyes adjusted back to the small single lamp positioned nearby they saw that, where before there had been the ceramic slab, there was now a dark, forbidding hole.

'Give me a torch,' Sarah said to no one in particular as she looked into the darkness below. A torch appeared under her nose as Jason passed her his. Taking it, she clicked it on and pointed it into the opening. The light revealed a vertical shaft hewn out of the bedrock. Ten feet from the surface a side wall had collapsed inwards, sealing whatever lay beyond it beneath an immovable mass of stone.

'It doesn't look like it goes anywhere,' Trish said, disappointed, 'but this mechanism or doorway is just – well – it's the crowning glory isn't it? Who could dispute this?' She looked to her friends in expectation, waiting for the celebrations to begin. Sarah and Jason, however still peered intently down into the shaft.

'I think there's a way through.' Sarah moved around the opening to get a better look. 'Yes, look, just there, there's a hole.'

'At the bottom, on the left?' Jason said, as he moved to Sarah's side; both were now crouching down.

'Yes, it's definitely big enough to drop through. We'll need a rope.'

'On it,' Jason said, and hurried away towards their camp.

After putting her socks and shoes back on Sarah didn't have to wait long for Jason to return. Securing the short rope he gave her to a tree, Sarah lowered herself down inside, while Trish and Jason lit her way. Gaining her footing at the bottom, she withdrew her own torch and investigated the gap in the rocks. Unlike the unstable ceiling in the South African cave, the collapsed wall consisted of hard, dense stone with no signs of loose sediment. Satisfied it wasn't going anywhere, she switched on her head torch and clambered lower, positioning herself over the hole.

'I'm going through,' she told them, 'Jason, get down here and tie me off with the longer rope.'

Once secured, Sarah was soon dropping into the pitch-black fissure. With Jason ensuring she didn't fall, Sarah helped herself move into the earth, close packed rock hemming her in on all sides. The stone around her didn't open up again, as she'd expected, and after a few moments her feet found their way down onto a flat outcrop where water seeped in from an unknown source, soaking the area with a cold dampness. Able to scrunch down into a squat, she illuminated her surroundings. Initially she'd thought she was resting on a stone that blocked her way, but in fact it was a flat surface, the bottom of the shaft.

Immediately in front of her face the dislodged rock wall, which had fallen to wedge itself against the opposite side of the shaft at her back, angled away down to this horizontal floor, creating a triangular space that led to a letterbox shaped hole. The collapse had reduced what must have been a tunnel to this slit of an entrance, the ceiling left hanging, precariously suspended above.

'I'm at the bottom,' she called up. 'I'm taking the rope off and moving in further.'

'Be careful,' Jason's voice came back as she unhitched the rope.

Struggling in the limited space she pulled her shoulders round with difficulty and manoeuvred herself until she lay on her back inside the slot, the water saturating her top and clinging to her skin. The hole was so tight she had to angle her head to the side to stop her face touching the surface above. Thankfully she wasn't claustrophobic, but even so she had to fight down that telltale sense of panic most people experienced when met with such confined quarters. The fear of not getting back out, of becoming trapped unable to move; tons of rock pinning you down, was powerful, tangible ... primal. Forcing her mind to ignore such thoughts and to concentrate on the job in hand, she squirmed her way forwards an inch at a time.

After what seemed like the length of a football pitch, but in actuality was about forty feet, she broke free. Getting to her feet, she now stood in a large tunnel. From this side it was clear to see that the ceiling had subsided from its original position to create the crawl space she'd just negotiated.

Bending down, she called back to Jason. 'I'm through, there's a big tunnel down here!'

'Great,' she heard Jason say, 'I'm coming down. Trish is staying up top to keep an eye on our gear.'

'How are you with really tight spaces?' she said.

'Fine,' came the response.

Ten minutes later Jason was scrambling up alongside her. 'You weren't kidding about tight space. I thought I was gonna get stuck at one point.'

'That's all this paunch,' she said, giving his stomach a pat.

Jason looked down at his waist with an aggrieved expression.

Sarah laughed and slapped him on the arm. 'Come on, fatty, let's take a look around.'

'Fatty?!' he squawked, making Sarah laugh even harder.

Increasing the power of her torch she noted the tunnel's high ceiling and the deep cracks throughout its structure. Water dripped in from above, trickling down the walls.

'It goes on for quite a way,' she said, her voice echoing slightly, 'and it looks like it slopes down near the end, too.'

Moving down the passage with Jason at her back, she clambered past a large chunk of rock which had fallen from the ceiling. As they made their way along, Sarah noticed the uneven surfaces of the walls altering, becoming smoother. The layers of different types of rock could still be identified, but they'd been rubbed down and polished. A lot of effort had gone into its construction.

As they reached the slope, the tunnel took a sharp downwards turn to the left and, after angling the torch, it was apparent they needed to watch their step to keep from slipping over, as the surface glistened with a thin film of flowing water. Sarah weighed up the risks of continuing before deciding it wise to go back and get some more rope and a few supplies to aid their descent. *After all*, she thought, *who knows what lies ahead?*

Retracing their steps, they made their way back through the hole and rejoined Trish, who waited anxiously for them above.

At the camp they gathered up what they needed, put on more suitable clothing, and headed to the shaft once more. This time, however, Trish followed them in.

'I thought you were going to guard our stuff?' Jason asked her as she dropped down beside them.

'It'll be fine, there's no one around. And anyway,' she said, grinning, 'I can't let you two have all the fun.'

Jason's expression turned dubious. 'It's really narrow down there. I'm not sure you'll like it.'

Trish's smile faded. 'You think I can't do it? That I'm some weak little woman?'

'Not at all,' he said, regretting the comment. 'I know plenty of blokes who wouldn't want to go down there, either. It is pretty tight.'

'Well, if your lard arse can get through, then mine can.' She pushed past him to follow Sarah, who had by now disappeared into the hole beneath.

'What is this?' he said in complaint and pulled up his shirt to look at his stomach. 'I'm not sodding fat!'

His complaints fell on deaf ears, however, as Trish had already gone down. 'I'm not fat,' he repeated by way of clarification. 'I just like my food, there's nothing wrong with that.' Grumbling to himself, he followed the two women underground.

With all three of them now in the tunnel, they quickly came to the slope where Sarah and Jason had initially turned back.

'Hold onto this,' Sarah said, handing them the rope and taking one end for herself. Torch in hand, she moved round the corner, splashing through the trickling stream of water, and carefully made her way down the slick incline. Shining the torch ahead, she studied the new section of passageway as it shrank into the distance. 'It levels out, but I can't see the end, even with this torch.'

'That's ten thousand lumens isn't it?' Trish said.

'Yeah, it goes a long way,' Jason told her.

'We'd better get walking then,' Sarah said, and motioned for them to follow her down.

After they'd regrouped, a half hour's walk later they neared the end of the second part of the sodden tunnel, where it branched off in two directions.

'Left or right?' Sarah asked.

'Left,' Jason said.

'Right,' Trish replied at the same time.

'Can you two never agree on anything?' Sarah said, exasperated.

'Eeny meeny it,' Jason told her.

'Eh?' Sarah wondered what on earth he was going on about.

'Bloody hell, you must know eeny meeny miny moe,' Jason said in disbelief.

'Even I know eeny meeny,' Trish said, piping up from the back.

'Look, you freaks, I don't know what sodding eeny meeny is; we're going left.' Sarah moved off in that direction.

'Freaks?' Jason said, as he trailed along behind. 'Coming from the person who hasn't heard of eeny meeny, I think that's a pot kettle black job if ever I heard one.'

As Jason chuntered on, Sarah pressed ahead, her concentration restored.

The seemingly unending tunnel continued in a shallow downward slope, and the ever-present water had steadily increased in volume and now ran around their shoes, a small stream bubbling and burbling as it made its way over a less than even surface. The waterlogged path levelled off again as it twisted and turned more and more until they eventually walked, splashing, around a corner to find themselves in an enormous expanse. A massive drop to the left drew their eyes downwards. Far below, a dark waterfall could be seen cascading into a narrow, silky black lake; its faint roar drifting up to the three explorers high above. To the right, their torches highlighted a large cavern filled with stalagmites and stalactites that sought to greet one another to form a single dripstone pillar. But what lay ahead was spectacular, the remnants of a bridge spanning a great chasm.

'Oh, my God,' Trish murmured in amazement as she took in the sight before them.

Sarah had to agree; it was pretty special. The structure appeared to be a good hundred metres in length by about ten wide. It almost looked like a natural formation; a quick look from one side, however, indicated otherwise. A lack of any kind of natural support hinted that some kind of fabrication was at work. No other features caught the eye except for a tantalising object glinting on the far side. Intrigued, Sarah headed straight for it.

'Sarah, STOP!' Trish cried out, her voice echoing around the gigantic chamber.

Sarah froze, her foot in mid-air. In her eagerness she'd let her caution slip, forgetting to watch her step. As she looked down she saw the reason for Trish's warning, a long rift in the stone cut across her path, cleaving the bridge in two. It wasn't that wide, perhaps a couple of metres, but considering the drop below she'd have fallen to certain death.

'Thanks,' Sarah said with her heart in her mouth.

Trish and Jason came to stand by her side. 'Just watch where you're going next time,' Trish said, her tone stern.

'This is starting to get interesting,' Jason said, as he strained to see the bottom.

Trish gave him a withering look. 'If falling down a big hole and getting dead is your idea of interesting, then you're a bigger idiot than I thought.'

'Guilty as charged,' he said. 'My motto is if you're gonna die, it might as well be doing something you love.'

Trish humphed. 'I'd rather do something I love and not die.'

'Some people just want it all,' Jason said, as if talking to himself.

Sarah ignored them as their bickering picked up again. She walked back a way and then ran at the gap, leaping across it in a single bound. As Sarah shot past them, Trish and Jason did a surprised double take.

'Hey, wait for us!' Jason said, but Sarah was already off to the far end of the bridge, this time with her attention firmly on the ground before her.

Sarah continued to where the end of the bridge opened out into a large plaza. In the middle a huge metal platform, five metres wide and four deep, glinted in the torchlight atop a raised dais. A weathered stone monolith stood immediately behind it and a square object attached to its front face gleamed dully as the beam from Sarah's torch caressed its surface. In its centre was something that made her heart skip a beat: an indented circle.

Sarah mounted the platform and reached up to feel the circle with her hands. It had the same diameter as the one they'd activated on the surface.

'Another circle device,' Trish said as she approached. 'If it works the same way as the other one, anyone on top will be dropped into a pit, or worse.'

'Some kind of trap, perhaps?' Jason said.

Sarah contemplated his suggestion. 'I don't think so, what would be the point? No, it must be another door like the other one, it just needs some faith to use it.'

'Faith isn't the word I'd use,' Trish said, 'and if you think I'm standing on this while it goes all funky and then vanishes, you've got another thing coming.'

Sarah looked over at her. 'Trish, please. We've come all this way, discovered these amazing things. I won't ask anything of you again, I swear, just this one thing, for me?'

'That's not fair. You know I'd do anything for you, but we don't know what will happen, it could be dangerous, surely you must see that?'

'Come on, Trish,' Jason said, 'nothing bad has happened so far. It'll just be another tunnel or room. Imagine what we might find!'

Trish looked at them both. 'Fine!' she said, throwing her hands up in exasperation. 'But only if we secure ourselves with the rope, agreed?'

'Deal,' Sarah said, giving her friend a hug.

Taking out the rope, Sarah quickly tied it around the stone pillar and tested her knot with a few hard tugs. Satisfied it would hold, she returned to the platform and removed her emergency climbing kit from her rucksack, handed a small belt harness to each of them and then secured the rope to these.

'Will this hold us?' Trish said in concern.

'Definitely. This rope uses nano fibres; it's the strongest stuff around. Anyway, if we stand right next to this block, it has a few handholds, we can grab onto it if the worst happens. Relax, it'll be fine.' Sarah gave Trish's shoulder a reassuring squeeze. 'Are we ready?' she asked them both as she took off her jacket and rolled up her sleeves.

'Go for it,' Jason said, excited.

Still uncertain, Trish hesitated. 'I suppose.'

Sarah placed her hand in the centre of the monolith's circle, and either side of her Trish and Jason once more grasped her bare arms.

Nothing happened at first and Sarah was about to take her hand away when she felt a small increase in temperature. 'I think something's happening.'

'Damn right it is,' Jason said. 'Look at the floor!'

Sarah glanced down to see the metal they were standing on shimmered and rippled like liquid mercury. Dark abstract patterns formed to swirl across its surface, creating vortices which spun and eddied around their feet, as a single bright blue line ran around the edge of the metal and alongside the monolith to complete the platform's outline. The circle's warmth increased and the pendant on her chest grew hot.

'I don't like this,' Trish said, fear creeping into her voice.

The blue glow crept in from the edges, filling the whole area with light. Sarah felt a pulsing sensation throbbing through her feet, and an audible hum grew louder and louder around them.

'I really don't like this!' Trish yelled as the sound grew ever stronger. She took her hand off Sarah's arm, but whatever process had begun was not stopping now. Trish jumped off the platform.

Jason also removed his hand from Sarah's arm. 'Sarah,' he shouted over the noise, 'I think you should stop, this is some mad shit!'

Sarah was beginning to agree with them; this was nothing like the small doorway they'd opened earlier. She tried to pull her hand away, but it was stuck fast.

'I can't move my hand!' she told Jason, who still stood next to her.

He grabbed her arm and pulled, but it wouldn't budge. Seeing their plight, Trish came back to help. A few more seconds passed, then Sarah's hand came free and the sound stopped. As they fell back to the middle of the metal platform – which was now pure blue light – Sarah felt an odd sensation of weightlessness. The rope, tight about her waist, went slack and before she even had time to scream she was falling through the floor.

As Sarah plummeted down she heard nothing but the rush of air and a deep constant hum. An intense blue light forced her eyes shut and time lost meaning as the drop continued on and on. Waiting for the inevitable fatal impact that must soon come, she tensed. And yet it didn't come. The sensation of the descent slowed. The winds encircling her lost their ferocity and the accompanying sound altered pitch, peaking even louder and then cutting out. The light vanished and she felt her body gently come to rest on a hard, warm surface. A vortex of air swirled around her, but then that, too, faded and ceased.

'Guys?' she called out to her friends in the darkness.

'I'm here,' Trish said, her voice quavering.

'What the fuck was that?' she heard Jason say, close to her side.

Sarah didn't know; she was more concerned with locating her torch rather than thinking about anything else. She pushed herself to her knees; for some reason she felt exhausted and it took an effort to extend her arms. Her hand touched something cylindrical and rubberised. Grasping it with both hands she pressed a button. A wide beam sprang into existence, illuminating a rock face to the left and a dark abyss to the right. Moving the light around, she saw they sat on a near identical metal platform to the one they had just been on.

'You two all right?' she said, getting up.

'Fine, just shook up.' Trish struggled to her feet and turned on her own torch.

'I'm okay,' Jason said. 'What just happened? I thought we were all goners!'

Sarah shone her torch on the cliff that soared above them. 'Well, we're not where we were before.'

'Then it was some kind of transportation device?' Trish said.

Sarah gazed down at the platform. 'Looks that way.'

'Then where the hell did it transport us to?' Jason said. 'And – more importantly – how do we get back?'

Sarah moved past her friends to take a closer look at the wall adjoining the metallic slab on which they stood.

'That isn't good,' Trish said as they looked at the wall, which failed to reveal a circular inset.

'A one way transportation device,' Jason said in despair. 'This just gets better and better.'

Sarah shifted her rucksack and picked up the rope, which was frayed at one end.

'So much for the rope,' Trish muttered.

'Well, we're not going to get anywhere by just standing around talking,' Sarah said. 'We better start moving, try and find a way out of wherever *here* is.'

Strength had begun to flood back into her body since the fall and with Jason and Trish following, Sarah struck out in the only direction available, forwards. With one hand on the rock on her left and conscious of the cavernous drop to the right, she walked with care, staying away from the edge. After a while it became apparent they were slowly descending in a massive spiral. As they travelled further and further down, Sarah slowed and stopped. The road ahead was blocked – or more precisely, gone. The rock face had given way and taken a large swathe of the pathway with it; small sections still stood, but between them only the void remained.

'Wonderful!' Jason said. 'What now?'

Sarah narrowed the focus of her light and directed it further ahead. 'It looks as though it's only this section that's dropped away. If we can get past this we'll be able to carry on again.'

'"If" being the operative word,' Trish said, also shining her light over the scene which greeted them.

Sarah measured the distance to the first ledge with a small laser built into her torch and then estimated the severed rope's length with her arms. She heaved a sigh. There was only one option available to them.

'I can climb across and then secure the rope,' she told them, 'then I'll throw it back and you two can follow me over.'

'The rope that broke?' Trish said.

Sarah nodded. 'It's the only one we have.'

'It didn't save us before,' Trish said. 'I'm not risking my life with it a second time, no way.'

'That was different,' Sarah said. 'Whatever mechanism put us here obviously cut through it somehow. It will hold, I guarantee it.'

Trish didn't appear convinced.

'Surely we've got to anchor the rope here?' Jason said. 'You climb over and tie it off and we follow you across. If you're throwing the rope back to us that means it's unsecured on the way over, which won't work.'

'We can't do that as we only have a small emergency climbing kit,' Sarah told him, 'and it contains one device to anchor a single point once only.'

'So then Trish and me tie it to ourselves and you go over; secure that end and then one of us climbs over, we then chuck the rope back to the last person and they climb across too.'

Sarah shook her head. 'That won't work either. The first gap is almost the same length as the rope. If it was long enough to tie it around you and Trish and for me to reach the other side – which it isn't – you'd both be perched right on the edge, and if I fell we'd all go over.'

'So that leaves only one option then,' Jason said, frowning as realisation dawned on him.

Trish looked confused. 'And what's that?'

'Sarah climbs over without using the rope, secures the anchor point and then throws it back for us; we then climb over one at a time.'

'You mean to climb over without a safety rope?' Trish said, aghast, as she looked at Sarah. 'Are you serious?'

'There are enough cracks and other handholds, I can make it.' Sarah's expression turned grave. 'Besides there's no other choice, it's either that or stay here and die of dehydration within the week.'

'What if you slip?' Trish said, nearly in tears.

'That would be bad,' she replied.

Sarah knew she could do it. Well, she knew she had to do it as they had no other options open to them. *It's just free climbing without the safety rope*, she told herself. *Just!* she thought, the notion of it making her mouth go dry. Climbing without any safety equipment was actually a discipline called free soloing. Sarah had never fancied it. Her competency at free climbing was all right, but she rarely made an ascent without needing the rope to catch her fall and this time she had no chalk or rock shoes to aid her. On the plus side the distance she had to cover wasn't great or particularly challenging; if she'd had the right equipment, that was.

After some more impassioned discussion Sarah realised they were getting nowhere.

'Enough!' she said. 'It's the only option. I'm doing it and the longer I think about it the more nervous I'll become, so let's get on with it.'

There wasn't much Trish or Jason could say, as neither of them could suggest a suitable alternative, so they were forced to watch in abject silence as Sarah prepared herself by shedding her thick clothing and rucksack. She now wore a short sleeveless top and waterproof combat trousers. Deciding her shoes were too thick and heavy to climb with, she took them off, too, along with her socks.

She stretched the muscles in her arms and legs, warming up her body for the job ahead. She couldn't afford to attempt this when cold; stiffening up or getting cramp could prove fatal. As she limbered up, she realised her combats were restricting her movements too much.

'Don't get excited,' Sarah told Jason, before slipping off her trousers, 'that's as far as I'm going.'

Jason, however, looked pensive, lacking his normal joviality and didn't even register a smile.

As she continued stretching she was glad she'd worn her hotpant briefs rather than anything skimpier – or worse, gone commando. *Modesty is the least of your problems*, she told herself. *Get your mind in gear, Sarah!*

Attaching the harness to her waist, she slung the small climbing bag onto her back and Trish tightened the straps for her, making sure it was firmly in place. Sarah asked Trish if she could use her hair tie. She held it in her teeth as she used both hands to pull back her locks and then held them back with one hand, while she used the other to fasten her ponytail in place with the tie.

'All right,' she said, all business now the task was at hand. 'You'll need to make sure you keep the light on me and the area above and to my right at all times. If I need it below me or to the left I'll let you know.'

Trish gave her a fierce hug and so did Jason.

'Good luck,' he said as he released her.

'Thanks,' she said, and then she turned to eye up her challenge. After a few minutes of studying it, she felt satisfied at her chosen route across to the next section of intact pathway. The expanse measured about seventy feet; the next two sections to climb were shorter, at roughly twenty feet, but she wouldn't be able to assess them until she got closer. With Trish and Jason aiming their torches along the rock face, she faced away from the edge and lowered herself down, her feet searching for a foothold. Satisfied with the support from below as her toes held onto a tiny outcrop, she swung her right arm out to grasp a near vertical crack. Shifting her weight, she located another crevice with her right foot.

As she edged out across the void, her concentration was total. Her first scare came when she misread a handhold. Her fingers slipped downwards and she flattened herself to the wall, her other hand tightening painfully onto its position. As her weight bore down to one side, she felt her toes slipping from beneath her. She didn't have much time to think, removing her hand and putting it back wasn't possible now her body had shifted its balance.

'Down to the right!' she shouted at her friends. The light that wavered above and to her right shifted at her request. There! Now illuminated, a large outcrop cut through with a long wide crack ran perpendicular to the wall. With no more time, she twisted as best she could to face it and launched herself into the air. As she dropped towards her target she felt utter horror, she'd misjudged the distance! Flinging out her hands she slammed into the rock face, the air knocked out of her as her right hand scrabbled for purchase on a smooth vertical surface. She didn't fall, though, as her left hand just managed to hold onto the crack she'd aimed for. With one arm dangling by her side, she saw the cliff face below her flailing legs disappearing down into a deep black nothingness.

Grunting, she braced her left leg against the wall and sought a hold with the other. Sweat dripped into one eye as she steadied herself. Breathing hard, she tried to regain her composure. The sudden fright, however, meant her mind and body had other ideas; she was rooted to the spot, secure in her position and yet paralysed, unable to move away from it. Her heart beat loudly in her ears and the fear sought to destroy her nerve. After a while she heard Trish's voice calling out to her.

'Sarah! Are you okay? You have to move!'

'Come on, Saz, you can make it!' Jason shouted in encouragement. 'Just reach up, there's a hold just above you!'

Sarah still didn't move, but she tilted her head up to look at the section Jason had suggested. *It's too far away*, she told herself, *I won't make it.*

'It's too far!' she screamed back at them, hearing the terror in her voice.

Her friends didn't say anything for a moment and Sarah remained clinging to the rock face, her arms and legs beginning to tremble with the effort.

'Sarah, listen to me!' Jason shouted across. 'Trish, shut the fuck up will you?' Sarah heard him say, and then he continued addressing her again. 'Sarah, if you don't get moving Trish and me are totally fucked. You have to move or we're all dead!'

Sarah closed her eyes tight. He was right, it wasn't just her life she risked, it was theirs as well. Steeling herself, she brutally suppressed her feelings and gritted her teeth, summoning something, anything. Anger welled to the surface and with a snarl she sank down a little and heaved upwards with her arms, propelling herself up into mid-air once more. Her hands grabbed onto the ledge above and she was moving again. She heard Trish and Jason whoop and cheer, but she was back in the zone again and everything else fell away for her except the wall. Amidst the terror of imminent death, Sarah worked her way across the gaping chasm before finally scrambling up onto the middle section of intact pathway, where she collapsed onto her back, her chest and stomach heaving from the exertion.

Once she had regained some energy, she took a tiny oblong-shaped device from her kit and placed it against the wall. Holding it in one hand, she pressed a button on the top, which released a loud charge sending a spiked cam deep into the rock. Sliding off the outer sheaf of the device revealed an elongated shackle on which to attach a cord. Ensuring it was locked in place, she tied the rope to it, coiled it up, and threw it across to Trish and Jason, who caught it after a couple of attempts.

The two both had rock climbing experience, but nothing like Sarah, which made her more than a little anxious as she waited for them to negotiate the hazardous route.

Securing herself to the rope, Trish came across first and she made good progress until she reached the section Sarah had found difficult. Sarah had been telling Trish to feed the rope through her harness, keeping the slack out of it. This advice paid off when she slipped and fell, the rope springing taut as it held her weight, her scream echoing out through the darkness that surrounded them. After a few more scares, and much to her relief, Trish made it to the other side and Sarah helped haul her up onto the safety of the ledge.

Their clothes and gear were the next things to pass over the crevasse, then it was Jason's turn to attempt the crossing. Like Trish, he lost his grip on occasion, sending the rope twanging tight as it supported his weight. Eventually, however, all three stood on the same small ledge that used to be joined to the rest of the pathway.

The next two sections proved a lot easier for Sarah as she had the added protection of the rope. Confidence high, she quickly scaled the first obstacle and then braced herself with the rope so that Trish could cross over more easily. Sending their baggage sliding along the line, Jason followed, with Trish and Sarah both holding the rope to aid his crossing. They handled the next gap with the same process. Once they were all safely across, Jason and Trish secured the rope to themselves and Sarah retrieved the other end, having to cross the two smaller sections twice more.

Back on the path again, and perspiring heavily, Sarah wiped herself down with her jumper as they all took a breather. Having taken on some water, they geared up and pushed on. Since they didn't know where they were, time might very well be of the essence. Their water wouldn't last long and they only had a few chocolate bars in their bags.

Once they reached the bottom of the stone trail, Sarah checked her watch; it had taken them two hours to get that far. Although there was still only one direction to take, which took the stress out of making the right choice.

'Would you look at that,' Trish said in reverence, after they had squeezed past some fallen boulders.

Sarah looked up to where Trish's torchlight cast shadows on an enormous arch that had been carved out of the stone. It rose a hundred feet above them and, as Sarah traced its outline with her own beam of light, she noticed it had been decorated with a multitude of shapes portraying leaves, trees and even animals, some of which seemed vaguely familiar. Sarah withdrew her computer and took a few photos. She just hoped she got the chance to print them out.

As they passed through the archway, Sarah thought she caught sight of something ahead.

'Did you see that?' she asked them.

'See what?' Jason said as he walked past.

'I thought I saw a light up ahead.'

'I didn't see anything,' Trish said, also moving past. 'It was probably the torchlight reflecting off some stone.'

'Yeah, maybe,' she said. But Sarah was certain she'd seen something.

'This place is huge,' Jason called back over his shoulder. 'My light doesn't reach the ceiling of this cavern either.'

No chasms or deep drops littered the way now, just a flat plateau. As they moved deeper in, their lights highlighted strange shapes a few hundred yards away. Jason forged ahead reaching one first. It stuck out of the ground, jet black and stretching upwards like a skeletal arm beckoning to the heavens.

'I think it's a dead tree,' he said, walking around examining it. 'It looks almost fossilised. I've never seen anything like it.'

'How is that possible? We're in a cave.' Trish touched it tentatively and then ran her hand across its surface.

'There are more of them up ahead,' Sarah said, increasing the range of her beam.

There weren't just a few more, there were a lot more, thousands in fact.

'This must have been a forest at some point,' Trish said in awe as they moved amongst the now densely packed trunks, some of which towered far above them.

Keeping up the pace, they continued pressing forwards until finally the dead trees thinned, and then Sarah saw it again.

'I definitely saw a light ahead that time,' she said, speeding up but ensuring she watched her footing.

As the final trunks disappeared she could see it clearly now; a blazing light in the distance, shimmering hundreds of feet in the air. She stopped moving, entranced by the sight of it.

Trish and Jason came to a stop by her side, also lost for words.

The hushed silence persisted, before Trish shattered the spell. 'What do you think it is?' she asked them in a whisper.

'Perhaps Homo gigantis still lives down here,' Jason said, the wonder in his voice mirroring the feelings of them all.

The hairs on Sarah's neck stood up at the thought. She took a deep breath and then expelled it.

'Let's go and find out,' she said and they began walking once more, but at a faster pace, the ethereal radiance temporarily making them forget their plight.

The light turned out to be much farther away than they had initially thought, and when they eventually neared it, they could tell it was a lot higher, too.

'It must be a mile up,' Jason said, tilting his head back to keep it in view, 'if not more.'

Out of the dark another monstrous entrance loomed in front of them and the star-like luminance they'd been following vanished behind it. It had a similar form to the arch they had seen previously, but if anything this one was even bigger. Passing underneath and coming out on the other side, the light failed to reappear and instead a vast blackness rose up before them. As Sarah tried to work out what it was, she heard a noise to her right and a small shape came rolling towards them out of the dark. They all focused their light on it.

'That's strange,' Trish said, as it came to a stop a few yards away.

As they peered at it a small, red, blinking light came on at one end and then a deafening explosion tore through them, knocking them off their feet.

Stunned and disorientated, Sarah stared upwards from where she lay sprawled on her back. Odd looking shapes filled her blurred vision. She couldn't make them out, but they were moving now, and coalescing into indistinct bipedal forms. As her sight cleared, a light bathed her face and what seemed like talking strove to make itself heard over the ringing in her ears. Finger like appendages grabbed and hauled her upright. Her wrists were bound and she was pushed roughly forwards with Trish and Jason by her side. It was clear now these weren't some ancient race of humanoids, not Homo gigantis but Homo sapiens. Humans.

With their torches left behind, the men around them seemed ghostlike in appearance, resembling the forgotten shades of long dead warriors. A dim glow sprang up in front of them, tracing two towering rectangles in the shadows ahead, and a million thoughts swam through Sarah's head as her mind returned to clarity.

'Who are you?' she demanded.

They didn't respond.

'Where are you taking us?' Where are we?'

Again she was met with silence.

Up ahead the lead man raised an arm and waved an object through the air in a curious motion. The rectangles parted and dazzling light erupted between them, streaming out to encompass the three friends and everything else in its path. As their eyes adjusted, a massive city could be seen beyond, teeming with life, a phenomenal tower in its centre soaring above them, its spire shining with a beacon-like brilliance.

'Where are you?' a man said at last in a strong American accent. 'Welcome ... to U.S.S.B. Sanctuary.'

CHAPTER TWENTY-SIX

REBECCA'S LEGS ached and her feet were sore; however, she only had concern for her small flock. The past couple of days had been very confusing and traumatic for a variety of reasons. They had been whisked up by a mysterious group of GMRC employees and a large collective of mercenaries, after having been assaulted by a gang of criminals. They had then been attacked by God knows who and experienced the death of one of their number, a much-loved elderly lady. If that wasn't enough, they'd travelled in claustrophobic conditions for hundreds of miles and then been dumped in the middle of some cold Mexican mountains and left to trudge miles to a secret facility, after which they had been transported deep underground by the biggest elevator ever created and marched along seemingly never ending tunnels.

To top it all off, an earthquake had struck, sending rock cascading down onto their heads. Luckily the only large piece to hit the carers and their wards had Joseph's name on it, and he'd been wearing the helmet Richard Goodwin had given him so it had bounced harmlessly off. Joseph had initially looked at Rebecca in shock, but a big grin had soon reasserted itself on his face when he realised what had happened.

Since the initial quake another smaller one had hit, but it had been a faint echo of the first and hadn't resulted in any more injuries or falling debris. Their relentless walk had resumed soon after and Rebecca had been trying to keep Joseph away from the soldiers who moved along with them. Many wore some kind of weird helmet which made them look like they had glowing eyes. Rebecca thought they looked sinister, but Joseph, apparently undeterred, seemed fascinated with them. She could have done with eyes in the back of her head as he gravitated towards these grim men like filings to a magnet. On one such occasion Rebecca had been helping a younger mentally handicapped girl and turned back to find him gone. Looking about frantically she spotted him off to one side with one such soldier.

'Joseph!' she said, her voice raised in alarm. 'Haven't I told you not to leave my side?'

Joseph grinned and held up a large rifle to show her.

'Oh, my God!' she shrieked, striding over. 'Give me that.' She snatched the heavy weapon off him and shoved it back at the man who'd given it to him. 'Are you out of your damn mind?!' she shouted at the Darklight soldier.

'It's not loaded,' the man said, oblivious to why his actions were inappropriate.

'I don't give a rat's ass. You do not give real guns to him, do you hear me?'

'Yes, ma'am,' the soldier said, nonplussed at her anger.

Joseph had got angry and upset when he'd been taken away back into the mass of civilians; he'd been irritable with Rebecca ever since. Rebecca didn't mind this reaction, she was used to it and much preferred it to the alternative, where he or someone else got hurt, or worse. She blamed herself, however; it was she who had encouraged Joseph with the pretend shotgun back at the care home; how was he to know the difference between a real and a fake weapon? She'd just ended up confusing the poor boy and now she felt guilty when reprimanding him for doing what she'd praised him for previously.

As they trudged ever onwards through the endless caves, Rebecca craned her neck now and then to see ahead, occasionally catching sight of Richard Goodwin alongside the hulking shape of the military leader, Commander Hilt. And, as she glimpsed the pair again, she wondered, not for the last time, where this underground base was and why they hadn't reached it yet; *surely*, she reasoned, *it can't be too much further?*

The sound of thousands of footfalls and the murmur of chatter filled the caverns through which they now passed. Goodwin had been receiving continued updates from Hilt about the progress of the Darklight scouts. As yet they were all coming back the same. No sign of manmade chamber systems or any human habitation at all, just more of the same.

As they descended ever further, Hilt's radio crackled to life once more.

'Commander, we've found something down here,' a soldier said.

'Something?' Hilt frowned at the lack of detail. 'Clarify.'

'It's – well – it's better if you come and take a look for yourself. You're about a click on our six.'

'Very well, I'll be with you shortly.'

Hilt called a halt to everyone's movement and, giving out a few orders to his lieutenant, he made to leave.

'I'll come with you, Commander,' Goodwin said.

Hilt hesitated, obviously weighing up the risks, but Goodwin had already walked past him with a torch in hand.

As they proceeded along the deserted intersecting passageways, Goodwin noticed something. 'Is it me or is the draught getting stronger?'

'You're right,' Hilt said, 'it's almost a light wind; we must be getting near to the base.'

As they rounded a curve in the cave wall they saw light ahead. The reconnaissance team had gathered and switched on their personal lights as they waited for their arrival.

'Sir.' A man saluted at their approach.

'Report,' Hilt said.

'We came across a structure, sir.'

'And this warranted my attention?' Hilt asked the recon leader.

'Yes, sir, follow me.' The man headed off to one side past his men and into a dark opening leading to an adjoining section of the cave system.

The beams of light from the three men sought out and highlighted the features of the chamber they now found themselves in.

'This is manmade,' Goodwin said as he studied the structure of the floor and walls around them.

The soldier didn't comment, but pressed further on until they came to a wide expansive and curiously constructed room, adorned in places with cracked and crumbling carvings of strange description. As their lights converged ahead, they illuminated something Goodwin couldn't quite believe was there.

In front of them a large stone plinth rose up from the floor some thirty feet in length and ten in height, the surfaces intricately carved with a bewildering array of patterns and forms. This in itself would have been a marvel, but what rested on top was a revelation. Perhaps measuring twenty foot long, lay a carved stone representation of a man. Bizarre garments adorned it and while only the side of the face could be seen at an angle, the detail of form throughout was simply amazing, including the thick, long locks of hair on its head. Goodwin had seen such artistry in ancient marble sculptures in museums and galleries, but nothing on this scale.

'And this is what you called me down here to see?' Hilt said, the sharpness in his tone indicating his displeasure.

'Sir, this is amazing. What is it even doing down here? Surely it's worth investigating further?'

'Sergeant, I don't care for statues or tombs or whatever *this* is,' Hilt said, gesturing vaguely at the monument. 'I'm trying to deliver thousands of people to safety and you're showing me some meaningless relic. Forget about it and continue the search at once.'

'Yes, sir!' The soldier saluted, spun on his heel and returned to his men.

Hilt got straight on the radio to tell his lieutenant to start everyone moving again, and then turned to Goodwin. 'I'm sorry, sir, this has held us up needlessly.'

'Don't worry, Commander, it's not much of a delay and besides, this is an incredible find, don't you think?'

Hilt looked at the statue again. 'Perhaps,' he conceded, 'but hardly important in the scheme of things.'

Goodwin removed his mobile computer from his jacket pocket and took some pictures so he could examine them later. 'I wonder who put it here? It looks terribly old. I can't quite grasp how it's located all the way down here, especially considering Sanctuary is only about thirty years old.

'Is it?' Hilt said. 'What do we really know about this base? It's shrouded in secrecy and as far as I know no Darklight teams have ever set foot inside it. Do you know anyone who's ever been here?'

Goodwin considered Hilt's words for a moment. 'The professor has, and the secrecy is just part of the GMRC protocol regarding the subterranean programme.'

'There's secrecy and then there's secrecy,' Hilt said. 'Has Professor Steiner ever disclosed any pertinent information about Sanctuary?'

'He's mentioned systems and management issues on occasion,' Goodwin replied.

'None of which is descriptive of the base itself. I've never heard anything about its structure, design or capacity and now that I come to think of it I haven't met anyone else from any other base that has ever been here, either.'

Hilt was right. Goodwin had never spoken to anyone else who'd been to, or come from, Sanctuary. He'd never really thought much about it before, as plenty of GMRC assets were regarded as black projects. He had high level clearance, but accepted he didn't know everything that went on. This find was very strange, however. He gave it a final look before they left to rejoin the rest of the group.

It wasn't long until they were moving again, but little time had passed before the sergeant came back on the com once more.

'Sir, we've come out of the tunnels into some kind of ... cavern. There's still no sign of the base.'

'Copy that,' Hilt replied.

'Sir?' the Darklight operative said again, his hesitance plain to hear.

'What is it, Sergeant?' Hilt said calmly, with only a hint of exasperation.

'Sir, we've err – found something else. You better get up here.'

Hilt's jaw clenched as the radio went silent. Goodwin hoped whatever the team had found this time was good, for the sergeant's sake. He'd never seen Hilt angry and he decided he didn't want to, either. Nevertheless, it must have been worth risking the wrath of their commander for, and therefore worth checking out, so Goodwin once again accompanied Hilt forwards.

They found the recon teams a few hundred yards outside the exit from the caves they had been endlessly trekking through. The area they were now in was vast, as their torchlight didn't reach any walls; *most likely an unused chamber of the base*, Goodwin presumed. *At last we're getting somewhere*, he thought, relief washing over him like a thirst-quenching wave. Ever since the earthquake he'd begun to fear they'd be trapped down there forever.

Coming to a halt, Goodwin noticed they stood at the edge of a large drop and strangely none of the soldiers had their torches on.

'This better be good, Sergeant,' Hilt said to the man, who had turned towards them at their approach. The rest of his men still had their helmets on and were peering up into the darkness.

'It is, sir; trust me, you won't believe this.' The sergeant detached an odd looking gun from his armour, turned away from them, adjusted a few dials on the side of the weapon and then aimed and fired into the air above them.

A small trail of smoke shot up into the dark and disappeared from view. Silence followed and then after a few seconds a small detonation sounded high above and a plume of yellow light sprang to life, shedding a powerful glow around and beneath it.

The scene that greeted them made Goodwin inhale sharply in surprise and wonder; they weren't in a chamber at all, at least not a small one, definitely not a small one. As he craned his head back towers, huge impossibly tall towers, rose up out of the earth in front of them. As the parachute flare drifted down the recon leader sent up two more, further apart and even higher.

'This is not possible,' Goodwin said, his voice a breathless whisper.

Hilt stood silently by his side, also taking in the unveiling of the spectacle before them as the other flares burst to life.

'There must be scores of them,' Goodwin said.

Another soldier handed him some goggles. 'More like hundreds, sir.'

Goodwin put them on and was greeted with the sight of more towers. They stretched as far as the eye could see, hundreds of spires reaching to the heavens in a great city that humbled anything found on the surface of the Earth many, many times over.

Goodwin gave a shake of his head. 'My God,' he said, the spine-tingling vision sending a shiver of awe coursing through his body, 'what is this place?'

It wasn't long before the thirty thousand strong column of Darklight and GMRC personnel walked between the enormous structures. Using spectral range finders, some of the buildings measured around two miles high.

As Hilt relayed the information to him, Goodwin marvelled at the prospect. 'That's over ten thousand feet!'

'According to the major,' Hilt said, 'the ceiling of this space is another mile above that.'

Goodwin couldn't help but laugh, the sound verging on the hysterical. 'That is just – wow.'

'How is that even possible?' Hilt asked him.

'Well, we know Sanctuary is far deeper than Steadfast, due to the duration of the journey from the surface in the elevator,' Goodwin said at last. 'Couple that with the steady slope through the cave system and we must be about five or six miles down, maybe more.'

'Shouldn't we be experiencing some kind of heat issues this far below ground?'

'Well, yes, you're quite right,' Goodwin said, impressed at the Darklight man's knowledge. 'At this depth it should be reaching around one hundred degrees Celsius. The continental crust ranges from twenty to thirty miles thick and where it meets the mantle, temperatures will exceed four hundred degrees.'

'So how are we not toast?'

Goodwin considered the question. It was a good one. 'There must be something beneath shielding us from the heat. That's the only explanation I can think of that makes any sense.'

'And does the GMRC have that kind of capability?'

'To protect against one hundred degrees C, on this scale? No, not even close, no one does. And the chamber size, an impossibility with current technology.'

'So this place, it isn't—' Hilt said, not knowing how to finish the sentence.

Goodwin held his gaze. 'Made by us? No.'

'Then who ...?'

'Perhaps that tomb was more important than we first thought.'

Hilt nodded mutely as they moved past a huge opening to one of the towers, the size of the doorway mirroring the building it provided an entrance to. The whole place seemed ominous and more than a little spooky as ghostly edifices loomed around them, hemming them in from all sides, even though the widths of the avenues between them were also immense.

Rather than move any deeper into the eerie metropolis, they decided to make camp and sent out larger Darklight teams to map out the terrain and surrounding area. The three main recon units were given the task of searching the closest structure.

As they settled in, Goodwin's phone sounded an alert signal. Considering they weren't in the vicinity of any transmission relay stations, he thought this odd to say the least. Withdrawing it from his pocket he looked at the screen.

It was a video message from the professor.

Selecting it, he moved away to a more secluded area on the edge of their temporary base to ensure he had some privacy. Against the backdrop of the powerful lanterns that the Darklight forces had erected, Goodwin opened out the phone's larger screen and pressed play.

Professor Steiner's face appeared in front of him.

'Richard, if you're watching this video it means you've reached Sanctuary. I will have told you that a message awaits you in my office at the base; however that was to misinform any unwanted eavesdroppers on our conversation. This is the message I want you to hear and I will embed it in the access programme I will be transferring to your phone shortly. The file was set to alert you to its presence when you reached a certain depth, which can only be achieved at Sanctuary.'

Steiner's face became grave as he paused before continuing. 'Richard,' he said, hesitating again, adding to Goodwin's mounting tension. 'What I am about to tell you is well beyond top secret and is far above your clearance level, but given the new circumstances forced upon us by Malcolm Joiner I feel full disclosure is very necessary at this point. When the asteroid 2011 AG5 was first discovered twenty-nine years ago, NASA had already begun testing a new high Earth orbit deep space detection array. This system was categorised as an unacknowledged Special Access Programme – or black project, as we call them – due to its unique capabilities, which included satellite disruption technology that was to be utilised against enemies of the United States, as required.

'During its first year of full operation, the array surveyed large swathes of space. In 2012 this new system revealed an extremely disturbing image. Following in the same trajectory as AG5 were six other asteroids. The first four of the six will be impacting Earth in 2042, the last two in 2045.

'The asteroids striking in 2042 are a variety of sizes. The smallest is half that of AG5, while the largest is five times as big. Considering the predicted fallout from AG5, this next wave will utterly destroy the fragile order that is human civilisation. Any remnants of human life that survive past 2042 will then be faced with the final asteroids in 2045, the largest of which is forty times the size of AG5 and is classed as a world ender. No complex life on the planet's surface or oceans will survive its arrival.

'The reason these objects are so staggered is due to the speed they are travelling at. Over the millennia, varying velocities have ensured the distances between them have been amplified. This stagger is also the reason that the Mount Lemmon Survey that discovered AG5 did not pick up on the presence of the further six objects. Once it was confirmed that the telemetry from the deep space array was correct, it was decided, in the utmost secrecy, to inform other major nations around the world in order for humanity to prepare for the defence of its existence on this planet. Thus the GMRC was born and many subterranean facilities were subsequently designed and built.

'During numerous summits it was agreed, rightly or wrongly, that these powerful governments would keep this terrible truth hidden from the rest of the world in order to maintain stability. Without a well-oiled and performing world economy, the task of creating these underground bases would have been nigh on impossible. Technologies had to be created and advanced in order to ensure our survival; if word had got out then a breakdown in civilisation would have severely hindered our goals.

'You may be wondering how, over the years, these new threats haven't been spotted by the many observatories around the globe. The answer is quite simple; with the world's greatest powers behind you it is easy to subvert and control many things and those we couldn't influence we forced closed. As we also controlled the media, any that slipped through the net were muffled and silenced. Unfortunately when your entire race is under threat of extinction, difficult and sometimes abhorrent decisions must be made.

'After AG5's arrival the dust cloud will ensure the general population doesn't get any forewarning of what is to come, thus ensuring normality continues, at least for a time. This is important as while the GMRC and the world's subterranean bases are ready for the arrival of the next wave of asteroids, there are still many final preparations to make. These preparations might not be as critical as our immediate survival, but they are still extremely important to our continued existence; such tasks include the relocation and protection of as many animals and as much plant life as possible. The placing of as many of humanity's greatest works of art, structures and objects in our B Class subterranean bases, including U.S.S.B. Washington and U.S.S.B. Haven, are still ongoing. With a breakdown of law and order these tasks, and many others, would be much harder to complete.

'The other sad fact is that it is in the interests of the majority of the world's populace that people do not know what is to come. Chaos, disorder and lawlessness would only serve to make everyone's remaining days a living nightmare. It will be hard for you to accept that over ninety-nine point nine per cent of the world's current surface population has less than five years to live. Due to the first wave of asteroids that will arrive in 2042, many of these have under two years of life remaining.

'The truth is,' – Professor Steiner clenched his jaw as he fought to keep a hold of his emotions – 'difficult to hear, I know. When I first found out, I refused to believe it, I wouldn't believe it. Why couldn't we deflect them, blow them up? Anything to prevent their arrival. Believe me, it was attempted, but the distances and speeds involved are beyond immense. For this reason, among others, plans were set in motion for a multi-tiered response to the threats we faced. If we were unable to prevent the arrival of the seven asteroids, we would build subterranean facilities all over the world in order to preserve our species and all other life on the planet.

'While these monumental construction projects began, the world's major space capable nations pooled resources and expertise to tackle the asteroids head on. Under the guise of exploration and communications improvements, over one hundred missions were sent up with varying degrees of success. Many fell short of even landing on 2011 AG5, which was deemed the best trial target since it was the closest to Earth. The few that were able to reach AG5 within mission parameters failed to affect its trajectory, although two came close. Due to further failures and unforeseen complications, it became apparent our resources were being ill-used and the majority of space missions were wound down and finally mothballed in 2035, leaving the subterranean response as humanity's last and only hope.'

Steiner hesitated before proceeding and looked up to see if his captors approached. Satisfied, he carried on. 'Richard, I appreciate this will be a lot for you to take in and I hope you can accept my apologies for not telling you previously. My hands were firmly tied, as they have been for many years. You may be wondering why I ordered the evacuation of Steadfast and why Joiner sought to prevent me from doing so. I realised Steadfast had to be abandoned after I gleaned some sensitive information from General Ellwood, information our beloved Director of Intelligence sorely wanted to keep secret, even from me.

'What I discovered was that one of the asteroids due in 2042 will impact in the immediate vicinity of Steadfast. Such a strike will significantly damage, if not completely destroy, the whole base. At the very least, all subterranean to surface shafts will be catastrophically damaged, ensuring the entombment of everyone below. Joiner must have realised that I had found out about his cover up and launched a pre-emptive strike to head off an evacuation to Sanctuary, the only base with the capacity to take that many people. His reasons I can only guess at, but the man's paranoia and lack of human compassion leads me to think that he didn't want to risk exposure of the GMRC's subterranean program to the public, even though this threat would have been negligible.

'Once he'd launched his attack on the Command Centre my hand was forced, so I issued the evacuation alert in the hope that I could save as many people as possible. It is also my belief that our gifted Steadfast personnel will be able to provide Sanctuary with an excellent pool of workers from which to draw for the good of the base. In my opinion, they will also increase Sanctuary's odds for long term success.'

A noise sounded in the background and the image went dark, accompanied by a rustling noise as Steiner must have slipped the computer phone into his pocket. Some muffled voices could be heard for a while and then the phone was taken back out again and Professor Steiner reappeared in view.

'Sorry about that, one of my guards checking up on me. Anyway, where was I? Sanctuary – right, by now you will have realised that Sanctuary isn't like Steadfast or any other project the GMRC operates. Unbelievably, it has long been known by certain powers in Europe that humanity wasn't the first species to forge an advanced civilisation on Earth. A human cousin had evolved long before us, over nine hundred thousand years ago. The reason this fact is unheard of is mainly due to work carried out by the Catholic Church who, for over a millennia, sought to accrue, destroy and hide all evidence of this ancient dynasty. Why? To preserve their religious doctrine and to retain their power over the masses.

'Their job had been done well. The known sites for this race were located primarily in Europe and South America. Those finds that were outside of these areas were minimal and either discredited or destroyed by nefarious means. To this day, we would have been none the wiser except for a phenomenal discovery made in the United States in the seventeen hundreds. An ancient tomb was found in the Nevada desert, by happenstance. Word spread and it was eventually looked into and covered up by the government of the day. Many years later, one of our presidents stumbled across the secret and decided to set up a special team to investigate the site further. Many more artefacts, bones and structures were unearthed, culminating in the greatest discovery in the history of mankind, Sanctuary itself. Make no mistake, the base in which you now stand is but a tiny part of an underground complex that reaches for well over two hundred miles in length, one hundred miles in width and perhaps twenty miles in depth. Due to its size, over ninety-eight per cent of it is still uncharted.

'What we know about this race is that they were far more advanced than us in many ways. They were also physically much larger and yet their numbers on the surface as far as we can tell were not great. Many mysteries about them remain unanswered, including why they died out. One thing we do know, however, is that our human ancestors knew of their existence. Some speculate that there may have even been direct contact with these human cousins.

'While the Vatican tried to destroy all knowledge of these *giants* they were unable to wipe them completely from history. Myths and legends woven into our culture live on and even the Bible itself has references to this most ancient of races. Other cultures, including the Egyptians, Babylonians and Mayans, amongst others, also hint at the existence of this lost ancestor. There are scientific and many other names given to this race, although perhaps with more than a little irony we refer to them as they were known in the Bible, the Anakim. Obviously all this information is known by only a select few outside of Sanctuary itself. The existence of the ancient underground structure has also not been disclosed to any other government, including that of Mexico, which believes the base is merely a manmade expansion of a naturally occurring cave system.'

Steiner paused for breath and then continued once more. 'I imagine you will watch this message more than once, as I would, too, in your position; please ensure, though, that no one else sees it, as this information is extremely powerful and dangerous in the wrong hands.' Steiner looked around his small room. 'Considering my current position and Joiner's quest for power, it appears I may not see you again or be able to help progress Sanctuary in the future; this job I now leave up to you. You must try to gain control of the base or at least be included in its management and direction. I have long admired your expertise and management skills, but what I prize most highly is your duty of care to those who you work to protect. Sanctuary, much to my disapproval, is run by the U.S. military and that means Joiner will essentially have control; this status quo cannot be left to stand and civilian governance must be established, as humanity's future may very well rest upon it.'

Steiner looked up from the camera once more and then back again. 'I must go, Richard. Be careful, good luck and Godspeed.'

And then the display went black. A blue screen followed and the writing *END OF VIDEO* appeared. Goodwin stared at the blue image for a long time before eventually pressing the replay button.

EPILOGUE

SARAH MORGAN STRUGGLED against the two U.S. soldiers marching her down a long corridor lined on both sides with reinforced metal doors.

'Where are you taking me?!' she said, unable to keep the fear from her voice.

The sound of their echoing footsteps was her only answer as the men remained tight-lipped.

'Where are my friends?!' Sarah leant back against their grasp, forcing them to slow.

One of her captors gave a growl and she was hauled forwards.

'I'm a British citizen; you have no right to do this!' Terrified, Sarah fought to escape, but the soldiers dragged her on, their powerful grips tightening around her arms.

They finally reached the end of the corridor and a heavy metal door was opened.

Sarah looked into the tiny cell in horror and planted her feet in desperation as they forced her forward. She jammed her foot against the door jamb, stopping her momentum, but a heavy shod boot kicked it away and she was thrown inside.

Sarah staggered forward, then spun round and surged back to the opening just as the door to the cell slammed shut with a resounding boom!

The sound of keys rattling, a lock clicking and metal bolts sliding into place preceded two sets of receding footsteps as the men retreated back the way they'd come.

Sarah screamed and hammered on the door. 'NO!! Where are you going?! You can't do this, I have rights! YOU CAN'T DO THIS!!

Outside the cell door her screams and shouts fell on deaf ears as the soldiers disappeared around the far end of the now empty corridor.

Sarah Morgan's quest was at an end, and only her despairing cries for freedom echoing along the desolate halls of a top-secret facility, hidden deep underground, were testament to her ever having existed at all.

'NO! Let me out!!'

The further down the hallway, the quieter her calls became.

'You can't do this ... where are my friends ... where are you going?! LET ME OUT!!!'

'Are the other two secure?'

The corporal gave a nod.

'And their belongings?'

The second soldier handed a transparent plastic bag to his commanding officer.

The sergeant emptied the contents into a cardboard carton and peered inside, then poked around at the different items on display, the most interesting of which included a metallic tablet, parchments and a couple of pentagonal pendants.

He dismissed his colleagues and then sealed the box with red tape before writing some numbers on a white label on its side, and the words *FOR ANALYSIS* on the lid with a black marker pen.

He passed through an office, opened a door at the back of the room and entered a huge unlit storage facility containing row upon row of shelving housing boxes similar to the one he held. Under the dim light streaming in through the now open doorway, he walked down one of the aisles, his footfalls tip-tapping through the deserted area. Eventually he stopped and pulled across a ladder connected to a set of rails, then climbed up to the fifth level of ten and slid the box into an empty space alongside its fellows. Having deposited his cargo, he climbed back down and returned to his office, the sounds of his passage fading away to silence before he closed the door behind him, plunging the warehouse back into darkness.

High in Earth's orbit a large mirrored oval structure glided through space. Located on the side of its control module was a large NASA insignia and the letters D.S.D.A., and underneath these letters were the words *Deep Space Detection Array*.

Inside the white hull of the satellite, a brightly lit screen operated. In one corner red words reading *Transmitting Telemetry Data* blinked on and off. In the centre of the screen a small circle indicated Earth's location, and spiralling out from this circle was a single line, which eventually came into contact with six red dots. Each dot had a small black window attached to it with the words *Tracking* at the top and a continuous flow of spooling data underneath.

Far out into space, the immense black asteroids under surveillance rotated slowly, glinting in the magnificence of the Sun, their momentum undiminished as they continued their inexorable, and unstoppable advance towards Earth ...

The Ancient Origins series continues with...

Ancient Origins: Dark Descent
(Book Two of Ancient Origins)

available at
amazon

https://geni.us/darkdescent

It would be wonderful if you were able to leave a review of Revelations: Ancient Origins Book 1:

https://geni.us/review-revelations

ALSO BY ROBERT STOREY

Ancient Origins: Revelations

(Book One of Ancient Origins)

Ancient Origins: Dark Descent

(Book Two of Ancient Origins)

Ancient Origins: Let There Be Light

(Book Three of *Ancient Origins*)

Ancient Origins: Genesis

(Book Four of *Ancient Origins*)

Ancient Origins: The Tenth Protocol

(Book Five of *Ancient Origins*)

Ancient Origins: The Lost Prophet

(Book Six of *Ancient Origins*)

https://geni.us/robertstorey

BOOK 2: DARK DESCENT - PREVIEW

Some people say the cosmos is a mere reflection of life on Earth, a mirror with which one can gaze into the depths of everything that life was, is, and will be. Others hold to the belief that God created the night sky in a matter of days, or that what we are actually seeing is merely a projection, a trick or sleight of hand on an epic scale. Scientists tell us with an unyielding certainty that the light from the stars is millions, even billions, of years old and that as we gaze into the night sky we are looking back through time and witnessing the past; a past before any one of us first drew a mortal breath or long before our species had even evolved.

Whatever theories of the universe you hold to, one thing is clear; it brims with glorious beauty in all shapes and forms. Pinpricks of flickering light populate the heavens while dazzling magnificent rotating discs, so bright and vast that they can only be appreciated from afar, punctuate an expanse beyond measure. But without the darkness there would only be light. And without contrast there is no beauty, no good, no evil, no life. If there is one, there must be the other; as with all things, equilibrium must always resolve itself.

On the fringes of space, framed against this backdrop of blissful cosmic serenity, a small craft orbited the once majestic vista that was planet Earth. Where before beautiful clear skies, glistening deep blue oceans and lush green forests could be seen, now only an all-encompassing thick, dark cloud remained. Far from featureless, the predominantly brown and black veil remained in a constant state of flux. Hurricane-force winds created huge vortices which revealed fleeting glimpses of the surface below; such momentary insights into what lay beneath were quickly swallowed up, snuffed out of existence like a small candle within a great and volatile tempest. Enormous thunderstorms coalesced over half a continent, sending lightning flashing and flickering across the upper atmosphere, with the occasional super plume reaching out into space itself.

Drifting through the celestial sphere, untouched by the maelstrom far below, the tiny vessel continued its balletic odyssey; and on the side of this distant wayfarer's white hull, large, black letters read:

U.S.S.S. ORBITER ONE

Underneath this, the evocative flag of the United States of America, the star-spangled banner, glinted majestically as the light of the sun streamed across its cold, pristine surface. Rotating through the icy vacuum of space, Orbiter One turned in slow motion, small white lights blinking on and off in leisurely regularity along its silken, metallic length. Inside, through this thin alloy skin, past bulkheads and cocooned within a mass of electrical and finely-tuned mechanical equipment, a small yet comfortable area provided room to live and work for two resident NASA astronauts.

Tyler Magnusson and his colleague, Ivan Sikorsky, currently on long term assignment, sat at the observation and control deck. The large, transparent, domed window provided the two men with a clear view of their target, an imposing disc-shaped structure that approached from their port side. Concave and smooth, the massive ship's topside was crammed full of high-yield solar panels while the underbelly sprouted an intricate latticework of intersecting walkways and modules of various shapes and sizes. The United States Space

Station, also known as the U.S.S.S. Archimedes, moved within final docking range.

'Orbiter One, this is Archimedes on final approach,' a strong female voice said over the internal speaker system. 'Prepare clamps and adjust position as per the navigation graphics showing on your screen projection.'

'Copy that, Archimedes,' Tyler replied before dialling into the computer the new parameters for the craft's trajectory. 'Action pitch and yaw adjustments on my count,' he told Ivan. 'Three – two – one – manoeuvre.'

Small puffs of air vented into space as Orbiter One lined up with one of the space station's external entry ports.

'Synchronising,' Ivan intoned, carrying out the final docking procedures.

'Reduce thrust by fifteen per cent aft,' Tyler said.

Ivan rotated a small joystick, its white rubber surround stretching as it inched back, notch by minute notch. 'Reducing thrust by fifteen per cent aft,' he confirmed.

The two space vehicles came together and Tyler felt a soft but perceptible jolt pass through the orbital vehicle. A clunk of dense metal on metal, and a muffled hiss of hydraulics, indicated the sophisticated dampers, locks and clamps activated flawlessly to secure Orbiter One in place.

'Welcome home, gentlemen,' the female flight controller said. 'Once you have acclimatised from micro gravity to the partial gravity environment here on Archimedes we can proceed with a full mission debrief at zero four hundred hours.'

'Copy that, Flight,' Tyler said. 'We'll look forward to some hot chocolate and cookies, which I'm sure the captain will have waiting for us when we get there.'

'I'll be sure to let him know of the request,' the woman replied with no hint of humour. 'Archimedes out.'

Ivan flicked off some switches overhead. 'She's a barrel of laughs.'

Tyler shrugged. 'She must be new.' He powered down Orbiter

One's systems, putting the ship they'd spent many months aboard into hibernation. 'All I know is, it's good to be back.'

A mere three hundred and sixty minutes later, at four hours past midnight, Central Standard Time, Tyler and Ivan found themselves loosely strapped into chairs in front of a large, oblong, transparent table in a circular conference room. Each held an Orbiter One mission folder. Across from them the captain of the Archimedes, Bo Heidfield, sat on a similar seat, flanked by various members of NASA, the U.S. military and the GMRC, the Global Meteor Response Council.

It had always irked Tyler that the GMRC had such control over NASA and the U.S. space programme in general. Well, perhaps *control* wasn't the right word, *influence* may have been more appropriate. The GMRC would recommend, request and suggest with increasing frequency until the powers that be relinquished or came up with alternatives to satisfy the GMRC bigwigs. Of course, it wasn't just the U.S. that had to submit to this kind of intervention; the Europeans, Chinese and International space programmes also had to toe the GMRC line. Unilateral cooperation was paramount to the survival of the human race, or that's what he was told, anyway; what all select NASA employees were told when they were given the real truth.

In order to ensure an efficient and effective planetary response to the asteroid threat the GMRC would lead the way and every nation on the planet had signed up to abide by its guidance. While this sounded fair and just, it was far from democratic, as the world's entire civilian population had no vote on the issue, or any idea what was to come. As far as Tyler understood it, and gossip was rife within the segregated space station fraternity, over ninety-five per cent of each country's politicians also had no idea of the scale of the threat to humanity and planet Earth itself.

Everyone, of course, was aware of the first meteorite, 2011 AG5, which had struck in 2040 – over six months ago – off the South African coastline. 2011 AG5's existence and predicted repercussions had been disclosed to the public in 2022. No, what the rest of the populace was blissfully unaware of was that six more asteroids were on their way and that life on the surface of Earth was nearly at an end. It was a stark and terrifying thought that life as we knew it was to cease in 2045 when the last of the asteroids arrived. Thankfully, for Tyler and his family, his job had ensured their continued survival. They were guaranteed precious harbour in one of the United States' underground facilities. Even Tyler and his small circle of colleagues in the know were left in the dark as to the location or scale of the base they were destined to live out their days in. He only knew its name, United States Subterranean Base Steadfast, or USSB Steadfast for short.

Tyler glanced up as movement caught his eye through the large transparent ceiling above. A streamlined Sabre space-aircraft had just arrived from Earth and was coming to rest at a refuelling arm. Tentacle-like hoses snaked out from Archimedes to lock onto it, like a giant squid with its prey. Yet this squid was supplying life, not taking it, as the craft's exhausted tanks were replenished with vital oxygen and fuel.

The NASA captain cleared his throat, bringing Tyler back to the present.

'Gentlemen,' Bo Heidfield said, addressing the two Orbiter One astronauts in a formal, business-like tone. 'First I'd like to congratulate you both on the completion of your mission. You have been in micro gravity for one year, so I hope your transition to life on Archimedes has not been too taxing. As you will have been informed, we are joined by GMRC representatives who are here to ensure all information transfer conforms with their strict protocols.'

'My apologies for interrupting, Captain,' said a woman sitting immediately to Bo Heidfield's left, 'but we are more than mere observers and administrators. We are here to report directly to the GMRC's senior Directorate and to advise them on the information gathered here today.'

Tyler noticed Bo's eyebrow twitch and a clear expression of anger appeared on his face at the woman's comment, an indicator that he was far from his usual impassive self. Tyler knew Bo well enough to realise tensions were running high between the factions in the room; looking around at the faces assembled he wondered how he'd missed it before. What the GMRC were up to now to cause such feelings he was sure to find out later. Now, though, he was here to report on Orbiter One's mission.

Ivan began their presentation on the weather patterns of the all-pervasive dust cloud caused by the fallout of the asteroid, 2011 AG5.

'As you can see,' Ivan said, while everyone in the room turned to the current page of his report, the paper documents rustling in unison, 'the dust cloud has reached a stable density in Earth's upper atmosphere. The Coriolis effect produced by the Earth's rotation and axial tilt has reasserted its force and the cloud now conforms to a new, but predictable, weather pattern. The circulation cells are now clearly visible due to the cloud's particulates providing a visual reference of their direction and path.

'From observations made on Orbiter One, over hundreds of tracks at varying compass points, we were able to extrapolate a lot of useful data on the intense weather currently being experienced on the surface. The unusual and powerful lightning strikes which have caused disruption to the GMRC's Subterranean Programme across the Americas and Eurasian continent are symptomatic of the negatively charged particulates and the enormous super cells that have been forming on a regular basis over the last few months.

'Utilising large data groups,' Ivan continued, 'we have been able to accurately predict the occasional breaks in the global cloud cover. This will obviously be useful in scheduling Sabre flights to and from the surface, and to position and launch rockets into orbit for various purposes.'

Ivan went into further detail about forecast weather patterns and areas of specific scientific interest, and then Tyler took over the report.

'If you turn to the next section,' Tyler told them, flipping over a couple of pages from his own folder. 'You will note the thermal images we have taken over the last six months. Underneath each image are corresponding charts and tables outlining temperature drops in comparison to the previous month and to the location's normal rolling ten year average temperature, prior to the asteroid AG5's strike.

'Figure five point three dash A is an enhanced image taken of the Sahara Desert two weeks after Impact Day—'

The GMRC observer who had irritated Bo Heidfield, interrupted Tyler's flow. 'Pilot Commander Magnusson,' the woman said, addressing Tyler by his formal title and with a supercilious air. 'Can you tell me why there appear to be no images here for the two weeks after Impact Day? Surely this was the most important time to collect such information?'

Bo looked like he was about to intervene, but Tyler was prepared for the question. 'Due to the unforeseen speed of the dust cloud kicked up by the primary strike we were unable to record said data as scheduled. As I'm sure you are aware the cloud was meant to take six to twelve months to cover the entire planet and yet in actuality this event took only days to unfold. Orbiter One operates on a strict prearranged course to maximise fuel and operational efficiency. We were unable to react to the cloud's speed at such short notice without significantly compromising future mission parameters. Two weeks was the time it took to reposition.'

Tyler waited for a response, but the woman merely nodded and motioned for him to continue.

'As I was saying,' he said, 'figure five point three dash A is a thermal image of the Sahara Desert two weeks after Impact Day. It clearly shows a dramatic temperature drop compared to the previous month and to previously observed averages. The following images for this particular location show further temperature drops over the next three months, not of the same magnitude as the initial fall, but significant nonetheless. After this the figures become steadier and in line with averages, albeit at a much colder level. Across the surface of the planet we have witnessed a drop in temperature equivalent to eight degrees Celsius or fourteen point four Fahrenheit. Africa has experienced a higher than average fall of ten degrees Celsius or eighteen degrees Fahrenheit; this is mainly due to the thicker cloud cover over the region due to the extensive wildfires instigated by the initial strike. Impact winter is very much upon us, although it is not as severe as some models predicted.'

Tyler carried out the remainder of his report in greater detail before closing the Orbiter One report folder. He then pulled a secure case onto his lap, the exertion required to lift it a tenth that of normal due to the partial gravity experienced on Archimedes. He activated the security locks using a combination of biometrics and codes, a process Ivan had to repeat before handing it back to him. Tyler opened the case and withdrew a bundle of reports, each wrapped within bright red film. Tyler passed one to Ivan, took one for himself and handed the rest to Bo, who distributed them to those sitting either side of him.

Once everyone had a copy, Tyler took his file and tore away the top edge using the supplied metal strip manufactured into the film. Everyone else followed suit, the tearing noises briefly filling the room. Removing the red sheath revealed the black folder inside. On the front of this a white panel had been placed containing the following bold, red text:

CLASSIFIED DOCUMENTS

GMRC Clearance Level: 10 Alpha
Special Access Personnel Only

NASA Clearance Level: AMBER 1
SEGREGATED PERSONNEL
EYES ONLY

Inside the front cover the NASA insignia was printed on white paper, its familiar blue disc and white lettered logo standing out against the background. Below this a heading read:

D.S.D.A.
Deep Space Detection Array
& PROJECT ARES

Collated Report
February, 2041

Tyler began detailing the information to the room. He noted the main attributes of each of the six approaching asteroids, including the latest composition, spectral light and deviation analysis. Potential fracturing events had also been assessed and predicted and proffered up graphically for the various scenarios. Everyone in the room knew that any splitting of the asteroids prior to impact would result in vastly different outcomes and subsequent fallout. This collective foresight was due in the main to one such occurrence having already happened when 2011 AG5 had gravitational forces exerted on it as it passed the Moon. A smaller chunk had broken free and ended up wiping out a large city in northern India. Nothing could alter the final outcome, of course, but there would be some form of human activity on the surface of Earth until 2045, and the GMRC wanted to avoid any hindrance to its subterranean programme prior to its final protocols reaching fruition.

Finally Tyler reached the most anticipated part of the report, the plain white page he'd turned to displaying an elegant silver logo in its centre:

PROJECT ARES

While on their analytical, fact-finding mission aboard Orbiter One, the two astronauts had also been tasked with testing a new piece of technology devised by the U.S. military and the highly secretive GMRC R&D Division. Strangely, the substantial piece of equipment in question was missing a large, critical component. Ivan had pointed out as much when the two astronauts had first been prepped for the operational procedures prior to their deployment. They had been told they were to test the system's functionality in the rigours of space. They were not there to test its full capability or to even understand what it was they were actually testing. This was perhaps the strangest part of the whole operation. The ambiguity and secrecy of what it was they had on board and were tasked to carry out a multitude of diagnostics on, was more than a little disturbing especially considering the military's involvement.

As Tyler went through the results from Project Ares, which encompassed an assortment of observational data, computer readout analysis, error codes and system parameters during partial operation, he was asked the occasional question by a couple of the GMRC personnel who were lead scientists on the programme. As he completed the debrief the questions increased.

'Did you experience any undue fatigue when the device was activated for longer than thirty minutes?' one of the scientists said, peering intently at the two astronauts over the rim of his glasses.

'We both felt a little tired,' Tyler looked at Ivan for confirmation, 'but that may have been due to the intensity of the daily schedule we were adhering to.'

The scientist nodded and jotted something down on his notepad.

Before Tyler could continue, the second scientist asked, 'Did either of you witness any unusual visual activity during the final testing period?'

Tyler didn't really understand the question. 'Such as?'

'Any hallucinations or disturbances around the module when it was deployed outside of Orbiter One?'

Again Tyler glanced at Ivan who shook his head. 'Not that we noticed.'

The other scientist once more scribbled something down on his notepad. Tyler was beginning to get an uneasy feeling about the direction the line of questioning was taking and looked to his captain for reassurance. Grim-faced, Bo avoided his gaze.

'And did either of you encounter any difficulties sleeping or breathing during or after the operation of the machine?' asked another man at the opposite end of the table, a U.S. military officer who had, until now, remained silent.

Tyler looked around the room. 'Is there some danger attached to using this device?' Like Bo, some of them – mainly the NASA employees – avoided eye contact with him, while others looked on impassively. He suddenly understood how a rat might feel when being experimented on by men in white coats, an array of disturbing apparatus close to hand; it was not a pleasant feeling.

'Of course not, Commander,' the GMRC woman said. 'We are just being thorough. We can check through your bio readouts and visual records for the mission at our leisure rather than bore you with any further questions.'

After some final statements everyone handed back the mission reports, which Tyler resealed in the case before handing it to Captain Heidfield, who in turn handed it to the military man who had been the last to question them. As everyone filed out from the room, aided by semi-magnetic footwear for ease of movement, Bo indicated to Tyler that he wanted to speak with him; he moved to one side and waited until they were left alone.

The captain approached him. 'Follow me, Commander,' he said and moved off down a deserted corridor, his shoes echoing metallically on the grid flooring. With Tyler at his heels, Bo Heidfield passed through a more populated section of the vessel and then down another confined walkway, its small windows filled with the view of the blighted Earth, its long, curved surface stark against the blackness of space. The next intersection they came across had eight diverging passageways. Two of these offshoots were guarded by four heavily built GMRC security operatives, who moved to bar any entry to the areas beyond. Such restricted access on Archimedes was unheard of and clearly this constraint also seemed to include the captain himself, who neither slowed nor looked in the guards' direction as he passed.

Tyler, however, found himself gawping at the spectacle and he craned his neck to watch as the eyes of the GMRC men followed his every move until he'd disappeared from view. While projectile weapons aboard a spacecraft were strictly prohibited, for obvious reasons, Tyler had been quick to recognise the advanced Taser and stun gun devices each guard had holstered at their waist. The reason for the animosity towards the GMRC personnel the Archimedes captain had displayed during the debrief suddenly became clear. Not only had the GMRC brought with them armed soldiers, but they had also cordoned off parts of the ship, which even the captain was apparently prevented from accessing.

It wasn't long until Bo halted his march at a white, nondescript, reinforced hatch. Looking up and down the passage to ensure no one was around, Tyler's commanding officer tapped in a six digit passcode and swung the door open. Entering, he motioned Tyler to follow. Once they were both inside he shut the door, turning the large wheel attached to its inner skin and locking it in place; the circular handle reached the end of its rotation with a dull thud, the noise echoing in the small room in which they now found themselves ensconced.

Without saying anything further the captain turned on a computer station and fired up a large screen located on one of the walls.

'Sir, what's going on?' Tyler asked. The captain was now accessing some part of the ship's internal computer system. 'Why is that section of the ship off limits? Have you seen what they are guarding? And they have weapons too, that's against one of NASA's fundamental directives.'

The captain stopped what he was doing while a small dialogue box on the screen read *accessing data feed* in bold green letters. He looked at Tyler with haunted eyes. 'The GMRC and U.S. military have deemed it in the global and national interest to utilise the USSS Archimedes as a base of operations for some kind of bastardised scientific research programme.'

'What kind of programme?'

'The kind that NASA would never sanction unless it was forced upon them. The kind that seals off whole parts of the damn ship and prevents even her captain from knowing what's been brought on board.'

The computer beeped and an error message popped up on screen. The captain swore and started typing on the keyboard once more. The previous message reappeared: *accessing data feed.*

'Ten days ago,' Bo continued, 'I was contacted by Mission Command at Houston. On a conference call I was informed that the military and GMRC would be requisitioning Archimedes for something we are all too familiar with, Project Ares. Amidst high security a cargo was flown from the surface and placed within the main laboratory modules and access has been limited ever since, with guards like you just saw posted around the clock. Whatever they are doing on this ship one thing is for certain, the safety of every one of my crew has been compromised as a result.

'Since they arrived, five of our team have experienced vivid nightmares and two have exhibited breathing difficulties. One of our youngest pilots also experienced extreme psychological events and he had to be sedated and, with the rest, sent back to the surface. As far as I was able to ascertain through the official and unofficial channels all of them are under quarantine, pending further tests. A team of doctors has been on board to carry out exams on the rest of us; so far we all seem to be in the clear of whatever it is that's causing these symptoms.'

'Jesus,' Tyler said as he tried to take in what he'd just been told. 'So what are we doing here?'

Bo glanced at the screen, which still displayed the same message. He looked back to Tyler. 'Before they took control up here I was informed that the lab was to be cleared and all cameras and recording equipment were to be extracted, barring life support and critical systems sensors. Having to adhere to their request, I cleared the area under GMRC supervision. However, the safety of my crew is my priority, first and foremost, and so in order to find out what they were bringing with them I managed to install a small remote camera with the help of Sandy Turner.'

'The spacewalk specialist?' Tyler said.

Bo nodded. 'When Sandy was on her way out for some routine maintenance I slipped her the device and she positioned it on a limb which has line of sight to the laboratory's window cluster. Initially I was unable to get a look at whatever they had in there, but my luck changed yesterday when it was repositioned.'

Tyler's curiosity was peaking, but not in a good way. Whatever was occurring on this space station was tied directly to the machine he and Ivan had been extensively testing on Orbiter One, a piece of equipment intrinsically linked to a project that had already compromised some of the crew's health, both physically and mentally.

'Here we go,' the captain told him as the screen dissolved into a four picture live stream of the outside of the Archimedes main laboratory complex.

Tyler scanned the images for anything unusual. 'What am I looking for?'

'There.' Bo pointed at the bottom right feed. He tapped a couple of buttons and expanded it so it filled the whole screen.

At first Tyler could only see the movement of technicians, all of whom wore white hazmat suits and breathing apparatus. 'I can't see—'

'Wait,' Bo said, cutting him off and pointing to one particular window.

Tyler watched and then one of the people moved out of the way and he could see part of – something. 'What is that?' he said in a hushed tone as he stood transfixed, staring at the screen.

'I have no idea. It's like nothing I've ever seen before.'

'It looks—'

'Alive.'

Tyler couldn't take his eyes off it. 'Yes.'

'If you look at the technicians,' the captain told him, 'you can see they are documenting their work on a computer terminal on the right hand side of the room. I know ten years back you were tasked with the simulations for all of Archimedes' internal sensors.'

'That's right,' Tyler said with a small nod of his head, still intently watching the oddity.

'Are you able to access them and get us some audio to go with this picture?'

Tyler thought for a moment, recalling memories he thought he would never use again. *Yes, I can do that*, he concluded. It was relatively easy for someone who had spent eighteen months fault finding to the nth degree. Taking over the console, he executed a few commands and altered a subroutine and then rerouted the sensor's signal.

'That should do it,' Tyler informed his captain.

Bo turned up the volume on the display.

A strange oscillating noise came through the audio system. At first Tyler thought he had made a mistake, but as he watched the screen once more he realised he had utilised a sensor in the room where the object was located. He also noted that the technicians were wearing some kind of hearing protection underneath their suits; he presumed the noise must have been a lot louder in the room itself.

At that point the sound changed; its pitch made the hairs stand up on the back of his neck and sent an odd tingling sensation running down his spine. A movement in the room dragged his eyes away from the strange vision that had so mesmerised him. The captain, hyperventilating, his breath coming in ragged gasps, had dropped to one knee.

'Sir, what's wrong?' Tyler asked, gripping the man's shoulders in an attempt to stop him shaking. The audio coming through the room's speakers changed again and Bo convulsed, froth seeping from his mouth.

'Sir!' Tyler shouted in alarm, but he was helpless to do anything as his superior's legs beat wildly on the floor. Realising the feed from the lab had sparked the fit he slammed the audio off, almost breaking the touchscreen as he did so. Turning back, he saw that Bo now lay unmoving; his eyes open in a fixed stare. Tyler felt for his pulse; there wasn't one. In a panic-induced state, he made sure the man's airway was clear, repositioned the body and began CPR. After what seemed like mere moments, but must have been many minutes, he stopped to regain his breath; his arms ached and his head throbbed. He looked down in despair at his long term colleague. Getting unsteadily to his feet, he reached out and hit the emergency response alarm, sending lights flashing and sirens wailing throughout the ship. The captain was dead.

CHAPTER 1

New York City, USA. Year: 2041.

Sirens wailed and chirruped, drifting on the wind while red and blue lights pulsed and flickered over the buildings of Manhattan Island as emergency vehicles sped through its troubled and turbulent streets. In the foreboding black skies above, police and civilian helicopters fought a battle of cat and mouse, one seeking to impose a no-fly zone on the other. Ominous storm clouds gathered on the horizon, warning those in its path of the rain to come by bellowing out deep, far reaching claps of thunder and thrusting down dazzling bolts of lightning.

In the centre of this maelstrom of activity a seemingly endless line of large, jet-black, twin propeller helicopters approached from the Hudson River to the east. Emblazoned on their sides was a familiar white logo.

GMRC

One by one they fell into a holding position around a large circular skyscraper, carrying out an intricate aerial dance while other pilots sought to unload their passengers as quickly as possible while avoiding the next wave coming in to land on the tiered helipads adorning the building's roof.

Far below, at street level, tens of thousands of protestors had gathered outside the edifice and right in the heart of the chaos, a small, handsome woman stood facing a cameraman. She wore a bright red, fur-lined, three-quarter length hooded trench coat and thick, blue, thermal mittens, her long, dark hair falling in immaculate waves across her shoulders. In one hand she held a clipboard and in the other a microphone. Behind her, an imposing blockade had been erected from metal fencing, steel bollards and – for good measure – heavy-duty plastic and wooden barriers, replete with red and white stripes, each pillar topped with a flashing orange beacon. Behind these obstructions, a vast array of NYPD officers had assembled. Further back, in the shadows, heavily armed U.S. soldiers lurked, assault rifles locked and most certainly loaded, ready and willing to repel any unwanted visitors to the gathering unfolding inside.

A bitter wind whistled down Ninth Avenue. Paper bags and other detritus swirled around the feet of the protestors, who shouted their fury at the untouchable dignitaries being ferried in high above. For what seemed like the hundredth time, the woman swept back her hair with one hand, placing it to one side in order to keep it from covering her face. A few strands caught in her mouth; she pulled them away as she looked around her to make sure she had the required space to work.

The camera and light operator held up five fingers, then four, three – the woman's face changed from a look of concentration to one of serious intent as she shook her hair back and squared up to the camera's lens – two, and finally his index finger pointed straight out to indicate she was on air.

'This is Jessica Klein reporting live from New York City for the BBC's Worldwide News Service,' the woman said in a flawless English accent, her voice raised to be heard over the cacophony of noise filling the air around her. 'In the skies above me, as I speak, the world's leaders, greatest scientific and military minds are being flown in from this iconic city's surrounding airports for the Global Meteor Response Council's annual summit. As ever, this vital meeting is being held behind closed doors, with the tightest of security and the minimum of disclosure. What will be discussed in the GMRC's imposing HQ behind me is a matter of great debate and of increasing national and international concern.

'It has been six months since the meteorite impact and in that time the world has experienced devastating climate change, plunging the northern hemisphere into sub-zero temperatures. The all-pervasive dust cloud transformed our days into twenty-four hour long nights, resulting in catastrophic failure of ecosystems on an unprecedented scale. The GMRC has long prepared us all for these events, but the reality of them has been far more traumatic and chaotic than anyone could have imagined.

'The initial panic and terror caused by the unexpected speed of the meteorite's fallout, specifically the dust cloud itself, threatened to bring humanity to its knees. Swift action taken by governments around the world acting on GMRC protocols did well to prevent a global collapse of law and order. The methods utilised to accomplish this task, however, are still being questioned. As ever, the GMRC has covered up the true cost every nation has paid. The countless deaths of civilians only equalled in ignominy by the far greater number of those injured as National Guards ruthlessly quelled widespread rioting and violent disorder. The blood of the innocent, many say, is on the GMRC's hands.

'Since those horrific times, now referred to as the Days of Blood and Dust, civilisation has teetered on the brink of disintegration in the majority of the world's nations. Those countries that were already fragile, where stability had already been sporadic, have disintegrated into wastelands of social anarchy and economic collapse.

'While civil wars rage across South America, China – emboldened by its heinous missile assault on Japan and South Korea – has expanded into other neighbouring sovereign nations to harvest their natural resources and exploit their labour force. Strangely the GMRC, United Nations and the U.S., and its allies, have only instigated token sanctions against the Chinese, followed by empty threats of military action. The reasoning behind this weak resolve is to avoid a world war at a time when humanity needs to be uniting rather than tearing itself apart. While this is a sensible standpoint, it begs the question whether China will ever be punished for its crimes.

'On the other side of the coin, the Chinese argue they were

merely responding to an assault on its people in a prior engagement of hostilities that, it says, were instigated by the Koreans and Japanese. As the BBC understands it, at this time there is little evidence to support these claims; however, some inside sources at the GMRC indicate there may be some truth to China's version of events. A special programme entitled *China's War,* tackling this and other issues, will be aired on this channel and via our other media streams at the local time now displayed on screen.

'In Europe and the USA food and water rationing is taking its toll and protests, like the one surrounding me now, are testament to the ill will and anger currently aimed at the politicians in their ivory towers. Unfortunately our elected officials seem to be in a position of impotence as the GMRC gathers more and more powers to itself in the name of *humanity's best interests*. As the world's economies crumble and stock markets plummet to record lows, plant and animal life continues to die off at alarming rates while the contingencies installed by the GMRC to ensure food stocks last until the dust cloud breaks up, in five to ten years' time, seem disturbingly inadequate.

'Despite the best efforts of the GMRC and the world's leading nations to ensure the global economy continues to operate effectively, it is clear this goal was optimistic, to say the least. In the USA, the western world's leading manufacturing powerhouse, inflation is skyrocketing, unemployment is at a one hundred year high and consumer confidence is at an all-time low.'

Jessica paused for breath and steeled herself as the unusual sensation of nervousness rippled through her body. Her lips became dry and she fought down the urge to run her tongue over them while live on air. *This is it*, she thought to herself, *why wait? Just go for it.*

'So is there any good news on the horizon?' she continued. 'Perhaps; independent studies have proposed the dust cloud may break up more quickly than the GMRC has predicted. If this is the case, the impact winter may lose some of its teeth within the next twenty-four months. As ever, the GMRC has played down such reports and dismissed these findings as specious and ill-informed. Coming from the GMRC, however, such a statement smacks of double standards bordering on outright hypocrisy.'

At this point in Jessica Klein's report her cameraman, James, looked out from behind his equipment and shook his head at her. She resisted the temptation to flick her eyes towards the movement. Jessica's producer, Martin, located hundreds of miles away back in an office in London and connected to her via an earpiece, also chose to add his twopenn'orth.

'Jessica,' Martin said, 'be careful what you say. We only have one shot at this.'

Jessica computed this dialogue on the fly and as ever showed no sign to the camera that she was receiving any remote communication.

'Switch to Keira's feed we have on the roof,' Martin continued, 'and we can take a break and discuss this one last time.'

As she heard this Jessica shifted her stance, adjusted her hand on the microphone and altered tack from what she had been about to say. 'We're now going to hear from Keira Jones, our latest dedicated GMRC correspondent, who is on the roof high above us. Keira, over to you.'

Jessica paused.

'And ... we're out,' James the cameraman said.

Jessica slumped into a more comfortable posture and pulled her hood up to warm her head. The crowd around them was chanting as loud as ever. Many held placards with slogans like *NO MORE RATION CARDS* and *DOWN WITH WATER CREDITS*. Others displayed the usual anti-GMRC rhetoric, or the simplistic yet effective GMRC logo itself surrounded by a red circle with a line through it.

The street was well-lit due to the substantial increase in lighting introduced by many major cities to distinguish between daytime and night-time hours. The simulation effect even ran in conjunction with the cycle of the sun; the extra lights dimmed at dusk and turned off at night, leaving just the normal street lighting in place.

James took the microphone from Jessica and handed her a flask of hot tea. Sticking one of her mitts in her mouth, she gripped it with her teeth and pulled her hand out. Unscrewing the lid, the steam escaped its container and she took a satisfying sip and wetted her parched lips.

'I thought you were going to wait,' James said as they huddled together while the mob around them kept up its relentless verbal barrage against its caged enemy.

Jessica shrugged. 'I thought it was the perfect time to transition into it.'

'Hmmm.' James sounded sceptical. 'Are you sure you want to go through with this?'

Jessica frowned at him in answer.

He held up his hands. 'Okay, you know what you're doing and Martin is backing you, but if I were you I'd leave it alone.'

Jessica ignored him and took another drink of the tea, feeling its heat warm her from within. She didn't care what he thought. He'd voiced his concerns before, she'd given them due consideration and dismissed them. She'd already had such discussions, and much more in-depth, with her husband, Evan, and it was his advice she valued above any other.

'At the end of the day,' he'd told her one evening when they sat up in bed discussing it, as they usually did when work matters were a problem, 'the decision is up to you, but from what you've told me it seems like the right thing to do regardless of the consequences. It's not like we need the money, if the worst happened.'

'That might not be the worst that could happen,' Jessica had said.

'No. But even they wouldn't be able to cover up that. It would be too obvious. You're too high profile.'

As usual, he was right. Well, Jessica hoped he was right, anyway; otherwise her life could change dramatically and quite quickly. Pushing the thought from her mind she felt her phone vibrate in her pocket. She gave the flask back to James, withdrew the device, saw it was her producer and moved away for more privacy before answering it.

'What the fuck, Jessica?' Martin's voice blared in her ear. 'We agreed what we were going to do and you nearly fucked it all up. I've already had the editor on the phone giving me all kinds of grief after your little tirade. It was touch and go for him to keep the GMRC bastards off our backs. If we're going to do this we've got to stick to the plan. We won't get a second chance at it.'

'I know, I'm sorry.' Jessica walked across to the far side of the road to get away from some of the noise. 'I thought I might as well get it over with. The intro was perfect and as I spoke it unfolded so I could just flow into it. I didn't think you'd mind.'

'You mean you just didn't think.'

Jessica bristled at his tone. 'Look, it isn't just your neck on the line here. And you came to me, remember? I'm the idiot who everyone will be watching, not you, so ease off, will you?'

A momentary silence ensued as Martin computed Jessica's point of view. 'Fine,' he said, 'but just stick to what we agreed, that's all I ask. We owe it to them to get it right and get it said. They can't get away with it any longer. Something has to be done.'

She suddenly remembered why this meant so much to him. 'I know. We'll find out what happened to him and the others too. It's what we do. We find the truth and we tell the world.'

'I hope so,' he said with feeling, and yet Jessica could hear the defeat in his voice. Like her, he knew what they were up against.

'It's time,' he told her.

'Okay. You're sure you can stop them from cutting the broadcast?'

'For a while, but by then the damage will be done.'

'Right.' She didn't know what else to say.

'Good luck,' Martin said and hung up.

Jessica put the phone back in her pocket. 'You too,' she murmured before walking back towards James, who still stood amidst the screaming masses. Squeezing past some protestors, she caught the eye of a woman, the rage in her face a vivid and powerful image that spurred Jessica onwards and strengthened a resolve which had begun to falter as she contemplated the words to come. Pulling her glove back on, she accepted the microphone from James.

'You ready for this?' he asked.

Jessica nodded despite her stomach suddenly feeling like it was barrel rolling within her. 'You?'

'Fucking A!' he said, noticing the tremor in her voice and trying to induce some courage. 'Let's give it to the fuckers, both barrels. I wanna see Jessica Klein at her bitchin' best. No prisoners.'

She knew what he was doing, but it worked all the same. Years of hardened debate on numerous television shows flashed back through her mind. She was Jessica Klein – *I am Jessica Klein, and yes, I take no prisoners.*

'Let's do this.' She positioned herself back in front of the camera, double checked her earpiece and put on her game face.

It wasn't long until she heard Martin's voice. 'Keira is cutting back to you in ten, Jessica,' he said, as if it was just another day at the office. She was then patched into Keira's feed and she could hear her colleague's voice as she wound up her set.

'—final one has landed. This has been Keira Jones reporting on—'

Jessica steadied herself, going through in her mind one last time what she was about to say. James' hand came up as a fist which turned into five fingers, four. *This is it*, she thought, *no turning back now*. Three – two – one. She was live on air – and she froze. Her perception of time faded into a treacle-like pace, the protestors' movements slowed and the noise around her became muffled and distorted. The microphone felt heavy in her hand and the smell of the fires set by the crowd to keep warm tasted strong and pungent, like incense on her tongue.

James popped his head up from behind the camera as her silence continued, his eyes asking a question.

'Jessica, you're on.' Martin's voice echoed in her ear. 'Snap out of it!'

Everything came back into focus coupled with a roar of noise. She blinked a couple of times and then started to speak. 'Thank you, Keira,' she said woodenly. 'It's good to have you on the case up there.'

Jessica hesitated again before finding a stronger voice. The moment was upon her and she must deliver.

Martin West, Jessica's producer, sat back in his chair in his state-of-the-art broadcasting control suite. In the room with him his usual production crew of ten, including audio-visual technicians responsible for producing and transmitting all live output content for the BBC's Worldwide News Service, across all media platforms. In front of him a sweeping curved screen dominated the wall, the flickering images of multiple video feeds within laid out like a living patchwork quilt. Those to the left showed footage of other channels being aired on the BBC, while those to the right spun up local, national and overseas news networks. The core area consisted of a large grid which displayed the previous, back-up, current and future feeds, the current live transmission taking centre stage. Of course, this had a slight delay on it in order to prevent any technical issues or unwanted content escaping the confines of the studio.

Using his personal control terminal Martin tapped a few keys and brought up a secure login screen to which he entered his username and password. Accessing a little used command programme which looked like a simple black box containing a flashing white cursor, he entered the following code:

Live_channel > worldnews_1

Override_external_source_control > Y

Override_internal_shutdown_control > Y

Broadcast_multiple_feed > UHF > ALL

Sound_carrier_frequencies > LINKED

Terrestrial_MHz_Band > 400.00–900.25

International_Bands > ALL

Live_feed_delay > ZERO

SAVE > Y

Martin hit the Enter key and a message popped up followed by the same cursor, the small, hypnotic, blinking line sucking in his attention like a whirlpool, demanding he make a decision.

Disable live feed delay? Y/N _

Martin hesitated before entering the letter Y and pressing the Return key. The main screen on the wall flashed once and a message in red text briefly appeared:

ADJUSTING TRANSMISSION

'Martin, did you see that?' his assistant producer asked, noticing the interruption to the stream.

'Yes, it's just a scheduled update to the system, nothing to worry about.'

The assistant nodded, apparently satisfied with his answer.

Martin got up from his seat and ambled over to the only door into the office and quietly locked it before slipping the key into his trouser pocket. Returning to his chair, he settled in to watch Jessica's report.

'As you may know I have been one of the BBC's main news anchors for the last five years,' Jessica began, addressing the camera and now easing back into her usual professional style. 'In that time I have been privileged to report to you, our viewers, the headline stories as they have broken around the world. Unfortunately in many instances, regarding the most important matters, I have not been given or allowed the freedom to report on the issues that I believe you have a right to hear.

'I, like many in my profession, hold dear the simple principle of the freedom of the press. A principle which a free and fair society must cherish and protect, lest those in power become above reproach, and injustice and corruption rots civilisation from the top down and from the inside out. Without a free press governments may act with impunity and commit atrocities in our name for the benefit of the few belonging to organisations and companies without borders; the few in power who publicly preach patriotism and yet privately practice treason, treason against their nation and against humanity itself. The greatest threat to humanity's future is not the dust cloud or the nuclear bomb, but the hidden sociopath in a position of power. How can the human race function with compassion if we are ruled by those without any?

'But I digress. In what will probably be my last broadcast for the BBC, I want to bring you the alarming truth about a global cover-up perpetrated by the world's leading nations. A cover-up planned and directed by the GMRC itself. What is this secret that we are not being told? I do not know. What I do know is that there is a cover-up and they will go to any lengths to make sure it stays hidden from view.

'How can I prove this bold claim? As ever, direct proof is hard to come by. The GMRC has seen to that. What I can prove is the surrounding evidence. A wise man once said you don't need to see something directly to know that it is there. Anything with substance, physical or otherwise, leaves telltale ripples which reveal its presence. The fact is, for over fifty years governments, powerful companies and organisations have been manipulating these ripples to cover their tracks. How do they do this so effectively? The utilisation of the media is key to their plans.

'I am reporting to you now for the first time operating under true freedom of the press. What you have been told is a lie. Whatever the GMRC is hiding, they are willing to suppress, silence and murder those seeking the truth to keep it hidden. So what is my proof? I can reveal the ripples surrounding the lie. Within the BBC alone over fifty journalists and researchers have disappeared or died in supposed accidents in the last ten years, over half this number within the last three years alone. Coincidence? No. Many of these people have been linked with, and reprimanded over, anti-government and anti-GMRC reports. What's more, my contacts have revealed a disturbing trend within the entire media industry, across seemingly every nation. I personally know broadcasters from CNN and Fox News in the USA, and CTV News in Canada, who tell me there is a deep unease and fear within the networks about reporting any overly negative views against their government and even more so with regard to the GMRC itself. As with the BBC, these organisations have experienced similar disappearances and *accidents* to their workforce.

'This high labour turnover in the journalistic profession is also replicated across Europe, Australia, India, China, Brazil and anywhere that has a high quality, so-called independent, press. I myself have been told on numerous occasions to avoid anti-GMRC viewpoints and not to report my findings on my missing colleagues. I have witnessed first-hand the seizure and destruction of BBC News computers by government and GMRC officials on no fewer than three occasions. Reporters have also been arrested while others have just disappeared without trace.

'The question is not whether the media is being suppressed, but why. What is the GMRC hiding from the people of the world that it will go to such lengths to cover it up? I hope this report will go some way towards exposing the truth and to galvanising and fostering public support for an end to unilateral GMRC control. It's time our politicians said "no more" to GMRC protocols and sanctions and stood up for the rights of the people they were elected to protect.'

'Jessica.' Martin's voice came through her earpiece. 'They've blocked the signal internationally; it's only a matter of time before the terrestrial feed goes too.'

Jessica gave an imperceptible nod. 'Even now,' she continued, 'the GMRC seeks to halt this broadcast. They don't want anyone to know the truth. What are they hiding from us? What are they hiding from you, from everyone? What are they planning for our future, for our children's futures and for the generations to come? Why is it that—'

'Jessica, we're off air,' Martin told her, 'it's over.'

'How did I do?'

'Brilliantly,' he replied with real warmth, 'you did us proud, did us all proud. I—'

Martin's voice cut off. 'Martin?' Jessica said, her concern audible. 'Martin!?'

There was no reply.

In London, Martin West relaxed in his chair as his phone rang for the umpteenth time. His ten colleagues looked at him with nervous eyes; the banging on the door to the broadcasting suite continued unabated as the people outside shouted their demands for entry.

Casually, Martin picked up the phone. 'Yes?'

'Martin, open the door.' It was his editor's voice, fraught with emotion. 'The GMRC are on their way. Don't make this harder than it already is.'

'I told you to do something,' Martin told his boss. 'My brother went missing and you did nothing. No investigation. No reports to even suggest there might have been foul play by the Government or by the GMRC. What did you expect, for me to forget the whole thing, forget my brother even existed?'

'I couldn't do anything; I'd have lost my job!'

Martin snorted in derision and slammed down the phone just as the door to the room burst open with a bang. Wooden splinters flew across the floor as grey garbed GMRC soldiers stormed inside. The other workers screamed and cried out in fear, some putting their hands in the air while others fell submissively to the floor. Pulled from his chair, Martin was thrust against a wall, handcuffed and marched from the room.

Back in New York, James had come round to the front of the camera to give Jessica an uncharacteristic hug. The noise of the crowd increased and Jessica turned to see the barriers had opened up at the front of the building. The NYPD brutally held back the protestors as a team of GMRC operatives swarmed out of the entrance and headed straight towards the BBC news crew.

James swore and turned to run, but he was brought up short by the sight behind them; U.S. troops had cut off their escape.

'Relax.' Jessica laid a reassuring hand on his shoulder as the grim-faced men bore down on them. 'This was inevitable. Just stay strong and we'll get through this together.'

Before James could reply they were forced to the ground by angry, shouting, armed men. As Jessica's face was held down hard against the freezing cold tarmac, all she could see were feet shod in heavy, black, military boots with the occasional glimpse of a terrified looking James, a few feet away, trying to maintain eye contact with her. Jessica gave him what she hoped was a reassuring smile and at the same time wondered if she'd ever see her children and husband again.

APPENDIX A

GMRC CIVILIAN PERSONNEL

Professor Steiner – GMRC Subterranean Director General
Nationality: American
GMRC Clearance – Level 10 Alpha
Designation – Civilian
Deployment: GMRC Oversight / Transient
Skill set:
Subterranean structural engineering
Management and leadership
Planning, design and development
Mathematical modelling and forecasting
Computer code and software development

Malcolm Joiner – Director of U.S. and GMRC Intelligence
Nationality: American
GMRC Clearance – Level 10 Alpha
Designation – Civilian
Deployment: GMRC Oversight / Transient
Skill set:
Espionage and covert intervention
Intelligence gathering, restriction and dissemination
Information pathways
Management and leadership
Psychological warfare

Richard Goodwin – GMRC Subterranean Base Director
Nationality: American
GMRC Clearance – Level 9 Alpha
Designation – Civilian
Deployment: U.S.S.B. Steadfast
Skill set:

Management and leadership
Planning, design and development

Commander Hilt – Darklight Officer
Nationality: American
GMRC Clearance – Level 8 Delta
Designation – Civilian / Private Contractor
Deployment: Unavailable
Skill set:
Overt military action / Multi terrain warfare
Covert military intervention / Sniper techniques
Hostage retrieval and counter terrorism
Close quarters and unarmed combat
Leadership and management
Strategic planning

Nathan Bryant – Subterranean Facility Coordinator
Nationality: American
Global Acquisitions and Intelligence Liaison
GMRC Clearance – Level 10 Beta
Designation – Civilian
Deployment: GMRC Oversight / Transient
Skill set:
Organisation and management
Negotiation, arbitration and presentation
Linguistics, communication and translation

Dr. Kara Vandervoort – Ecosystem Director
Nationality: South African
GMRC Clearance – Level 8 Alpha
Designation – Civilian
Deployment: U.S.S.B. Steadfast
Skill set:
Biomechanical engineering
Management

Data analysis

Special Agent Myers – CIA Agent
CIA Special Operations Group (SOG)
Nationality: American
GMRC Clearance – Level 9 Delta
Designation – Civilian
Deployment: Transient
Skill set:
Covert military intervention
Close quarters and unarmed combat
Leadership
Strategic planning

Mariana Lima – GMRC Public relations
Nationality: Brazilian
GMRC Clearance – Level 6 Beta
Designation – Civilian
Deployment: GMRC London Office
Skill set:
Public relations
Communication and presentation

Shen Zhǔ Rèn – GMRC Subterranean Base Director
Nationality: Chinese
GMRC Clearance – Level 10 Delta
Designation – Civilian
Deployment: P.R.C.S.B. Oversight / Transient
Skill set:
Management and leadership
Planning, design and development
Structural engineering

Dr. Daniel Sidwell – GMRC Subterranean Base Director
Nationality: English

GMRC Clearance – Level 10 Delta
Designation – Civilian
Deployment: E.U.S.B. Oversight / Transient
Skill set:
Management and leadership
Planning, design and development
Physics and chemistry

Sophie Merchant – Primary aide for Professor Steiner
Nationality: American
GMRC Clearance – Level 7 beta
Designation – Civilian
Deployment: GMRC Oversight / Transient
Skill set:
Organisation and presentation
Linguistics, communication and translation

APPENDIX B

U.S. MILITARY PERSONNEL

Colonel Samson

SFSD, Special Forces Subterranean Detachment
(Codename: Terra Force)
Nationality: American
GMRC Clearance – Level 8 Alpha
Designation: Military – Special Forces
Deployment: U.S.S.B. Steadfast
Skill set:
Overt military action
Covert military intervention
Counter-insurgency
Close quarters and unarmed combat
Leadership

Brigadier General Ellwood

Nationality: American
GMRC Clearance – Level 10 Delta
Designation – Military
Deployment: U.S.S.B. Sanctuary

General Shultz

Nationality: American
GMRC Clearance – Level 9 Beta
Designation – Military
Deployment: U.S.S.B. Steadfast

General Redshaw

Nationality: American
GMRC Clearance – Level 10 Beta
Designation – Military

Joint Chief, retired in 2032

General Hampton (1955 – 2030)

Nationality: American

GMRC Clearance – Level 10 Delta

Designation – Military

APPENDIX C

ARCHAEOLOGISTS

Sarah Elizabeth Morgan
Nationality: English
Profession: Archaeologist, Anthropologist

Trish Brook
Nationality: English
Profession: Archaeologist

Jason Reece
Nationality: Welsh
Profession: Archaeologist

Carl Benson
Nationality: Scottish
Profession: Archaeologist

APPENDIX D

ALBUQUERQUE RESIDENTS

Rebecca

Nationality: American
Profession: Mental health worker

Joseph

Nationality: American
Mentally handicapped man

Julie

Nationality: American
Profession: Mental health worker

Maria

Nationality: American
Profession: Mental health worker

Edna

Nationality: American
Mentally handicapped woman

APPENDIX E

OTHER PERSONS

Selena Adams

Vice President of the United States of America, 2016 – 2020.
Nationality: American
Retired from GMRC in 2034

Mark Sanders

Sarah Morgan's boyfriend
Nationality: English
Profession: Office worker

Frank

Nationality: South African
Profession: Retired pilot

Javier

Nationality: Honduran
Profession: Bus driver

Yochi Cayut

Expert in ancient Mayan civilisation
Nationality: Guatemalan
Profession: Lecturer at Mayan University, San Benito.

Victor Fernandez

Expert in ancient Mesoamerican languages
Nationality: Mexican
Profession: Philologist at National Museum of Anthropology, Mexico City, Mexico.

Jessica Klein

BBC Newsreader and TV Presenter
Nationality: English
Profession: Journalist

Professor Guraj Singh
Academic from the Indian Institute of Astrophysics
Nationality: Indian
Profession: Astrophysicist

Michael Bailey
Works for the U.S. Department of Homeland Security
Nationality: American
Profession: Civil Servant

Dr. Mowberry
The Lord Archbishop of Canterbury, 2029 –
Nationality: English

Tyler Magnusson
Nationality: American
Profession: NASA Astronaut

Ivan Sikorsky
Nationality: American
Profession: NASA Astronaut

Captain Takahashi
Captain of Darklight aircraft carrier Phoenix
Nationality: Japanese

Enitan Owusu
United Nations Secretary General, 2038 –
Nationality: Nigerian

Keira Jones

Nationality: English
Profession: BBC News correspondent

Clare Andrews
Nationality: English
Profession: BBC News correspondent

Martin Johansson
Nationality: Scottish / Swedish
Profession: BBC News correspondent

Simon MacDonald
Nationality: Scottish
Profession: BBC News correspondent

Andrew Stapleton
Nationality: English
Profession: BBC News correspondent

Dr. Middleton
Sarah Morgan's mentor when she was at university.
Nationality: English
Profession: Archaeologist, Anthropologist, Lecturer

David Broad
Chief of Staff to Vice President Selena Adams, 2016 – 2020.
Nationality: American
Profession: Civil Servant
Retired from GMRC in 2025

APPENDIX F

ORGANISATIONS

BBC – British Broadcasting Corporation. Television, radio and multi-media network broadcaster operating in the United Kingdom and globally / www.bbc.co.uk

GMRC – Global Meteor Response Council. International organisation set up by the world's nations for the protection and preservation of humanity, civilisation and all life on Earth.

MNA – Museo Nacional de Antropología / National Museum of Anthropology (Mexico) / www.mna.inah.gob.mx

NASA – The National Aeronautics and Space Administration (civilian space agency of the United States government) / www.nasa.gov

United Nations (UN) – International organisation for law, security, human & civil rights, political freedom and world peace / www.un.org

APPENDIX G

FACILITIES, UNITS & DESIGNATIONS

U.S.S.B. – United States Subterranean Base

China Lake Facility – C Class subterranean base
Footprint: circa 2.2 sq. miles (5.7 sq. km)
Height: 800 ft (0.24 km)
Depth from surface: 2,000 ft (0.6 km)
Cubic capacity: 0.34 cubic miles (1.4km^3)
Year of build: 1990 – 2007
Population: circa 2,300

U.S.S.B. Steadfast – A Class subterranean base.
Footprint: circa 20 sq. miles (52 sq. km)
Height: 7,500 ft (2.3 km)
Depth from surface: 3,000 ft (0.91 km)
Cubic capacity: 28.7 cubic miles (119.6 km^3)
Year of build: 1996 – 2035
Population: circa 500,000

U.S.S.B. Sanctuary – A Class subterranean base

U.S.S.B. Haven – B Class subterranean base

U.S.S.B. Washington – B Class subterranean base

P.R.C.S.B. – People's Republic of China Subterranean Base

E.U.S.B. – European Union Subterranean Base

P.R.C.S.B. Shanxi – A Class subterranean base

Darklight – Private security firm

SFSD – Special Forces Subterranean Detachment
(Codename: Terra Force)

COG – CIA's Special Operations Group

DOD – U.S. Department of Defense

Territorial Army – British volunteer reserve force

Fort Bliss – U.S. Army post, New Mexico / Texas

1AD – U.S. Army's 1st Armored Division

Phoenix – Darklight aircraft carrier

APPENDIX H

WORDS, TERMS & PHRASES

Genesisity – Global conservation movement akin to the *Green* political and environmental movement which drives the policies and targets of many companies, organisations and governments in the early part of the twenty first century.

Commercial Driver's License (CDL) – Required in the United States of America when operating heavy and hazardous goods vehicles.

Confab – An informal private conversation or discussion.

[Author note: This is a strange word since it has an almost identical sister word which many people also use, *conflab*. Apparently, according to my research, conflab evolved from confab as an informal colloquialism. It now appears to have taken on a life of its own, so much so there is some question as to which is correct. I originally wrote conflab, but since confab is the original I opted to use that instead.]

Rooves – Plural for roof.

[Author note: I always find the word *rooves* as a more intuitive and smoother sounding word than its more frequently utilised cousin, *roofs*. Rooves appears to have gone out of favour over the years and some now consider it incorrect.]

Get – Informal term for offspring / children.

Lucked out – A phrase to mean someone or something has been the beneficiary of good luck.

[Author note: Conversely many people also use this term to mean the exact opposite, i.e. you ran out of luck, which—when looking at it —makes more sense. It appears that some consider the meaning of *lucked out* to be a divide between the UK and USA, where people in the UK believe it to mean you've received bad luck and people in the USA to mean they've received good luck; this doesn't appear to hold true, however, and many people on either side of the Atlantic have their own opinion on it. Some even expand on the phrase and use it in other ways, i.e. you're a right luck out.]

Fubar – Fucked up beyond all recognition. Verb: to fubar, fubared.

Numpty – Foolish or stupid person.

APPENDIX I

LOCATIONS & BUILDINGS

Oxford – a city in England. Located approximately 50 miles north west of central London, in the county of Oxfordshire.

Dulce – small town located in Rio Arriba County, New Mexico, United States.

San Benito – a city in the El Petén department of Guatemala.

Sky Pillar – skyscraper built in London, completed in 2040.

The Shard – skyscraper built in London, opened 2013 / www.the-shard.com

The Spire – sister skyscraper to The Shard, built in London, completed 2025. Similar in appearance to The Shard.

Ruins of Copán – ancient Mayan city located in the Copán Department of western Honduras.

City of Tancama – ancient city built by the Huastecs circa 700 AD. Located near Jalpan de Serra, a small town in the state of Querétaro, Mexico.

Sierra Madre Oriental – mountain range located in the north east of Mexico. Spans one thousand kilometres.

Cerro El Potosí – highest mountain in the Sierra Madre Oriental mountain range, Mexico.

Teotihuacan – Pre-Columbian Mesoamerican city located near Mexico City, Mexico.

Sterkfontein Caves – also known as the Cradle of Humanity. Located near Johannesburg, South Africa.

APPENDIX J

TECHNOLOGY, ARTEFACTS & OBJECTS

Thermal Density Reduction (T.D.R.) – excavation technology utilised in the creation of large scale subterranean chambers

P.S.S.B.O. – Partial self-sustaining biological organism

Thermal sword – Darklight personal weapon

SABRE – Synergetic Air-Breathing Rocket Engine, an engine that operates in both air-breathing and rocket modes. Developed by Reaction Engines / www.reactionengines.co.uk

SPVU – Sediment Pulse Vibration Unit, excavation device

VSEs – Visual Spectrum Enhancement goggles

DPD – Digital Parchment Paper

Computer control circlet – Digital, infrared human interface device, similar to a mouse, worn on the finger.

Stelae – carved stone monuments, singular *stela*.

Stratigraphy – Geological study of rock layers / strata, which can be used to date objects found within.

Radiocarbon dating – A scientific procedure whereby the material from dead organisms is analysed to determine when it lived. Also known as carbon dating, or carbon-14 dating.

Crossmatch radiocarbon dating – A powerful scientific technique utilised by archaeologists to date the material of deceased organisms. Developed by the Chinese in the second quarter of the twenty-first century, crossmatch radiocarbon dating extended the seventy-five thousand year limitation of normal radiocarbon dating to seven hundred and fifty thousand years. Combining the fields of carbon dating, stratigraphy, big data, quantum modelling and molecular retracing, the technique is able to peer further back in time than was previously thought possible.

Molecular retracing – A scientific process whereby molecular decay (and in some instances, movement) is recorded by a special high resolution imager and then recreated in a computer simulator, before the process is reversed beyond recorded data to give a snapshot of the material's past.

2011 AG5 – Asteroid
Impact Year: 2040
Length: circa 4.2 miles
Diameter: circa 1.9 miles
Velocity: circa 36,000 m.p.h.
Estimated Mass: 1.24 x 1014kg (124,000,000,000t)

APPENDIX K

EMBLEMS & LOGOS

ABOUT THE AUTHOR

Robert Storey's first published novel is *2040: Revelations* This became book one in his Ancient Origins series and was renamed Ancient Origins: Revelations in September 2016.

Robert went on to complete the series of six books in 2018.

A year later Robert died at the age of 43.

For more information about Robert and his work, please visit:

fuse-books.com/robertstorey

Ancient Origins: Revelations is dedicated with love to my parents Maureen and Terry, without whom this book would not have been written.

ACKNOWLEDGMENTS

Thank you to my parents for proof reading my work and for editing and suggesting as they went; without them I wouldn't have been able to see the woods for the trees. And to my copy editor, Julie Lewthwaite, thank you for your outstanding work and words of encouragement.

Robert Storey, 2013

Addendum:
Fuse Books partnered with Terry and Maureen Storey, following the tragic death of their son Robert. It is our privilege to bring his books to new readers.

As Rob himself noted these books would not have made it to publication without the support of Terry and Maureen. Devoted parents who could not have done more for their son.

James Blatch & Mark Dawson
February 2020

First published in Great Britain in 2013

This edition 2020

All the characters in this book are fictitious, and any resemblance to actual persons, living or dead, is purely coincidental.

Fuse Books
www.fuse-books.com

Printed in Great Britain
by Amazon

56656242R00267